For my son, Lonan

And with my thanks to the Aspenites, headed by my dear friend, Sammy Schiralli. Also all the professors, and their staff, who wish to be nameless, but without whom I could not have begun to understand what is possible in the field I chose to use – thank you.

As always, my life is enhanced by the support of the rest of my family: Gavan and Rogan.

And to Anthony, a further thank you for steering me through.

By the same author

Bermuda

ASPEN

Vanessa Fox

ARROW

Published by Arrow Books in 1995

1 3 5 7 9 10 8 6 4 2

Copyright © Vanessa Fox 1995

Vanessa Fox has asserted her right under the Copyright, Designs
and Patents Act, 1988 to be identified as the author of this work

First published in the United Kingdom in 1995 by
Arrow Books Limited
20 Vauxhall Bridge Road, London SW1V 2SA

Random House Australia (Pty) Limited
20 Alfred Street, Milsons Point, Sydney,
New South Wales 2061, Australia

Random House New Zealand Limited
18 Poland Road, Glenfield
Auckland 10, New Zealand

Random House South Africa (Pty) Limited
PO Box 337, Bergvlei, South Africa

Random House UK Limited Reg.No. 954009

ISBN 0 09 9 177811

Papers used by Random House UK are natural, recyclable
products made from wood grown in sustainable forests. The
manufacturing processes conform to the environmental regulations
of the country of origin.

Designed and Typeset by SX Composing Ltd, Rayleigh, Essex
Printed and bound by
BPC Paperbacks Ltd,
a member of The British Printing Company Ltd

ONE

The first thing was the smoke. They had seen it from the valley: spiralling like a wraith against the winter sky as the convoy rolled steadily along the mountain road.

The wheels of the army jeep slithered and caught as the road gave way to a rutted track and they swung in with a lurch between banks of snow pitted yellow with mud. It was precipitously steep, the track rough and awkward, and as they jostled their way up over the stones and pitted earthworn gulleys caused by mountain rains Alex Dawnay clung to her seat, more than ever aware of the smells of spilled fuel and damp serge. The floor was wet beneath her regulation boots, and the flak jacket she wore as easily as her underwear now seemed to tighten on her breathing as the jeep clambered up the rough mountain road. Through the narrowed window the heavy steel wipers battled against the drifts of falling snow.

As they reached the top, the track levelled out. It was bitterly cold, but she felt the prickle of heat on her skin as the village drew towards them out of the grey shrouds of snow like an old photograph; a drinking fountain, the shape of a pond in the square. A church with steps up where the door swung open and there was dark beyond. The buildings were pocked with shells from which the smoke rose steadily.

The soldiers who jumped from the vehicles while they were still moving, ran to take cover. She went with them, used to it now, at a crouching run, seeking shelter of the walls. The falling snow was wet and the icy wind tore at them, flailing already frozen cheeks, but despite the cold she was now truly sweating beneath her flak jacket. Nothing moved and Alex felt a deep sense of unease.

Her eyes were trained on the small square, and that open door. The wind blew and banged it emptily against itself. It told her more than the many footprints that had been here before them. Footsteps and tracks that were still visible, despite the fresh snowfall salting their dark prints.

The fountain was rusted and the long drop of water a thickening icicle that led to the buttress beneath, but on the lip of the stonework was a splash of colour. She strained her eyes and made out a small child's abandoned toy. There could only have been women and children here, but not a child ran to greet them. It was a world that had stopped in time. She looked up at the windows all around that stared emptily back. There was dark green paint on the snow-flecked shutters and empty terracotta flower pots on a wrought-iron balcony that braced a line of washing, clothes frozen like white boards. Empty staircases, window shutters half open, cracking gently in the bold wind, all told their story. Alex felt her sense of foreboding build.

Three soldiers centred on the small doorway and were gone. The church timbers were blackened, the charred smoke staining the pale walls around the windows. The fire that had raged was now gone, just the soft spirals of smoke that lay up in the sky above, and the black of destruction. The commanding officer went forward to a signal and down into the bowels of the church. The cameraman, Shaun, spoke questioningly to one of the soldiers, but Alex was alert.

She would know by his eyes as he returned, and she did; pain tightened a face already used to suffering as his eyes sought her out and signalled that it was safe for her to break cover. They ran across the snowy square and his hand touched her shoulder in a brief chill warning as she entered the darkness, the small camera crew behind her. They fell into the open maw of the staircase. The snow falling over the past hour had created a kindness. Bodies lay, mercifully covered by a delicate blanket of white. The soldiers moved past them on the broken staircase. Above, the pall of dark grey smoke thickened on the white sky. Ash floated gently within the snowflakes.

The rafters open to the sky were blackened and the day-light did nothing to penetrate the gloom. A flashlight bobbed on the staircase to the cellar. Alex found herself going down, driven by her gut instincts. She signalled her crew to follow.

It was hard to see after the sullen bright of the snow-cast world outside, but her eyes became quickly used to the shadows. Employing the silence, she listened hard for any sound. There was none. Alex gathered herself, and her outward breath frosted the cold black air. Another step and she saw the curve of bodies. She smelled the bitter charcoal, the taint of flesh. The cloth was singed from their skin, and in death they held each other tight.

Bodies, blackened beyond recognition. Remnants of cloth, a sandal, an outstretched arm. Within its embrace two tiny shapes. Her heart quickened. She turned away, holding that vision in her head, back up the grimed staircase where the ash still fluttered and out into the brashness of the clear white day.

The briefing with the CO was short and to the point. Outside, she took her place beside the building and drew back her hood. A small wind stirred tendrils of her hair. She felt it almost as a sign of life.

Her blue eyes tore with the wind, the cameras turned over, and Shaun counted down. She did not bother to peel back the long damp strands of hair that now fluttered over her face, a face bleached as pale as the frozen world around her. Her drawn eyes spoke volumes, the steel of their look telling the story to the millions back home.

Her words were carried away on the small breeze as the soldiers went about their job. Probing, banging doors, running. In their midst her voice spoke for them as the young subaltern ran across the square from the gathered convoy. He saluted as he handed his commanding officer the bulletin, its edges fluttering in the wind. The officer took it, read briefly. A dispatch from London. He saw her name: Alexandra Dawnay, and looked over at her.

Briefly, the old soldier watched her, admiring her resilience. With the suffering of these people, his own pain smothered him daily. He was a man of war, the Gurkhas a tough regiment, but nothing had prepared him for this. He saw what he had come to know. A girl in his opinion too young to see this sort of thing, a girl in a flak jacket, with a

7

collar that framed her determined face, her dark hair pulled back in its familiar plait, wide winged brows and deep-seeing compassionate eyes. As she spoke on, her lips were frozen by the cold. But as she delivered her broadcast in that distinctively rich voice she never faltered, and in her eyes he saw what he felt himself and knew how good she was; it was her ability to transmit this hard-edged emotion that had won her the job.

Three of them, a mother and two children.

The camera whirred as she faced into the watery light and wound up her regulation three minutes, her eyes screwed up in an angry fierceness that marred her looks, her emotions barely hidden.

So tiny.

The image would not leave her head.

'. . . this is Alexandra Dawnay, for the BBC, reporting from Bosnia . . .'

Microphone down, she turned away and looked up into the mountains as if searching for those who would do this thing, the images swimming. The CO watched her back, her stillness. He did not disturb her, knowing how much it took to contain oneself in the face of atrocity. He envied her her tears, dashed away with her fingers. He wished he could do the same, but he was a creature of war, this was his business. He could not allow himself the luxury of sentiment. Marshalling the few soldiers left in the square, he turned back towards the convoy. He had to set an example, move them on. As he strode away, he handed the paper to the young subaltern with instructions not to interrupt until she had composed herself.

A lone small figure, she walked to the edge of the silent square, the voices diminishing. Left alone with her grief, she drew a deep breath, and felt her stomach turning.

Burned alive.

She made it to the back of the house where she discharged her meagre breakfast into the bars of white snow. The acid burned her throat. She dashed handfuls of ice across her mouth and dampened her face, breathing deeply.

The paradoxes of her life warred within her. Man's in-humanity to man never failed to appal her, and she had seen scenes just as heart-rending on many previous occasions, but suddenly it was one too many: she knew she was good at her job because she could make people aware, make them feel what she saw, but conversely if she could not remain more detached her own strong emotions would fail her. She breathed deeply, letting the cold sober her, calming herself. It was a few moments before she turned to rejoin them.

The village had been old, levelled out of the side of a hill to protect it from the worst of winter storms, the low stone houses clustered in against the lee side of the mountain. Winter's uncompromising image showed it in the hard light of poverty but there had been community here. A long bench outside a bar gave testament; a rusty metal poster advertised beer. On this bleak mountainside there had been little enough. Now there was nothing.

Back across the square, the lorries smoked, steam from their engines still running. The subaltern stretched out the paper, saluting. She took it with a stiff smile but without words; there were none she felt like exchanging. Feedback from the news room. The paper crackled as she ripped the binding, stretched its contents between gloved fingers.

Hart Bennett's smiling face beamed out of the mono-chrome photograph. Alex bit her lip. Beside him, the blonde clung to his arm. She was thin and her lines were rich. The celebrities attending were written up in black type in the opening paragraph. Her heart read the news in shock. A society wedding.

Only a week ago they had made love. Out here, amongst all this; whispering their need for each other. Work and love, a team. She'd never known at what point she had lost.

She turned her face away towards the hills where now the snow fell steadily. This time, there were no tears left. She, too, had learned the price of war.

9

TWO

Christmas, Aspen

The gentle scream of the jets floated in over Sardy Airport. Lights streamed out over the pale evening-blue drifts of the most beautiful snow in the world. Aspen wore its best party dress. Thousands of feet up in a range of mountains that bordered the desert to the west as it fell, the snow was dried in the warm rush of air. It drifted down like silk. Rich man's powder.

Hillaire Bowman stretched out his legs as he watched the land below sweep into view beneath the wing of the company jet. Almost dusk; the best time to arrive. He smoothed back the hair from his forehead and checked the time. Drinks in the bar, dinner with Miki Leng and then probably a club. Their billionaire oriental host was bound to be very hospitable, but he would have preferred an early night. It was going to be a long one.

He heard over-sharp laughter and looked over at its source. Freddie Renby-Tennant, the aristocratic Englishman, swept the pool of dollars from the table. Under the soft lights his long hands were smooth, and dextrous; hands that had made him famous. Beside him, Felicity, his wife, clad in tweed and sensible shoes, smiled with complacent pride and as Hillaire looked up he felt her close-set eyes rest on him for approval. There was curiosity there too. That was good; it meant Tennant, the weak link and the society man, had not confided in her. Across the aisle, Kowolski, the only other one of the immediate group, waited as the vain and sardonic Englishman dealt the cards once more.

Briefly, Hillaire switched his interest to the other man. People were as revealing in play as at work, but the ubiquitous bespectacled face gave nothing away. He was known to be both quiet and clever and never to be underestimated; definitely the interesting one. David Kowolski's ability was legendary. They had never met until briefly at the airport, though they had known of each other long before that. Now he was here because Hillaire Bowman had found the chink in his armour, and tempted him beyond his ability to resist.

Hillaire had held the edge by choosing to sit apart. He looked out; darkness as they cruised down into the shadows mirrored the window and reflected the man. Heavy set with a crest of silver hair receding from a broad forehead, his dark eyes told the story: a man of command. Single, powerful, and one with whom you would not cross swords. A purposeful man. Chatter floated over him from the seats at the back; the children were here too, sitting at the back with their nannies. The men's families were their cover.

Seats buckled, the plane swooped down to make a long graceful landing under the rising peaks of Buttermilk mountain, soft scoops of white under an early moon, trammels of dark blue liquidising beneath into pure black where sheer cliffs broke down into the valley. The land then poured out into a soft white carpet that glittered like a coat of pale blue diamonds under the floodlights and met the edge of tarmac where the company jets were parked wall to wall.

Outside, the long black car sighed into the kerb. Early stars pricked the sky. The night air was cool and the snowbound land created its familiar padded quiet and promise of excitement. There was tension, the men separated by the knowledge of what they were about to attempt. The innocent children made a splash of colour and noise in contrast as they gathered outside the airport's entrance with their elegant fur-clad mothers and nannies in attendance. Hillaire, in astrakhan and cashmere, turned to the group.

'These cars are yours for the duration.'

The heads turned to see the two other cars slide up to the kerb behind the dark-windowed limo. 'Please, feel free to enjoy yourselves tonight. Not too late though, our first meeting is at seven at the Red House. These same drivers are yours, and will pick you up, separately, at quarter of, sharp.'

He handed his briefcase to the silent chauffeur, who slid it into the recesses of the car and then stood impassively waiting. Hillaire ignored him.

'I have taken the liberty of assigning you restaurants for the evening. They are all excellent and your bill is already charged, as is membership of the well-known club, Chasers, for the duration of your stay – but, please, check amongst yourselves who's doing what. We don't want to be seen together, for obvious reasons.' His glance took in the women and his cold charm directed itself to them. Now he saw the distance in their eyes, and knew they were afraid of him. It did not matter; he was used to it. Sometimes it even helped.

He had already made their position clear. Separation from now on was to be a fact of life in order to protect the identity of the group. His instructions had been specific: discourage association, especially introductions that might cause questions they must not answer.

A small wind scurried snow petals on to his broad black shoulders. He lifted his hat. 'Goodnight then, ladies.'

He raised a hand as his chauffeur opened his door and he slid with easy familiarity into the darkness within. The car peeled away into the twilight.

Jackie Kowolski watched him go, then turned to the other couple, lifting her shoulders briefly as if to rid herself of tension. 'Well we were planning on the Jerome bar once we've freshened up,' she said, her voice bright. 'How about you?'

Freddie put on his best sardonic smile. 'If we see you, we can always sit at the other side of the room.' They laughed as one, their awkwardness tinged with relief. 'But we thought we'd make a night of it.' He glanced at his wife. 'This club, perhaps.' Freddie was a known night owl. 'Chasers. You interested?' She shrugged ambivalently.

'Fine with us.' Kowolski's glance took in his own wife. Small, dark and vivid; her face was bright with intelligence. 'Jackie, early night tonight, honey?'

She nodded. 'The children are tired, anyway.'

'Well, that's OK; the club's all yours then if you want it.' Kowolski turned to the taller man. 'We might go tomorrow. That suit?'

'Absolutely. Can't wait to do the town, old fellow. The others are apparently already at the hotel. No trouble there, we won't recognise them until after the morning's meeting.' This was just the New York contingent; the Renby-Tennants had flown in from London the previous night and joined forces at Kennedy.

'Presumably after tonight Hillaire will prepare us for the future.'

'Of that I have no doubt.'

A bikini-clad girl climbed provocatively from the pool at the exclusive Hotel Jerome, the heavy water sliding like caressing hands from her slick, oiled skin. Her laughter lit the air as a man, rotund and a whole head shorter, carefully draped a towel around her tanned shoulders, and held it tight. She laughed again at something he said, throwing back a mane of tousled blonde hair. In their incongruous setting, snow fell delicately all around the pair. Steam clouded the cold air and the pool was underlit with blue vaporous light. The redbrick hotel rose behind them, imposing and grand, the epitome of Victorian architecture. The elite guests sauntered in, pretending they did not look her way, nor notice her indiscreet and flagrant pleasure, her *joie de vivre*, her ignorance of the international laws of etiquette: the rich must not be seen to be enjoying themselves too much, for that would give the game away.

For the Hotel Jerome said money. The waiters slid softly along thick carpets in the lobby; there was understated chic in the earthy terracotta and desert sky blue ambience. Chandeliers and stag heads, rich red oriental carpets and striped wing chairs, deep comfortable sofas plumped up ready for use, all told of the rich and their familiar comforts. A welcoming fire burned in the grate, pictures lined the walls, and polished English antiques were placed discreetly amongst huge ferns as Victoriana met Santa Fe. On one of these sideboards a silver canteen of hot cider stood waiting for the guests to help themselves. The rich spicy smell drifted enticingly through the lobby.

There was a sense of excitement, characters bright. Skis were stacked in the hall, the cold snowy day outside drawing in for the evening. The lights went on in the old iron lanterns that dotted street corners and threw their glow across the banks of snow. It was an old mining town, and had been kept that way. Saloons and Victorian houses with low picket fences and discreet shop façades that housed everything the rich could want in a fairytale setting that dated back a hundred years or more. Their private playground was a storybook Dickensian world.

Hillaire Bowman walked through their midst. Although an imposing figure, he could withdraw into himself and pass unnoticed when he wished. Clearly travelling alone, no one bothered him. The other guests mingled and chattered excitedly as he crossed to the desk and asked to see the guest list for his party. Having ascertained that everyone had checked in, he turned to leave the hotel.

The woman saw him briefly as she turned in the lift but did not call out. The sight of him had caught her by surprise though she had known of course that he would be here. Twenty years; she would know him anywhere. She had not thought she would. Her husband, Wilhelm, pressed the button for their floor and instinctively Hillaire seemed to feel her gaze and turned. Their eyes caught for just a moment: a moment that said a great deal. The doors slid softly shut, eclipsing her and the man beside her.

Upstairs in the junior suite, David Kowolski watched Bowman walk from the hotel and into the street. He studied him unseen for just a moment, and then lost interest. That could come later. The scientist took in the atmosphere. They were positioned right over the swimming pool and he could see over the rooftops to Ajax, the mountain that dominated the town. The last of the skiers were curving down its blue white base, swooping like scavenging black birds. The gondolas had stopped for the night and golden lights had sprung up all over the town, as people went out walking together for the evening, took in the cafés and bars or headed up the hill to the Aspen Club for their exercise class or self-help therapy groups.

Beneath, beside the swimming pool, the blonde girl he had seen on arrival kissed her fat lover, and his hands reached around her neat behind. Kowolski sensed her promising murmurs and knew he was right as they kissed again, and the man was reaching for his towel and leading her out. He took in the girl's boldness, her knowledge of her youth and her power.

It was a heady mix: youth, health and beauty, and very much on his mind. It was what they had come to deal with. And what better place than Aspen? Their leader had chosen well.

Outside the snow fell with Christmas card softness in a fairytale setting, the children chattered in their bedroom alongside; families were the perfect cover. If they kept themselves separate no one would begin to suspect there was anything odd about so many of them in one place at one time. Aspen attracted the best, and they were the *crème de la crème*.

He turned back into the room. It was perfect: decorated with rich fabrics, dusky pink flowers and stripes, a bathroom *en suite* continuing the old west pioneer theme, and lace curtains that flaunted the windows and the view. He took his washbag into the bathroom and came back towards the bed.

His briefcase stood there, and for the moment he saw it as a baleful animal about to spring. Black leather that crouched over contents that were pure dynamite. The noise of the children faded in his mind. It was a strange thought, and he dismissed it as foolish. He walked over, sat down and leaned over to it, springing the locks. A plain manila file lay on top, its contents composed by himself. Papers that could change history. He wondered what the others would say, and do, when they knew what he had brought them. He reached in and drew out the bulky object that lay beneath.

The dressing-table mirror caught the movement and he looked up. Beyond the flash of his steely spectacles he saw the deeply grooved lines of his face; the aesthete grown realist, the realist turned . . . God? Once again, as so often since this venture was planned, he had doubts. Bowman had convinced him that what they were about to do was right; he didn't know. Today's dream, or tomorrow's nightmare? He did know he would watch Bowman very closely. He picked up the sheaf of papers. Toeing off his shoes, he lay back on the bed and began to read.

As she stepped off the Greyhound bus at Agoura Alex Dawnay felt the heat of the desert. The doors slid with a small pressure squeak of air and the bus trundled on up to the crossroads. She wore a crop-top T-shirt with a thin blue cotton skirt and hiking boots. A cotton knit sweater was thrown around her shoulders, taking the weight of her bag. The warm air billowed the folds of her skirt and her hair was loose. She had put more than miles between herself and Sarajevo.

Alex squinted into the sun and looked around. Down at the end of the road was the lock-up. It was a typical California scene: pancake house, pizza parlour, cafés with strong hot coffee by the jugful, a couple of garages, a Chevron and a 7-11, and the Ventura freeway heading south and north, the crossroads taking the traffic across Kanan canyon to the beaches at Malibu, or up the coast to Big Sur and beyond. Across thousands of miles to the east, fat cars sat on the broad highways flooding towards the coast, kids with dreams of Hollywood, the ocean, the big city lights. She'd been here once with dreams; dreams of the man then beside her, Hart Bennett. Dreams of a different sort.

Blue sky, always blue, and a breeze that should be ashamed to call itself winter. Up on the hill the rough scrub grass and sage were recovering from the arson fires that came with the Santa Ana fall winds, summer heat and drought. A sandstone rock dominated the view. Someone had scrawled in huge red writing across it: JESUS LIVES.

The country road dipped down, bordered by bleached grass and stones. There was a sweet dry smell in the air. Alex picked up her haversack and suitcase, and started walking. She could see the high iron crossmesh of the lock-up from here. It covered the end of the block. The road was dusty, and the heat felt good on her shoulders. She loved the

States, its easy ways; the mountains, the stretches of desert, the coast. She'd hiked it coast to coast when she was a teenager. Now it felt like coming home.

The stones crunched under her feet as she came up to the gates and went through the pedestrian walkway of Kanan Storage. A wooden hut stood to one side, for the moment empty of life.

And then the woman appeared. Her eyebrows were quizzical. The cigarette in her fingers held a long spiral of ash.

'Hi, there.'

'Hi. I'd like to settle up.'

'What's your name, dear?'

'Dawnay.' Alex put down her bag. 'Alexandra Dawnay.' She pointed away. 'The old motorhome, the Dodge Discoverer.'

'Ah yes.' The thin mouth smiled. The woman turned back to her books, flicked the pages. 'You owe me . . . forty five dollars.'

Alex dug in her bag, handed over the cash. The woman stamped the receipt and handed it to her. The cigarette made it to her mouth, and her eyes narrowed with the smoke.

'Paid in full. Need to park here again?'

'I'm not sure. Can I let you know?'

'Sure. I'm always here.' The girl's straight dark hair, falling from a middle parting, shone in the sun with deep red lights. She seemed in her mid-twenties, yet her eyes were older, very clear and thorough as if she had seen too much; wise eyes. The woman pulled on the cigarette, remembering her now, hearing the soft English accent. 'Come rain, come shine,' she laughed. 'Ain't that what you Limeys say?'

'I've heard it. You wouldn't need it here.' She looked up at the dry hills, at the scrawled red writing on the standing rock.

'That's for sure. We just got our earthquakes. One day we'll drift off into the ocean. Going far?'

Alex brought her attention back; the woman's eyes were shrewd.

'East, a way. See what I come up with.'

17

'Well now, you take care. There's some mighty strange people out there.' She remembered the man the girl had been with before. He was not with her now. She guessed at what had happened. 'Big contraption to handle alone.'

Alex smiled; her face gave the story. 'I'll manage. Alone's OK, it's lonely that's not.'

'You got that right.'

At the far side of the compound, in the centre of the line of flashy cream and chrome motorhomes, Alex found it. It was a fifties Dodge Discoverer, aerodynamic in style. Closer she slowed, feeling a strange thrill despite the reason why it was hers. She'd never driven it. She'd travelled alone, but always with a purpose: a newshound reporting back. This time, she was on her own. The world stretched ahead – deserts, mountains, rivers. America at its most beautiful, with winter coming on. There would be snow in the Rockies.

She fitted the key in the lock and stepped inside.

A smell of musky, closed air greeted her. She parked her bag on the sofa to the left and unlatched a window above it, letting the breeze flow in, and looked around, taking pleasure in her aloneness and sense of possession. It was all hers now. Opposite the sofa were two bunks with cupboards above and below. Up the central aisle to the right stood the kitchen, a dining unit and then the cab itself. This end there was a small bathroom with a drizzling shower. A deeper breeze stole in from the window. She felt a feathering over her stomach and thought of sex.

For a moment, a hot image pulsed into her. Hart's smile in his tanned face, the water pouring down, over his body and then hers as he pulled her close. Making love. That time they had been at the coast with the ocean breeze drifting over their cries, and afterwards it had dried their bodies as they lay together, dreaming and making promises they had not kept. It hadn't been so long ago.

Alex felt the knife thrust through her. She'd had dreams: one had been this journey. She could make at least one of them come true. The Dodge was old, but it was roadworthy. She stood, discarding his image as she climbed up into the cab, and hit the motor. She felt the *frisson* of excitement.

The engine turned over on the second shot.

Alex pulled a pair of favoured jeans from her bag, and dug out a heavy cableknit sweater for the late afternoon chill. California was never cold, not as she knew it in Europe. No biting winds, and rain, and cold that got into your bones, but the evenings could be cool. Cool and clear.

Briefly another image filled her as she recalled the market square, the softly falling snow, the hope of just one whimper, one life to save. She remembered the silence it was no good to remember. She tried to put it from her mind, busying herself with preparations as the old motor ticked over.

Back in the driving seat, she parked the drink she had bought *en route* in its styrofoam cup in the pocket beside her, an apple, a bag of chips – leftovers from the bus ride. A map: one of many. This one would take her across country to Utah. She had planned where she would go. She was heading for mountain time. The emptiness, the far-spread wide beauty of Colorado where she would be alone with the land. A land she had crossed once in love, laughing, feet up on the dashboard, listening to the Eagles.

She still had the tape. She tucked it into the cassette deck, determined to shed the memories. She had never been sentimental.

There was no more to do now but leave. She grasped the steering wheel and pushed in the gear. It was like driving a bus from the comfort of an easy chair. As she rolled out, she could see the whole world through the huge windows, and she sat up above it, her life in her own hands now as the old bus ground its way over the stones of the compound to the exit. She tapped in her number and the gate slid slowly back. The Dodge Discoverer rumbled out on to the road.

The woman watched, touched her bright yellow hair in the mirror. Her routine was the same every day, no one to change it for. Four o'clock. The sun had only just lost its heat, and the air conditioner had packed in. Thank God, the cool of evening was on its way.

She listened as the Discoverer turned out on to the highway and the motor picked up as it climbed the slight hill towards the crossroads. She dug her hand into a bag of Doritos, ate some and washed them down with diet soda. One worked against the other; she always took sweeteners in her coffee; that way, she could eat dessert. The Bakelite ashtray was full of filters; smoking was OK, long as you used filters. And she never emptied it during the day, the ash was bad for you. She emptied it at night when she left, so the hut could take the smell, not her. She didn't have far to go home: just to the small house alongside the trailer park that came with the job. Sometimes she wished she could go far afield but this was her life. Stuck here incongruously in the middle of the desert, surrounded by high steel and bales of barbed wire, minding people's possessions who travelled the way she wanted to, but never did.

She switched on one of her daily soaps. They were her family. She hit the remote to change the channel and lit another cigarette. *The World Turns* filled the screen. She wondered where the girl was going.

Ahead the Agoura crossroads spread over the Ventura freeway. Alex pulled into the gas station, a list of necessities filling her head. Hart had always done it before. Check the fluids, buy propane, fill the water tank, check the tyres, buy rations – a Thermos of coffee, an essential that would be refilled often on the way, a paper bag of fruit, food to cook later when she camped out. The fridge was working; so was the cooker. She pulled over to the side of the parking lot and jet-sprayed the motorhome, then swiftly cleaned it out, checked the oil, fitted the sanitation and the paraffin.

She was set. Packed beside her, her Walkman and speakers, carrot juice from the market and dry 'save your ass' biscuits. Black khombu boots for warmth once she hit the hills, one-bite hash cookies stashed under the seat and a bottle of Cook's dry champagne in the fridge.

Three hundred miles to Vegas. It would take five hours driving. She would stop early for the night and sleep, and head out with the dawn breaking as she drove east. Dawn was the best, with the light breaking over the land as if the world was coming alive for her.

Slotting a tape into the deck, she flipped the ring on her can of Root Beer and headed east on Ventura, towards Colorado and mountain time.

THREE

Iron street lamps glowed in the quiet early evening in the small town setting. Still pockmarked with mine shafts, the mountain, nicknamed Ajax after an historic silver mine, created a dramatic backdrop that dwarfed the town laid out at its base. It looked much as it did a hundred years ago when mining was in its heyday and ore was hauled from the town by two railroad lines.

Soft gold lights caressed the air as the lights of the town came on, bathing the old preserved mining cabins and bawdy houses, deep drifted with snow. Ruth could almost hear the jingle of spurs and the laughter from the salons. Nineteenth-century carollers serenaded the town in hats and frock coats; there were lattice windows, holly wreaths on the doors and children in fur snoods, boots and mittens.

Ruth Lindstrom in her very twentieth-century jogging pants stacked her skis in the hallway and paused for a moment before entering the hubbub. She turned to look back up the mountain, appraising it with a practised eye. Mid-forties she still cut a great figure. She thought about the eye contact from the man outside the lift – Hillaire Bowman; a moment only, but enough to say so much about the years between.

Twenty years. The mountain had been cordoned off for the winter Olympics and the team had stayed at a small private house in the West End. Ruth had been one of them, young and idealistic, an unworldly but outspoken student.

Into the house one day had strolled a young man, wealthy already as a result of his ability and with an insight beyond the rest. He had bought a house at the end of the street, small and Victorian with a white picket fence. He had not agreed with her principles then, so why had he asked her to be here? They had argued relentlessly. Had he changed? She

22

did not think so for a moment, but still her mind was alive with questions.

The previous day they had flown in from Munich and, though very fit, she had been feeling the strain in her body. The quick walk had refamiliarised her with the town she loved and revitalised her after the long flight. She shook the snow from her hat as she came into the lobby, and took the stairs to the second floor feeling young and vigorous again. Ruth was a true believer in the theory that the physical energised the mental, and as she entered the suite her mind was alive.

Her husband was already dressed for the evening; facing away from her, he was talking on the phone. She opened and closed the door quietly, the smile still on her face.

'. . . yes, Sandford. No, I have tried. I will yes . . . yes, I know, but . . . where? All right . . .' He glanced at his watch, and seemed to brace his shoulders briefly.

Ruth, hearing the pressure, felt puzzled. She came around and into his eyeline, making a face.

'Wilhelm? Who's that?' she mouthed.

He turned quickly into her, his look of concern turning to one of shock.

'How long have you . . . just a moment.' He turned his back to her and with his face into the phone he spoke overloud: 'I'll call you later . . . yes . . . all right, goodbye.'

Ramming the phone back on to its cradle, he turned to the bed shovelling hastily reviewed papers into his case. 'Come on, hurry up, Ruth. Where have you been?'

'Just out for a quick walk. There was no hurry. This evening's our own. Who was that on the phone?'

'No one. Get changed. I'm starving.' He slid the case under the bed. His tense manner was unusual and in contrast to her invigorated pleasure. She tried to make light of the scene, her good humour rapidly dwindling.

'Nonsense, Wilhelm,' she chided, her voice gently teasing. 'You're never hungry this early.' She patted his stomach then slid her arms around him and looked up into his face. 'Besides, I thought we decided on a little dieting whilst we're here, despite the yummy menus . . .!'

23

His hands took hers and pressed them to her sides, and his face held no apology as he looked down at her, his pale blue eyes dismissive. 'Well I am hungry tonight. Must be all the time changes. Look,' he checked his watch again. 'I meet you in this Motherlode restaurant. It's here.' He took the small town map from the side table, tapped the street with his finger and cast the map on to the bed.

She felt the last drops of pleasure finally evaporate.

'But can't you wait? I'll be ready in ten minutes.'

'No. I haf been waiting for you all this time whilst you re-lived your old haunts. I'll see you there. Fifteen minutes.'

She stared at the door that closed with a soft shush as he went out. It was rare to hear the echo in his voice of his Austrian past; Wilhelm had perfected fluent American. With a moment's disquiet she ran over the scene again in her mind, recalling his strange behaviour on the telephone . . . almost as if he was hiding something. But they were both in this together, so why was he being so secretive?

The restaurant, of course! He had been planning a little *tête-a-tête* and she had spoiled it. How romantic, and how typically Wilhelm to get mad just when he wanted to be loving!

With a wry smile and a sigh at the perversity of her husband, she pulled her sweater over her head on her way to the shower to bathe and change. No need for her to check the map. She knew the restaurant; the Motherlode was an old haunt – of theirs. Hers, and Hillaire's. He'd got that right at least. The smile died slightly and an altogether more intense look filled her brown eyes. The dark and sombre face filled her memory as she discarded the rest of her clothes and stepped into the hot jets of the shower.

Sundown came quickly in California. A lilac sky painted with sweeps of clashing pinks and orange, and then a fireball sun that turned into a soft square as it hit the smog and the horizon before it dropped into the Pacific, and the world went dark and soft.

Alex flicked on the switch, and her brights picked out the

endless highway. She was already well out of LA. The Eagles had sung their greatest hits twice over. She had to find a place to stop. Southern California was left behind as she crossed the Nevada state line. There was an evening cool to the air, and the window was half open, the breeze on her skin.

She pulled in to the first camp site, and taking her flask of tequila and the salt shaker and lemon, she opened the door to the outside world. She did not go far for the moment, preferring to sit out on the steps.

The camp ground was deserted, and the scenery splendid; the pleasure of being solitary made it all hers. A huge sandstone rock was prominent, the long sepia orange valley collapsing into riverbeds and gulleys beneath her. And the wind had been heaven: sweet and soft it travelled for miles across the open plains gathering sage and desert flowers; clearer than a bell. Way off in the distance a hundred or so miles, the road drove straight to the horizon, bordered by huge boulders and sliced stepping rocks that clambered down pinkly to the desert floor, topped by a wide blue sky that, though the light was now fading, seemed endless, the roof of the world presented so low and wide it was like a stage set where anything could happen.

Alex squinted dark brows at the horizon. She checked her watch, monitoring time against mileage. If she slept now and got up really early, she would reach Las Vegas first thing.

After a quick supper, she switched off the generator and the power, set up her hammock outside and climbed in with her bag and a plaid rug that trailed over its edge. Listening to her music she closed her eyes. The night smells wafted over her; only moments passed before she knew she wanted to feel the land she was in completely, and she unclipped the headphones from her head and let the sounds of the desert night ride in. Hart's face had also come to her mind.

Willie Nelson's expressive dirge faded away and she flipped the switch off. Suddenly the music seemed obtrusive; that or it had engineered her thoughts and now she wanted them full flow for the first time. A low moon hung over the horizon and stars sprinkled the night. She took a shot of tequila and a bite of lemon and felt the kick. She was grateful for the winter and no mosquitoes; she'd always had a problem there. Sweet skin, Hart had said . . .

Hart Bennett. Alone, it was far too easy to replay the past. She had been trying to stave it off for hours, listening to music and concentrating on the road. Now as the engine cracked itself into quiet she was conscious of it all. Crickets glipped in the night, and a soft wind feathered the tumbleweed bushes. The tequila hit the spot, and was followed by another. Except for the moon throwing its shadows over the land, she would be in pitch darkness.

She was not afraid of the dark or its fellows; though slim, she was of a good height and deceptively strong. She had seen more cruelty and danger than could be found here. Besides, the philosopher in her said life's course would find its own pattern. She watched the night but there was nothing to see, this was desert. A lone car swung up the hill and passed. Despite her courage, a photograph had caused more fear to course through her body than any war zone.

But the tequila made her brave. Now she gave herself the time to reflect.

Through the falling snow passengers threaded their way through waiting taxis and limos. They jostled bags, cab drivers and each other. The true dark of night had fallen and it was now cold. A stiff wind had got up. Crystalline flakes swirled off the sidewalks and flurried up around them or shivered down from the cottonwood trees. They wanted to join the animated *après-ski* chatter over hot drinks, then retire to cosy hotel rooms with their own wood-burning fires, and latticed bedroom windows which gave a sneak preview of the mountain that would provide a great day's skiing tomorrow.

The young man seemed to head straight through them, find a solitary cruising cab and step straight in with no preamble. He had that air about him. A big man, travelling light; his skis hefted over his shoulder, he carried most of his needs in one black sports bag. The cab pulled out and headed away from the throng. The swirling snow hurtled towards them out of the darkness as they headed for the main road into town.

Five minutes later, Liam Gower stepped out of the cab into the smart West End of Aspen and looked around with interest. Ornamental street lamps on every corner; cats that slept on rocking chairs, home cooking, gingham curtains at the windows and ruched Austrian blinds. Even the steadily falling snow seemed to filter down more gently from the network of pine trees above. Here the rich brought out their childhood fantasies and played them to the hilt. The houses were festooned with coloured lights, and Christmas trees stood festively in windows where snow was piled on sills and doorways. He could even hear the distant tinny sound of carols. He had the feeling that it was all predestined, that if it snowed nowhere else it still would in Aspen, tinkling and shimmering and reflecting in sparkling snowdrifts packed up around picturesque houses.

A white picket fence surrounded a small garden now pillowed softly with snow, a tiny gate opened on to a path that had recently been cleared and was now being silted with powder once more. Steps climbed up to a wide veranda on a clapboard house, where Alpine hearts were cut into blue wooden shutters. Smoke streamed from the tall chimney. It was compact and charming, a Hansel and Gretel woodcutter's house. He opened the gate and went up the path with interest. Wood blocks were stacked on the porch. A ginger cat sprang from the porch and disappeared through the rails of the balcony. From here he could hear the carols more distinctly and realised they were coming from the pink-washed house next door in an endlessly recorded celebration of the season.

It was misleading. Aspen fed its contradictions to them like cookies for tea. Self-help groups vied with astronomical prices and exclusivity. It was the help-yourself society: help yourself but don't help others. No minority groups (unless they happened to be famous and above it all) and heart attack prices. Zen and meditation ruled and if you could remember the seventies you weren't there.

Liam stepped up on to the porch. From here he had a longer view into the valley. The music had drifted away with the small distance he had covered, and it was quiet, with the quiet of nature. The trees creaked gently. Beyond was the Roaring Fork river, its progress slowed now by the frozen cold of winter. Over in the back country it would be impassable and still, a blue white world of cold and quiet where nature was still an awesome force. There a silent chill would hang in the air. By day there would be black runs and danger, something to test a man's nerve. But here it was tame: cosy shutters, oil lamps and shops whose price labels would give any reasonable person good cause for laughter.

These were not reasonable people. These were the elite.

And he was one of them.

He rapped on the storm door to no answer, and looked in through the stained-glass doorway. A soft light burned on a bureau, showing a patchwork blue sofa and a warmly glowing room with peach cushions where a cat slumbered. A welcome mat and a sleeping cat. Aspen-style comfort. No one at home, but the doors open. Hospitality for the in crowd, no criminals allowed.

Liam pushed on the door, and finding it open walked in. A note was pinned to a cushion on the patchwork sofa.

'Liam. Meet me at the Motherlode at seven. The car will come for you at five of. Your bedroom's first right at the top of the stairs. Help yourself to a drink on the bureau. Hillaire.'

He put down his bag and looked around. A silver salver stood on the antique nineteenth-century sideboard along with a shot glass and a bottle of very decent malt. This was home for the next two weeks.

Christmas in Aspen.

Alex had woken to a sound; shells blatted on a city already reduced to rubble, one howled close. Hart gripped her hand, and held it.

The two pepper trees between which she had stretched her hammock rustled softly into her conscious a moment later. It was still warm, and the night sky was painted soft dark lilac. An animal squealed in its death throes yards away. It was that that had awoken her; death in the darkness. The silence when it came was awesome.

The road was a distance off and there was no one close. The old motorhome stood monolithic in the moonlight a handful of yards away across the tumbleweed bushes and the rocks beneath which snakes would curl. Was it a snake that had caused the blood-curdling scream? Rattlers? But this was winter, and they were unlikely to be around. Her heavy hiking boots lay in the hammock with her. Stepping into those first thing to find something had crawled in before her would not be fun. No, it must have been something larger; a coyote perhaps, or a racoon, but now the night was eerily still.

Her hand was still cramped from where it had lain pressed beneath her sleeping body, and from too much hanging on to the wheel of the cumbersome motorhome. She rubbed it; coming to, she was unable for the moment to muster her customary resilience and felt a flash of quite unaccustomed fear. He had always held her hand in trouble. The pain of that memory sliced her heart. The analyst in her wondered why it was not her brain, the font of all feelings, and she knew she was already trying to overcome a deep wounding of her psyche. She curled up, pulling the rug closer and tucking it protectively around her chest.

Alex picked up her drink and sprang the ring, drinking deeply. She had always loved adventure; she craved it. But Hart had sold his photos for a bomb, and his story to *Hello!*

The full magazine piece had been back at their digs, her cameraman, Shaun, looking as shamefaced as a naughty dog. Hart and his amorata had made the cover: a glamorous story of love, a rushed wedding and an island honeymoon. From the look of the two of them, they had found nirvana, each other irresistible from the start. Entwined on a paradise beach, him in designer shorts and her in little more than a huge smile, it had been a million miles from her life together with him. News interest. The ego of the man. In the silent desert night Alex recalled once more the self-satisfied grin, the cruise ship swimming pool, the two newly-weds cavorting for the camera. She felt her own foolishness engulf her and then anger take its place, her saving grace from pain. She had not known him at all, but then in the beginning she'd been so young.

Hart Bennett. *How* young she'd been, how naive; an investigative reporter just starting out but known for her ability. They'd told her they'd teamed her up with another reporter for the nine o'clock news, but not told her who. They'd shipped her out to the Gulf before she'd had time to draw breath.

She'd known *of* him, of course. Hart was a big lithe man, a bit of a ruffian, but he'd seemed perfect. She was absurdly pleased when he seemed happy to show her the ropes. Once a lowly field journalist just like her, on screen his handsome face set against a backdrop of missiles that rained like fireworks, his persuasive mellifluous tones, his urgency and need had sold Third World countries to the English populace just like he had sold himself to her. He was infamous, positively toxic.

Alex swayed in her hammock and squinted at the horizon. Her direct eyes and expressive mouth made a wry self-deprecating twist. Her fatal flaw, because he played that scene again and again. And then, as the record grew old, he played it with someone else. She shifted uncomfortably at the memory of her trust in him. She had always considered stupidity of choice a congenital defect of the mind.

When they had been sent on her first mission together she had fallen for the handsome world-weary traveller, admired his guts and know-how, his instinct, his ability to laugh in the very face of danger. That first time was a strong memory and now as if to salve her wounds, she gave in to it. One night, after a harrowing chase had put them both in mortal danger, he had pulled her towards him and kissed her. Burned her with his passion; just like war victims themselves they had hurried to the nearest dark spot and made love in a field by a bright singular moon. Far off had been the steady thump of mortar shells, but soon the sounds of war had been dissipated by the sounds of her breathing, and her need. All the

30

fear, the tensions and control had burst out of her as he entered her, relieving her of it all, causing her to believe in love at first sight and establishing Hart as her lover *extraordinaire*.

Hart's testosterone level had been legendary, and there was nothing more challenging than an undomesticated animal. It was an easy step to the next stage: at night making love once the need had taken hold. They'd worked as a unit in Bosnia, covering stories, atrocities that had her crying as he took her in his arms, the veteran. The cruelty and the hypocrisy had destroyed her at first but Hart, the consummate showman, had mended her. The tears of frustration that were the natural solution to the horrors were a prelude to their lovemaking and, almost shamefully in such circumstances, adversity had given it its edge.

But then just as suddenly it was all over, and then the next day there was worse news: a trouble spill in a minor African state, a bloody civil war – more bodies to photograph. She had been flown home.

Back in London, her producer had called her in to break the news. Shaun and Bill were going out alone. Someone else would cover the story: the camera's favourite, Hart Bennett. Clearly she could not go. He knew; her broken heart was news all over town – everyone at the studio was avoiding her. He told her to take a break over Christmas, told her she needed it.

She had taken the enforced holiday and caught the next flight out. The one legacy from their relationship had been the old motorhome. They had planned to tour America one day, when they had a couple of weeks off, but they'd never had time for that. Both professed to love the job they were in more than any easy-living vacation: where would the excitement be?

A fax before she left London had solved one particular problem. Hart's guilt gave her a respectable deal, one she could afford: she had bought his share in the motorhome. She had to rebuild her confidence and this trip, so different, was one way. Now the time to travel America was here. And she had not stopped moving since she had returned to England.

She took her map and torch out of her rucksack. Even these were relics of their relationship. The torch flooded over the veins of the map: 15 climbed optimistically north, then cut across on 70 to Denver; the mountains loomed in shadows, higher and higher.

She was finding unexpected pleasures in her solitude. She could sleep out under the stars in this old hammock, listen to country music which he always hated, the dust on her boots. And she was getting a kick out of the physical side of handling this old wreck and keeping it on the road, learning its idiosyncrasies. There was pride in overcoming adversity. She was getting lean, her mind growing strong.

Colorado and its whispering mountains, its grandeur like a massed concert choir, had always seemed like home. Once she had visited there as a child with her parents, and remembered the car ride, weaving through mountain roads with a never ending view that was stunning in its intense beauty. Beyond Las Vegas lay a day's worth of driving through Zion and Bryce National Parks; beauty that could not be equalled. Great roars of rock, shields of pink rising against the tangibly blue sky, achingly lovely clear air, pine scented and cedar wood sweet, and rushing boulder-strewn rivers. Clean, fresh and joyful: the Rockies, where her mother had been happiest. They had always been laughing in those days long before the break-up. They had cooked out, slept under stars as bright as brass buttons. God's waistcoat.

Las Vegas was next.

The dream beckoned. In a cupboard under the bunks she had found her old Rosignol skis and boots. She had an aunt in Aspen and she loved to ski.

An hour before dawn found her heading into Vegas, the last range of hills cutting reality from fantasy. She took a shot of Jose Cuerva Gold to match the scene and hoped solitude wasn't going to turn her into a boozer. The thought made her laugh: she'd never had to rely on crutches, and humour was her saving grace. The tequila stung her throat and made her eyes wake up Vegas style. She was ready for the sudden skyglow of the city as she hit the brow of the shadowed hill.

FOUR

'Wicked!'

Darren Mason stuck his straw into the last of the frothy cocktail that his new friend, Charlie Renby-Tennant, had just bought him, and found the lemon-creamy bit at the bottom. His hair was white blond surfer cut, and his eyes as bold as his mother's. He was kitted out in Joe Bloggs and faux American University gear. Tonight he wore his Dodgers baseball hat back to front, looking cool.

Fanny Mason of Yorkshire, new to Aspen, entered the Jerome Bar at the same moment and felt the adrenalin rush to her head. The swim in the hotel pool had been magic and now she and Stud were raring for a good evening out. The newcomers could not help but survey their surroundings, rubber-necking the crowd for famous faces when of course they were not there at all. The room was full of *arrivistes*. The local celebrities, such as they were, lay low over Christmas vacation when the rich tourists invaded their paradise.

Fanny spotted her rightful heir over at the bar and made her way over, tingling with excitement. She had bought up the last bit of glitter she could find in her local town and she was wearing it all. Her skirt was so high that the full length of the strong thighs Studley adored were on display.

She wrapped herself around her son, embracing him in a dangerously low *décolletage* and a heavy wave of *My Sin*. Darren, all of ten years, fought himself free of the pneumatic breasts and retrieving his black Dodgers baseball cap from the floor shoved it back on his head with all the cool he could muster.

She was voluminous, perfumed and glitter bright, and Charlie, a new friend and a smartarse, was twelve and very well versed in hormones. He didn't want to look a sissy and was somehow conscious that Charlie was every bit as socially

33

superior as his mother. Darren was aware there were Rules; he wasn't yet quite sure what they were but he didn't want to get them wrong and lose a friend. Charlie's cool insouciance was somehow attractive, but Darren's natural exuberance overcame him as he recalled the real fascination.

'Mum! Charlie's asked me to go and play his computer with him. Can I go? I know some great moves I can show him. And they've got a nanny.'

Charlie lounged stage right, locking louche eyes at half mast with his eye-popping elder sister, Victoria. The Renby-Tennant Norland nanny, Sarah, along for the ride and ready to prove her value to her employers, gathered her charges to her.

'I suggested a bit of fun before bed, Mrs Mason. Hope that's all right.'

'Sounds just my sort of party,' whooped Fanny. 'Yes, of course, lovey, you can go. But bed by ten, mind. Early start tomorra.'

'Bogus,' said Charlie carefully.

'Crucial,' said Darren, happy because at least they'd both watched the same American TV series.

'Aah,' said his mother, sinking into the chair reserved for Freddie Renby-Tennant at Felicity's prime table for two. 'Get us a drink, Studdy, while you're up. I'm that thirsty after all that exercisin'!'

Darren Mason downed his drink fast. He couldn't wait to get upstairs and eyeball Victoria in private. She was a knock-out: thirteen with breasts like cricket balls, not like his mum.

The nanny scooped up the children and headed out. Fanny squeezed Darren tight as he left; he extricated himself from a 'be good, lovey, OK Mum' standard issue conversation.

'Well, what d'you think, Fanny?' said her husband as she gazed out from behind an electric smile that never wavered, eyes bright. He was enjoying her expression.

'Ooh, I love it. I'm gobsmacked. It's *great*.' Her accent was broader than ever in the chic surroundings. 'Isn't this ex-citing,' she said happily, altogether missing Felicity's look of surprise. Fanny was a natural force, her whole person radiant. She had no idea she was being monitored by the snooty Felicity Renby-Tennant. Tall and elegant, in belted cream silk, Cyclax lipstick and family pearls framing her horsy face, she could not believe the woman had simply commandeered the other chair at her jealously guarded table.

'Could Stud get you a refill, Fel?' As she shook her head, Fanny giggled and grabbed a handful of snackbites. 'Whenever Stud's away I have to put something in me mouth! It's an old joke!' She leaned over and gave her reluctant compatriot a bruise-provoking push on the shoulder. 'Oh, cheer up, chuck, you could be dead tomorra.' She laughed gaily. 'That's me family motto!'

Felicity decided she wouldn't crack under pressure. Her family motto, loosely interpreted, was 'Strength Through Adversity'. Looking round desperately for Freddie and finding him nowhere, she drew on her endless well of social conversation.

'Do you come here every year?'

'No! Give over! At this price!?' Fanny said, crossing her legs so that her skirt rode even higher. The electric smile beamed. 'How about you?'

'Oh, we do. We come here every year.'

'It's our first trip to Aspen.'

'I'd never have guessed,' said Felicity drily hiding her expression behind the rim of her champagne glass.

'Really. It doesn't show?' she giggled. 'I'm that impressed.'

'Not a bit.'

'I think we might make a habit of it after this.' Her voice lowered and became confidential. Felicity guarded her arm with her hand.

Presumably the woman could afford it; how ghastly. She hadn't meant to take on her son, but for some reason Charlie had struck up an immediate friendship with him. Felicity closed her eyes briefly, recapping her plans for the next winter season, and opening them caught sight of the short husband returning from the bar. She leaned forward for a hors-d'oeuvre, determined now to bear with it. She segued into Part Two. The pale eyelashes fluttered.

'And what does your husband do?'

'Me hubby's big in meat packing,' Fanny offered proudly. 'It's a licence to print money, really. Long as everybody eats meat, and they do.' She tilted her head. 'What about you?'

'Felicity, darling . . .'

Freddie's hand fell on her shoulder. His wife looked up at him, relief etched in her eyes as lean, sanguine Freddie bent to kiss her, his vulture eyes supercharged.

'And who do we have here?'

Still thrown, Felicity's fingers revolved in the air. 'Stephanie. She, er we . . .' Felicity shot him a warning look. 'I had a table for us,' she said stiffly in 'couple talk.' 'Er, she . . . decided to join us.'

Fanny broke in.

'Oh, is this your hubby!' Fanny had a smile like a strawberry ice cream and big blue eyes that flashed like the gobstopper jewels on her fingers. She shone like a Christmas tree herself. Her pretty face was full of good humour and mirth. She was gorgeous, and very loud. And young. Freddie took to her immediately.

'Fanny, please,' she said, holding up a dainty, manicured hand. 'Fanny Mason. Only me Mum calls me Stephanie, but Studdy here calls me Fanny. It's Studdy's idea of a joke. It kind of stook.' She screamed with laughter, and bashed Felicity on the arm. Felicity threw her husband a furious look of despair, but he was making no move to save her. 'Felicity here and me was just getting acquainted – '

And up on her high heels, showing an endless expanse of leg, she grabbed a chair from an adjoining table and pulled it across. 'So – ' She patted the empty seat – 'park your bum down here and tell us all about yerself, Renby-Tennant. What a mouthful. Do you have a nickname?'

'Well I *do*, yes . . .' Inwardly, he felt amused as he sat down beside her feeling his wife's discomfort beaming at him. He thought her exuberance enervating, and his eyes shone. 'My friends in the Cotswolds call me Rising Trot.'

'How unfortunate!'

Felicity intervened with a Margaret Thatcher smile. 'We do a lot of hunting. The Beaufort, you know.'

'Oh, hunting.' The constant smile faded for the first time. 'I don't like hunting. I feel sorry for all them poor little foxes.'

Felicity, in the best tradition of fox-hunters, glowered at her.

'You clearly don't live in the country and know what damage they do.'

'Oh, but we do. Probably quite near you, in fact.' Fanny grabbed another handful of snackbites. Felicity lifted her glass once more to conceal the expression on her face.

But Freddie was interested. 'D'you live anywhere near Tetbury?'

'Yes actually. You know that house on the left just as you're going out on the Bath road . . .' She mumbled her way round the snackbites: 'The big black gates.'

'Not the . . . not Rivernham Grange . . .' Felicity's eyes widened despite herself. 'Not opposite . . . Prince Charles?'

'Yes.' Her hand clutched her knee as her giggle now threatened to splutter the chips all over the place. 'That's the one!' She was laughing now, and Felicity felt it was directed at her, despite its innocence. She had always wondered who lived there. Rivernham Grange was huge. 'You must come and visit us when you get back. We've got stables but I'm afraid we don't hoont. But you're welcome to go for a ride over the estate. We got a fair bit to mess around in.'

Hundreds of acres, a wildlife lake, a thick and endless beech wood, land where the hunt was never allowed to go. Felicity was sick as a parrot.

Felicity was also a dyed-in-the-wool snob. Even more so as Freddie had lost a packet with Lloyds, and all the rich wives who had been their bread and butter were now slowing down on the mid-forties facelifts. They'd had to sell the mill house in the South of France and she didn't know where to put her face in London. Everyone was so mean, asking questions. Freddie had chanced his arm with a big syndicate, been greedy really, and they'd gone down harder than most. He'd lost the lot; now times were definitely hard. She was trying desperately to hang on to their class when all else failed and this trip was a last-ditch effort to show off lost wealth. Fanny Mason was certainly not on the curriculum. She'd felt resentful of the Masons on sight, but despite Fanny's thick skin she'd roped them into her conversation. Now Felicity felt cornered, and her husband wasn't helping.

The woman in question giggled wildly at something her husband said, and her flashing eyes lit around the group and back. She looked about as brainless as a donkey, thought Felicity, but all the men (including Freddie, she saw with annoyance) were taken in by the bouffant blonde hair, the delighted smile and the pneumatic breasts straining under that awful low-cut black angora dress. It was a clash of classes within which Felicity easily paled beside the bubbly Fanny Mason but Felicity set her shoulders in defiance and Fanny – turning back to check out her husband threading his way back and seemingly oblivious of her new friend's pain – smiled sweetly at her and changed the subject.

'I just love your frock, Felicity pet. Me, I can't wear shoulder pads. They always end up looking like a third tit. I'm not one of them Irma Krumps.'

Stud placed her drink before her and sat down, stage-whispering.

'Ivana Trump, Fanny.'

'Do you. You are a greedy boy. Well, I did offer, and you missed yer chance.' She gave him a sidelong look over the rim of her drink, not minding who heard. 'Wait till we get back upstairs.'

'Fanny's unique,' he said, laughing happily.

'I do wish you'd stop saying that,' she giggled. 'Makes me want me meself!' But she was pleased, and he knew it. She leaned forward to Freddie, displaying a provocative amount of honey-cream flesh. He was enjoying himself now, despite his wife's clear discomfort.

'We went down to London before we came out here. Studley's trying to give me an education, poor sod. He took me to the British Museum. I love all those old things, don't you? We're still collecting for our house. Stud's having our portraits painted for above the fireplace. I've seen that in other houses around. It looks really grand, it does.'

'You like art, do you?' Felicity's tone was caustic; she imagined some gilt-framed prints from Athena, or murderous sunsets from Piccadilly.

'When it's *good*. Studley was in a buying mood, as usual.' Her voice was casual, the smile warm. 'We got a couple of Cannelonis for the dining room.'

Felicity's eyes grew wide as she exchanged a glance with her husband. Heathens, with Canalettos. She had to put her down.

'Well of course art's in the family, you know. Some of our marble ended up in the British Museum.'

'Would we have seen it?' Fanny sounded pleased and genuinely interested.

'I don't think so. They swap the collections around from time to time. They're in the basement at the moment, I believe.'

'Bargain basement stuff, eh?'

'Not exactly.' Her acid tones did nothing to quench Fanny's verve; she seemed to have a hide like a rhinoceros. 'They've only got so much room. My grandfather collected busts.'

'So did mine.' Fanny folded her arms under an ample bust, and smiled her thousand-kilowatt smile. 'Me grandmother looked just like me.' Studley chuckled as she gleamed at the reluctant Felicity; everybody warmed in the end to Fanny, even if she had to beat them into submission. 'So, is it Ajax or Buttermilk for you two?'

'Oh, Ajax, I think. The old girl's a great skier,' Freddie expounded. 'She was a chalet girl. It was how we met.'

'Freddie doesn't ski,' Felicity warned, getting her own back.

'Oh, I do, darling.'

'Not *very* well.'

'Not like you, of course, but . . . it's true, I never was much one for skiing. Legs are too long.'

'So what are you going to do for pleasure then?'

'Pleasure? God forbid. I am an Englishman, after all. You know what they say: an Englishman thinks if he comes first it means he's won.'

Fanny howled her appreciation and slapped his leg, her long manicured fingers remaining clutched to his thigh. Her voice became conspiratorial. 'So what *are* you here for?'

'Er, research.' Unbeknown to her, she'd hit the button, and unfortunately he'd fallen right into the trap. He looked over at the door and felt the interest of his wife. Felicity was torn, not wanting to blow the cover, but enjoying seeing him at a disadvantage at last.

'Research . . .? Of what? Snow!? What *do* you *do*, Freddie?'

'My husband's a doctor,' Felicity pronounced over a mouthful of olives. Forget the manners, it was time to show a little pecking order.

'Oh, how interesting. What field?'

'He's in . . .' Out of the corner of her eye she suddenly saw Freddie staring at her, an intent look on his face. She hesitated, going cold. And then, eyes wide: 'I'm not at liberty to say.'

'*I see!*'

The blonde's big eyes widened. Freddie sensed with horror that she was about to pursue it: Fanny, far more astute than she seemed, was always innately curious. He felt all their attention suddenly in the silence that fell. But thankfully he was saved from an explanation by Fanny herself, enthusiastically waving her hand.

'Look, Stud, there's the Molotovs. Coo-ee! Jackie! Over here, love! Ever such a nice couple. We met them in the lobby, just before we met you in fact. Stud, find another chair for Mrs Molotov.'

Freddie was on his feet. 'No, that's OK. We were just leaving anyway.'

The arrival of the Kowolskis changed everything. He saw David making his way across the room and was instantly on his feet, remembering their instructions through the haze of whisky: if in company detach yourselves; no introductions unless essential. They simply must not be seen as a group, nor one with a common denominator. That much Felicity knew at least, and knowing there was also money involved, the success of this trip would ensure her cooperation.

40

'Well, as I was telling your wife – '

'So sorry, there's our party. We really have to go.' His hand was on her arm. 'Felicity?'

His glance stopped her from finishing her sentence, and she was up. 'Oh, well ... it's been so nice meeting you. Sarah will bring Darren back to your room after dinner. All right?'

'Lovely. See you later, then. We'll be going clubbing.'

'Chasers?' Freddie threw in mid-rout. 'See you there.'

They walked off, threading through the tables side by side. As he stood back to guide her he looked at her beaky self-righteous profile.

'You nearly gave it away.'

Her blue eyes flared. 'It was inevitable. Besides, I don't see why it matters so much. Everyone who's anyone knows you're a plastic surgeon.'

'Please,' he said as she edged through. 'Not in here – you'll start a riot.'

Freddie sensed his wife's stiffness, but could not explain just why and how it mattered. Telling her that would be tantamount to telling her everything, and Felicity was a dab hand with a secret, as she'd already shown. As they reached the door he could not help himself as she turned to face him.

'Well what did you think of Fanny?'

Her eyes flashed at his as he spoke. 'You seemed taken.'

He delivered the *coup de grâce*. 'I thought she was delightful. Refreshingly honest and a wonderful smile; so warm.'

'Not everything that shows its teeth is friendly, Freddie.' She stalked off ahead, snarling at the injustices of life. 'You should know that. You've seen enough of them in your office.'

'She means no harm. I bet you even like her in the end.' His smile flickered to include the others hovering at the door. He wondered whether to warn the pair to be on their toes, but decided not to. Let them find out. Besides, if he spoke Fanny was sure to notice. He could feel her radiating from here.

'You just lost your bet,' Felicity said, as her smile joined his, her eyes catching those of Jackie Kowolski and the sardonically raised eyebrow between them as the other couple now entered the room, a table's width away.

David Kowolski had seen them all together from the moment he and his wife walked in. He'd stood back, giving them time to detach themselves as the blonde waved in their direction. There could have been no other choice once she'd called them over. Now, the scene clear, the scholarly figure followed his wife across to the table, catching Freddie's eye briefly as they passed. He'd recognised the girl from the pool and her rotund partner immediately and was as interested to find out their story as if she were a butterfly under a pin. He walked between the tables to where the silvery blonde tresses shone under the lights and the smile was welcoming them.

The atmosphere in the famous bar was alive with greetings and restrained laughter. The rich wore their badge in the way they stood and talked. For the moment the man with the ponytail was unnoticed as he wished to be. On the far side, he'd missed nothing. His eyes quickly gathered in the crowd.

And from the shadows of the bar the elegantly oriental Miki Leng left his table and walked quietly out heading for his rendezvous up at his own house with Hillaire Bowman at half past the hour.

He did not pick up the check. The bartenders all knew Miki; he was the richest man in town.

Ruth Lindstrom donned a *café au lait* silk polo with leggings and a warm hooded woollen cape trimmed with mink and headed out into the evening ten minutes later. The cold air was fresh as sherbet on her face and the snow was falling thickly into a stiff breeze, swirling around the street lamps where the white flakes flared in a ghostly orange nimbus. All around was the softness of heavily drifting white against the purple of night, cushioning sound. Restaurants glowed softly, and couples huddled cosily under big coats headed out together. She held her head up, the magic all around her making her feel young again, and alive. Her boots crunched virgin snow as she headed along the familiar sidewalk for the café, and when she entered her dark eyes were bright, her skin freshened, and her cheeks rosy. Snow petals lay in the rich upsweep of her short hair.

There was a small shadowed foyer and then the bar, softly lit. She went straight through and saw Hillaire immediately sitting at the curved bar with a younger man. Recovering fast, though puzzled, she was ready with a quick smile and without pausing in her stride. It was Hillaire who had set the agenda. It was Hillaire who had chosen to be here too where they would bump into each other, and who tapped the younger man on the shoulder and came over, that old familiar smile on his face. She was conscious of the darkened shadows behind her pushing her forward into the light, into him.

'Ruth.' She felt the look, and broke its intensity with a smile.

'Hillaire. I thought we weren't supposed to meet.'

Wilhelm would be watching. Quiet-mannered Wilhelm, her husband, who missed nothing. He'd be in the restaurant of course, beyond the doorway. Waiting, watching. She was conscious of that. Or tried to be, but she was failing as Hillaire's eyes held her tight.

'I'm allowed to break my own rules.'

'You haven't changed a bit.' She exhaled as if she had been running, and loosened the cape at her neck.

'And nor have you.'

She meant his power. But he hadn't changed. His expression was just the same, only nature's years had aged him, not the man within. It frightened her a little as she felt her heart's pace. He'd always been able to control her. Especially now, it was important that he didn't. Tension, formality, curiosity. Her smile belied her lack of composure.

'Twenty years, Ruth.' A small twist to his smile. 'I've watched your progress.'

'And I yours.'

'I'm so glad you could come, particularly.'

'You made it hard to refuse. That very public donation . . .' Her voice, though tart, edged on warm. She still looked

43

young, because she had kept her figure and her way of standing. She had always been proud. A difficulty that. 'The clinic is still recovering from shock.'

'I'm sorry. I wanted –' the past caught at him – ' I needed you here.'

'The funding certainly helped to ensure that.' Her tone was caustic, and she tilted her head suddenly. 'Are you sure?' Her tone was arch and not a little defensive. He knew her views. 'You do surprise me. Isn't this all slightly immoral?'

'Aspen!?' He smiled, deliberately misunderstanding her. She was silent, waiting. 'Who's to say?'

'Me, for one.'

He laid his hand on hers. 'It's why I asked you. You have an instinct second to none. I need you to help me with the others.' He felt her resistance.

'You know I'll fight you.'

'Yours is the moral voice, Ruth. I hope to persuade you that morality can be linked to progress.'

'From what I hear, I don't think that's possible.' Her voice was low. 'I know you, Hillaire. You run away with yourself. You're not God.'

His eyes grew very dark in the shadows. It was his turn to give a wry smile. 'Well, that's what we're here for. To decide!' He signalled the waiter and pointed him to the bar, his voice growing serious again as he turned back. 'If you stand out from a crowd, Ruth, people will always point the finger. I once tried to tell you that. It's not so bad to be different; it can be good. We, you and I, are not part of the herd. We think, we *choose* to play God.'

Her eyes took him in, her stomach tightening at his words. 'Is that why you chose this place, Hillaire?'

'It's why, yes. It's a land of achievers. Happy families at Christmastime.'

'*Rich* families.'

'It's the perfect cover, don't you see? Where else but Aspen to ski,' he spoke slow and soft. 'No one would suspect we are all here except by chance.' He said the last word softer than ever. 'Look around you. We're even safe enough talking . . .'

44

Around them the guests eddied like fall leaves in a wind. This restaurant, like all the others, catered to and for the best. It was assumed that at certain levels people knew each other anyway. Only the best came here; they were amongst their peers in the professions and entertainment and no one exacted any special attention. All were rich. Equality for the unequal; where none could afford the prices, they knew they all had something in common – an impenetrable sense of 'arrival'.

A lull, and a second look. He was the linchpin that held her fast, steadfast. A laugh from an elegant woman clearly used to centre stage, and Ruth, casually dressed, with little make-up, turned her face slightly into the room to take the moment away. But Hillaire was bending to her still as if she was fascinating and his eyes never wavered. The other woman, tuned to power, sensed him and looked over and away, and Ruth laughed suddenly, finding an inexpressible pleasure in the feeling. She was perversely glad to find he had not changed. She looked back into his eyes.

'You always knew how to focus your attention when you wanted something.'

'You see,' he said, pleased, 'everyone expects to see the top echelon here at Christmas. We do not stand out.'

Her low voice matched his. 'I can't *fail* to see the irony.' She watched him raise his eyebrows in that old way. 'Aspen, the land of the body beautiful, nature's way, when what we do is –'

'Hush.' He put a finger to his lips. 'Walls have ears.'

She almost blushed. He'd always been arrogant; it had separated them once. He made her feel like a child. Ruth, with her Cinderella complex, brilliant in her field; childlike in her emotions. Her recent work had made her infamous; a moral issue with which she wrestled. Off balance, now he would test her, but just as suddenly he changed tack: 'Come along' was all he said, and led her to the bar.

There, he spoke. 'Ruth . . .'

'Yes?' She looked up at him.

'Are you glad you came?'

Their eyes held: his were black and unreadable, hers spelt a warning.

'I'll answer that tomorrow,' she said.

She said it so softly she wondered if he'd heard. The moment passed, and the young man with whom he had been sitting earlier at the bar turned in his seat.

'Liam.' Hillaire raised his voice as the young man put down his drink and stood. Hillaire put his hand on his shoulder. 'Liam is my house guest for the Christmas season. I asked him along for this get-together. Ruth Lindstrom, Liam Gower . . .'

Ruth looked at him with curiosity and found the same look returned to her as they shook hands. His eyes were as dark and a face as haunting as those of a young Hillaire. He had the same mixture of unapproachability and sensuality. A dark horse: contained, clever, subtle and attractive, all formed to give an inner strength. She listed mentally what she felt instinctively, but wondered at his angle, his reason for being there. He was certainly not one of them. He answered her question with a smile. 'I'm Hillaire's protégé. Not in your field at all.'

'Liam is an excellent sportsman, Ruth,' Hillaire offered with a smile, between them.

'Perhaps then you'll teach Hillaire to ski. I once tried, and failed.'

'More likely you than me. I heard of your prowess . . .' His smile was powerful, and despite their disparity in age, she found herself warm to it.

'Perhaps tomorrow.'

'I'd be delighted.' He bent his head. The aristocratic lines of his face caught the lamplight.

Conversation so casual and yet he seemed to know exactly who she was. He also seemed aware of the implications of why they were all there. Hillaire would never entertain a stranger to this deal. He was a man with few friends and many enemies; they were always a little afraid, even her. Yet Liam treated him with the ease of friendship, as someone scared by little in life.

46

Her questions were broken off by the subtle press of Hillaire's hand. Behind her a door opened and she felt Wilhelm before she saw him.

'Tomorrow for me too, Ruth.'

And Hillaire was gone, back to the bar, in immediate easy conversation with Liam, laughing with the younger man. Ruth, standing alone, turned to her husband, who took her arm, as if nothing was amiss. So bound up in the moment was she, it took her another to become aware of the cool of the outside air on his cheek and on the cloth of his grey cashmere coat. His short blond hair was sleek with damp and he was late. She realised that he had been elsewhere, somewhere outside, not intending to surprise her at all. She felt as if events had overtaken her in the last few minutes, events she was unaware of even before he swept her into dinner.

The two men at the window looking quietly out over the night were ill-matched in size – one small and slender, the other heavy in stature – but they were perfectly coordinated in their tangible element of power, and stood easy in each other's company. The backdrop was pure grandeur. At the foot of the snow-blue mountain Aspen displayed its glitter against the velvety darkness.

The deferential oriental voice broke the silence.

'I heard about the tragedy in Switzerland.'

'Four of our top men killed. It was waiting to happen.' Hillaire Bowman drew in a deep reflective breath. 'But we have David at least.'

'David?'

'Professor Kowolski.'

'Ah, yes . . .'

Soft lights flicked on in the house far across the slope and a couple strolled on to a balcony. Gently, they fitted together. Both men watched for a moment, then Hillaire turned away into the room, his associate on his mind.

'I flew down with him. He was supposed to be in Basle.'

Miki Leng turned with him and together they walked back slowly across the huge shadowed room, in heavy thought.

47

'Thank God he wasn't. I hear he is quite brilliant.'

'He's gone further than anyone. Time we're finished they'll be all too aware of just how far. They need to be, to know what he has discovered. It's pure dynamite.'

'Somebody else clearly knows that too.'

Hillaire ran a finger over his chin thoughtfully. 'I've known that for a while.'

'Know who it is?'

Hillaire lifted his whisky from the side table. 'Not yet. That's why absolute secrecy is such an important factor.' His dark eyes searched out the other man. 'You know what the media are like.' He drank deeply, draining the remains of the whisky. 'This is a first: experts who will talk more openly if only a very few trusted people are invited to listen. And time is not on our side. If this organisation steals a march on us by infiltrating individual experiments they could gain hold of the supreme knowledge before we have a chance to harness it ourselves.' His voice, though cool enough, was edged with urgency. 'It's why we're trying to keep our meeting so quiet. If it was leaked it would be disastrous for us.'

'But you know of each other,' Miki's voice was politely enquiring. 'Have you not all met before?'

'Naturally, but each is fairly possessive of knowledge. Sharing does not come naturally when each wants to outdo the other. *And* don't agree, and are competitive. I've allowed for that, though.' For a moment his thoughts seemed to dwell elsewhere; then, clearing his throat he put down his glass again. 'They're all running scared now, and since the Swiss episode well they might. Though they don't know the half of it, they will soon enough, as you suggest, if we're not all doubly careful. I've warned them. Up to them that they adhere to it.'

He appeared restless, and Miki Leng, understanding his guest, held out his hand, bringing the evening to a close.

'They'll be safe enough here. My men are all trained in martial arts. You'll have no trouble, Professor, I guarantee it.' Protected from the outside world, Miki's Aspen hideaway was impenetrable as a fortress and the perfect venue. Hillaire

48

acknowledged the part he had to play with a low nod of his head. Miki's voice waved away any such gratefulness.

'Secrecy also benefits me, as you must realise.' His eyes relayed the intimate message that the two of them and few others shared. 'I'll reassure them tomorrow.'

Hillaire, still dwarfing Leng's hand with his own, gave a small smile. These were not men who allowed easy intimacy.

'Good of you. Right now they're like chickens who've found themselves nesting on porcupine quills . . .'

FIVE

'Shit . . .'

The voice swore loudly as the hood came up and the steam poured out of the ancient gas guzzler. It was a dark green oldsmobile with wooden trim and a huge smoking maw. It could house án army, but at the moment the estate was packed to the roof with gear.

The garage forecourt was empty as Alex jumped down to fill up on coffee and fuel. A tall girl was bent into the hood of the Vista Cruiser. It had a dent on the side that had been there a while. She had a sheet of white blonde hair topped with a pink quiff, and a black T-shirt with Meatloaf's tour dates on the back. She wore frayed cut-offs and her legs were those of a dancer.

As Alex passed her on the way out again she straightened up, the short black T-shirt emblazoned with letters in text recreated by a full bosom. The sleeves had been cut off the T-shirt and the cloth frayed around her brown shoulders. The drift of hair floated down her back. She was striking and immediately noticeable. Around six foot, the long legs, strong and dark from the sun, ended in ornamental scuffed cowboy boots. She slammed the hood with disdain.

'Shit,' she said again. 'Shit, shit.'

She kicked the bumper.

Alex strolled over as the gas filled up. 'Got a problem?' She was smiling at the girl's anger.

'Damn car. Mine got stolen. I borrowed this . . . thing. Two miles and it's burned out.'

'May I?' Alex lifted the hood and looked in. 'Does it have oil?'

'I don't know.' The girl looked her in the eye. Her face was angular and the lips full over buck teeth. She wore Ray-Ban Golds on a pert nose. 'You know cars that well, huh?'

'Well that is fairly elementary,' Alex grinned, 'but yeah, kind of. I took a course some time ago.' Her face closed slightly as her eyes searched the interior: it had been an essential of their training. She took a rag and checked through the huge dirty engine. Oil was splattered everywhere.

'You took a course in car mechanics by choice?' The girl's admiring smile blew away the Third World cobwebs of the past few months.

'More through necessity.'

'You're English.'

'It shows. But we have cars there too.'

They both laughed. The grin stayed on the blonde's face.

'Not so big, though.'

'That's right.'

She looked over at the motorhome filling the space beside the pumps.

'That yours? *That's* big.'

'It is, yeah. I'm just getting to know it.'

'I don't want to know cars no more.' She appraised her again. 'Are you on your own?'

'Yes.' Alex's voice was muffled from inside the engine.

'Where you heading?'

'Heading east.' She straightened up, wiping the dipstick on the rag. 'Well, it's blown all right. Oil's gone everywhere. You can see.'

But the girl was watching her instead. Hands on hips, her Yankee twang was noticeable. 'You mean, I can't drive it.'

Alex laughed, and closed the hood.

'No, you can't drive it!'

'Damn!' She scuffed the ground with the toe of her boot. And then she smiled too, showing square white teeth with a large gap in the centre. It made her look predatory and friendly at the same time. The sheet of blonde hair lifted on the breeze. 'East, huh? My name's Montana.' She held out her hand and Alex took it. 'Montana Marr. I'm a showgirl. From Vegas. I'm going east too.' She had a bad girl's smile; when she took off the Ray-Bans her brown eyes were pure mischief. 'Or was . . .'

As Alex took in the implication her mind did overtime. Did she want company at this time, her first time alone; company that was now there for the asking? It would stop her thinking about the past. Peace, the first in a long time brought its own difficulties. Her voice overrode that brief joyful solitude in the desert.

'I'm heading for Aspen.'

'No shit. Me too.' The smile stayed.

'Well, er . . .' She looked at the baggage in the back. 'You want to come along?'

'No kidding? That's great. I'll get my stuff.' She had it hauled out in moments, throwing it up the steps into the motorhome where it filled the corridor. She saw Alex's look of consternation as she turned back for the last load, and shoved her hands briefly into her shorts pockets, grinning at her.

'That it?' Alex asked wryly. 'I mean, you sure that's all?'

Montana laughed, a broad smile, the gap between her teeth prominent. 'Hey, this girl is tidy. I mean she does hospital corners! I'll get it put away soon enough, you won't know it's there.' She winked as the next case went flying down the corridor, but she was hardly out of breath. 'I used to be a nurse. Thought it was a means to an end. Dippy old men, you know. I ended up cleaning slops. I was *outa* there.'

Alex climbed in and she followed, coming up to the front and looking around admiringly. 'This baby is cute. Yours?'

Alex levered herself into the driver's seat, hand to the ignition.

'That's another story.'

'I'm sure I'll hear it.'

Alex wound down the window beside the passenger seat. 'What about the car? Your friend?'

'Oh, he'll find it. Jim!' she shouted at the guy across from the pumps. 'Tell Johnnie the wreck's here. Tell the asshole it's all his.' She flung herself down in the passenger seat. 'Probably hoped I'd break down in the desert far from anyone but rattlers.' She spun the chair around, eyes quickly touring the trailer. 'Neat.'

Alex turned the motor over. It roared into life. 'So, who's Johnnie?'

'Johnnie Angel. Owns a club. Place I worked. He's a mobster.'

'And you don't think he'll come after you.'

'No chance.' A look came over her face. 'Besides, I didn't want to go that route any more.' She smiled slowly, and looked her over with a warm interest as Alex backed up. 'Johnnie's got the control round here. A hook on all the girls. I was getting out of town. I've done it all. I thought ... Aspen, *yes*, and I was on my way!'

Alex looked into the back at the hoard of gear. 'No skis?'

Montana stretched out, hoiking a boot on to the dash.

'Well honey,' she drawled, 'I've learned that where there's need and a great body, there's always a loan. And I sure got a great bod.' Alex laughed aloud as they pulled out on to the road. 'Besides,' she said, as they headed up to the highway. 'It was all kinda last minute.'

'You could have fooled me,' Alex said, amused. The smile was still on her face as she looked over, appraising her. Montana appeared to be checking out her new surroundings. Alex tipped her head to indicate the well beneath her feet. 'There's fresh coffee in the pot.'

'Sure.'

'You live around here?'

'Till now. I came from a small town originally.' She stretched pleasurably. 'Doomed to be a trucker's pit stop for life, a handful of houses on the side of a highway, one 7-11 and a load of dust, and those narrow-minded back country brains. It wasn't even a town, more a pile of shack houses each side of the highway, dirt and dogs running in the yard. I *longed* to get away. I sat on the fence and watched the cars go by. My biggest journey was down to the corner store. By the time I was ten I'd listened to all the road songs ever written. My daddy drove a truck. He liked the Eagles mostly. He told me too many stories of far away to ever make me comfortable in Pitstop. My momma was fat, and he strayed often as he could. I never wanted to be fat. I knew by my daddy's eyes

53

the world was out there waiting for all the thin girls there ever were. Someone was listening. I hit six foot at thirteen and the only thing big 'bout me was these.' She lifted her breasts with long fingers. 'I found a copy of *Playboy* some guy'd left behind. I dyed my hair bottle blonde with a pink quiff. It's my trademark. They used to love me in the clubs. I stood out all right. This big guy gave me my name. Said I reminded him of Montana where he came from – big and rangy. I liked the name.' She settled back. 'Yes, with the body I got I knew my future.' She laughed, the slide of white hair falling back against the black leather seat, and drew a roach from her breast pocket. 'Do you smoke?'

Alex, looking away, was negotiating the traffic. 'No.'

'May I?'

'Go ahead.' Las Vegas pulled away behind them, soaring silvers and windows that caught the morning sun. A rainbow of revolving colour pulsed between the gilded building block façades and a black pyramid of glass. It looked quite unreal in the midst of the open prairie. She smelled the dope immediately the girl lit up and looked over.

She stared, feeling surprise. 'God, you do that stuff in full view?'

Her look was cool. 'Long as you don't mind, I do.'

Alex raised an eyebrow and shrugged.

'Just amazed you're so open.'

Out on the highway the sun hit her eyes and she pulled down the visor. Beside her, Montana pulled on the joint, seemingly unperturbed.

'Are you straight?'

Alex thought about the ounce under her seat.

'No,' she said. 'I just heard about the cops round here, that's all.'

Montana smiled through smoke-narrowed eyes, unconcerned.

'Russian tobacco,' she said. 'That's what my dad used to call it.' She breathed in the smoke. 'It seems some guy came past one day, a Russian sailor, and gave him some of his tobacco. He called it that so's he could do it in front of me

54

without my knowing it was *de weed*. Must have been a real friendly sailor. He smoked for the whole of the next ten years, and I never suspected. Not till a guy offered me some anyway, and I asked him if he'd been to Russia too.'

Alex laughed, her eyes flicking over to her and back. Montana looked up at the roof of the cab, her smile soft.

'Did you hear that Aspen's halfway between Virgin and Climax, that's its claim to fame. But closer to one than the other, I'd say, wouldn't you?'

'And just north of Happy Hollow.'

'According to all I've heard.'

Now they both laughed, the ice broken. 'That's better. See, it's not so hard, is it.' Montana watched her profile, amused. 'You should loosen up. You look pretty when you smile.' She smoked, eyes narrowed in humour. 'Where are we headed first?'

'I thought the old Indian reservation just north of here. I bought fireworks there five years ago and let them off in the desert. It's pretty dramatic, it's so black and it was the only burst of light. Check the map,' she said, pulling it from the pocket beside her, 'it's just south of Moapa.'

'Can we let them off right away, tonight!?' Montana unfolded the map, her voice as eager as a child.

'It's illegal . . .' She saw Montana raise a sardonic eyebrow. 'Yeah, I know . . .' She pulled the map over towards her and frowned as she searched the red lines of the highways. 'We head into 70 going east. Across the Utah prairie. We start to climb then up into Zion and Bryce.' The national parks were spectacular. 'Out the other side we're into the mountains, and snow. That'd be great at night. Just around Green River, twenty minutes to the grasslands, twenty minutes to the snow. I'll never forget that. That'll be our last stop before Aspen.' She let go of the map and concentrated on the road ahead, dipping them down and up over the land and running straight as a die to the horizon. 'We could do it there. When no one's around. A celebration, if you like.' Her smile faded as she felt the old cart pull beneath them as they climbed a small incline; cars whizzed past, and she topped up the revs, her forehead creasing.

Montana was busy with her joint, fastidiously holding the roach now with a pair of tweezers. 'Sounds good,' she said. 'You've been out there before?'

'Yes.' She looked over. 'What's there for you? Old friends?'

'I have no old friends,' Montana mused. 'I live my life in sections. You'll see me with a mass of people, always, but I hardly know them. They're only ever recent. This time next year they'd be non-existent. I like moving on.' She leaned back into the seat. 'I went last year, fell in love with the place, had a friend who was a bartender there. Took me to the Bartenders Ball. All the locals go, I thought I might pick up a bite. Trouble was they saw me with him. You need to get in at the right level. He stayed on, told me Aspen's best-kept secret is the summer season. I had to get back to Vegas. He was never going to make it big. No ambition. Bet he's still there waiting tables.' She sighed expressively. 'No, my new friend Alex, exploitation's my game, of my own natural abilities. I plan to use what I have to get myself rich for life. Aspen at Christmas attracts the cream de la cream. I'm going to skim it off, just for me. Skiing's only a part of it. You ski well, of course, I bet.'

'I used to be into extreme skiing.'

For a moment her mind envisaged the black runs, the out-flung snow-capped rocks and the nail-biting jump off into the canyon below. She'd got to know some of the black runs in Aspen, the uninviting cold and beautiful black country whose whole ambience was one of irresistible challenge.

'That must be a blast.' Montana's voice held awe. 'I always wanted to. Stoned, preferably.'

'Searching for the ultimate, they call it.' She watched the country roll by. 'It's a life's pursuit for some.' She looked over briefly at the soft dope-induced smile. 'Why don't you try?'

'I can imagine. Not for this kid, though. I like life itself way too much. I can ski like a dream but I'll keep it for show on Ajax mountain.' She wound her body expressively against the seatback as she spoke. 'I'm real supple. Comes from being a dancer.'

56

'What's Vegas like?' Alex checked her out briefly. 'Being a showgirl?'

'It's OK. Like all glitter it wears off one day. You have enough of shaking your titties at a bunch of assholes.' Alex laughed. 'You don't have to hook up with any of them, but it helps. They're all loaded.'

'Bet they make you pay your dues though.'

'Oh, *sure*...' The joint had run its course and she was busy tweaking the last puffs from the dying embers. 'All rich men are mean somewhere, somehow. You're a commodity, bought and paid for. They understand the meaning of paid up, and so had you better. Paying your dues is *it*. This time I gathered my money all together, got that crap car off Johnnie but didn't tell him *exactly* where I was going; he thinks I'm just heading out for a couple of days. No way, I'm gone. Planned to dump it in a car park somewhere. I offset my own to add to the piggybank and decided this time I'm going back unknown, on my own terms. I'm going to book into the Jerome, take the best room I can, eat out at Abetone's and shake my booty at Chaser's. At worst, I can last the Christmas season. But this time I'm going equal, using what God gave me and my wits. That's why all the gear. I've hoarded the best of the stuff I acquired over the years. Honey, I'm going to look like a goddamn heiress and act the same way. I'm going to blow it all, win or bust.'

'And what will Johnnie say!?'

She laughed, and flicked the joint out of the window.

'Fuck Johnnie. Now enough of the questions already! I'm a girl who leads with my hips, not my conversation.' She grinned the toothy smile. 'You didn't stop in Vegas, did you? You ever been there before?'

'No.'

'Not interested?'

'Not much. I'd rather hang on to my money. Perhaps on the way back.'

Mountains loomed on the horizon, long and black like a tidal wave on a flat beach of scrub land. The Nevada border lay ahead.

'I thought you must have been before. Most folks driving through for the first time, time it for twilight. You drive out the dark desert into this bright city right slap in the middle of nowhere. When I came here first I loved that. Got a real kick out of it.' She lifted her boot back on to the dash. 'So then, what's your story?'

'I'm just crossing the States.' She made it sound light.

'And?'

'That's it.'

'You planned it that way?'

Alex hesitated long enough for Montana to notice.

'I thought I'd head for the Rockies. Ski in Colorado. I have an aunt there.'

'You're not planning to stay in Aspen?'

'I don't know.' She pointed at the Thermos to deflect the question. 'Want to pour us a coffee.'

Montana unscrewed the lid. 'Well I plan to stop with the wanderlust for a while anyway. I don't know the future, but I do know it's up to me to set the agenda. Aspen seems a good place to start. Do you ever consult a clairvoyant?'

'Can't say that I have.'

'I did. Last week. She told me the future looked rosy.' She poured the coffee into a cup. 'My mom started me off, with a Ouija board, calling up dead spirits. Used to make my dad mad as hell. They were real close, so he said, tell you what if I go first if there's anything in it, I'll get back to you.'

Alex felt her interest. 'And did he?'

'Yeah, he went. And you know what, he never got in touch.' She sounded so indignant and wide-eyed that Alex laughed.

Montana laughed too. 'My mom never believed in anything after that. She was pretty uptight, I remember, always looking like she was searching for her brain.' She handed over the cup of coffee, doused with milk. 'I'm not like her at all. I've always known the score.'

Alex remembered. 'So, what happened with the fella?'

'Well honey, I was the worn-out shoe, wasn't I. He went for a new tight fit. These showgirls are so tacky. When I found out, I told him goodbye. It's over, I said. And he said, well I accept that. Yes, it'll hurt, but it'll pass. I'll get over it eventually. Life goes on.' She hooted aloud. 'I thought, Woah, just a minute. Let's think about this. Get over me!? When, how soon? Let's hold on a minute here. I may just leave tomorrow instead.' Her long hands palmed wide. 'The worst thing is he didn't even *argue*!'

'Well, what did you want him to do?'

'I wanted him to get hold of me like this,' she said, curling her fingers, 'and beg me to stay, say don't you dare fucking leave, and just, you know, overcome me. *Make* me stay.'

'The scientific approach.'

'Yeah!' She laughed. 'In the end he believed me. He got smart. And you know – he wanted *me* to apologise. Said he'd have me back. Hey, the girls were lining up in advance. One thing about me. I never ever say I'm sorry or wrong. It's my only defence. Nothing to do after that but leave.'

'Man is master of the ever-changing plan.' Alex headed the vehicle up through rearing sandstone rocks. Beyond, the road trailed like a bright ribbon between miles of arid desert. 'Like a child with a sandbox,' she said drily, thinking of Hart. 'Knock down this castle and make a new one over there. The sand remains the same, it's the shape that changes.'

Montana looked wise. 'Sounds like you know what I'm talking about.'

Alex was saved from comment as they slowed at the crest of the hill. The engine coughed and almost died as she kicked up the revs and she found herself fighting several tons of machinery over the brow. She kept her foot down hard. 'Darn, maybe I flooded it at the gas station.'

Montana looked at her with interest. 'You can handle it though, can't you?'

'I'm learning.' Concentration etched her face a she revved it higher. 'Shit, the damn thing's dying on the idle.'

They made the crest and rumbled sweetly down the other side. Alex uncurled the tension in her body, pushing back into the seat, and breathing deep.

'No guy, huh?'

'I don't need a guy.'

'Not a little rich girl, are you?' Montana looked around with that half-smile. 'Doesn't go with this wagon. Or is this breaking out, showing independence?'

She paused as if negotiating her thoughts. 'No. It's not a show. It's for real.'

'So you work.'

'A bit of writing.' She checked her driving mirror.

Montana stared ahead at the undulating road. 'I pride myself on knowing what people do. Years of watching the punters. It was a game with the girls to keep from getting bored. I could spot the freaks any day of the week. You're going to try and pick up a story in Aspen, that it?'

'Could be.' She thought about it, measuring her memory. Something would always be happening there. But could she be a paparazzo? She doubted it. And that would be it for news. There would be nothing world-shattering happening in Aspen.

'You have to go to Chasers then. All the stories start and end there.'

'What is it?'

'It's a club. As exclusive as they come anywhere. All the top locals go. The celebs, the filthy rich. They all gain entry. It's membership only but if you're someone special, you get in anyway.'

'So membership's a fallacy.'

'Not if you're a nobody! The joke is on those paying the high ticket. It's owned by Jack Fenner. He's an enigma, end-lessly fascinating. And his friend, Rowan Bader. They laugh at the jerks who pay the membership fees. Like him or love him, Jack gets himself talked about. He fills lots of spaces between the drinks at dinner parties. Nobody smokes any more, so Jack's become the new intercourse cigarette.'

'You seem to have found out a lot about this guy.'

'I always do my research. One of the showgirls came back. She'd got a guy and they were off building their own six-bed ranch style in Red Mountain, stucco, brick and lots of glass. Mountain views from every room,' she said, her voice wistful. 'Yeah! Way to go!'

60

'So what's your interest in this fellow Jack?'

'My friend started in Chasers. It's the best place to be seen. Girls get jobs there because it's chic to work for Jack and it's not really work. You just gotta look right. If you're not nubile, you're not noticed. His favourite saying is "Go away and lose twenty pounds and you can have a room." He gives you a room for free, and you have cachet. Any other job you have to bus in from Glendale and that's over an hour. Rooms are cheaper there. Jack gives girls a deal.'

'He sounds horrendous. So it's a high-class pick-up joint? Why leave LA? You can see a Chasers club anywhere.'

'Because it's Aspen and because it really has got soul, and because it's *not* LA. And because a certain kind of guy goes there, the ones who throw their money around – *and* because only the very rich can afford to rent and at some point I might just have to start thinking about that. So, I thought I'd get in with this Jack fella first. He's a real cool dude.'

The first cool breath of mountain air had reached Alex. She breathed in, savouring it as she ploughed the old motor-home up another difficult incline on to yet higher ground. It was all upward from now on, and she was wondering if they were going to make it.

'Seems Jack has everybody where he wants them. He can afford to be cool,' she said, her hands feeling the sudden judder of strain on the engine through the wheel. She pushed her boot down harder to catch the revs. 'You don't need to be a member, you just need to be someone. What kind of exclusivity is that?'

'His. He has control on that. On *whether* you're someone. It's what he says that goes . . . that's what makes it interesting. And him . . .'

She put a teaspoon on the end of her nose as she spoke. Alex stared at her.

'What *are* you doing?'

'It's the latest cure for stress.'

'Not my driving, I hope.'

'Nope.' She wiggled it into place, her head back: 'but you just reminded me of my contingency plan. Aspen streets are

61

paved with self-help groups. They're all neurosis ridden there. Angst, that's the "in" word. People warm to me because they know I don't give a shit. I'm going to teach them to be cool. You have to calculate the things you're good at. It's a competitive world.'

'Are you trained?'

'Man, I've had my training in Vegas,' she said, clutching the gravity-defying spoon in her hand. 'Every psychopath goes there. And I've got balls. Everyone in my family has. It's not exclusive to the guys. Jack Fenner, get ready . . .'

Jack Fenner paused outside the door of his restaurant in front of a strategically placed mirror. He shook his hair dry for a moment, ruffling it with his hand. His smile stayed in place, his eyes permanently crinkled as if looking up a mountain slope into the sun, something he'd done a lot. Jack skied every day, or at least, even if he didn't, he went up the mountain to Bonnie's. Everyone stopped at the halfway restaurant; the view from there was fabulous. Like many, Jack looked at the arrivals, not at the mountain view.

Jack had a fiefdom. He also had a wealth of grey curls, a face like a handsome bloodhound and an old roué's smile. He was the feudal owner of Chasers, and it was *the* place to be, *après après-ski*. He made his guests welcome while ruling them completely. He appeared to be extremely easygoing, but appearances were deceptive. Unmarried, fiftysomething, he was surrounded by nubile young things helping out. They had strong legs, skimpy costumes and were seriously under-paid, but they were where they wanted to be. They did it for the prestige of being a Chasers girl and for working for the great man himself. And the rooms he gave them for free were as rare as gold dust, with real estate as it was in Aspen.

In his customary style he had arrived for dinner late. Having trained as a chef, he bossed and bullied the staff in the kitchen and prepared sauces with skill till everyone fled – and only then, greeted with enthusiasm by the room at large, did he head through the main dining-room door to sit down with his guests at the favoured table in his chef's whites, the stains of his expertise still on his bib like battle scars, curls still damp, his skin healthily tanned. Seating twenty, it was a massive Elizabethan refectory table he'd picked up in England and shipped over. He sat in a black oak bishop's chair with his back to the fireplace.

The barbecue for the ribs and steaks was laid out in the huge fireplace. Summer or winter he always had a barbecue, and he always made his guests help. 'The kitchen's through there' was another of his sayings, and they soon got the message. Now they rallied into the kitchen, bringing out the food, pouring drinks at the bar for late arrivals. They paid a lot for the privilege, and he understood that need. He had grown up amongst the rich as an observer. A barman's son himself, he had found that the rich had a kinky need to be slavish given the right circumstances. It was fun to be allowed in the kitchen, to serve at the bar and wait table; as though you were exclusive, such fun to be servile. It meant you were a friend of the owner. It showed you were 'in'.

Jack shouted, bullied and ordered them about just as if they were staff, and they scurried like mice, and came back for more, amused by it all. He had it off pat. He also ran the small Hotel Lenore alongside. There he'd call the guests in their rooms and force them down to supper on time. He ran the establishment like an English country house, and yet they paid willingly. They almost felt as if had they refused to play the game, they wouldn't be invited again. Everyone was a friend, and yet none were. There were no guarantees. Jack and Rowan had nowhere to climb; they were already kings in this jungle. They knew they held the aces, and laughed their way to the bank.

The ambience itself was masculine; warmed over Ralph Lauren, eclectic English country manor, oversized sofas, attempts at art, hunter green and burgundy. A steep wide dark wood stairwell led down into the darkness below: a bar, a restaurant, a womb-like dance floor. But Jack did not mean to please the men. He only pleased himself. Jack didn't relate to men.

Exclusivity; that was his game. He knew which buttons to

press. Jack was a poseur, Jack was smart, Jack had created an atmosphere, but more than that. He had created originality. And in Aspen that was everything.

Fanny Mason and Freddie Renby-Tennant got ready to get down and shake their booty on the dance floor. The music hammered, lights revolved, and so did Fanny's backside. Felicity, sitting alone and unable to talk to anyone through the endless pulsing din, ground her teeth. She hated the noise of the music and was not enjoying herself at all. She wished it wasn't so essential to be seen at Chasers.

She wanted to stop it all at once and go home, but for once, turned on by the effervescent and wholly natural Fanny, Freddie was standing up to his wife, much to her chagrin. At least if she asked him any pertinent questions in here he could pretend he couldn't hear her, but he needn't have worried; Fanny's frenetic dancing precluded any sort of conversation. The northern girl, bedecked in glitter and fun to boot, was entrancing. She made life fun for everyone. It was a world he had forgotten. As they moved back to her table he found himself confiding in her.

He was looking for her an hour later as they left the club. From the bar, Jack Fenner watched and made mental notes. It was his business.

At Evie Bader's house in Starwood, the hot tub picked up the sybaritic atmosphere. Laughter, drugs, naked bodies and cold beer stacked in snow was piled up around the steaming hot tub. Music thumped in the background. The house was one of Starwood's finest: contemporary glass and marble with soaring cathedral ceilings and next door – if you could call it that with a few acres of private grounds in between – to an Arab prince who was never there. They could party as much as they liked.

Aspen was the land of the body beautiful and no more so than here. Hopefuls, waiters and ski bums got down for the night. You had to look good in a place like this. Drive a cab, wait tables, winter jobs – then you got chances. The girls, high on a combination of superb fitness and expensive drugs, showed off their bodies. A playboy bunny – once the most famous of all but now steadfastly married and her body hidden from view except for her husband's playtime – was free for the night. It was her party and she was sick of the old man's clutches. She stripped off slowly to wild applause.

It was freedom. She leaped into the hot tub, and out into the snow pursued by a naked young god, running as hard as he could with a lusty grin and a whooping laugh like a hyena just to frighten her. It only served to heighten her excitement. She screamed delightedly and headed for the bedroom with its own private terrace and entrance. And warm satin sheets.

A fancy dress party. Satyrs and nymphs. He was a dryad. He could have been anything, it didn't matter as long as you were bare-ass naked.

That was the whole point.

It was just like the old days.

Fanny Mason watched the black Range Rover with its sable dark windows draw up at the kerb. Its chrome bumpers jutted out a good foot in front, polished to a perfect shine.

'Ooh, look, Studley. Rhino bars. I didn't know they had rhinos in Aspen.'

She watched the short dark man climb out, his grey hair pulled into a ponytail. He wore a heavy black coat with a high collar, and his face was square and set as he turned. He disappeared into the hotel, wearing aviator sunglasses even though it was night. 'Weird,' she said and returned her attention to the room.

'Darren's snoring away. Dead to the world. He's going to love it here tomorra.'

The thump thump of the Chippendale tape drove through the plush quiet of the suite as Stud came out of the adjoining bedroom and quietly closed the door. Fanny was boogieing in her undies while the tape played enthusiastically on the video. It was the one demand she made, and Studley, adoring her, conceded. The saucy tape had become part of their luggage, and the video recorder booked in every hotel. It was all part of the ritual, and it had its rewards, after all.

'Nice evening, lovey?'

'Lovely,' she said breathily, concentration etched on her face. 'Magic.' The music pumped into a jungle beat and she headed straight into the funky chicken for a quick workout. Her breasts jiggled in their lacy cups. She was wearing a sexy pair of diamanté-studded heels. She knew he loved that.

He walked over to the mirror, eyes on her as he started to unfasten his dickie bow.

'You're unique, Fanny love, did you know that?'

'I wish you'd stop *saying* that!' She screamed with laughter and ground her hips more fervently to the music, shimmying away from him. He watched the rounded rear end revolve across a pair of strong thighs, the long smoothly tanned legs endless. A neon thong decorated the bedpost. It was Fanny's most precious belonging after Studley; a momento of a rave night at a Chippendale concert. She'd never told him how she got it, but he trusted her implicitly.

She threw her mane of blonde hair back over her shoulders, eyes on the television screen as her favourite Chippendale strutted his stuff with a huge naughty smile. The dancer toyed with his skin-tight shorts; any moment now.

'Good of that Felicity to help out with Darren.'

Fanny snorted loudly but did not stop her rhythm. 'No skin off her nose, Studdy. The nanny did all the work. She's a right snob. Who does she think she's kidding? She asked me if me rings were real. Bloody nerve.' She lifted her pretty chin defiantly. 'So lovey-dovey with that husband of hers . . .' She chuckled, remembering. 'What did they call him?'

'Who?'

With a teasing smile, television's Body Beautiful turned, bent from the waist, and oh so very slowly peeled down his shorts to reveal a tight tanned butt in a minuscule black thong. The provocative over-the-shoulder smile was pure 'come-on'. Up went Fanny's blood pressure. The rhythm change, the shorts were flung aside and he was around –

dancing lustily, full frame right up into the lens, jiggling everything inside that little black pouch.

'Freddie,' she breathed, her cheeks flushed, and dancing to match him.

Stud watched, transfixed at Fanny on the move. It was quite a sight. The other man still on his mind was there as he looked into her lovely face, bright eyes just a little wild. Studley was acutely aware of the wholesome, lively beauty that drew men to her, and ruled by his love for her. He couldn't bear to share her, and he turned away, looking back into the mirror.

'I think he should be called Ruddy Twit.'

Fanny broke into laughter. 'Well, I just know that she gives him hell. They were at each other's throats all night. Did you see how she reacted when she knew we lived at the Grange? Bloody snob.'

'Next time you see her tell them we're getting divorced, that I'm bankrupt and we're going to be squatting in Sunderland when we get back. They'll probably make up.'

She laughed even louder. 'They'll fuck like crazy.'

Studley warmed to his subject, twisting round on the chair, his chubby cheeks alight. His hands spread wide, his eyes sparkling, he described it as he stood up, his bald head reflecting the lights that pulsed from the telly as the erotic dance sequence thumped towards its close.

'He'll start to come quickly, her up against the wall, in rapid jerking movements: "Oh, Oh," he'll shout. "Studley's a loser, Studley's a loser . . .!" He'll come with a cry, and then he'll go all quiet . . . "Sorry I was so quick, dear . . ."'

Fanny giggled. Laughter always made her randy. 'You've made me all hot with your talk.' Her eyes shone. She wriggled towards him, discarding the undies and stopping briefly at the bed to slip into 'something more comfortable'. The neon thong now decorated that part of her he loved best.

'You want to try room service?'

She was a good head taller than him, putting him at a perfect advantage as she drew him into her. He pulled her closer. 'As a matter of fact I *was* feeling a bit peckish.'

67

He picked up the glossy room service menu, and studied it. She lifted it from his fingers and tossed it back on the bed.

'*You're* the ruddy twit.'

She pushed him on to the edge of the bed and sat on his knee winding her arms around his neck.

'And *you're* so wicked,' he said, tapping the pert nose. For a moment there was little but the sound of their kisses and the soft feeling of her flesh under his hands. He squeezed the delectable rear. Her thighs pressed closer and he felt himself burn for more. Pulling away ever so gently, hands on her hips, he gazed at her in adoration.

'Are you happy with me, pet?'

'What a silly question.'

'*You* should have a nanny. Someone to help out.'

She ran a long finger down over his nose and lips to his chin, looking deep into his eyes.

'Now why would I want that? I like being a family, Studdy. What's the point of kiddies otherwise?'

'Time and a place, you mean.'

'Exactly,' she said huskily, her eyes running over him. 'You know, you look ever so sexy with your dickie bow all undone like that.' Expertly she manoeuvred the pearl button aside and slid her manicured fingers over his chest.

'That Freddie took a shine to you,' he said.

'That Freddie'd take a shine to a duck if it quacked. Me, I like quality in a man.' She slid a hand down. 'Know what I mean, chuck . . .'

But she sensed the change in him, and as suddenly her eyes found his, and humour lit their depths. 'You're *jealous*, aren't you!?'

'I'm scared of losing you, petal.'

She saw the seriousness and the light in her eyes died, genuine worry taking its place. 'Now what brought that on?'

'I don't know.'

'You'll never lose me, Studdy,' she said, cradling him close and springing the ties at the side of her garish monokini. 'You mean too much to me. There's a thousand Freddies out there, honeypot, and only one of you . . .' On the video the routine drew to a final raunchy close and an array of upturned bottoms. 'Ey, I love that bit,' she said, and flipped the switch, sending the Technicolor display into blackness. 'Lie back sugar daddy, now it's your turn . . .'

The two girls stopped to buy fireworks at the reservation. Feeling good, Alex began to sing as they drove along in the black desert night. She had a clear bell of a voice and Montana listened, quietly smoking and humming along in the passenger seat. At Mesquite, Alex changed her watch to mountain time and headed deep into Mohave country.

They were a day's drive from Aspen.

SIX

The chink of the spanner sounded on the desert night.
'Where d'you learn all this shit?'

'I can't see. Hold the torch still, Montana.'

'It'd be easier to look for the nearest man.'

'There isn't one. And even if there was, I wouldn't trust
him out here without a gun in my right hand.' The engine
that had finally stuttered to a stop would not start again.

Alex took the air filter off, and with the flashlight dancing
looked down into the carb. She saw it right away, quarter of
an inch of gasoline pooled in the intake manifold.

'The gas is flooding the carb. The needle valve might be
stuck.'

Montana peered in, baffled. 'Can you fix it?'

'Yes, I think so.' Alex straightened up, wiping her hands
on a rag. 'I'll try soaking it up in the morning, by daylight.
We might as well stay here tonight.' She stood free, slowing
the movement of her hands on the stained cloth and listened.
'Where is this place? It's goddamn beautiful; listen.' The
Rockies loomed ahead and there was the distant sound of a
rushing river. 'There's a river down there. Hand me the
map.'

She opened it, and together they pored over it. Alex
pointed the flashlight. Her hair, floating free, swept across
Montana's arm.

'Snake river, Nevada, looks like. We'll have to camp for
the night. The sleeping bags are under the bunks. You fancy
sleeping out?'

'You kidding. At least we agree on that. There's no other
way with a sky like this.'

Montana looked around her. The desert lay in soft relief
under the stars, and the craggy rocks braced the view from
every side, some pointing up into the sky like great mono-
liths. A sense of drama coupled with the rushing sound of
the river and air that was sweet and cool.

'You're right, it is beautiful,' she said, against the quiet.

'Tomorrow I'll pick up a rebuild kit in the next town. Do a bit of work on the carburettor.'

'Shit, you're such a bloody mechanic.' Montana seemed to find it funny and laughed hilariously, chuckling again once she'd stopped.

Alex watched her, eyes full of amusement. 'You OK?'

'Yeah! It's just it's a guy's job.'

'And a guy would expect a return for his investment. Count yourself lucky.'

'Oh, I do!' Her fresh burst of giggling infected them both. When it died, she looked around, breathing deep.

'God, it's a pretty night. Just look at those stars.' She looked up at the sky and breathed in. 'Studded like a pair of Las Vegas jeans.'

They walked to the edge of the ridge and felt the wind blow up from the river below. Montana took out the half of tequila and tipped it into her mouth.

'You planning to get drunk on that stuff?'

'Sure gonna try.' She grinned at her. 'Puts the world in Technicolor.'

'It's already bright enough for me.'

'Well, maybe I'm just missing Vegas. My eyes need to quieten down some. I'm not used to dark with no lights. Let's walk down to the river.' She fished in her pocket. 'Damn, I forgot my dope.'

'Try some of this.' Alex handed her her Venice beach clay pipe and a Zippo lighter. There was a small knob of hash in the bowl. 'Here's one I made earlier.' She grinned. 'It's an old English joke.'

'You are a dark horse,' Montana said, inhaling the dope. 'Smells like good stuff.'

'I've had it a while. I tend to nurse it.'

'Moments of stress or intimacy only.'

'Something like that, yes. Got it off a guy in Marrakesh.'

Montana was about to light it when Alex held her arm and stayed her. Her foot was already raised. She stepped back. 'What's that godawful smell?'

71

'Is it your hash?'

'Don't be daft. If it was it would kill you. It's skunk. You can smell them a mile off.'

'It's not skunk.' They went closer, shone the torch.

The rat was huge. It lay on its side, in a bed of stones and scrub, its fat tummy spread like a lump of punched grey dough. Its head was moving.

'Ugh. It's alive.'

Montana pushed it with the toe of her boot. It rolled back, its sharp yellowed teeth bared. The torchlight picked out the rustlers, a bunch of maggots shifting hard under the skin in their gluttony.

'No, it's dead.'

'How disgusting.'

Alex flicked the torch out.

'That's our future.'

'You enjoyed that, didn't you?'

Alex chuckled, and took the pipe, lighting the dope and dragging hard on the flame. She spoke around the pipe stem.

'I'm learning.' Her eyes were amused. 'Get you back for calling me a grease monkey.'

'And you're good at learning, I can see,' Montana said slowly. 'Loads of practice. Man, what is your story? I reckon you can see in the dark. You sensed that thing before we smelled it and you didn't even turn a hair. You produce dynamite dope filched no doubt off some fakir in Morocco, and I thought I was the ballsy one. Were you in the army or something?'

The bowl lit, Alex laughed and handed it over, her voice cracking with the smoke. 'I just like to cope with life, adversity doesn't frighten me.'

But Montana was watching her closely. 'What do you do, back in England?'

'Smoke that thing, it's going to go out.'

But for once it didn't interest Montana; she stood in front of Alex. 'Come on, show me yours, Alex. I've shown you mine. Fair's fair. And I'm bigger.'

Alex pulled a face. 'Not much to tell.'

'Like hell.'

'It's not interesting.'

'Try me. I've a feeling it is.' She weighed her up. 'I took aikido,' she warned, the grin hovering.

Alex untied her pony tail, and ran a hand through her hair. The black mane fell around her face, shadowing it. There was depth there, and warmth. Montana took a look at her as she pulled on the pipe and the flame lit her face. It emphasised the smoky eyes, and the strain. Keeping her eyes on the other girl, she proffered the pipe.

Alex caught at her eyes, and took it without a word.

'I was a journalist,' she began.

'A paparazzo?'

'No, nothing like that. We were front line . . .'

She told it like it was. How she'd been front line in war-torn countries, heard children cry for water. How she'd reported it, how they had eaten food off the floor, worn their clothes till they fell off their backs, itched with sweat, dirt, and skin raw from chafing boots, or frozen almost to death just as she had a couple of weeks back. All for the sake of the truth. It was not comfort; the comfort was knowing she was driven to do the right thing. Altruism aside, she had always loved adventure. As she recounted her story she remembered how she'd craved it.

'It all sounds very past tense.' Montana's voice was cool as she slowed into thoughtful reflection. 'Do I sense a guy in here somewhere?'

'How did you guess?' Her voice was dry.

'There's always a guy when a girl like you gives up.'

'I haven't given up.'

'No? Sure looks like it to me. So tell.'

'Well, there was a guy,' she admitted, as Montana nodded, 'and I got him all wrong,' she said, at first defensively, pushing her hands deep into the pockets of her jeans, but as she told the story for the first time it began to flow.

How she'd fallen in love. How he was a man with a reputation for the story and for women, and how their love affair had been played out against strife. The pain as she related it had been twofold: his betrayal, and the memories of those children that she could not erase. Hart had always had the ability to make people perform for the camera even with their loved ones dying and their lives in ruins. She had called that exploitation; he had called it news, human interest. It had been the source of their one endless and unfulfilled argument. He had always wanted recognition where she had looked for the story. She should have known better.

'I thought he meant it when he said we'd make a great team reporting from trouble spots all over the world, me taking risks alongside him. It gave it its edge. It gave us notoriety too.' Glamorous, hard-hitting, tough; they'd been called all of that. 'We were a well known team, and I suppose I got off on that as much as anything.'

'That's what made it special?'

'No,' she said slowly, spelling it out. 'We shared: danger; the challenge. A deadly duo for me. I thrived on it, but it was fantasy.' She gave a short mirthless laugh. 'Reality apparently was back in London and the social round where he told of his exploits at smart dinner parties.'

'What was he like?'

She thought. 'Extrovert, handsome, able. A bastard. But he had me drawn in tight; together. There's something about adversity shared, that intensity. It's a killer.'

Gazing out over the dark, she searched the night stars, as if for her memories.

'Tell me about it,' said Montana drily. 'Guys like that want it all for themselves. But how did he manage in no man's land without an adoring fan club?'

'Oh, you'd have to understand the man. He was an operator. For Hart, war was a gift from God. Living on the knife edge gave him a rush.' It had made sex extraordinary. 'He'd say, look my friend, my chiefs want corpses, tell me where to find them. Just so that the anchor man could say – some of the viewers may find these pictures disturbing.' Alex laughed hollowly. 'The electric pylons would start to sing immediately. If any new war fizzled out without blood and guts he would be disappointed. They all would.'

'And you?' Montana's head was tilted back. Alex had let her take the pipe once it was lit and she was pulling on the embers so that they glowed, bright in the night. Alex, herself, wasn't in the mood after the first hit.

'Maybe I was wrong in the job. I did it for truth.'

'Yeah, and you a journalist too. Sounds so noble. Are you sure? You are, after all, a snooper after the sensational, the story, with all that that implies. A curiosity beyond control. Feeding the media.'

Alex was unmoved. She'd heard worse. 'It doesn't have to be like that. Many journalists are not gutter press. I respond to challenge. And action. I could never bear to be immobile, and I have to be outdoors.' She looked out over the silent scene before them, the soft wind finding the nape of her neck and gently lifting her hair. 'Yes, curiosity drives you, but it's a *need* – to uncover the truth, to pursue it and flush it out. You're right, it's not all altruistic, a need for fair play. It's also dangerous.' She spoke quietly. 'Perhaps I'm a bit of a gambler.'

'That the reason why you didn't stop in Vegas? Didn't trust yourself?'

'Not a lot left to lose.' She gave a dry laugh; Montana heard the note within it.

'Was he a gambler too? Or perhaps that was an essential to the job, was it?' She handed Alex the pipe.

'We were revolutionaries.' Alex sat down on a rock and tapped the pipe out on the stone. The embers catching on the dry desert wind drifted and danced on the stone like fireflies. They both watched. 'We – I, understood the minds of those men, and women, who went to war to fight for something they believed in.'

Montana looked at her steadily. 'So what happened?'

'On a whirlwind visit home, Hart married a socialite blonde. A deadly combination; a bored bimbo with dollars and attitude, and a need for stimulation. She would have found Hart exciting; he was rough and infamous. He would have been ideal. As she would to him. How little I really knew him at all.' Alex looked back out over the lilac dark, the grandeur of the quiet desert night, musing. 'So he ran off with a fluffy bimbo who gave great social parties.'

'And great head, I'll bet . . .' Montana grinned.

She gave her first laugh and picked up her mood. 'Whatever – I was shattered. I realised Hart was basically a sexist, old-fashioned guy who liked his girls to be feminine and stay at home.' The wry note of laughter edged the husky timbre of her voice. 'I'd thought he liked me as I was.'

Montana snorted derision. '"I like you just as you are" is the oldest line in the book. You never want to fall for that one. People lie,' she said, '*especially* guys. Why did you give up the warpaint?'

Alex lifted a quizzical eyebrow.

'There never was much warpaint.'

'More war *cry*, huh?' Montana said, sitting down on the rock beside her and following her gaze. 'So he liked you how you were when he met you; ballsy and tough,' she said, raising a fist. 'But still *woman*. What a challenge. He changed you to make him feel safe.'

'Possibly,' she demurred, tasting the idea.

'*Definitely*,' Montana pronounced. 'A man like that has to conquer everything. Especially fear.' Alex looked at her and Montana held her look. 'You made him feel inadequate. Look at you – sexy, strong, positive. You could do anything he could do, and more. Whereas the bimbo made him feel safe.'

The slight shadow of pain that had touched Alex's eyes lifted as she laughed.

'Do you always philosophise like this?'

Montana's returning smile was slight, her voice light.

'When I like somebody.'

A silence fell. Montana broke it, kicking at the small stones by her boot. 'So, why did you leave the job, if you loved it? Not because of him, surely.'

'No,' Alex said, guardedly, rubbing the warm surface of the rock with the palm of her hand, 'and I'm not sure I've made the departure permanent. But – ' and here she lifted her head as if watching again, and spoke into the dark as if the words she chose were very important – 'I saw something that broke my nerve. War wears you down; it takes away your nerve – but it sharpens it too. You can only bear the contrast as long as the imbalance doesn't become too severe. I was in endless conflict; daily exposure to tragedy either desensitises you or destroys you. You have to be tough to take it, feel it and put it across as I did. There was this one day when – I don't know – we came to this small village and went down into a church cellar . . .' She hesitated, remembering. 'There was this mother, with her arm round two children, just trying to shield them, not *thinking* of herself, protecting them as best she could with her body . . .' her voice trailed away '. . . they were burned alive . . .'

She took a breath, but this time there were no tears. Montana sensed her deep sorrow. Alex set her face as she looked out into the dark and her voice was quiet.

'It broke something inside me. When I went outside I felt I could no longer be impartial. I wanted to get in front of that camera and shout at somebody to do something, to stop the killing . . . of innocents. Of course I was tired and hungry, we'd been travelling for days, and . . .'

She stopped, lost in the past. Montana spoke into the dark.

'How's your nerve now?'

'I don't know how I feel.'

'There's always killing of innocents, Alex. It's a part of war and inhumanity, and always has been through history.'

'Oh, I know. But I realised as I gave the broadcast that in order to function I had to shore up all those tragedies inside me; I'd become a newshound first, and last. That particular day it all came back on me. It's like that in life, isn't it? One thing tips the balance. And then on top of it, the letter from Hart.' It had been waiting back in her hotel room, a curt coward's note from Hart the Brave. 'Till then I'd spent so much time in fatigues and heavy boots, perhaps I simply lost . . .' she paused, '. . . a certain femininity.'

'Femininity!?' Montana exploded. 'If you'd been worried about that you'd *never* have reached the top. This guy destroyed your nerve, not war, Alex. You could cope with that.

It's just because it's synonymous with the event over the kids, that's the way you've got it stuck in your head. But I'll bet it's not the truth.' She looked at the long graceful figure angled across the rock. 'You exude femininity, you've still got a great figure. Anyone can see that. Did you try to hide that too?' Her voice held unbridled sarcasm.

'No.' Alex paused. 'But I believed in him, in his ability to take my toughness as my way of dealing with the job. I lost faith.'

'No you didn't,' Montana came back. 'You fell in love with a destructive man, that's all. Very few can handle a strong woman. He weakened your belief in yourself to give himself the edge. It wasn't war that took away your nerve, Alex, it was him . . .'

Her voice rolled on and into Alex's memories.

'The two events came together at the same time. You probably just needed a break, and that's fine. You'll get over it and do it again, I'm sure. You shouldn't feel guilty, just enjoy the time off, and to hell with the bastard.'

'I am,' she murmured.

'Sure you are.' Montana's caustic voice scrubbed free the sentiment of her memories, now flooding back: 'Honey, that guy screwed you both in and *out* of bed . . . he controlled you . . . got you just where he wanted.'

The truth hit home hard, as scenes flicked over in her mind. She recalled the atrocities that had had her crying as he took her in his arms. Sometime it had been the only way to come down, and her tears would spill out as she broke the control that had held her all day through the endless awful sights, and the newscast that needed calm equanimity. News had to be delivered impartially and she had learned to control her own feelings; though sometimes she'd wanted to shout out the truth she held herself in while politicians sat at home mouthing platitudes and pleasing the voters. Hart had taught her how to speak her own message with her eyes and the timbre of her voice.

Like an illicit love affair their moments were stolen and she had begun to depend on him. No reason why not – he was the one constant thing amidst the ever changing war zones; no reason not to think he would always be there. She had seen them as a team.

Then when it was all over, and as she had tried to recover – a rapid backtrack to sanity so that those around her would not see her fall apart that day in the mountains – the scenes had become indelibly woven together. She had never before doubted herself, and saw for the first time the damage he had wrought. She realised how much she had come to rely on his strength. Truthfully, had he been there to pour balm on the wounds of sight she would not have become so morbidly attached to that scene in the church cellar. She knew it, yet this time she had not been able to deal with it. Montana was right.

'First mistake,' said Montana quietly, watching her. 'Never change, no matter what they say. It's the kiss of death.'

The dispatch had told her that. Alex studied her anew.

'I think you missed your calling.'

Montana gave her gap-toothed grin.

'So; how did all this come about?' Her sweeping arm took in the motorhome, their journey.

Alex twisted to look at it, managing the swift change of subject despite her thoughts. 'Oh I got out of town. Couple of years back we bought the old motorhome together. One day, when we had time on our hands, we were going to cross the States together.' It had been their promise to each other, a standing joke as work took them all over the world. 'Things came to a head earlier than I thought. My producer told me to quit, take Christmas off. He didn't ask, he gave me a plane ticket.'

'And what's in Aspen for you?'

'Time to think; my aunt.' A clear memory came back to her. A front room, the cold outside, warmth in there, the colours. A family reunion, laughter and noise. She remembered that lovely house, the wandering hallways and crooked creaking staircases, the rooms filled with artefacts brought back from innumerable European holidays and film visits. As a young girl, she had loved it. Suddenly it was just what she wanted. 'My mother's sister. I haven't seen her for a while.'

'Where's your mother?'

'Oh, long gone. She joined a religious sect.'

'No kidding? Your dad?'

'My father left a long time ago. He was a character actor who never quite made it. He ended up doing cameos in B-rated movies. It killed him. Quite literally. He jumped out of a plane.'

'Jesu.' Montana stared at the sky as if to see him. 'My family's tame after that. My mom still lives alongside the highway, she still wipes the dust off the windowsills every morning where the trucks roar by. Until dad died he got drunk every night. They'd watch TV and argue. My little sister's still there. She had no ambition. Not like me. I took that look in the mirror one day. I packed the next. One thing: time heals. One day all you'll remember is that he had ugly feet. Me, I don't care what kind of feet a guy has, just as long as he has a pretty wallet.'

'And you've been telling me to pick up the pieces and get back to my job, while you're looking for a meal ticket . . .'

'That's for me, not you. I can handle it.' She picked up the pipe and lighter. 'Come on, revolutionary, let's lay out our bags and I'll cook you a dynamite supper.'

The warmth of the dying barbecue still stood on the still dry air. They had laid out their bags in a clearing in the brush. First, a heavy Indian rug and then two sleeping bags Alex had picked up in Russia, built for severe cold and damp.

Tucked in against the evening chill it was cosy and intimate. Above them a thousand stars stood against the canopy of night. The Rocky Mountains loomed ahead. There was the distant sound of a rushing river.

The edge of the hill swept down to a riverbed below. They could hear its dramatic sound as the river, warmed by the desert heat and swollen with winter snows, swept down to the valley floor now that it had reached the edge of the desert. They were climbing now: tomorrow they would be in the mountains themselves.

Supper was over. Montana swept the remains into a wastebag. It had been simple, but delicious. Fish, cooked on the griddle of the barbecue, a saffron sauce she'd whipped up in a moment, a leafy salad with a light dressing; cheese and crackers, icy California wine.

'That was pretty good.'

'Another rudimentary lesson. If you want to get a man, learn to cook. I took lessons in gourmet. It's worked many times.'

'The element of surprise,' Alex said laughing. Montana just didn't look the type. 'Men. Is that all that motivates you?'

Montana looked at her. 'Isn't it enough? From there, anything is possible.' She stopped briefly. 'You could learn a little from me, you know. We're like two halves of a jigsaw, Alex. So different, yet we fit together.'

'I'm not sure I see it quite like that, but still.'

They settled into their bags. The desert seemed overwhelming in its calm serenity.

'Stars here are the biggest in the world.'

'Everything's bigger in America.'

'You know that, do you!'

The night was still and for the moment so were their separate thoughts. Alex's voice came out of the darkness.

'Do me a favour. All this stuff about my past. When we get there, it's between us.'

'Sure.' Montana let the moment ride, understanding. When she spoke, her voice was slower. 'Our partners are like a mirror into which we look for our own self-worth, Alex. A bad reflection is how we judge our own selves.' She sat up and reached for the pack of cards that lay beside her bag. 'Let's have a hand of gin. I'm going to show you something.'

Alex turned up the wick of the lamp. 'Playing for stakes?'

'Forfeits. High stakes.' She laughed. 'Like truth or dare. We hand over what's most important. I trust you to tell me what that is, if you lose . . .'

She shuffled expertly without looking at the pack.

'Why do you hesitate?' She looked at the quirky expressive mouth and gave a small smile. 'Don't you trust me?'

'Hell, I don't know.'

'Stop being polite. What does your instinct say?'

She thought. 'You seem OK with me.'

'But generally, what would you think?'

'I'd say to others, be careful. Watch out.'

'Exactly. I'm glad you were honest. And you're right, I'm very self-motivated.' She cut the deck and snapped them back as quick as a cardsharp. 'Never make trust personal, always general. Those who love you today, screw you tomorrow. Trust nobody, and watch me carefully.'

'I read an article the other day,' she went on, chewing on a toothpick; she spoke with clenched teeth as she dealt the cards. 'It said, appearance counts for 55 per cent of first impression, voice 38 per cent and what you say a mere 7 per cent.'

Alex rolled over to watch and sat up on one elbow, cupping her face.

'So a quiet girl, 38 double D and not a whole lot of conversation has the edge. That lets both of us out.'

'In part,' she laughed, picking up her hand, and nodding at Alex to do likewise. 'There's nothing like a thrusting pair of tits straining out of an expensive blouse to throw a guy off, make him feel vulnerable and submissive. A clever woman can use that to her advantage.'

Alex's laughter was cut short by a tap on the hand as she lifted her hand and looked at the low-grade deck. Montana had dealt the cards expertly.

'You didn't watch me, did you, and I told you to. See how easily you were distracted. That's a loser's hand and you let me trick you.' Her eyes were bright as she studied Alex's face. 'Now . . . I'm going to show you how to play liar's gin. I'm going to beat you, Alex, but don't worry, I'm not going to hold you to your debt . . .'

Her throaty voice was laced with amusement, but there was another note as well, one Alex could not decipher and it retained its gentle threat as she stared at the lousy cards.

'. . . I'm not even going to ask you what's most important to you. You can teach me some things, but I can teach you men. In some things you have to learn how to win; in some, submit. When you meet the right guy you gotta be *ready*.'

Alex's eyes flicked up to her face.

'I'm to beat him at cards?'

Her laughter rippled between them. 'No, you jerk! Just know how to if you *want* to. Weapons; that's what it's all about. It's a battle, babe.'

'How about old-fashioned love?'

Montana's laugh was derisive. 'Forget it!' Her eyes were suddenly intense, the falling hair silvered by moonlight, as she studied and selected cards from the fan in her hand.

'You changed for this guy, didn't you,' she accused. 'I bet there was a moment when you thought "I can't go through this without him,"' she said with sudden perception.

Alex shrugged, but she persisted.

'. . . when he had a hold over you, when you thought you needed him to be there. That's how you lost him; he weakened you. And it was your fault, you let him. You changed for him. Bastards do it every time.' She revolved the toothpick with her tongue, as she took a card from the top of the pack. 'Take a tip from me, Alex. Men like what they first see. As I said . . . *Never* change . . . it's fatal. I learned the hard way but the guy was the sharpest dude in Vegas.' She spread the cards in a perfect fan, and smiled. 'Now, watch this. It's bitchin' . . .'

SEVEN

Boom. The sound was muffled and distant, the roar of the snow guns up on the mountain punching into the morning quiet. The echo drifted away.

Silence filled the space. Mochi Leng lay in the hot tub and let her body float. Then her mind, piece by piece, just as her therapist had taught her. She slid down, opening her knees wide and let the warm water flood up over her body and lap around her ears. Under the water she was in a womb. Her beautiful face like a perfect oriental mask lay on the surface of the water, her long black hair floating amongst the hibiscus petals.

Her hands brushed out over the silvered surface that reflected the day outside. The sides of the black marble pool were embossed with raised golden fish and scorpions. Would the baby be a dreamer with a bite in his tail, or a secretive soul who never took revenge? She was very into astrology. Her soothsayer had told her the baby would be a boy; a foregone conclusion as far as Miki was concerned. It had been arranged like so very much else in their lives. But the other thing was to watch out for a tall blonde woman. Mochi smiled to herself. If that was the case they would have to move out of Aspen! Besides, she knew something the astrologer did not, and she was not prepared to part with that knowledge. So she had simply listened, as she always did.

Her thoughts were strewn like the petals that her maid had floated on the pool. Above her, huge palms interlocked to create a bower. He liked to come in and find her like that, floating in a jungle pool surrounded by exotic flowers, her hair strewn over the water. It was an extravagant statement that was typically, particularly him. Miki saw her as something exotic, beyond touch. It was this that had caused their problems: a billionaire's strange wishes as much as any traditional oriental's ways.

Miki had always liked to play God. The conservatory had been built for that purpose, an oasis of steamy dark-leafed hothouse green set amongst the white of winter, the black pearl pool at its centre. Miki's money had bought it, just for her, like everything else. Even her?

She didn't think he had bought her, not entirely. And it wasn't something she allowed to bother her very often. She had been taught not to think for herself since he had brought her here as a child of twelve. He had even given her her name – *Mochi* – cream, in Japanese. Cream; the best – that irony had not escaped her. As with everything else, he had created her. He ordered perfection in the house, and expected her, as its *maîtresse*, to be its epitome. It might have been a burden, but Mochi had been a studious pupil and grateful to her master. He had taught her how to walk and dress and please him. He had taught her how to think, how to react – even how to make love to him – and at the right age, sixteen, he had married her. It was a foregone conclusion once she had reached the proper stage of knowledge. The marriage had become an honour for her; her graduation, so to speak. Thinking for herself was not part of the plan. Miki had established his power over her in a very subtle but thorough way; she belonged to him in all that she was. And knowing that much of beauty is a creative art he had known that in his care she would grow up beautiful, and he had shown her how to make the most of this beauty. Therefore, she had always been driven by a hedonistic need that her looks encouraged. He called her his orchid, and she was: that exotic, tender breed of beauty, with her long limbs and lustrous black hair. She was ornamental, precious, exquisite. In his world, she was perfectly set. He was never unkind, but always concerned with her comfort and happiness – as he would be with anything he owned. Miki was a collector of the world's finest and she was the very best. And one thing was certain: Miki had absolute power over her.

But what about love?

Mochi felt its ache. She looked down on her perfect body and ran her hands over her skin. Feeling the sensation and closing her eyes, she sighed.

Things were definitely wrong there; that much she did know.

She lifted her head and felt the water pull on the weight of her waist-length hair, and then subsided again as if she could not be bothered with the effort. Her analyst was right, her thoughts gathered themselves better when she was as one with the water.

Suddenly, in the last year the idyllic set scenery of their life had changed. Miki kept himself to himself, he had long moments alone; privacy that she was not allowed to break. Despite her extreme beauty, she was entirely dependent on him for the elevated existence which she could not forfeit – so she never questioned him.

In those abandoned hours she amused herself, lunching with girlfriends, musing over furs and paintings and gossip. Idle days they were not; skiing, horse riding, shopping, good works (she was on many different committees) kept her very busy. And Miki's appreciation of her understanding worked for them both; after these separations he was always generous. But these days he was different. She had noticed small things at first, signs of discomfort, found him watching her watching him. He had left lunch tables, gatherings, rooms suddenly. Miki was gracious and stood on ceremony. It was most unlike him.

And then had come that discussion two months ago and now their life had changed irrevocably. House guests for the Christmas break that were not guests at all, but something far more unsettling; endless trips to New York . . .

And Miki's revelation . . .

She climbed from the bath and towelled herself gently. Smearing the glass slowly she made a circle with her finger and looked out on the day. Cold, white and beautiful. An early sun rose over the scene, casting long lemon yellow shadows and pale rose and lilac in the shadowed snow.

The fire red snow cats growled up the mountain grooming the run for the day's skiing. A mantle of snow sugarcoated spruce trees and smoothed over the rolling contours of the mountains beyond. Deep, dry snow had flurried in from the east the night before and a silent chill hung in the thin clear air. The day would break up later. The sky was a wash of grey; clouds sat on the mountains, beyond which was the faintest peach blush of the early morning sun. The slopes lay cold and smooth like the table she lay on in New York. Two weeks since she'd been there; today she'd go back. And tomorrow . . .

Mochi crossed into her bedroom, dropping the towel at the doorway to another spectacular mountain view. The emperor-sized bed was crowned with a sun and moon entwined from which billowed gossamer curtains that were tied to the carved posts. It was covered with a white velvet duvet and her grandmother's white silk shawl, banded in gold, the fringe trailing to the ground and, though six feet in diameter, so fine it could be pulled through the eye of a wedding ring. The floor was of bleached and polished wood.

At the far end of the room was a rosewood grand piano, a Steinway. Sometimes after she had bathed, Miki would ask her to play to him. Then she would tie up her hair and fix it with combs, and wear her traditional robes. She would play something sweet and melancholy – she'd had the best teachers – and Miki's silence would fill the room. At these moments they would never speak and often he would leave before she had finished. Mochi never argued. She had known his ways since she was a child, and knew this relationship of unquestioned authority was predestined. Her parents had impressed upon her her luck and her sense of respect before she had left home; she owed it to their family honour to obey and achieve status. She hardly remembered Japan and her home, though sometimes the music would stir her as she played. Miki had paid for everything, even her education in America. She owed him for what she was entirely.

The huge room was arched and beamed with fantastic zodiac carvings in the customised woodwork of the doors and cupboards. East met West, as animals adorned the sculpted wood; pigs and snakes twisting behind the scorpions and fish in predominant relief to match her and Miki. Stained-glass windows threw light through the balustrade, making the animals appear to dance; the pig arched within the embraces of the snake.

Mochi shuddered. The scorpion snake: would she ever know him? He showed her nothing, except that which he had to. He was her husband, but they never shared anything that they both felt deeply. He had taught her through his reserve to restrain her passion as if it was unworthy of her delicacy. They seemed to step around each other like strangers. She accepted his formality, thinking it was what he wanted, yet they were both passionate. But their passion was not directed at each other. His was used for making money, hers for spending it in an endless useless circle. Mochi's eyes rested on the sunlit figures; there was more passion within the bas-relief wooden sculptures than between them.

This time, perhaps the circle would be of life, and together they would make something good – before the end.

She heard his footsteps pass her door and turned her face, hoping to see him enter. She stood there naked, pale and beautiful and boyishly slender, shrouded in her long black hair, the sun behind her casting blue lights in its depths, her small perfect face eager for admiration. Perhaps he would walk towards her, take her in his arms. Perhaps he would tell her he loved her.

The footsteps passed and she stepped closer to the window, lifting her black kimono from where she had left it spread upon the warm boards. On this side of the mountain the glades were already streaked with sun as an early morning skier cut down the slopes, slicing through his own pelt of virgin snow. The man was an expert, dancing fluidly down the slopes, and she, for a moment, felt in touch with him, a stranger. She could sense his pleasure as she tied the belt around her waist and lifted the long train of black hair free, wrapping the ends loosely in a white towel. Then she let it, too, fall to the ground, leaving it where it lay.

Today, all of this beauty served to deepen her feelings. In her idyllic world, she was desperately lonely. She opened a secret cabinet set into her bureau; within it were rows of pills. She rubbed her arms and looked in the mirror. Her face was still perfect, but she shivered, suffering the withdrawal effects of her drugs. A mixture of emotions were reflected in her eyes. Her fears seemed to creep into the cream silk of her heart-shaped face and draw lines before her eyes. Mochi saw her age; it was her own imagination, but real enough to her. Her beauty was her lodestone; nothing must mar her perfection. She'd weighed in that morning at a hundred and five pounds. Normally on a day like this she would starve herself. But now ... now there was the baby to think of. She ran cold fingers over her high cheekbones, looked into her almond black eyes and turned away. She could take no more risks. Every carrot stick was monitored by a nutritionist hired by Miki, and his silent manservant, Lee, watched over her.

Gracefully, she piled her hair up on top of her head, securing it with tortoiseshell and silver combs, and rouged her lips. At the gigantic windows of her room she became part of a Japanese frieze. Soft lines of drifting morning light, soft grey mountains beneath and the pool lying like a silver sheath under its reflection, a mother of pearl montage; and Mochi standing in the silver light in her black kimono.

She knew they would come now.

At the end of the long drive, the black gates suddenly began to slide open, slowly, the gold lions' heads catching the morning sunlight. As slowly as a funeral procession the three long cars headed up the drive. Mochi watched, tense, as she stood in the shadows. They were here. She was terribly aware of them. She felt her eyes absorb the cars' progress as they inched their way up the huge drive that stood in front of their house.

The Red House took up thousands of feet of prime Aspen realty. It was built of marble and stone, and the glass windows were softly shaded so that the full brightness of the sun's glare on the snow did not hurt the eyes, yet they did not withhold the beauty of the best view in town. It took in the whole valley and the towering blue mountains rising on all sides. It showed their danger, angry mountains, as she thought of them, and the full glory of the sparkling drifts of snow.

The cars stopped. She stood back just a little, conscious of her own breathing and her tense excitement, her eyes never leaving them. She knew none of them, but looked for the one woman, who stepped out of the second car. Mochi held her breath and stood perfectly still, withdrawing slightly into the shadows. Below her the men left their cars and turned, breath smoking in the cold air, all in greatcoats. They seemed like black sentinels in the wintry landscape, something seen from the past in a storybook. As a body they stood back, waiting for the large man who was the head. She had seen him before with Miki, and knew what he represented to them but she had never spoken with him. Miki, a traditional oriental, did not include his wife in business, though in this case she was very much involved.

He climbed out now, and she sensed the respect. He signalled something to the chauffeur and the man nodded and moved away. He was pulling off his leather gloves and palming them into one hand, and her own husband was coming down the steps, diminutive beside him, to shake his hand. She was awed; Miki never went out to greet anyone.

Though she was aware of the group and the onus they placed on her, she did not want to be seen. She felt their import through the way her husband was acting. Deferentially he was leading the way, as if to an honoured guest. Together the two men of power climbed the long shallow steps to their residence, and the group fell in behind with short glances towards one another. In their spearheaded body she felt as if they were penetrating her house; penetrating their lives. They would never be the same again.

She took her eyes from the group and, looking back, saw that the woman had glanced upward. For a solitary moment their eyes met and Mochi fancied there was a world of meaning there. This woman knew it all. This woman was the one they relied on. It was only a moment, but it captured her like a photograph Mochi would reflect back on many times; then Mochi stepped back into the shadows of the room.

Her heart beating fast she flew across to her door and opened it gently. The long corridor beyond led to the head of the stairs down to the large hall below. She felt the sweep of cold as the door opened, the low voices. She picked out Miki's voice but could not hear the words, only his soft murmurs. Miki's voice was deceptive, quiet and unassuming. It gave no sign of the man.

She heard them move as one towards the room he had assigned them, his own conference room beyond the study. It was a fabulous room: as the door opened the whole sweep of the valley was on view with Aspen nestled at its base. She imagined them all, one by one, as they walked into that room, overly conscious of what they meant to do. Aware too, of her husband's words; to keep out of sight – and not to tell a soul they were here.

She heard his soft steps on the staircase and quickly closed the door, both hands pressed to it to deaden the sound. A small click, and she breathed again. Her eyes focusing inwardly on her thoughts, she moved away from the door. Her hands crossed her stomach like a star; as if in protection, or as if in an offering.

Her long black silk nightgown floating around her like petals she lay back on the swan-white bed. The room was bare and stunning in its simplicity, the richly carved woodwork its only ornamentation, the bed and its matching dresser its only decoration. With one of the most awesome views in the world, it needed nothing.

Mochi did not see it. Her thoughts were of the small life that had started now inside her. Her hands still lay across her small flat stomach and she wondered.

Downstairs, the group entered the conference room. It was indeed a spectacular view. Conscious of the tenor of their meeting, the worldly group were equally imbued with a sense of the grandeur of the historical moment and their surroundings. None of them lived like this. A great soaring room of marble, glass and steel, and balconied, with a view of the ski slopes and the early morning skiers. It took in the world.

Outrageously valuable Picassos from his blue period, and one brilliantly dominant Van Gogh, that had not been seen in the world for years, were casually dotted around the walls, the only break of colour in the room. It was white as ice, with a heavy crystal chandelier poised over a black marble table, so highly polished that it reflected the whole sweep of scenery causing the mountain to seem to flow into the room.

Only Hillaire seemed unmoved; perhaps he had seen it all before. He went to the head of the table and stared down its polished length. There were chairs for twenty, but only seven folders lay on the table. Before each place was a selection of stationery items, a Mont Blanc fountain pen, a narrow ebony tray with clips and pencils in three primary colours, and a chapter's worth of white paper perfectly aligned within this framework. Hillaire picked up his briefcase and laid a bulkier sheaf of notes in his place at its head. Square across them he placed a gold Mont Blanc.

A camera was already set up, and he took out a tape and slotted it into the video as the others filed in. Briefly he was absorbed in the moments to follow as they were taking in the room. A blackboard dominated the wall, with a map of the world and a clock that gave the time worldwide. A complete reference library ranged floor to ceiling and there was an entire video and computer system with a ticker tape and a fax in the room alongside: the door stood open invitingly for any of the guests who wished to do business.

Ruth found her place, two down from Hillaire. Wilhelm sat opposite without preamble. This time, no glances. The atmosphere was one of business. She could divorce herself from all personal feelings, even from her husband. It seemed he could do the same. His face devoid of expression, his blunt fingers opened the file and gave it a cursory glance. No more; she had not expected it. He would wait to see. As she would.

Now they would all look to Hillaire. The others pulled out their chairs.

There was a soft sound at the door and they remained standing. Miki Leng's small and elegant figure entered the room. He felt their reaction and smiled. He bowed from the waist to their silence. Hillaire moved to invite him in, but his hand stayed him.

'There is no need, my friend. I am not included in this gathering. But may I say you are invited to lunch. During the morning refreshments will be provided. Should you require anything else you only have to ask. The office adjacent is entirely at your disposal,' he said, indicating the open door, and a dark well-dressed woman in her thirties. She smiled and closed it gently. 'My staff will meet all your needs and are very well versed in international affairs. My assistant, Pilau, will come in at twelve-thirty to bring you upstairs for lunch. It will be my honour to invite you as my guests. I am delighted to have you here, gentlemen – and lady' – he gave a small bow towards Ruth. 'Do not worry about being overheard. These walls are security proof. There are no bugs. The room has been swept. But please –' and here he permitted a small smile – 'if you wish to do so once more, be my guests, I will not find offence. Good day.'

He bowed and left.

Ruth took her seat, as David Kowolski pulled out her chair. Miki Leng was quite something. So that was what a billionaire looked like, she found herself thinking. Why, one would expect them to look larger than life, like film stars, but it was just the opposite. He was ordinary, you would pass him in the street without a ringing of bells. She opened her folder and glanced briefly at the agenda. More money than he would ever know what to do with – or was that true? He had brought together and financed this venture. He knew what money could buy, undoubtedly. Them, for a start.

The conversation eddied as everyone sat down. David, herself, Wilhelm, the Russian – Valery Kalinin, a bone surgeon from Moscow who had perfected the lengthening of bones, so far only in dwarves – the Italian, Mario Bene, a prominent embryologist, who warmly adopted the practice of giving post-menopausal women the chance to give birth, using aborted foetuses for the purpose amongst a deal of controversy in a Catholic nation. She had not met them properly yet, but knew they were staying around town in separate accommodation; the Little Nell, a condo, the Ritz. A buzz of talk as chairs were pulled out, paraphernalia laid down, pens and pencils measured up on the table top; the members shifted the items before them to resemble their territory.

'Do you think he's got us bugged? That inscrutable oriental look. A bit of double bluff? Should we have someone check it?'

'Even if he has it won't tell him anything. It's all in talk. Even people in our own profession wouldn't understand the terminology. Relax, gentlemen ... and ... Dr. Lindstrom...' He inclined his head briefly to Ruth.

Hillaire's dry voice put them all at rest. The sense of respect and excitement increased now that the door was shut and they were all together at last. Bar one; and then the door opened and closed quickly once more to include the last man: Freddie, of the social persuasion, a late arrival, elegantly smart and long-legged in mufti that wore the badge of Savile Row. He shook hands with a group that already knew of him by reputation. The atmosphere was tight, formal and curious. There was a sense of purpose as brash as the cold wind outside.

They were all there.

Hillaire tapped the table gently.

'Why us?' he began, drawing them all in. 'You have all been asking this question of yourselves.' He paused. 'I chose each of you for a particular reason. The "us" will become obvious as we progress. The main reason is that we are all the very best in our fields at what we do and collectively we could be extraordinary...'

He let his words sink into the silence that had fallen as he began to speak. He had one of the best minds Ruth had ever come across, and like all the most brilliant men was quiet and able to put across his thoughts in layman's language. Now he was charming the group by saying very little, as was his way. Hillaire's determination was now on course; forget the charm. He had them in his spell, and she wondered how far he planned to make them go. He was unstoppable when he was like this. She sensed the coldness that had once both attracted and repelled her. His voice fell low, and she felt chilled.

'I want to introduce you all to the only way of thinking.' He ran his glance across all of them. 'This is a first,' he began. 'Never before have we all been together.' He spread his hands wide. 'I am honoured.' He paused, whilst the egos rose, and when he spoke again his voice had changed. 'Yet, we all know of each other's progress. What we are here for is to discover what we can create – together . . .' He paused once more. 'Can we introduce ourselves – with our credentials. Please feel free to be as egotistical as you wish. You have all earned it.' He gave a small smile. 'Ruth, would you like to start . . .?'

Miki walked slowly down the upstairs corridor. Now that they were settled his thoughts soon left them and focused on the one subject that mattered to him. Ahead was her closed door, and it symbolised her.

Mochi.

Mother of his baby.

His son.

She was possessed of that rare beauty that combined mystery and perfection. Indeed, she was hung up on perfection and horrified by deformity. She would not, could not, think for herself – and it was all his fault. He had taught her that beauty was everything, that the best was the only way. And then in the past year tragedy had struck him. He berated himself now for not allowing her to be more – equal, in the Western way; yet his upbringing had not allowed for this. His family were an old proud dynasty, set in their ways. That he lived in a town like Aspen, with all that it represented, was merely geography. His oriental heart had not changed.

He slowed for just a moment at the high arched window that took in both floors at the central part of the house. Mochi. She looked to him for the answers. He, in turn, looked to this contingent of men, and one woman, in his house, and knew that the answer for himself and his young wife had to be here. Their house together was a testament to beauty and nothing could mar it. Outwardly cool and lovely, inside she was another character altogether that he had never reached. This was their one last hope. Perhaps if he could cast away her doubts he could have his male heir *and* her love. Perhaps then they would talk, then they would find each other through a child of their own flesh and blood. A ray of pale sun fell through the window upon the white Carrara marble in the downstairs hall that led to the gardens that he loved in summer, and he felt the tremor.

Miki looked at his hands, and saw them shake. Though his face did not change its expression, inside he felt despair at his mortality. He clutched the balcony rail and felt the tremor pass through him, tried to steady his disloyal body. Tried to command it with his will, and failed. He dropped his head, feeling it bob relentlessly in a parody of some hopeless old crone. Shame washed over him. Next, he would lose his bodily functions and his humiliation would be complete. He fumbled for his house phone and found he had unclipped it and left it downstairs, a mark of dignity as he met his guests. He could not summon his manservant.

His thoughts swayed to Mochi and he prayed she would not choose this moment to leave her bedroom. He had ordered her to stay there for the arrival, but lately she had been different; not so compliant. Though she had made no overt remark or gesture, he sensed it as one does a child testing its parent. He ached with the impotence of standing here defenceless outside that door that could open at any second. He felt a cry inside him that he had to steel his mouth to suppress. Nowadays it was coming more often. He had hidden it from her with lies; he did not want her to see him fall apart and see her disgust. He could not bear it.

The moment was passing; he loosened his grip upon the wooden balustrade and straightened up, feeling the sweat pour down his back. These moments drained him, leaving him weak. Feeling the sun upon his face as he stood in the corridor, he knew he would give anything he possessed for a return of the health he had taken for granted all his life.

The disease had now made him almost impotent. Layton's Syndrome, a sister to Huntington's Chorea, only this one went down the male line. It was a rare genetic disorder and had gross physical signs. He would not lose his brain, and there was no senility. It was far worse: the motor system would go and all of his bodily functions. He would be totally conscious as his body fell apart. He faced the all too cruel reality that his self-respect would be gone, as the disease stole away control of muscle and limb; the simple gifts of walking, talking and facial expressions would be eaten away as he became a vegetable and then he would long for death.

He headed down the corridor, his dressing-room door just ahead.

Suddenly he felt the pain; and it was worse than ever. The door swam in his view. He pressed his hand to the wall and pushing his way along, his footsteps changing their pattern, he staggered down the hall to his sanctuary and closed the door.

On the other side of her bedroom door Mochi had been waiting. Now she heard the footfall, and her new determination increased. Maybe it was because she was about to become a mother; she did not know. But she opened the door and stepped out.

He heard the silk whisper as she entered but could not turn. He was doubled over. He had fallen and was curled in a tense ball beside the bed, his head pressed into the carpet. Drool fell from his open mouth. He lifted a hand to wave her away, but she came in anyway. He was shaking, his whole face grey.

Mochi guided him to the bed and helped him on to it, showing surprising strength. He could not smile or hold her, or stop her. Even his words seemed fumbled. The uncontrollable tremors that racked his body forced him to swallow his pride and try to speak.

'No, Mochi, don't. You're not allowed . . .'

'Hush.' She lifted his feet. 'I don't want the servants to see you like this. And I'm fine.'

Guided there, he relaxed, but his whole body shook, and

his hands quivered with palsy. Lee had often had to dress him when he was like this, tying his tie and his shoelaces, brushing his hair. He closed his eyes. Now she knew it, and thankfully she had left the room; but it was only for a moment and when she returned it was with a cool cloth in her hand, with which she gently cleaned him. Then she took his cold hands between hers, feeling rough calluses which had never been there before. Ignoring them, she stroked gently, calming him and restoring him.

'It's started. The thing you warned me of.'

'Yes.'

Her small hand was gentle on his forehead, and her face, swimming in and out of focus, gradually resettled. There was nothing he could do, she had discovered him and he felt impotent, but her gentleness was soothing. Slowly, he relaxed and felt the tension ebb from his body.

But with the renewal of his strength he resisted her presence, wanting to suffer alone with dignity.

'Call Lee, Mochi. He will take care of me.'

Her hand did not even falter in its movement.

'No servants. I will take care of you, Miki. Tell me what to do.'

'There is nothing to do, Mochi.'

His words touched them both with its inevitable message.

'This is not the first time, is it?'

'No.'

'Lee already knows?'

'Yes.'

'Then this is what you have been hiding from me.'

He was silent and she fell into the pool of knowledge with him but said nothing to accuse. In her calm demeanour was mere acceptance.

His eyes scanned her face. 'When are you going to New York?'

'This afternoon.'

'How do you feel, Mochi?'

'I feel proud, Miki.'

Miki looked into her face and saw the resolution there.

She was doing all this for him. Their baby had been produced on a cold lab table in sterile conditions in a New York clinic. As white as the snow that lay around them. Mochi had often felt as if she lived in a sterile world; despite its grandeur and her beauty, she had been unhappy. Now there was hope. She could give something back to Miki; the one thing he really wanted. That was her pride.

They had gone to extraordinary lengths to produce Miki's heir. His genetic offspring were frozen in undignified fashion in a New York laboratory, an insurance against a time like this.

Tomorrow they would check the embryo in Mochi; their baby would then spend two days on a dish in an incubator. One cell would be checked for the chromosomes and if all was well they would put it back and Miki would pray. Ten days later came the blood test, four weeks later the check to see if the tiny morsel of life was growing.

Then they could see the flicker of the baby's heartbeat.

Only then would be the time for rejoicing.

She was doing this all alone. He did not even have to be in New York. He hated travel now; his fits, such as they were, could come on at any time. His money could buy anything, even the best brains in the world. Would it be too much to ask that his money could also buy life and even happiness?

His father, long dead, had been a fatalist. He would have been shocked at these extremes, but Miki was a man of modern science. The concept of this son had become all important in his life and he was imbued with a glow of gratitude to Mochi for her indulgence. He felt vulnerable now the fit had passed; was she doing it for them, or just for him? He searched her face for the answer.

'It seems so strange that at a time like this you are doing it all alone.'

'It is an honour.'

'No, Mochi.' He took her slim hand. 'You want it too, don't you.'

'Nothing would make me happier.'

He could not read her. Was it respect, or love? But love

was the one thing he hadn't, couldn't have, taught her. He had bought her from her parents, brought her to the West and educated her in everything. Her childlike devotion remained: she was grateful for his kindness. Even her soft voice no longer held the musical note of Japan. With an old man's need, he now wanted to be loved for himself.

'I want to be there with you.'

'No.' She pressed his hand gently. 'I am happier this way, Miki. You are better here, safe with Lee to take care of you. I'll only be there for two days, and I'll keep in touch. If all's well, the transfer will take place, and I will ring you with the good news.'

'This woman, Ruth Lindstrom. She's one of the doctors. She's discovered a cure. In a year or so these sorts of genetic disorders will be repaired in the womb.'

The words were not necessary. They both knew them. *But too late for us.*

She looked at him, feeling the sadness of their separation. How to cross the bridge and make a stranger into a lover? Especially now, when the lover could no longer make love.

'Mochi . . .?'

She held his hand.

'. . . what are you thinking?'

But old habits die hard. 'Only how to make you well.'

He sighed and turned his head away on the pillow. He felt the passion, but knew not how to unlock it. It was indeed his fault. He *had* bought her, in every way. He remembered her words about the servants; she was ashamed. And now she was only trying to be kind.

'Are they going to help us, Miki?'

He did not turn his head. He needed to trust them; he had no other choice. 'Let us hope so.'

The scream filled the air and echoed out into the dry dusty landscape. The farmhouse stood alone, way back from the dirt road. There was a sign that swung in the wind. Wires hummed overhead. There was nothing for twenty miles around; just the bowling tumbleweed and the wind. A corral stood outside the farm spread. A couple of horses were tethered there, and an old farm cart. It looked what it was, a Wyoming chicken farm. A prosperous one; the farm buildings were many, and the house itself well kept, the paint on the clapboard was new, and the fence had been painted this year. There were some good eucalyptus trees shading the house, and balconies to the upstairs rooms.

The house stood back at the end of a long drive. Up the drive a car now headed, dust flying from its wheels. It was a new Chevy, and looked incongruous in this landscape.

It skidded to a stop, and a man jumped out, reached back in for a bag and took the steps two at a time. He disappeared through the door on the veranda.

The scream was louder here. As he came down the corridor and through the door, it filled the room.

'Has he been told?' Their benefactor liked every detail logged.

'Yes. We called him just now. Told him you were on your way. He wants a report soon as.'

The doctor bent over the bed where the woman was writhing but did not seem to register him at all. He felt her carefully, and the swollen belly. She keened again, an animal sound.

'She's ready, all right. Wheel her in.'

The woman was lifted on to the trolley and pushed through the doors. He followed. Beyond was a room that belonged to a city hospital. Shining instruments were laid out; two nurses and a doctor, dressed in green and masked, stood beside an operating table. The woman was placed carefully on it.

Her clothes were separated to expose the distended belly. He lifted back the cloth of her hospital gown from her thin arm. She did not look good.

'Give her a shot.' He leaned in close. Comfortingly spoke: 'You're going to be fine.'

There was no recognition. The eyes wandered the room, seeing nothing. Anaesthesia was applied, and the screaming gradually lessened to a moan. The knife glinted as the nurse handed it across.

101

He prepared to cut then delivered the baby with quick and easy expert movements. Its gentler cry filled the air, and the nurses smiled. The baby was lifted free, checked quickly and thoroughly. The doctor examined its face closely. Merely a baby face, screwed up and red, too early to tell a thing. But he'd want to know right away it was healthy; a boy. Nothing wrong that he could see. Perfect.

A frown of worry crossed the matron's brow.

'Doctor, she's not going to make it.'

He looked back at its mother, eyes swiftly registering signs of distress on the monitors. Her heart was violently erratic.

The important issue was the baby. This one would do fine. Quickly wrapped and cleaned, its small red face howled protest at its new way of life. Its wail filling the air, he worked fast to save the mother. But it was impossible; the woman, fast declining, moaned once and then her head sagged sideways on the pillow. He shook his head as he looked down at the stilled face.

'The pain was too much. You left it too long.'

'It's difficult when they go into premature.' The matron's voice held a defensive note. 'The hormones should counteract, but they don't always.'

'I accept that. But each one's precious, far too valuable to lose. Don't try to handle *anything* yourself. Next time call me, quicker. That's all.'

He sewed her up, shook his head again as he pulled up the sheet and stepped back, snapping his hands out of his gloves. He ran a clean hand over his hair.

'I hate to lose them.'

'You did all you could. We'll take care of her.' She handed him the notes. He took up the paperwork. 'No relatives of course?'

'No.'

He read on down. 'Good.' He breathed out wearily, handed back the sheaf of papers. 'I'm going back there now. Tell Matron at the home to tidy up her things and get rid of them. Clear that room, we've another coming in tomorrow, I hear.'

Now his ears tuned into the noise he had missed before. A steady moaning and a thumping on the walls. He looked at the nurse. She pulled down the gauze of her mask.

'Mrs Carinic is giving us some trouble. She's in the next room.'

'Nothing more here. Let's see her.'

The woman was banging around the room, her arms flailing at unknown enemies. She weaved from side to side like a chained elephant, and her stomach was swollen in front of her beneath the shapeless clothes. Just like the one that had gone before her, she was a woman in her seventies, straggled grey hair, and grey down brushed over her top lip. Hormones. She had the beginnings of a beard on the edges of her jaw and chin. He took her hands and gently eased them down to her sides.

'Now, Mrs Carinic, what's the matter?'

'I'm OK, doctor. Now you're here.' She smiled at him like a lover. His returning gaze was the same, even though he was thirty years younger and handsome as hell. 'I'm hungry.' She said it plaintively, as if begging. He did not flinch as she moved closer, still soothing her. His hand touched her face gently.

'Then we must get you something to eat. Nurse, see to Mrs Carinic. Some grilled fish, Mrs C. I know you love that.'

'You're good to me, doctor.'

'That's because you're a very special lady.'

She took the advantage. Her voice was childlike, and cunning. 'And some dessert? That chocolate fudge is my favourite.'

'Well all right, this once. Not too much. Got to watch your diet.' He laid a hand on her stomach, and she giggled.

She was calm as she was led away to the dining room. The matron looked at him admiringly. She was a woman in her fifties, slender and smart. Her blue eyes twinkled. 'You're marvellous with them, doctor.'

'It's because they know my voice. And they need control.' He closed the door behind him and stood in the corridor thinking for a moment. He turned back to her.

'He'll want to hear about the child. I'll go to New York myself tonight.'

'Oh, he's not in New York, doctor. He left yesterday.'

She had his interest. 'Where is he?'

'In Aspen.'

EIGHT

The day was hot. She could smell the earth.

Alex took stock of life outside from the steps of the motor-home, feeling the sun's warm light on her face. She closed her eyes. Rich, dry air. The breeze rushed in like an ocean.

She shaded her eyes, taking in the landscape. Montana's freshly washed undies lay snagged on a rock with a small stone. The girl herself came striding back across from the edge of the hill. She was already dressed in her shorts and a T-shirt. In her backpack was a small bottle of carrot juice.

'Tastes so good in this dry desert air. Want some?'

Alex sat on the steps with her and drank deeply from the bottle. The taste was exquisite.

'Ah,' she breathed in and out. 'It's so motivating.' She grinned. 'Come on, let's walk.'

They had parked on the lip of a bluff. Beyond, over the scrub, the hillside veered down quite sharply, in places so steep that a torrent of small rocks would invade any descent. The ground was dusty and the earth smelled sweet. All around tiny paths made by animals led under scrub bushes down to the waterside. The river itself started without sight somewhere off in the mountains then found its way past the road and suddenly swept into sight beneath them, shimmering like a hungry swollen snake as it cruised down around the corner to be lost from view once more. This side of the water was a flat sandy beach which looked soft and inviting. Seaside pleasures in the middle of the desert. The water lifted over boulders, quickly making small tidal waves whose crests were icicle-white as they rippled together noisily before joining the fast current once more.

'Race you.'

And they were off, grabbing at each other's arms as they hurtled down through the sliding stones, finding themselves almost thrown on to the beach by the gradient.

Panting, Montana ditched the backpack on a rock.

'You want to swim. The river sounds so good. It's probably our last chance.' She looked up at the Rockies forging ahead against the blue sky as she pulled off her shirt. 'After this, it's going to get cold.'

Alex stood, hands on hips, looking round. Her eyes took in the empty top of the ridge whence they'd come.

'I forgot my suit.'

Montana laughed as she pulled the shirt free and tossed it to the ground.

'Such reticence. Modesty's no attribute, and a stranger virtue. I never had that problem.' She was a free spirit, and never more than now. The sun and wind made her smile. 'Share it, Alex. It's what you said you liked.'

She stripped off her clothes and stood there, ass naked, her blonde hair streaming down her back. Her shoulders were broad and strong and her flat belly almost concave, yet her breasts were heavy and sat up on a taut ribcage.

'Good, huh!?' She lifted them proudly. 'Go ahead, look. I'm worth admiring. People have paid thousands.'

'Minus the feathers, does the rate go up or down!?'

'The feathers cost. They're the tease. You're getting the childrens' matinée.'

Squatting down, Montana pulled her cowboy belt from her shorts and snaffled it around her waist, refitting her Walkman headphones over her neck.

'Every little thing's gonna be all right . . .' Montana sang. 'My Sony. I feel undressed without it.' Her voice was overloud.

Alex paused for just a moment, then slowly pulled off her shirt, then more quickly her shorts.

Montana looked her over, pulled the cans from her head and dumped them on top of her clothes, throwing the belt down with a flick of leather. 'But I don't need this today, I need this.' She scooped the ever present roach from a pocket, and lit it.

Alex stepped out of her knickers and felt the full freedom of the breezy warmth on her skin. She looked up to the sky, seeing a whirling bird.

'Sun's bright,' she said. She looked over at Montana's tanned skin. 'I didn't bring cream. You're not worried about getting too much?'

'Sun?' Montana offered the joint. Alex accepted, pulling in the smoke as the blonde girl watched her. 'I don't care about the ozone layer. Give me hot rays and suntan lotion, factor 2 with a tanfast ingredient; one day I'll be forty with sagging tits and an ass to match and it won't matter none if I've got wrinkles, 'cos I'll be rich. I mean to capitalise on what God gave me. Besides, by then they'll have found a way to cure cancer. They're finding things every day.'

'God?' Alex's voice cracked on the smoke.

'Oh yes, God. I'm a God-fearing Catholic. My ma and pa conceived me on a Protestant gravestone. Said it wasn't a sin. Sides, being a Catholic gives you a sense of purpose. Laws to break, you know. You Protestants don't have nothing to fight against.'

She slapped a long tanned thigh, and grinned; split her face with it. 'Know what I'm talking about?!'

'I'm afraid I do.' She handed back the roach.

Montana smoked contentedly. 'I was married at twenty, you know, Alex. An ex-jock. All he ever did was watch sport on TV and channel-hop till I went crazy. He'd use up all the frozen peas when he iced his knees and then refreeze them. I loved peas. I kept eating them and never knew what was making me sick.' Alex laughed at her, and folding her clothes on the rock, stood up. 'I divorced him for it in the end. Moved on to money. It was a safer bet.'

Alex smiled gently and moved away feeling the freedom. Montana turned her head to watch her. She had a raw beauty, so pale, her creamy flesh shadowed by long muscles. The morning sun cast peach on her curves. She turned, her back view tight as a boy, and in a long fluid walk reached the edge of the water where she crouched down, scooping at the sand. The water rushed into its new niche and flooded her toes and fingers. She wore a gold chain around her waist. It glinted in the sunlight.

Montana had spent her life wanting things.

107

Alex was something she wanted.

She looked at the broken fence a few yards away that divided one piece of land from another. It ran right down to the water's edge but beyond the river turned and the water spilled out on to the bend into a natural pool. She pointed it out. 'If we go through the fence there, we can't be seen even if someone did turn up, above. Water's calmer there too. Won't be dangerous. I shouldn't say that word to you, though, should I? You might jump straight in.'

Together they went through. The sand, thrown clear by the rushing water, was purer there, like a real beach. It was warmer too and sun and wind were fresh and enticing; dry as Martini on ice. Montana ran straight into the water and swam out towards the middle. There was a lee to the river as it swirled around the corner where the water had gathered in the pool.

'Works for me!' she said, diving under, bottom up. 'Do it fast.'

Alex, ready for the bite of mountain water, ran for the pool and dived smoothly in, surfacing just beside her with a small yelp which made Montana laugh. The water was freezing.

'Gets better,' she shouted. 'Just keep moving.'

Five minutes was enough; they came out shaking themselves like a couple of animals. The sun was bright and the wind dry. Choosing a warm rock, they sat together, the breeze curling around them brushing away the droplets of damp. The warmth of the sun stole into them. Alex closed her eyes once more, then, the breeze on her skin, she bent to feel the wet clotted sand in her palm. The sand was damp and dark like potter's clay and tactile. She reflected upon the physical sensation, drawing it in, and crouched down, sun hot on her back, skimming the sand slowly off the palm of her hand.

Montana had not felt anything so deep. She watched Alex for a moment, then dug in her bag for an orange, peeling it dexterously with firm long fingers. She pulled off the pith and handed her half, throwing the orange peel over her shoulder. It lay, a blast of colour on the sand.

'Don't panic, it's organic,' she said. 'Here.'

Alex stood up, taking it. So close, she could feel the cool of her skin. She had never felt so at one with another woman and knew that it was due in part to the sang-froid of her new friend.

She looked around. 'Isn't this idyllic.' Her eyes traced over the horizon; she felt the dry heat on her skin, and freedom, the hedonism of being *au naturel*. There was something to be said for discarding clothes.

'I never would have guessed it. So, Miss Prim, how's it feel to be so casual, huh?' Montana started to laugh. 'You see I got what I wanted even without you knowing – I wanted to see how you'd be once you were cool, *relaxed*. And sharing is what is most important to you.' She looked her over. Alex was built along finer lines, but she was athletic. She had long legs and small high breasts. 'Man, if you'd been on the stage at Las Vegas, they'd have died.'

Alex looked down on her, her dark eyes still sensual with the pleasure of the day.

'My body's not the part I want just anyone to see.'

'I feel honoured.'

'You're a girl. That's OK.'

'Is it?' The river rushed by. The dope seemed to fill their heads. Alex bit into the bright curve of the orange and the juice spilled on to her lips. The gold chain around her waist glinted. 'That guy was crazy to leave you,' Montana said softly.

As Alex looked at her, at the languid dark eyes that seemed to draw her in, her own eyes caught a spiral of grey beyond the hilltop. In a double-take her eyes suddenly looked back.

'What's that?'

Montana looked, more slowly. 'Smoke.'

'Smoke?'

'Probably someone making a campfire.'

'Did you put out our fire?'

'Absolutely.'

Alex realised her lack of clothes, and a feeling of dread

109

arose. Back through the fence she hastily pulled on shorts and T-shirt and started running for the bank.

'Where are you going?'

'I bet that's our stuff, Montana!'

She reached the crest of the hill and broke into a run. Behind her, Montana, coming slowly up the hill saw her move and speeded up. Both arrived on the flat almost simultaneously.

'Oh, my God!'

Over the camp site hung a pall of smoke as they raced back. The wind had relit their breakfast barbecue stove: the sleeping bags had gone up in flames. They ran along the paths, winding and twisting to the black oval that had now been burned in the earth. Small bushes with blackened limbs surrounded a tossed inferno of cloth and nylon and foam innards. A book lay to one side: Montana's night-time reading, *Women Who Run with the Wolves* lay smoking beside a melted torch. The pillows were shards of charcoal.

'I thought you put the fire out. Thought you said you knew what you were doing?'

Alex grabbed the broom, and the fire extinguisher.

'Keep your hair on. I thought it was out.'

Montana was philosophical and amused. She took the broom from her and poked.

The fire bit into the broom handle, gnawing at it like an angry dog as soon as she lifted the edge of one of the bags. It twisted like a spiral into the forgotten edge of cloth and flared around it, eating it up in perfect fire conditions, creating another hazard instantly. The motorhome stood yards away. Alex poured froth out of the fire extinguisher till it was empty, but the fire had spent itself, and their belongings were long gone.

'Idiot.'

'It's just a sleeping bag. I'll get you another.'

'It could have been the motorhome.'

'But it wasn't. Look on the bright side.'

'I'm looking,' Alex said, staring at the flames. How to tell Montana about sentiment? She had carried that damn bag all the way back from Russia. It held a whole host of memories.

'They're better forgotten,' said Montana, reading her mind. 'Look on it as beneficial.'

Now Montana sat down and, taking the broom, amused herself by lifting up what was left to watch it burn in dope-induced pleasure.

'At least it didn't get my knickers.'

Pristine white they still fluttered in the breeze. Alex, serious until that moment, suddenly could not help the laughter that bubbled up inside her. Both of them fell about, hysterically. Alex, always in past so in control, found herself in different mode with this girl and wondered at the changes in her life.

Laughter consuming her, she realised she was stoned. The flames looked beautiful in the dry air, orange bright. She sat down to watch and time passed without mattering. Montana's voice came softly after what seemed an eternity.

'Come on, let's pack up what's left.'

Montana was feeding the last of her gummy bear sweets to the red ants on the sidewalk as the Indians settled down on the side of the road to sell their wares. They spread out blankets carefully and then knelt to lay down their beaten silver jewellery, set with turquoise and coral. Symbolising their craft and heritage, the silver was scored with feathers and linked with beads.

As Alex stepped up into the cab, she spotted them and wondered how long they had been there. The motorhome had shaded them from their sight.

The two of them went over and knelt down to pick up the jewellery under the silent interested gaze of the family. They were not dressed traditionally, and the younger ones seemed of mixed blood, though the elder man and woman had the typical faces of the Old West and remained impassive in the background as they bargained in the expected tradition.

They walked back softly, Alex slightly ahead. Montana had stayed a moment longer to barter. Dry heat stirred the air all around them and it was very quiet. She could feel the purer air of the mountains, and a slice of cold from the river. Perfection. Alex held aloft a silver cuff earring set with a single turquoise. In the dry unsteady breeze it clinked like the mast of a boat.

'It reminds me of marinas in England,' she said as Montana caught her up. The dangling feathers were bright in the sun. 'Except England never gets this hot.'

Montana took her arm. An object was cradled in her palm. Alex was aware of Montana's shoulders gilded from the sun and her flat brown belly under the crop top.

'What is it?'

'It's a Zuñi fetish. Man's desire to control forces beyond his immediate power. For warding off evil, bringing good luck. It's a personal good luck charm, an amulet. It's yours.' She pressed it into Alex's hand.

'It's beautiful. Thank you.'

'You have to feed it, for protection. With corn meal, and ceremonially. You keep it in a fetish jar. Its power is regarded as a living thing.'

Alex looked down at the small carved oblong, shaped like an animal and roped with feathers and beads.

'Does it work?'

'It's purely a matter of belief. If you believe it possesses power, then it does. You know how that works.'

'It's a psychological Band-Aid.'

'It's to say sorry.'

Montana's eyes held hers. They had a distant dreamy look. Alex held the amulet to her. The sensuality of the warm sun asked for quiet confidences. 'What do you aspire to, Montana? What are your dreams?'

But her voice became suddenly light and the look was laughed away.

'The day when I need not worry about opening my morning mail without a strong drink by my side. Let's get this thing on the road.'

It was a small operation. Alex pulled the plugs and dried them off. Montana cleared up their stopover, beating out the last of the flames, and dropping the pieces into a steel waste bin. She poured a bucket of water over the remnants just in case. Then she brushed out the barbecue, gathering up their

112

food from the table and putting it all into the ice bucket. Alex tore an old towel into strips and forced a piece into the carb to soak up the extra fuel.

'Are you ready?' she called.

Montana came up alongside her, hands on hips. A light sweat stood on her skin. Her T-shirt was tied under her breasts, and she wore the ever present cut-offs. Her feet were bare.

'All done.'

'Jump in, then. We've only got one shot at getting it started. The gas is still dripping into the manifold.'

Climbing in, she quickly fired it, immediately got it going and put the r.p.m.s way high to keep it alive. The Indians watched them impassively as she bumped them over rough ground to avoid reverse and over the kerb, heading up towards the highway.

'Yes, we made it! Now we've just got to get to a gas station and get the carb rebuilt.'

'Look at you, you're all fired up. What a sense of achievement.' Her eyes alight, Montana put her head back and laughed. 'Never in a million years would I have thought I would have arrived in Aspen like this, nor seen someone get such a kick out of a challenge.'

'Just thank God it wasn't the motorhome,' she said drily. Alex headed up the hill, praying they'd make it, one hand on the wheel, the other fisted in her lap. Montana raised her eyebrow.

'You hold your thumb in your fist just like I do.'

Alex looked down briefly to where her thumb was tucked into her fisted fingers. 'It's comfort.'

'Well if you can't suck it, at least hold it. My first husband taught me that. I've never forgotten it!'

'It's rather hard to forget.'

The snow-clad slopes were all around them now. The blown carburettor fixed in Grand Junction, now the generator had packed in in the high altitude, but as they limped across the bridge at Glendale Springs, the huge blue pool alongside

113

steaming into the day, they were in the mountains, rising up all around them, as they turned a corner. Ever higher, climbing, climbing.

The girls were excited and tired. It had been an eventful journey; Alex had become quite a mechanic, tending the old machinery and getting to know it and she'd got quite a kick out of it. It was quite beyond Montana, whose respect, despite her taunting, had grown for Alex's ability. Alex was thorough and applied herself, and seemed to thrive on adversity; Montana used her wits in quite a different way.

Now the magnificent 14,000-foot mountains loomed ahead against the sky and showed off their intimidating beauty. They were nearly there.

Mochi's stretch black limo slid down the street towards the airport and the family Lear jet waiting on the tarmac. She was on her way to New York.

Montana watched it go by.

'That's the life for me.'

Alex laughed at the contrast as she heaved the old bus into the last stretch. The motorhome had made it up the final slope in the late afternoon, at the beginning of a snowstorm. Snow swirled thick and fast, looping into the windscreen, giant flakes that blotted the world from view. She drove into the parking lot at Buttermilk mountain, taking a dry space that a car had just vacated.

Almost immediately, Montana pulled down her bag and unzipped it. She didn't plan to waste time. Alex stretched.

'Jesus, my aching butt.'

'Want me to rub it?'

'No, thanks!' She climbed out of the driving seat like an old cowboy. 'I'm going to go over to the Inn and use their phone. Call my aunt.' She pulled on her parka and woollen hat. 'Why don't you put on the coffee and fix us a sandwich. I'll be right back.'

The whirling snow caught her as she stepped out, driving into her nose and eyes and up the cuffs of her sleeves. Hastily, she pulled on her gloves as she stomped off across the car park heading for the lights.

114

Five minutes later she was back, and the snowstorm was slowing, flakes drifting down like feathers from a pillow. She pulled open the door emptying a rush of cold air into the warm interior. Montana was standing at the table, ladling from the pan.

Alex stood on the first step, stamping snow from her boots. 'My aunt's out of town, probably not for long.' She came in pulling the door to. The night was getting cool, a soft pale blue shadow falling over the snow, the lights sparkling diamonds into the unbroken crusts of drifts that surrounded them. She looked through the window. 'Isn't it beautiful out there.'

'I made some soup. Sit down.'

'You're an angel.' She slid into the seat, pulled off her wet woollen hat and laid it on the table. Montana ladled the soup into a bowl and placed it in front of her and a plate with a warm buttered roll.

'Eat.'

She disappeared into the shadows.

'It's great. Aren't you having any?'

'No, thanks.' Her voice came from the back of the motor-home.

Alex sat in peaceful lamplight, the wick turned down, and ate her supper. It was a beautiful night, the snow falling softly. She wouldn't be going anywhere just now. She kicked on the radio, found the local station. The lamplight, pooled on the table, cast the rest of the room into shadows. At the back of the bus, Montana busied herself beyond the door of the bathroom. A faint sliver of light showed through, but not enough to break Alex's romantic mood. Music played gently.

'Where are you staying then, the Inn?'

'Can't afford it. Four hundred dollars a night just to put my head on a pillow just isn't my scene.' She spoke into the dark. The news came on the radio and she found herself only half listening.

'You're not staying *here?*'

For a moment Montana's face popped into the light, a garment strung between her hands. She was stripped to her bra and knickers.

115

'Why not? It's that kind of country. People live out in these things for years. They're pioneers, they crossed this country in wagons. This is just the modern equivalent.'

'Well, not me.' She disappeared again. Alex tuned in to the weather report. Aspen news.

'. . . and now, coming up to the hour. Ten inches expected tonight on top of Ajax . . .'

'Wish it was on top of Montana.' The door slid open and closed, the light clicked off. She came out of the shadows. 'Well, catch you later.'

Alex turned her head. 'Good God!'

'That good, huh!?'

Montana's silky hair was tied back off her face with a black velvet bow at the nape of her neck. It emphasised the sleepy dark eyes and cushioned lips. She wore black leggings and boots and a white polo. Not a fancy wardrobe, but she looked a million dollars. The trousers showed off every inch of her legs and every asset above and below. She dumped the soft leather overnight bag at her feet and turned again, to show a tight high butt, the well defined breasts.

'What do you think?'

'You look amazing.'

Montana looked pleased. 'A thirty-six-inch inside leg's got to have some mileage.' She pulled a huge dark silky fur from the shadows of the bed beside her and slung it around her shoulders, then let it slip back to the floor, holding it by a finger. 'Nice?'

It was certainly effective. Every head was going to turn when she did that. Everything that was best about her was displayed. She draped the fur back around her shoulders and as she stepped into the light, Alex saw its quality and deep rich beauty. Montana was wearing a black ankle-length sable.

'I rented it,' she said defensively, seeing Alex eyeing the coat.

'You must have done a lot of dancing to buy that.' Her voice was dry.

'Oh, well all right, it's not mine, but I'm paid up. Johnnie's wife's closet. It's just for the intro, then I can ditch it. Or mail it back. Whatever,' her voice was airy. 'Can I leave my gear here for a while till I get things fixed up?'

'Of course. Where are you going?'

'To a hotel, of course. This thing won't make it into town, nor would I want to spoil my arrival.'

'You have enough money? The hotels are expensive.'

'I got my room booked, I told you. I'll get a cab from the Inn over there. Five nights at the Jerome should get me off and running.'

'The Jerome! That must be well over $2,000. And then some.'

'I told you, I sold up when I left Vegas.'

'Christ, and I thought you were broke.'

'A showgirl! Broke!? Give me a break. I had to save it, don't you see. Once I have it made, I'll spoil you rotten.' She leaned down and kissed her. 'I knew there'd be someone along that day. Just didn't figure it'd be a girl.'

Her eyes held that note. Alex couldn't quite figure it. Regret, warmth. The big smile followed, and she was gone.

She kicked up the heating after Montana had left. The generator still would not work, running rich in the high altitude, so she let the gas jets burn for a while. Darkness fell, the snow continued to fall, drifting in a gauzy sheet gently down around the iron street lamps that lit up the banks of snow and it looked like Narnia; the memories were comforting. She tucked in and watched the world darken, and popped the champagne she'd been saving to share with Montana. It hit the spot fast. Memory drifted away, dulled. She cobbled together some bedding and climbed in in tights and a black polo. Tomorrow she would pull on her suit and hit the slopes when the lifts opened. She'd ski all day, then shower, throw on the gear, and go into Aspen to check it out. Tomorrow her life would start.

The heavy snow fell and fell. It was like a different world. The layers seemed to form a glaze as she fell back down into her down comforter and cuddled up. Sleep pushed at her and her eyes closed.

117

NINE

On the other side of the mountains, on the ski slopes of Ajax, Jack Fenner stood outside Bonnie's restaurant and took in the view for a moment. Another perfect day in paradise; the backdrop of pure blue-white against the slab of brilliant blue sky, was marshalled by snow-capped fir trees on the horizon. The sharp air sang with good health.

He carried his drink over to one of the corner tables on the veranda and sat down heavily next to Rowan Bader. The ageing film star had a lived-in face and a permanently naughty smirk on his lips. His eyes raked the women that came by so salaciously that many of them succumbed. Besides, he had a hellraising reputation. It had to have started somewhere.

Close by, gossiping with her girlfriends, was his wife, Evie, a well preserved socialite, but that didn't stop Rowan checking out the talent with his old friend, Jack. They were both well-known Aspen characters and all that went with it, part of a clique of home-owning celebrities and fast movers.

They heard her laughter before she arrived. Chiffon always made an entrance. At forty, she was fitter than most eighteen-year-olds and she had an immaculate body, by reputation manufactured, tucked and bobbed wherever possible, though nobody knew for sure. Private about this, the rest of her life was anything but. She was a self-publicist, dressed to shock. Now she was laughing with a passer-by about the party the night before. They'd all been there, as they always were. Everybody in Aspen attended every party.

She slid into a chair at their table.

Rowan grinned his wolf-man smile. 'How's the talent? Have you found me a live one yet?'

'I'm not available.' She smiled at him, her image reflected in his Technicolor aviator glasses.

'You mean you're not putting out the welcome mat. Unlike you.'

'Christ I'm fed up with this.' She looked around and preened for the onlookers. This trio were what the out-of-towners came to see. 'Tired of being a clothes horse with no apparent brain.'

Jack's voice was dry. 'Everyone knows you have a brain, honey. Look at the amount of money you make.'

'That's true.'

She settled herself in with them, her smile as bright and seductive as her clothes. A waiter brought her a glass of wine. She was half-caste, her blood somewhere between native American Indian and ghetto Harlem. The result was rich black hair that shone in the sun, a strong-boned face that had smiled out from screens and billboards all over the world, and a mouth that half the world could climb into and half had. She talked, laughed and sang in a husky contralto and Chiffon was famous for being infamous; her lovers legendary. The woman had an appetite to match the two old roués who sat it out daily halfway up the winter mountain.

These three were the selection committee. No new ski instructor or nifty little *ingénue* escaped them, and they talent-spotted for each other. The two men took their pick of the girls who flocked in for the season. The girls knew it, they knew it; it worked every which way. And in case one of the randy ski instructors fancied one of the girls, the guys took care of that for Chiffon. They were the snow town's rat pack, known as the Huntin' Hyenas because they got everyone else's rich pickings.

Rowan cast a quick glance at Evie out of the side of his eye then kept his attention on Chiffon. Evie was bent close to one of her gilded friends, in skin-tight Armani and a bear-skin hood. This was the land of the endangered species. The friend wore a leopardskin collar and magnificent pearls. Diamonds caught the sunlight as her hands described something, and the 'girls' all laughed.

'What's the latest?' asked Rowan in his slow gravel I'm a bad bear voice.

119

Chiffon leaned back, her hand loosely round her glass of wine.

'Johnnie's had the snip. I'm going to cross him off my Christmas list. I like my men intacta.'

'Which Johnnie's that?' Rowan's tone was provocative.

'You *know*, the actor; Johnnie Cross. Got a new house in Red Mountain. The one that used to be married to that model girl. The one with the body and the black thong bikini.' She flapped a hand at him. 'Oh, Rowan, you *know*, you're just winding me up. On location she used to do two hundred laps of the hotel pool every day. I saw you watching.'

'Oh, that one.' He picked his teeth. 'Everybody knew her.'

'What happened to her?' Jack lifted his face to glance at one of the nubile bodies floating down the well textured slopes.

'She found a new pool to swim in, I guess. Left Johnnie up a creek. I fished him out.' She played with her glass of wine. 'He left town a week ago. I wrote to him right after and I haven't had an answer.'

'That's your answer.'

'So that's what's made you mad. Not getting your oats.' She snorted.

'She's getting them. What about that new ski bum I saw you with, Chiffon. I ain't heard him speak yet.' Rowan crunched his cigar between his snow-white even teeth, grinning around it.

'Oh he talks. He even speaks English. He's a great fuck too. First he didn't need to talk, then I wanted him to. Then all I wanted was for him to shut up. Funny that, isn't it!'

Rowan chuckled his agreement. 'You gotta put something in their mouth. Might be difficult for you.'

'I'm tired of second hand. I want one of my own.'

'Everybody's a leftover, honey. Even us.' He looked towards his friend. 'What about the party, Jack? Any ideas?'

Jack's upcoming Christmas party was always the event of the season. Every year it was a different theme, and every year Rowan asked, and Jack gave nothing away. Nothing changed.

'If I did, I wouldn't tell you. You'd put it on local radio.'

'I'd tack it above my bed, that way everyone would know,' he said, grinning and showing his killer teeth. 'More people with big mouths tune in there than anywhere! Chiffon'll tell you that!'

Chiffon was more casual, looking for a clue. 'What's the scene going to be?'

'You'll have to wait and see. I've timed it for the winter carnival and the torchlight parade. Everyone will get high that night.' Christmas was in the air, and the crowds felt it. Every night was a great night for a party of any sort when Aspen glittered under its necklace of fairy lights.

'They could ski in their outfits, long as it wasn't too chilly.'

'Knowing Jack, they'd get hypothermia.' Rowan leaned over his forearms, his voice a growl. 'He likes everyone in their birthday suit.'

Chiffon let out a peal of laughter, turning heads.

'How about everyone coming as someone else's fantasy? They could send their fantasy in a sealed envelope to me, and as I got each one I could send it out to someone else. That way you could search for your fantasy all evening.'

'And find it?'

'Then it wouldn't be fantasy.'

'We couldn't trust you not to steam open the envelopes, and set us all up. You'd have to think of a new one.'

'That wouldn't be hard. I've got a repertoire.'

'Talking of hard, check that out.'

Montana had timed her moment for late afternoon. She skied down Ajax to get her man dressed in a pink satin bikini trimmed with maribou. Her maxim was: to hell with the ozone layer, the cold, or ethics. She was beautifully tanned, mentally tuned to the cold from an old Chinese mantra she'd learned in her relaxation therapy group, and her ambitions were keeping her hot. Her blonde hair flew out from under a white fur hat and she wore white boots and glittersocks and a white pompom on her backside.

She carved a silky trail in the bluish light of the mountain, her costume picking her out as she wove in through the last of the skiers and came to rest just beyond them. Her skin was darkened by contrast, and the long blonde tresses gleamed like silver. The maribou held sparkling grains of snow, and her breasts heaved gently with the exertion.

'This one's a must for the evening's fun, Jack.'

Rowan stood and dusted off his seat. But she didn't look his way, as if she didn't notice. The trio were unmistakable for any star-spotters in the area. She leaned against the rail, backside up, and gazed out on the view as if catching her breath. Rowan was riveted by the pompom.

'This girl sure seems keen to meet me.'

'She's probably heard the weather report and wants to fuck you, boy.'

Ten inches on Ajax was an old joke. They'd been known to bribe the weather girl at the station when things got quiet, just so's they'd have a line for the day. By repute, Jack could measure up.

'Yep; she's not even looking my way. Can't be anything else but the rumour. You ain't got no money worth having, and sure as hell you ain't got no charm.'

Chiffon got up quietly whilst the two of them fell over their jokes and casually joined the girl at the rail as if admiring the view with her. Within a moment, they were laughing together. An instant later, and she was following Chiffon back to the table like an offering on a plate.

Montana, well aware of the scene she had created, had settled to her new role. It was important that Chiffon be the one to strike up the friendship first, so that she could have one up on the men. Almost totally broke after checking in in style to the Jerome, she knew the game every bit as well as they did. Resistance was an important feature. During the day she had found out from her old bartender friend that they took the last drinks of the day up at Bonnie's. She had watched the two men head up together; she had followed, two chairs behind.

Jack pulled out a chair.

'You look chilly, but sweet.'

'Like California wine.'

Montana's homework had netted her an A plus sooner than she'd expected.

'Here.' Rowan stuck his cigar in his mouth and yanked the wolf fur off his back. He threw it around her shoulders to receive a smile that was pure greed, the spaced teeth giving Montana a predatory look. Yet the eyes maintained a feigned innocence. Rowan felt his temperature rise despite the loss of his coat. He circled his chair before sitting, his famous eyebrow cocked as he looked at his friend.

Jack handed over his hip flask, unscrewing the silver top as he did so. 'Brandy. It's customary in survival cases.'

'Like yours,' teased Chiffon, seeing the lust on their faces.

They all laughed, the Hollywood orthodontist getting his money's worth in advertising. Montana, gap toothed but chic as hell, grinned and tipped the brandy down her throat in her own expert style, and at the same time she stretched out her long legs where the coat gaped wide. She knew she looked great. She knew she was in.

'So what are you doing here?' they said in checking routine rota.

'Staying at the Jerome.'

Eyebrows went up. 'Alone?'

A small pause, a slow answer. The wolf fur slid a little more.

'Yeah.'

'How long you staying?'

'About a week. Through Christmas.'

'Then what?'

'Then,' she shrugged. 'Back home, I guess. Maybe Europe.'

'You should stick around a little longer. Have some fun.'

'That sounds good.'

'Jack has plenty of space, don't you, Jack?'

She slid her eyes round to him. 'Jack Fenner,' he said, holding her look. 'I own Chasers.'

'Oh, do you. I think I've heard of it.' They all grinned as one. 'I'd like to check that out.'

'Well I'm the Christmas fairy,' Jack said as Rowan guffawed alongside him, 'and honey, you just got your wish.'

'Hold still, Darren. I'm trying to buckle your skis, love.' Fanny was bent over, with her pink silk backside stuck up in the air, her son clutching her hips. 'Stop sliding about, for goodness sake.'

'I can't help it, Mum. Snow's slippery.'

'Well, I know that. There.' Fanny stood up, wobbled and giggled. 'Woo. OK, now where do we go? Over there, panda slopes. That's us.'

'Oh, no Mum. I can ski.'

'You can't even buckle your own boots. Now, come along.' She grabbed his mitt and together they slid towards the lifts. 'Lovely, isn't it, Darren pet. Invigorating.'

Up they went in the lift, Fanny with a little helpless cry of laughter as the seat caught her under her backside and lifted her up and forward. Her skis dangled heavy and ungainly beneath them, but soon they were fifteen feet over the slopes and the whole of the sparkling snowclad mountain was beneath them. Swinging gently in the climbing lift was the perfect way to view its splendour.

'Oh, marvellous, Darren, what a treat, love.'

'Now look, Mum. When we get to the top, it's easy, just grab your poles, so – stand up – and as we reach the top you just ski off the chair.'

'Oh, my God . . .'

'No, seriously, Mum. It's a breeze.'

The ski station clicked into view ahead, and she primed herself, grabbing her skis, and then at Darren's prompting she stood up. Lurching wildly she was off, sailing down into the snow beyond, a wild scream floating behind her. At the last moment she managed to remember her lessons and leaning to the right, she turned and stopped.

'Fantastic.'

Darren swooped in beside her, like an instructor, enjoying the novelty of being in control of his mum.

'OK, get your poles ready. I'm skiing ahead of you, backwards.'

'Backwards?'

'Yes.' He held the tips of her skis as he drifted back

towards the edge. 'Remember the snow plough: keep them turned in till you get the hang of it.'

The first bank was nerve-racking, like riding the big dipper, and then she was over, on her way down and nowhere else to go. He let her go.

'Snow plough, Mum!'

Ski tips in and stopping, sliding and then hurtling down the mountain; the yell pealed behind her. And, up the mountain once again; Fanny, never quiet, adapted her screech to a laugh, if anyone could tell the difference. The lift even became easy.

'What's that you were doing last time?'

'A stem christie, Mum.'

'You *are* a clever boy.' Her arm draped around his shoulders as she looked out, relaxing. Silvery mountains scored with ski runs, and the sky an electric blue. 'This is great . . .'

'Get ready, Mum!'

Off the lift, and she cruised to the lip of the panda slopes all by herself and pushed off. She stopped staring at her toes, and looked around. Gaining confidence, she levelled out and felt the joy of speed.

'Wow, I could get to like this, Darren . . . Darren!?'

'You're doing fine. Ski at will, Mum.' And he was off. She saw him peel off across the clubhouse, licking across the snow towards the mountain lifts. '*Darren!*'

But no expert herself, and hurtling along she could not remember how to stop and headed straight down to the bottom. When she collapsed in a heap of flailing skis, managed to right herself and turn around, he was halfway up on a swaying chair lift, and waving happily.

'Oh no,' she whispered. 'Darren, you naughty boy.'

Alex revelled in the challenge of the mountain, the pristine air, and being alone. At the pinnacle it was clear as a glacier mint; a blue white haze under a brilliant blue sky. Her memories crowded in, and exercise was her therapy. She'd been skiing since early morning.

The past forgotten, she was heading down the mountain, trying out the harder tracks through the forest, when she heard the cry for help. She saw him at once, skis akimbo and his poles waving. Leaning into her skis, she slithered and slipped through the edge of trees and swept in to stop in a dash of flurried snow.

'You hurt?'

'My ankle.' The boy's face was pale, and his hand clutched his right leg. Alex knew what to do. Crouching down to him, she made a splint of her ski pole, and wrapped her scarf around it, tying it tight.

'OK I'm going to get you on your feet, then ski with my arm around you, all right?' He nodded. 'We gotta go together, brace yourself as you climb up. Remember it's slippery.'

He saw the quick smile and took her hand as he came up.

'What's your name?'

'Darren Mason. Ow, it hurts.'

She locked him back into his skis, protecting him with her body beneath his against the lie of the mountain.

'There. You shouldn't be up here alone, if you can't ski. Where are your parents?' He was on his feet, and holding.

'Me mum's down on the panda slopes. It's not her fault, I just took off.'

'Yeah? Well, let's get you back down there. She's probably worried sick about you.'

'If I know me mum, she'll be making ever such a lot of noise . . .'

They saw the pink apparition, blonde hair glowing in the sunlight as they headed back down the last wide slope. Fanny Mason stood out from everyone else in Day-Glo pink neon, tight as a skin, with lime green, purple and citrus yellow accoutrements.

'Mum!'

Alex brought him in close as Fanny stomped in ungainly fashion towards them. Her character was as bright as her clothes, but there was no malice in her voice as she chastised her only son, her love.

126

'You naughty boy. I told you.' She straightened and turned to Alex. 'He's so ambitious. Won't listen. Just like his father.' Her voice was alternately proud and worried. 'I'm Fanny.' Her wide smile anticipated the response. 'Fanny Mason. Thank you ever so much!'

'Alex Dawnay.' She'd never seen such openness in a face, and one rich with prettiness and colour. She'd trust everyone. She rested on her poles. 'He'll be fine. It's just a sprain.'

'Are you a doctor?'

'No. But I learned first aid.'

'I always meant to do that. Studley would say, you got time on your hands, take some courses. Red Cross was one of them. You know how it is, I never got round to it.' She smiled ruefully. 'Now I guess I should have. I don't know if he'll make it to twelve. What *were* you doing, love?'

'I wanted to try out the Toilet Bowl,' he said, yanking a map from his breast pocket and pointing at the kids' trail. 'See . . .'

She looked at the layout, and stabbed at the black spot on the map. 'And I suppose you ended up at the Wall of Death.'

He looked glum. 'I was doing OK till then.'

'Darren. It says here that that trail is the most difficult.' Pride was mixed with concern as she studied her recalcitrant son, and Alex noted it. The boy had determination, and guts. 'Just like your Dad,' she said again. 'Once you see something you want you just can't leave it alone.'

'Did all right with you though, didn't he!'

'Darren . . .' She took a swipe but he ducked.

Alex snapped herself out of her skis. 'Darren can ski, he just needs to get smart about it.'

'Let his body catch up with his brain, you mean. He thinks he knows it all. Won't have lessons. I can't teach him. Can't even ski properly meself! Me, I'm still on the panda slopes with the tots!'

'Buttermilk's a great place to start.' Alex hefted her skis over her shoulder. 'Even I came here today to get back in training, get used to the snow again.'

Fanny eyed the black winged eyes and rosy cheeks, and

127

the tendrils of dark hair that had escaped Alex's hat. 'And I'm glad you did, lovey. We're ever so grateful, aren't we Darren?' He nodded as she pulled him close to her.

'Tell you what,' said Alex, settling her skis comfortably and looking at the kid. 'I'll give him a couple of lessons over the next day or so. Help him get started. You won't have to worry then.'

'You're a pet. But he's a handful, Alexandra love. Always in trouble, bless him. Even at a distance you couldn't cope with him. He sent a ball to some new friends we made. Love from Darren it said across it in black indelible ink. Great. This boy, Charlie, grabbed it and kicked it up high. It shot up the bank as his sister Victoria appeared on the terrace above in her white muslin party dress. It landed perfectly and printed Love from Darren backwards square across her stomach.'

Alex smiled wide. 'You staying in town?'

'The Jerome. You?'

Alex pointed. The top of the motorhome was just visible. 'There.'

'What, in that thing? Not sleeping, surely?' She looked shocked. 'You'll be frozen to death.'

'No. It's warm enough and as big as a hotel room. Besides, I was so tired after the journey here I'd have slept in the car park itself, and I knew I could ski first thing. I was first up the mountain. The prices are crazy, and I don't mind sleeping a little rough. In fact I rather enjoy it, as long as I have the occasional feather bed and American shower.'

'You must stay with us. Darren's got a double room all to himself. Studley insisted, he's such a good dad. There's a single bed just going begging, and a beautiful bathroom. It's all paid for, part of the package . . .'

'No, well, I couldn't, you see –'

'Just till you get settled, that is. To say thanks for Darren, it's the least we could do.' She punched Alex playfully in the shoulder. 'Hang out with us, love. I can't stand them snobby types like his friend Charlie's mum, Felicity. She's got a cork up her arse like all them county types. Give me some moral support, eh?'

128

'Well, we'll see.' She wondered about another night; she was more concerned about the hotel's reaction than anything. She had a bed and, with the stove on, at least enough heat to get her warm before setting up for the night. But without her sleeping bag, last night had been tough. Three a.m. she had been frozen.

'Just come back for a drink then, with us . . .'

That was fair enough. 'Just to help you get him back then. I've skied enough today, anyway. I thought I'd check out Ajax tomorrow. I'll take a fresh look at it tonight.'

'I have to get back to check on my hubby, Studley,' the pretty woman confided as they escorted the hobbling Darren down the steps to the ski centre. 'Too many cute blondes around here for my liking. I just know I can't leave him alone too long, all those girls are going to want him.'

With the onset of a new fall of snow, they hailed a taxi, rather than taking the skibus which would mean a walk down through the town at the destination. It was beautiful in the fresh light of the afternoon, the river a silver cut through the mounding snow driven by the wind, every branch of the trees along the river banks laden with sparkling crystals. Fanny talked warmly about her husband, painting a glowing picture of family harmony; clearly she was proud of him.

By the time they reached the hotel it was almost concealed by blowing flakes; snow was swirling among the trees and deepening rapidly. The wind churned the drifts along the sidewalk, causing the icy crystals to spiral into the air to mix with thick, fluffy flakes that blanketed a now almost invisible sky, and driving straight into their eyes and nostrils.

'God's preparation for the mothers' race,' Fanny said, as they started to run for shelter, half carrying Darren between them and arriving breathless.

Stud was swimming in the pool when they arrived despite the snowfall. Steam rose from the water; it was at extreme heat to combat the falling snow. His rosy body emerged out of the mist as Fanny hailed him loudly. He was short, bald and he was no physical specimen, but his presence was magnetic. Fanny went over and with screams of delight and shock as he splashed her she kissed him and went over the story of Darren's downfall with spectacular additions. Their love was a revelation. Clearly Fanny saw him as not only handsome but a real catch.

'Oh, Studdy, I did need you, love. I was that worried. You should have come with us. Whatever do we do without you there to take care of things. Luckily this fine young lady stepped in and got our Darren back down the mountain.'

'Did you, love?' He wrapped himself in a white terry robe, came over and lifted a square wet hand. 'Sorry about the water.'

She smiled. 'It's OK, and so's he. Just a sprain. You might want a doctor to have a look at it, though. I'm not sure he can walk properly on it, let alone ski.'

'What a shame. Poor lad. So,' he said. 'Just let me grab me towel.' He walked alongside the pool. 'Are you staying here?'

She felt the power of his charm, and understood in part what had snared the exuberant Fanny. He was without pretence.

'No, lovey. She's staying in a *motorhome*, can you *imagine...!?*' Fanny dug him in the ribs and made eyes at him. He appeared to ignore her, and carried on.

'On your own, are you?'

'In the car park, Stud.'

'I know, Fanny.' She slipped her arm around Darren's shoulder. 'Not meaning to sound rude, but will they allow that, then?'

'I shouldn't think so for a moment. They want to keep the prices up. Everyone'll be doing it. No, I expect I've got one more night at the most.'

'You're a resourceful girl, I can see that.' His tone was admiring.

'Not totally,' she explained. 'My aunt lives here and I'm just waiting for her to get back.'

'You know that, do you?'

'Yes. She's always here for Christmas.'

'Well then.' And now he stopped walking and planted himself squarely in front of her. Once again he ignored his

130

wife's wild gesticulations from behind Alex. 'You must take up our Fanny's offer and come for lunch. It's the least we can do.'

That she could accept. 'That'd be great. Thank you.' She smiled at Darren. The little boy's face was quite pale, though he was holding himself straight. 'I expect the hotel has a doctor. I'll go look.'

'Dr Lindstrom?'

Ruth turned her head with a start. She'd been reading in one of the chairs in the lobby, a glass of hot spiced cider at her side as she waited for her husband, who was out walking the town somewhere. The young man stood there, bending from the waist, and looking awkward.

'A slight problem. The hotel doctor is out on call, and a young boy has hurt his ankle. I'm so sorry to disturb you, but could you, would you mind just taking a look? His parents are very worried.'

Ruth was out of her seat in a moment. 'Well I'm not a general practitioner, but I can certainly tell if it is broken or sprained for you, and make recommendations.'

'Thank you. That would be so kind. As I say, I am sorry to have disturbed you, but the manager – '

'That's quite all right.' She was all business now. 'Show me where they are.'

She found them in the bar; bending over Darren's foot she gently turned it one way and the other. Her cool fingers probed and felt and her face was composed. Darren seemed comfortable with her.

'Well, it's not broken, or fractured.' She stood up, and Alex admired the highly attractive middle-aged woman. She had a strength and capability about her, yet Alex sensed more underneath the efficient exterior. 'Leave the sock off. The tumble has caused a little bruising that's all. He can't damage it any more . . .'

'Want a bet,' said Fanny, laughing.

'No, well what I mean is, it's up to him how he uses it. If he wants to ski tomorrow, I see no problem. But a good night's rest first.'

131

She smiled and tossed back the dark hair.

'Come on then, Darren . . . I'll be right back, Fanny. And thank you, Doctor . . .'

'Lindstrom.'

His father took Darren by the arm and together they headed for the lift. Ruth smiled warmly and prepared to move away.

'No,' Fanny held her for just a moment. 'Stay and have a drink with us.'

'Well, I can't really. I was just waiting for my husband, you see, and – '

She turned her face away and found the Kowolskis walking straight towards them from an afternoon's skiing. There was no escape. The children were crowding round eagerly. They stood there, eye to eye.

'Jackie and David,' called out Fanny brightly. 'How was the skiing?'

'Oh, wonderful . . .'

'We just bumped into Dr Lindstrom. Darren hurt his ankle. She helped us.' Fanny smiled from one to the other. 'Come and have a drink with us. We're just going into the bar.'

'Well, we er . . .'

But Fanny had not finished. 'Oh, sorry, do you know each other?'

Alex had already seen the man with the mid-European looks trying to brush past with his family. A flash of something had touched his eyes and she felt their need to be gone, but Fanny had stayed them. Due to her extrovert nature she had obviously already met them all and now she introduced them brightly to each other.

Ruth's glance held his.

'David Kowolski. How do you do?'

She put out her hand slowly. 'Ruth Lindstrom.'

'And my wife, Jackie.'

Nods, polite smiles, but lots of eye contact. As if they shared a common secret. It was a look of some intimacy, and Alex picked up on it with her quick senses. She caught an odd expression on the doctor's face as if a signal passed between her and the man. Alex puzzled over it for a moment not understanding quite why the introduction had provoked this chain reaction. Unless they already knew each other, and they were acting as if they did not.

Alex's antennae was working overtime.

'David's a doctor too,' Fanny said, with a lack of guile. 'In fact I met another one earlier today. The place is full of them,' she laughed with black humour. 'Good thing if anyone just happened to break a leg!'

At the edge of her laughter, Alex looked into the man's eyes.

'What field of medicine are you in?'

She saw the guard go up.

'Genetics.'

Fanny exploded. 'Not *another* one! The only other doctor I could find earlier dealt in genetics. There aren't that many old people around here, are there?'

'I think you're thinking of geriatrics, Fanny,' Jackie smiled.

'Oh yes! Then – '

'Well, been nice meeting you ... kids ...' The doctor's arm around his wife's waist he was already propelling her away. He lifted a slow hand as they made steady progress towards the stairs.

Alex watched them. She'd been a journalist too long not to feel the customary prickle; she had a nose for it now like a wine connoisseur. It was the undercurrent she sensed, more than words. They already knew each other, she was sure of it. Mildly curious, she ventured:

'Are your families here together?'

Ruth smiled coolly. 'No. I have only a passing knowledge of the man,' she disclaimed. 'It's a small field.'

Precisely, it was. Which was why ...

'Are you a keen skier, Miss ...'

'Dawnay. Alex, please. I've skied quite a bit.'

'Ajax is fun. Some good black runs. Trouble is, they're letting in the amateurs with these cosy gondolas. They ruin the mountain.' She pushed her fingers into the pockets of her jerkin. 'Well, gotta run ...'

133

Fanny's brow creased. 'You won't stay for a drink?'

'No, really got to go. I'm meeting my husband, right now in fact. See you all on the slopes.'

Her hand lifting her parting shot, she too had hurried away. Fanny's voice came from behind.

'Well you'll stick with us, won't you?'

Montana watched as the huge pile of snow melted and slid off the glass roof of Boogie's. The restaurant had its own avalanche as it toppled over the edge and exploded on the pavement below just missing the pedestrians.

The room surged with noise, music and loud chatter. It pulsed inside her head, and she had to shout at Jack to order. Hamburgers were piled high on plates as the waitresses scurried to and fro. She closed the menu: it was an easy decision.

Burgers, fries and a Coke. She'd been dying for food. She always got a craving when she'd been on a high and Jack had obliged. Montana's tastes were not fancy: Boogie's hit the spot. Jack was impressed. Most girls would have dragged him to Abetone's.

A bike was suspended from the ceiling and the whole place was neon glitter. Rock music from the sixties to the nineties blasted the eardrums, and downstairs, clothes, western style and California v. Colorado, changed hands amidst the cacophony of noise and colour.

Montana wore a red angora sweater with snowflakes and maribou on the shoulders, and white pants and boots. Earlier, she'd left all her gear at the bottom of the mountain.

The middle-aged man checked her out once more as he headed down the spiral staircase. He seemed to have no place there, yet Aspen was ageless; it was the air he didn't have. Jake Boxer would like to have stayed just to look at the big raw-boned girl with the gap-toothed grin, but he had business.

In early twilight he hit the street, brushing snowflakes from his shoulders. More snow loosened from the glass roof of the hot hamburger joint as the place steamed up hotter for the evening. It slithered off the roof and on to his jacket. As he brushed off his arms, a second man walked out of the shadows.

'You're late,' Boxer accused. 'I had to buy something so's I wouldn't look out of place.' He hefted the bag and the black stetson.

The second man's pale eyes remained fixed on his face for just a moment. He had a cold, Gothic face, his albino pale features and hooded eyes almost too sensually carved. He was Sandford Wainwright's right-hand man, and he didn't care for Boxer's attitude. Wilhelm Lindstrom drew a letter from his pocket.

'Give this to Sandford. It's details of the meeting tomorrow. I don't know anything yet, but I'm going to try and bug the room. It may not be possible. Professor Bowman is very astute.'

'And if you can't?'

'He'll have to trust me with what I hear. Verbally.'

Boxer looked at him hard. He wouldn't trust anyone, and his eyes said so.

'He'll need proof.'

'He'll get proof, but he haf to be patient.'

'Mr Wainwright's not –'

'I know, I know. It's an old cliché, buster boy. I'll do my best, all right. As soon as I have anything I know that will interest him, I'll be in touch. It's in my interests too, don't forget.'

It was. He had been promised the one thing he wanted. Sandford had tweaked his Achilles' heel and he was still rubbing it. He had found out what he wanted more than anything in the world.

'And what about your wife?'

'I'll deal with my wife.' Ruth had opposing views to him, he knew that. She was a moralist, but her knowledge was essential. He'd always demeaned her: she was a plodder, a grafter, he was the one with flair and genius. But now her hard work had won her a place in history. He could not let her know what his own plans were. It had been enough of a game to get here in the first place and into the conference.

Boxer gave him a look; a man who would spy on his own wife. He held him in little regard, Wilhelm Lindstrom could see that, not even honour amongst thieves in this one. But he did not, could not possibly, know nor understand the stakes. To a man in his profession, what Sandford had promised was nirvana.

'I went to this club, Chasers, last night,' said Boxer. 'Saw a couple of your boys there. Listened in, sounds like it's all being kept hush-hush. Your evidence is going to be important. Also some bunch of socialites up the mountain just now at the restaurant. Good thing I learned to ski. I mean to get to know everybody, to get a handle on the social side of town.'

Wilhelm eyed him, wondering what on earth sort of success he thought he would have. He wouldn't fit in. People sensed others of like mien, and this man, even in his expensive ski gear, was not one of them. He looked into the square, florid face bullet-holed with acne scars, and felt a cold smirk of superiority.

'Tell Sandford not to call me in the room unless I can answer in code. Ruth came in yesterday and I had to face up to her. It won't help if she suspects something.'

Boxer's small eyes fastened on him. There was no love lost here. 'Well that's your business. You take care of her.'

The men separated, walking casually down the street amongst the meandering evening crowd.

Boxer saw the girl right away because of her hair. It trailed silver in the evening light and her laugh with it. The two of them strolled together, laughing. She came down the street with Jack Fenner arm in arm, still in the wolf coat, and she topped him by a few inches. The man caught her eye. He knew Fenner, but who was she? Her coat opened suddenly over her long legs and before she had wrapped it back around her, he had taken in the body on display; seen just how the raspberry pink angora strained so sensually over her breasts, seen how the ski pants clung to her figure. He'd seen her a day ago, alone, and picked her out. She'd worked fast. That kind of girl was meat to him. With her kind of kudos she might be a way in.

He headed down to the black Range Rover with the shaded windows that stood at the kerb, and the ponytailed governor within. The couple were headed in his direction and with luck he could detail the afternoon's events and point out the girl and her partner, who could well be players in the game ahead.

'So what do you do, Alex?'

These two clearly never watched the nine o'clock news.

'I . . .'

'Why don't you stay with us and help Darren to ski?'

'And Fanny . . .'

Their conversation peppered the air with cross-fire. Rich, but tightening his belt in a recession, Studley was chubby and middle-aged and blatantly adored his buxom young wife. Alex was soon caught up in their enthusiasm.

'Did Fanny tell you how we met . . .' His look met hers.

'Go on, tell her, Stud.'

'I was attending a meat packing conference, at the Hatton Hall hotel in Gloucester actually.'

Fanny leaned forward.

'Stud earned his money in meat packing – '

'Let me tell it, Fanny.'

'He's made ever such a lot of money, and we give loads to charity. Word has it he might get a New Year's honour. He's a clever pet.' She grabbed his hand. 'A knighthood, Studdy, that'd sort 'em out. Stop them looking down their noses.'

'Well, it was like this . . .'

They were a double act as they joined forces and fought for delivery of their story, in their strong northern accents, and Alex sat back and began to enjoy them both, feeling her spirits rise.

'I'm already in love with Aspen, Alex pet,' Fanny interrupted. 'I went on a guided tour this morning of where all the stars live. Starwood. Have you seen it? Oh, it's lovely, right up there in the mountains with the most beautiful views. I've asked Studdy if he can get us a house there,' she whispered conspiratorially, her hand clasped to his. 'Just for a week! Ooh, I'd love it. A house in Starwood for the rest of the holidays.'

He raised a hand. 'I'll do what I can. Anything for you, petal.'

'Isn't he a love. I'm a right lucky girl.' She smiled broadly. 'Well, get on with the *story* then. *I* don't know . . .'

'I call meself Studley from Dudley,' he began. 'No pretensions, me. Just plain old Studley . . .'

'Get *on* with it.' Copious giggles from her, a grin from him.

'So we met when I was staying at this prestigious Hatton Hall hotel. Did you know it won the Loo of the Year award in 1982?'

'He was running the show and alarmingly rich. I thought what a chubby little fellow, but he was ever so kind. He had the best suite, Room Twelve . . .'

'It had a balcony overlooking the valley. I called up a bottle of champagne and I stood there, with me champagne in a bucket, feeling ever so lonely. It was a beautiful night, autumn, and you could hear for miles. Me first wife had run off with a barman from Cyprus.'

'Imagine, standing there, ever so sad it is.'

'I had me binoculars. I love birds, you see . . .'

Fanny giggled and tweaked his leg. 'You don't have to tell her everything!'

'No, the feathered variety. I had a weekend in the country to study them. Owls were me favourite. Well the night was still, it was autumn as I said. I could hear sounds for miles. Oh, the country was grand. Then I could hear this distant sound, and I swear this high-pitched laughter. I focused on the opposite hill. And then there was this eyesore, the lit-up ski slopes at this place called Matson. Because it spoiled me view, I lifted up my binoculars.'

Fanny squealed with delight.

'I was up there with me girlfriends . . .'

On the slopes in Day-Glo print, blonde hair streaming she had come wobbling down the nursery slopes.

'I watched her at the centre of her friends; she never

138

stopped laughing. Then, on the lift going up she fell flat on her backside and still hanging on, the lift carried her upwards slowly, her legs stuck up in the air!' His whole frame shook with merry laughter. 'I could still hear her laugh from right across t'valley!'

Fanny smiled at him, absorbed with the story herself. 'And he fell in love, didn't you?'

He gripped her hand. 'On the spot,' he affirmed, his voice more than loving. 'Me kids were all grown up, me wife had run off. It was time to go skiing. I made me way over quick as I could. I found her in the bar, still laughing with her friends. That noise filled up the bar, I could hear her as I opened the doors outside. It lit up my heart. I bought all the girls a drink, parked myself next to Fanny and the rest is history.'

'And you've been parked next to Fanny ever since!'

He chuckled. 'Now, what to do about this girl,' he said, holding hands with his wife. His glance took in Alex, and then Fanny. 'I met Felicity upstairs, petal – '

'Oh, my God save me. That woman's such a misery. I swear she's so negative one of these days I expect to hear her say "you know, I have to breathe in and out several times a day" . . .!'

'Yes, well never mind that, she's asked Darren to stay the night with Charlie. Apparently his dad's bought him some new computer game.'

'So it's a foregone conclusion then.'

'Come on, love. She's got a good heart.'

'That's what you say when there's nothing else.'

'She's a good mother.'

'Sheep make good mothers, Studley. And that kid is every bit as snobby as she is.'

He gave her hand a squeeze, and his voice was steady. 'Leave it off, Fanny. Darren was delighted, so I said yes. And what it means of course is that if you were to stay tonight, Alex, you could have that room all to yourself . . .'

His eyes met hers.

Fanny chimed in on cue, the second man. 'So, Darren's staying with Charlie. His room's empty. Going to waste.'

It was a persuasive argument. All her money had gone into buying Hart's share of the motorhome and the trip over. Last night was cold, and who knew how long the hotel, the Inn on the Mountain, would allow her to camp in their parking lot. They might even be waiting for her to get back there. Until her aunt, Fabrice, arrived it might be a good way to pass the time. Fanny seemed to read her thoughts.

'Till your aunt arrives,' Fanny's eyes were wide. 'How about it . . .'

'One night,' she said, smiling, and holding up a finger. She wasn't ready to give up her independence just yet.

'All right, one night. Just to have a bath,' Fanny suggested with a big smile. 'I couldn't do without it, can you? And it's *such* a big one . . .'

She stretched luxuriously at the idea. Alex laughed at the gleam in her eye and the calculating one that matched it in her husband's.

'I think I've been set up!'

'He likes to get his way,' Fanny said, digging him in the ribs. 'Didn't Darren say!'

'It sounds wonderful. And then I can be right there to take Darren out in the morning, long as he's up to it. And you can have a lie-in.'

'Lie-in, nothing. We're early birds. And he'll be up to it, if I know Darren.' She leaned over and patted Alex's hand. 'Well we're going out for a walk,' she said, hand in hand with her husband. 'You coming up . . . just going to grab some woollies.' They got up as one.

Alex stood up too. 'I'll head back to the motorhome first and lock up, grab a couple of things.'

'OK. We'll leave the key at reception for you. 'Tisn't often we get a chance to be romantic. You've got the place to yourself. There's a video . . .'

'If you like a workout,' he said. And she giggled at him.

'See you in the morning.'

Alone, Aspen was just as Alex remembered it. It hadn't changed a bit; real estate windows that displayed vast homes for sale and designer shops; world-class shopping – the clothes seriously casual; never Dallas. The most she spotted was a cowboy shirt with glitter lapels. She could tell the locals from the tourists: they seemed to think the opposite – the brighter the better. She wandered round the streets, feeling the past in this old silver-mining town; fancying that she could almost hear the jingle of a barouche, the painted ladies passing by with the feathers nodding on their hats ready to fleece any hard-working miner, the dust flying on the roads jostling with freight wagons and pack trains; the gamblers and the cardsharps stepping down into the dust of a sultry summer's day to head across the street to where an old joanna tinkled from the smoky shadows of the saloon. The bawdy houses and gambling saloons now housed fancy boutiques and arty bookshops and cafés but the ambience remained in the old iron lamp posts and the brick and stone buildings, the wide redbricked roads bordered by trees.

She glanced in the windows: $4,000 for a red suede-fringed suit, $2,000 for a beaded Indian blanket, $3,000 for a hideous antlered chair with stitched leather cushions. Six figures for an abstract painting that looked as if it had been painted by a blind rat on speed.

Alex walked back down the town and smiled at the American way; Christmas brought out the child in them all even in self-conscious Aspen. It was in the menu set up outside in the snow on the red-tiled walkway, the small latticework windows needing no fake snow or tinsel to make them look like wonderland. She brushed the softly falling snow from the glass with her mitten. No prices; at least here was reality. She shook her head and laughed, but the aroma of strong fresh coffee and newly baked bread from the gable-fronted coffee house with its neat snow-capped box hedges was irresistible. She headed into the warmth and found a cosy room with small tables, a welcoming fire and the steady hum of talk and laughter. Beside the fireplace, she had a hot chocolate with a dollop of heavy cream. Snow fell outside like a child's Christmas dream. Alex felt some of their same excitement and wanted to share it. She caught the bus and headed back to the motorhome, found no note tacked to the window, and went in. It was cold inside, and rather dismal after the brilliance of Fanny's company. She found she missed Montana and was happy to be going back to town. She put on her snow-boots and a heavy sheepskin-lined parka and took the last bus in.

Back at the Jerome, Alex eased her long body into the hotel bath. Heaven. Aching limbs, and trail dirt. She knew all those old cowboy films now, the contented hobo in his tin bath. She stroked the sand from her leg from the morning at Snake River. It made a *frisson* against her skin, a gentle grating that was pleasant. The desert scene filled her mind, and for a moment warmth and sensuality embraced her: the bright twist of the orange peel, the serene wind and the haze of sunshine, Montana's words, the way she had spoken, almost as if . . .

She made the call right after the bath. The telephone was beside the window. She checked with Montana's room but there was no answer. She listened to the buzz, then put down the receiver, her mind still drifting to that sultry moment between her and her new friend, Montana.

Now she was out on the town. So were they all. She stood by the window for a moment longer, infusing the scene, the diaphanous curtain of snow, the quiet Old West streets, the golden lights and soft blue of evening, her mind still drifting. It was a cliché of Christmases past, a nostalgic Victorian theme of which Americans were so fond.

At the kerb, the bespectacled Doctor Kowolski stepped into a waiting Cherokee jeep and that was what first caught her attention; it was a local car and he was ostensibly a tourist. No reason for him not to have friends locally, but . . . She recognised Ruth Lindstrom easily though, running from the hotel, hand raised. She climbed into the jeep too; they were chatting easily as old friends do. Had they made friends that quickly? She didn't think so. They weren't the type. These two shared something they wanted to keep to themselves. The car drove off smoothly in the opposite direction towards Red Mountain.

An hour later, Alex tucked herself up like a child in Darren's bed, but her mind was still alive. The bed was slumber soft and smelled sweetly clean. There was a Fisher-Price music box beside her and a book entitled *Brigitte Bardot: A Legend*. Darren was at the in-between stage. She could see the bright white of the mountain. A cool thin wind stole in from the sliver of open window. The night was brilliant with stars and her bed was warm.

She was being absurd, fanciful. It was most unlike her. Was she just missing the excitement of her life, touting for business in her role as an investigative journalist? This was Aspen! This was playtime for the rich folks, that was all.

No, she knew that was not it. There was more. She punched the pillow and rolled over, grappling with her thoughts.

Why would the doctors lie?

TEN

Mochi's belly pooled golden under the lights. It was quiet. The doctor leaned over her, his hands braced at the edge of her bed.

'Let me explain what we are going to do, Mrs Leng. The embryo will be put into an incubator. It'll stay there for two days. After twenty-four hours we can see signs of fertilisation. Then it is called a pre-embryo. At forty-eight hours we can see the first cleavage. Then embryo transfer takes place. Between these two times one cell is removed and checked for the disease. If there is no sign of the disease, the embryo is replaced without misadventure.'

Against the white pillow, her dark eyes were troubled. 'When are we sure?'

'Nine days. Then we know it's fertilised. At six weeks we can see the flicker of the heartbeat. Let's take it stage by stage, and carefully. Are you comfortable?'

'As much as I'm going to be.'

'Fine. We take it out through your bellybutton. So just lie still and dream about the future. It's going to be good, I promise.'

His voice was firm, but gentle. A woman stood beside her, her pinafore rustling. The face that looked down on Mochi was in starched white and pale blue, a Florence Nightingale of a face, concerned and maternal. The woman found her hand under the sheet and held it. Her eyes willed her to be good and authoritatively let her know she was in good hands. He was the best, this doctor.

There was the rattle of instruments, the bright blinding light that bathed her as if she lay on a warm beach. There was the clean smell of the room, the rustling of the starched cloth. The long needle glinted silver. Mochi closed her eyes and felt the prick, her eyelids squeezed tight.

'Just going in now. Hold still . . .'

She must help them, she mustn't move. She'd never been particularly brave, but the importance overcame any pain. And it was more discomfort than anything else. The hand that held hers was comforting. She looked into the nurse's blue eyes and smiled.

She trusted them.

Clinks, the brush of movement as bodies beside her passed her precious cargo between them. Someone left the room. The doctor's face loomed over her. She saw the light sweat on his forehead, the pores in his nose; his teeth was misshapen but his smile was friendly, and his expression was weary. This must take dedication and strength. Professor Bowman had said he was the best. Miki would always have the best.

'All over. Nurse Peters will see to you now. Rest for a bit, then we'll see you back to your apartment. Try to take it easy. Do you have people to take care of you . . . Mr Leng, is he . . .?'

'He couldn't . . .'

'Of course, of course.' His hand patted hers. 'I understand. Very wise.'

In case of Round Two. Just one more chance, if any at all. Miki had to keep himself very quiet now. No excitement, no travelling. The disease had him in its grip. God forbid it had their baby too.

Their baby. She felt the tears steal under her eyelids. The doctor seemed to understand as he saw her eyes gloss in the lights.

'It's a wonderful time for you both. Everything's going according to plan. Hold tight.'

And he was gone, brushing out of the door as half a dozen assistants stood respectfully back.

'Mrs Leng?' The nurse's voice was solicitous as she bent over Mochi. She had a trim waist and slender hips; she wasn't as old as Mochi had thought. 'Let's take care of you now.' Her face showed she was caught up in the excitement of the moment, the blue eyes sparkled. Compassion. One became aware of it in moments of vulnerability. Her thoughts

145

switched to Miki, lying helpless on his bed; had he felt how much she'd cared?

Mochi let them minister to her, pulling the sheets up around her breasts, and closed her eyes. She'd never been religious, but now she prayed.

It had been Miki's need at first, but now it was hers.

She imagined the baby's room back at the Red House, and started to pick out the crib, the curtains and the pretty blue wallpaper; not too floral, a little masculine. Stripes perhaps, and a frieze; for a boy.

The rookie nurse went about his business next door. The room was small and clinical. Shelves ranged up to the ceilings with pipettes, trays, drugs, some covered in cloths; overflowing, sterile – only an expert could play the game of 'what's on the tray' in here. On the stainless steel counter around him were ranged all manner of complicated machines, none of which could be touched. They were all carefully set to temperature.

Now everyone drifted away and the heavy rubber-edged door with its small viewing window had closed gently. He looked at the incubator, aware that he could be seen. Inside its steel cabinet, the heir to billions flickered on the edge of life. He must be careful. Altering the temperature and opening the door could destroy the frail embryo's chances of survival. At this point too, they did not know if it was going to be fertilised. The opportune moment would be just before it was transferred back.

Then the incubator had done its work.

In two days, he would make the swap. After the doctors had removed the cell and checked the embryo. They would only keep it if there was no sign of the disease. He would wait for that moment, when they knew – then the phone call. There would be minutes only after that discovery whilst he was alone and had laid plans to be in charge.

Hearing the sound of the next patient being wheeled in he laid down the instruments he was pretending to examine and went to the door, peeping through the glass window at eye level. This would be the other patient to whom he would make the swap.

The woman's face lay on the pillow.

She was black.

He turned away, his hands squeezing at his mouth. His heart hammered hard; he did not know how to deal with this. He looked at his notes; routine IVF check. 'Mrs Bellamy' gave no indication as to colour. It was an ordinary name. He felt the first prickle of worry, and headed down the hall to the pay phone. He dialled the number he had been given.

'It's me . . .'

He listened for a moment to the question.

'Yes, it went fine.' He hesitated, feeling the tension in his stomach. 'But there's one problem . . .'

The barked voice issued a single word.

'The . . . the other patient I told you about. I didn't know, from the notes . . . she's er, black.'

He listened to the instant's silence, then the hard laughter. He felt his stomach uncurl in relief. The cold fingers slid down his spine and away.

'Yes, sir. I will.' He put down the phone.

Even better – those had been the words. Blackmail, in the real sense of the word. The man had found it hilarious.

That would come days later, just before she heard from the clinic with the good news.

'I'll say one thing for you, darling; you've got class. Only someone with real style would get away with this dirigible.'

The woman who had banged on her door the next evening was instantly familiar, and welcome. Alex had come back after a day's skiing with Darren to fiddle around with the reluctant generator and the knock on the door had sounded ominous. As she opened it, she steeled herself for a confrontation with the manager of the hotel. Alex laughed when she saw who it was.

She stepped down into the snow and hugged her. 'It's so good to see you, and you look wonderful.'

The slightest breath of perfume, and a jangle of bracelets accompanied the kiss. 'Sexy sixties, darling . . .'

Fabrice Strauss held herself well. Straight and with a direct, even smile. The perfection of her face told of a life where beauty had been commonplace. She wore Colorado clothes: blue jeans, western boots, a cream flannel shirt, and a stetson from Fast Eddie's with a leather band and silver concho hearts. She stepped up into the motorhome.

'So this is where you've been living.' She looked around, and laughed uproariously. 'Not exactly Aspen.' Her innate glamour made her highly amused by her niece's living conditions. 'Well, now I'm here, collect up your things and let's go over to the house.'

Alex stood behind her on the steps, the fading light of day brushing her back. 'When did you get back?'

Fabrice sat down on the bed. 'An hour ago. Benny gave me your message; she's cooking up a dream of a supper right now. Come on,' she waved a hand. 'No buts, sleeping gear only if you're really attached to this thing.'

'Sleeping gear got burned.'

'Ah well, we've got beds if you can stand it,' she remarked brightly. 'Park it at my house. There's a huge yard at the back. You can mess around with it to your heart's content, but do please sleep in the house, darling. There's stacks of room. I've no guests tonight. Bring your overnight fuck bag, that's all you need. The French coined the phrase, I do think they're awfully sophisticated, don't you? They don't feel the need to say "weekend", just tell it like it is.' She stood up. 'Come along.'

They left ten minutes later. Fabrice seemed to breathe deeply as they climbed back into her fire red pickup, its colour softened by a coating of snow. She had always been a social snob, but she considered certain necessities ran alongside chic, and pickups were *déclassé*. Besides, they were useful. The broom stuck out of the back, catching her eyes as she turned.

'I had John sweep the yard behind the garage. You'd never get that thing up the drive otherwise. You'll have to bring it over tomorrow.' She backed up, eyeing the monster out of the side of her eye as she made to drive out. 'Thank God you didn't park it any closer in. I have a reputation to keep up.'

'Lucky I didn't park it on your street,' Alex said drily.

'You wouldn't have had much luck. No place to park, nor live for that matter. Keeps the tourists out.' Fabrice took a long look at her as they reached the road and checked the traffic both ways. 'Well, you don't look too bad, a little pale, perhaps.' She took in the direct eyes, so similar to her own, the swept back dark hair and lovely features. 'How do you feel?'

'Not as well as I thought I would. The air is marvellous, but I wonder if I ate something.'

'A little nauseous?'

'Yes.'

'Altitude sickness,' Fabrice pronounced. 'Nothing to worry about. Headache, short of breath. A couple of days you'll be OK. We're more than 8,000 feet above sea level here. It's the reduced humidity. Drink fluid, no alcohol; you'll be fine. A little dressing up and a touch of make-up would help, of course,' she said as she pulled out on to the road and headed for town.

Alex smiled. It was an old battle. Fabrice had lived many years in France and was always chic. She had a French-woman's wardrobe: bare; expensive essentials only. Even her staff called her Madame.

'How are you doing these days, Aunt Fabrice?'

'You can drop the aunt, and I'm doing fine as you can see. I've been in Europe, only place to be. I went on to stay with some old friends in Rome after the Paris collections. I stayed on for a couple of weeks, travelling; Florence, Venice. I have so many friends. I can't keep up with them.' Her bracelets clicked on her wrist as she drove. Fabrice had worn the same two gold bracelets as long as Alex had known her, one set with rubies, one with emeralds. She had said they had been given to her by a first lover and were deeply sentimental, but Alex's mother, Beatrice, had always claimed they were bought by her at Garrard's in London, and were simply a way of keeping her husband, Boris, on his toes. For the same reason she had had red roses delivered spontaneously when-ever Boris strayed, with no note, and Fabrice would mysteriously leave town till he got back in line.

'John can drive you back in the morning to collect this thing. How long are you staying?'

'I'm not sure.' Alex looked out of the window, watching the steady fall of snow ahead of the pickup. It charged through the three inches of powder that covered the street. Her memory could not help but revert to that other day as they started up the slope, and the windshield wipers batting at the snow blowing across their vision. The landscape sped by.

'Not working?'

Now she looked back at her. 'I thought I'd take a break. See what I come up with.'

Fabrice nodded. Alex had never been a freeloader; she had always been an independent girl and though her lifestyle had been different to her aunt's, Fabrice respected her.

'Well, you can stay as long as you wish. I've got an outside entrance on the guest wing. It's all yours. You can come and go as you please.'

'Thank you.'

'It's the least I can do for your mother, bless her. Do you ever hear from her?'

'Never.'

'Ah, religion. It's so contradictory.'

Fabrice was an east-coaster of French ancestry, and from a wealthy family in her own right. She was, if not Queen Bee, one of the matriarchs of the old mining town, and she was a consummate, but amusing, social snob. She and her husband had bought a house long before it became fashionable when the Paepckes had discovered Aspen and real estate went through the roof. She had one of the most beautiful Victorian houses in the West End. Boris, her husband, once a rich industrialist, was now dead, and Fabrice travelled. Now there were European palazzos and English country houses on Red Mountain, grand-scale contemporary glass and wood edifices on gated Starwood. She, like many others of her ilk, had kept the old Victorian Aspen exclusive.

The pickup headed down the streets, winding round the familiar gingerbread houses to one standing back at the very end. There was a rustic bridge over a frozen stream, snow banked in blue shadows around a dark green spruce, and they were home. Frills and ornate bric-à-brac enhanced the fashionable mansion.

In the twilight a coyote's howls floated across from the distant mountains. Snow fell in a thickening drift around them and snow crystals crunched underfoot. The path was glazed with a crust of ice sparkling under the soft house lights that streamed across it. Alex felt a sense of wellbeing as she looked around her.

'Well, here we are.'

Alex hefted her leather overnight bag out of the pickup and followed Fabrice into the house.

Dinner had been served in the small candlelit dining room. Now they sat in the drawing room with strong black coffee in porcelain demitasses, served by Benny. Fabrice had changed into a pair of soft aubergine silk palazzo pants and a matching blouse, which showed off her slim build. Alex sat on the carpet by the fire relaxing in a soft wool skirt and sweater. Benny had closed the door and they were alone.

Fabrice switched out a couple of the lamps and they sat by the light of the Christmas tree, which was garlanded with tiny white lights, silver lace and angels.

'So,' she said, placing the tray closer on a low table. Beside the coffee pot was a large covered dish, a half of champagne already opened and two tall glasses. 'Have you left the writing behind?'

'No. Not exactly.'

'And the boyfriend?' It was a question anything but casual.

'That's past tense.'

'I thought so.' Fabrice knelt on the carpet beside the low table and poured coffee. 'I saw him on television when I was over there,' she said. 'Reporting from some far-flung spot. He's very good at it.'

'Yes,' Alex said drily, and stared into the flames. 'He is convincing.'

Fabrice saw what she had been looking for. Evidence that

Alex was not free of it. She liked to know how things stood. Not necessarily a gossip, she simply preferred to be in tune with those around her, and made no bones about direct questions. She alone knew of Alex's past and admired her for it, and for her reticence. Most would love to brag about a job that brought danger and the romance of such a challenge to one still so young. But looking into the still face, Fabrice was not without curiosity. 'Do you never worry about the danger?' she enquired, changing tack. She handed Alex a cup.

'Of course.' Alex came back to the present and looked up at her, taking the cup of aromatic coffee. 'I'd be mad not to. Ignoring danger could be all too final.'

'And you'll go back.'

'Probably,' she said slowly. 'Right now though I need something different.'

Taking the lid from the dish, Fabrice knelt beside the fire and made dessert. Marshmallows blackened on the fire until the insides were golden, and the outside charcoal sweet.

'You'll find it here. It couldn't be more different. Aspen is not what it was at all. It's all meditation and gym classes. Hollywood came here looking for an alternative, quaint old restful charm and beauty. An old-worldliness away from the glam and glitter. Trouble is, they brought Hollywood with them. Now you can hardly see the join.'

Alex sipped her coffee.

'I travelled out here with a friend. When I asked her what it was about Aspen, she said it had soul. I saw something of that last night when I went walkabout.'

'Yes, but it has changed,' said her aunt sadly, pronging a soft pink marshmallow and holding it to the fire on a toasting fork. 'Aspen is harder on dreams than most places.' She now looked into the past in the dancing flames. 'We came out here with the Paepckes of course. Boris was half in love with her; Elizabeth was a legendary beauty. She convinced Walter, so we came too. We were all part of the same crowd. But Aspen has gone in a different direction to the one her dreams envisaged. Multimillion-dollar houses whose owners visit a few weeks in every year – it's become a town of glitz and glamour without substance, I'm afraid.' She poked at the fire, making the sparks crackle and leap, laid the poker back down in the grate and turned the golden marshmallow in the flames. 'Elizabeth was rich with a difference,' she went on. 'She represented the real Aspen, pre-image Aspen, the old values and old money. She and Walter invented Aspen, but now so much has changed; the newcomers don't understand the town – it's dreadfully sad. They take and never give, too many rich people of the worst sort, lawyers and realtors.' She shook her head. 'They always make changes, and rarely for the better.'

'I hear she was quite something.'

'She was.' Fabrice settled back on her haunches, reminiscing. 'And Aspen admired her, but sadly those very values of hers synonymous with the town, have not stood the test of time. It's become a world of who you know.'

'How did this place start out?' Alex sipped at the bitter dark coffee.

'With Jerome Wheeler and James Hagerman. They brought the railroads in first. Their silver heyday was a hundred years ago. They made fortunes. But even their past doesn't seem so very far away – Wheeler forgot to take into account the variation between magnetic north and true north; it means the streets of Aspen were laid crooked, and that hasn't changed. It kind of adds to its charm.'

A hundred years later the courts were still trying to sort out conflicting claims of land, and mineral and water ownership; the confusion about who owned what was never entirely settled. The age-old custom of squatters' rights had been supposed to guarantee ownership in those days of land already occupied, but still they fought over the veins they found – if a prospector discovered a vein underground he had a right to follow it. He'd locate boundaries of his claim to include the surface vein, ultimately causing each claim to run into others on the surrounding surface.

A hundred years ago too, it had been Jerome Wheeler who had really set history moving: he'd seen the future, fed railroads into town, and transformed the rough raw mining

153

camp into a silver rich enclave moulding a centre of beauty and culture with a hotel that would rival any in the world. He planted shady trees, created an opera house, encouraged culture and made the town sophisticated enough, complete with electricity, cars and telephone contact, to attract any world-orientated traveller. In the forties, Walter Paepcke had begun again. Imposing his rule much as his predecessor had done, he had taken the mountain ghost town and, reforming the now shabby buildings and streets, had turned it into a fashionable ski resort in winter and a place of celebrated culture in the summer with the Aspen Music Festival and the Aspen Dance Festival. Albert Schweitzer himself had come to speak at the Aspen Institute for Humanistic Studies.

'Yes, Aspen has gone through many changes,' she mused, holding the fork towards her niece. Alex pulled the sticky sweet loose and popped it into her mouth, the golden burned skin and soft oozing cream melting deliciously on her tongue. 'They started out with a brick courthouse, dignified and imposing, and set up a locale for cultural events – and at the other end of town were the painted ladies.' Fabrice fitted another marshmallow to the fork and doused it in heat. 'Then came 1893, a failing economy, and it took its toll. Depression made its way everywhere; Aspen mines closed their doors. Eighty per cent of the enterprises went bankrupt, and thousands were suddenly destitute.'

'What happened to those who stayed?'

'They lived as best they could. There was a tiny tourist industry, summer fly fishing on the Frying Pan river where they say fish leaped straight from the river into the pan, and there was the Roaring Fork too. Crops grew well, some businesses ticked over, even though mining stocks fell steadily after 1894.'

'But basically,' she went on, 'the residents that remained simply liked living here, and so they stayed. There was a good life, good schools and churches, a doctor and a dentist as well as a decent legal system and a theatre, ample merchants. Families hiked, camped and rode horses through the trails, the mountains were uncrowded then; children could swim in the rivers. And in winter they sledded down Monarch Street, or skied in the hills near the high school.' She lifted her face, remembering. 'Nothing could compare with its beauty, Alex; the vision of brilliant blue skies against sparkling drifts of snow, the pure pine air and the joy of simply feeling good through being in the mountains. People began to realise that this was the deepest, lightest powder they had ever known. The skiing was glorious and a miner's cabin was dirt-cheap.' She spoke slowly, as if in reverence. 'It had, and still has, an indelible magic. The Greek concept of the complete life – work, play and educational leisure – all in one perfect heaven on earth. That was Walter's dream. It really was the most enchanting place I had ever seen.'

The flames leaped and crackled in the fireplace as her voice stopped.

'It sounds idyllic,' Alex sighed.

'Oh, it was,' enthused her aunt. 'And then of course, there was the *culture*. Once Walter got a hold of the place it began in earnest. This time it established itself.' She delicately placed a marshmallow into her mouth as she finished speaking, and remembered the beginning for her and Boris. At this altitude, everything had been sharper, in clearer focus, a little nearer the sky. Goethe and cowboy boots; a mingling of cultures. 'Dreamers and doers came here,' she said, 'the best of everybody; the elite.' She opened her hands wide. 'Brilliant sunshine, a pristine blue sky.' She shook her head. 'Every day a perfect day,' she said softly and forked another marshmallow, turning it against the fire.

'Even if money and power are the only things respected here now,' Alex added drily.

'Absolutely.' Fabrice's voice retained its softness though she chuckled warmly. 'That essential element of the traditional Aspenite remains unchanged.' Fabrice studied Alex: the long silky black hair catching the light of the fire, the serious but beautiful face cast in shadows. 'Will you still be here for the winter carnival?'

'I'm not sure.'

'I'd like you to stay now I have you. It's a treat for me, Alex

155

dear. You look so like your mother, and believe me I was always very fond of her. And the torchlight parade's quite a treat.'

'That has something to do with when all the silver mines were open, doesn't it?'

'That's right. At night, the miners would change shifts and hundreds of them would be crossing the slopes carrying lanterns to guide their way. It's quite a tradition.'

'The mines aren't still in operation, are they?' Alex took the marshmallow off the fork and licked her fingers enjoyably.

'No. But the whole mountain is honeycombed with them.' This time she laid down the fork; Fabrice kept her own figure by treats in tiny amounts. 'The most famous was the Mollie Gibson on Smuggler Mountain. When the US adopted the gold standard the bottom dropped out of the trade, and slowly all of the mines were shut down, boarded up and abandoned. But they are still very much there. It's a strange paradox, isn't it, when you consider what this place has become.' She paused for a moment watching the snow fall on the wooden porch outside. 'Now it's people standing around being rich together, interested in little but themselves. The same underlying boredom, a need for stimulation of any sort, salacious gossip being the best as long as it's about one of their own. All the parties have the same conversations, the same people. Boris would have hated it.'

She turned to look up at his picture set over the mantelpiece in the cosy terracotta and wood-beamed room, and Alex followed her gaze. He looked like a cattle baron of old with his roughened good looks and silver grey hair. He was a big man; in his western suit and tie, and his cowboy hat with a dusting of snow on its brim, he dominated the room, as he had dominated life.

'When you find one, don't let him go, Alex. That's my advice.'

'Well, there's no fear of that!'

Her aunt gave her a long hard look. 'That's just when it happens,' she said, climbing to her feet and settling back into her chair.

156

Alex laughed outright. 'I'm so glad you're back.'

'Me too,' she smiled, leaning forward to pat Alex's hand. Once again, she was light-hearted. 'Of course most of us lie low at this time of year, but I just happened to be homesick.'

'Despite the changes.'

'Despite them!' she agreed. 'And what providence,' she said, her hand still lying over Alex's. 'In a couple of weeks the gang will be back, and if you're still around I'd like you to meet them.' Though she had only just arrived, Fabrice was already aware of who was in Aspen this season. 'Now,' she said, all brisk efficiency, 'tomorrow we have a lunch to which you are naturally invited.' She sipped at her coffee. 'An old friend, Hillaire Bowman – he has a house in Riverside – and his rather younger friend, staying with him: another doctor, a Liam Gower.' She reached across with a jangle of bracelets for a piece of fruit, and cut it expertly with a small silver knife. She fed the slivers into her mouth as if they were delicacies. 'No excesses,' she said. 'Makes us a clean vessel,' she said, sweeping her hands over her body like a dancer. 'Keeps the lines at bay.'

'Just them?'

'No. Also Freddie Renby-Tennant and his unfortunately ghastly wife, but Freddie's a hoot. He's a plastic surgeon, very famous in London, have you heard of him?'

Alex smiled at her. 'I'd have no reason to – unless he got in the news.'

'Oh Freddie wouldn't do that, too impressive a list of clients to assuage. He's infamous amongst a certain clique of ladies. Here he'd set the place on fire. He'd have to be hot, wouldn't he? We have to keep him really low key. He's asked especially. It's all health spas and plastics surgeons in Aspen, along with planned travel jaunts, who's who, and the usual *cause célèbre*, clean air and the environment.' She smiled widely. 'Darling Freddie has lifted every eyebag and bottom in society. The tales he has to tell! Forget the Hippocratic oath if you go to him. He loves to talk. But he seems to get away with it. He is such fun . . .' She stroked her own perfect jawline absently. 'He's a snob, of course, but a very funny one.'

Alex ran her mind over the cast list. 'Why doctors? I thought you liked to pick and choose. Put oddballs together?'

'Oh, they *are* oddballs, Alex. They are. All scientists are mad.'

'This place seems lousy with doctors, doesn't it? I mean I met two already in the Jerome.'

'Not necessarily. Just people at the top of their tree.' Her aunt passed it off. 'This young man might be fun for you too. Quite apart from evening up my numbers nicely!'

'Don't try to set me up, aunt,' she growled.

'Would I?' She slid the slice of fruit into her mouth. 'That would be the kiss of death with you.'

She leaned forward, beating the firewood down to break it up for the night. Alex's investigative sense showed its interest.

'So what does this Dr Bowman do?'

'*Professor* Bowman.' She sat back. 'Ah, he's a brilliant man. An old Aspen friend. Something fancy in medicine,' she said, leaning forward again to disperse the embers. 'He's ex-Harvard, ex-this, ex-that.' She waved her hand airily. 'A veritable *list* of qualifications.'

Alex couldn't help it. 'Genetics,' she pronounced.

'Yes. That's it.'

Alex felt her blood stir. 'And the other one?'

'Oh, he's a surgeon, or something. Quite brilliant in his own way, I gather. He's Hillaire's protégé. Must be clever: Hillaire wouldn't tolerate an also-ran. I haven't met him but I gather he's a dish.'

Alex hardly heard her; she could not resist it, she *smelled* a story.

'Fabrice, tomorrow – please – don't talk about the job . . .?'

'Of course not, if you don't want.' She took her in, pausing at the fire. 'But why?'

Alex made a face. 'I just don't want to answer the questions.'

'Fair enough, but they're bound to ask. What will you tell them?'

'I don't know. I'll think of something.' Her voice was thoughtful.

'Well, nothing too alternative or in this place they'll be queuing for lessons.' Fabrice got to her feet. 'Make it dull is my advice, you don't look like a snow bunny.' She stretched, checked her watch. 'The evening news is calling for flurries,' she said. 'Clouds have a good eight inches in them. Time for bed.' She walked to the french windows and looked out and up. 'Ah, it's a beautiful night. Come see.' Alex stretched and came to stand beside her. Fabrice put an arm affectionately around her shoulders.

'I'm sure you're going to enjoy this place, darling. Have a soak in the hot tub if you want. Switch is over there by the side,' she said, pointing out over the terrace, 'robes in the closet, but call it a day soon, all right. I want you to have an early start bringing that dirigible back here, please, I don't want anyone to see it *en route* . . . take the champagne with you . . . good night, poppet.'

She left the room with her easy stride, bearing away her own glass and leaving her guest warmed by her stories, the crackling fire's atmosphere and the soft lights of the tree.

Alex pushed open the french windows and stepped out on to the terrace, the briskness of the mountain night and its sharp perfumes washing over her. She wandered to the edge of the heavy wooden terrace where a soft wind swirled through the trees, scattering a silver mesh of ice crystals on to the sculpted drifts below. New snow began to fall and the tiny flakes settled on her skin, gently feathering like a lover's kiss. Alex lifted her face and closed her eyes and for a long moment she stood there feeling the sensations, hearing the soft silence, a silence that made her feel as if she was the only one in the world, as the snowfall deepened and the lights of the town beyond faded into an opaque distance through the surrounding glade of tall pine trees. She drew it in, letting out all the tension and knew just what she wanted now.

She turned on the bubbling hot water of the tub, returned briefly for the cloth robe in the closet and, bearing her glass of champagne, shed her clothes quickly and climbed into the tub. Fabrice's one concession to new Aspen. The bubbling heat claimed her briefly chilled body down into its depths, and she let out a sigh, taking in the freedom of loosening her naked limbs to the dark velvet heat and letting it flow hotly over her shoulders for a moment. She let her body float up, so that her shoulders and the tops of her breasts broke clear of the bubbling waters. Snow fell soft and steady, sprinkling on to her breasts, a sensation she quickly realised was not without its benefits. Reaching for her fluted glass of chilled champagne, she took a long delicious sip, the contrasts of chilled and warm stirring a *frisson* along her skin. From the secluded terrace she was hidden from view, and she gave herself to the feelings with sheer delight.

She lifted her face to the falling snow, another sip of icy cold champagne sliding down her throat and the crystalline flakes melting on her eyelids and cheeks. The hot tub, the snow, the champagne were all deliciously decadent. To hell with altitude sickness; she sipped and laid her head back, felt her body lifted on the hot churning waters and sighed a deep sigh of satisfaction. She started to sing gently, chanting an old madrigal, her voice rising softly into the air.

The hush of falling snow had muted the sound of the approaching footsteps. The man stood back, unwilling to disturb such unadulterated hedonism.

He was still watching, a smile in his eyes, as she climbed from the water five minutes later and slid into the plush robe of Egyptian cotton, bending to switch off the bubbles. Lifting her empty glass she padded into the house, where the warm boards caressed the soles of her chilled feet, the door clicking shut behind her and closing her away from him.

He stood in the night and waited until the lights flicked out in the downstairs rooms before quietly climbing the front steps of the porch and posting the letter through the door flap and returning at a slow walk back through the trees. Once, he looked back and then he was gone.

Alex couldn't sleep. She felt her excitement like that of a child. When snowflakes began to swirl enticingly by her window, she threw back the covers and, bare feet sinking into the thick alpaca rug, crossed the room and curled up on the padded windowseat, Mesmerised by cosy warmth and pleasure she watched the steady fall of white powder, the darkness enhancing the feeling that she was the only person in the world.

Steadily the snow filled in the footprints that made their way across the lawn and through the soft blue shadows of the trees.

ELEVEN

The telephone was ringing. It was morning; she'd already retrieved the motorhome, found a note from Montana, wrapped around a joint and pasted to its windscreen, parked it in the back yard, and gone back to sleep.

Back in bed now, she listened absently to the ringing. Unscrambling from her warm bed, she went to sit on the windowseat. The room was decorated with print wallpaper, pale blue with dark roses. A throw rug lay across the brass bed. A pale blue dressing gown was hanging on the back of the door, a fluffy towel on a rack, flowers on the windowsill, and a carafe of water beside the bed. Fabrice thought of everything. The house was just as she remembered it. Warm, with youthful breezy decoration amidst the lovingly gathered antiques. It was a home.

'Alex, telephone . . .'

She pulled on the dressing gown and ran down the narrow stairway barefoot to take the call in the hallway.

'Fanny, doll! So you've found your auntie. That's great! We're moving to Starwood, isn't it wonderful! Stud found a house. You know Rowan Bader, the film star?'

'Yes.' She combed at her sleep-tangled hair with long fingers as the hall mirror presented a picture of rosy-cheeked dishevelment. Fanny's joy-filled voice was bringing her to full alert in seconds. She tucked her fingers back into the pocket of the gown, feeling the square of crumpled paper. She drew it out as Fanny went on:

'Well it's his wife's house, Evie. Apparently they have houses next door to each other, because they can't live together. What an arrangement!' She laughed uproariously at the idea. 'Well, anyway, Stud was talking to this Jack Fenner who owns this club, Chasers, and he said he'd see what he could do. So he asked Evie, and she said we could have it . . .'

'I've heard of Jack Fenner.' Alex turned the note round in her fingers.

Great news, I'm working at Chasers. Said I would, didn't I! Call me there, Montana X.

'. . . yes, well, apparently he had a word in her ear, and she's moving in with her husband for a week!' Fanny laughed. 'And we've got her house. It's all stucco and wood, contemporary style, you know, with views for ever – right down the Elk mountain range. It's quite stunning. Darren's crazy about it. It's going to be brilliant. You must come up.'

'I will. Give me the address, I'll come by and pick up Darren.'

'Well, really? Now you found your aunt and all. You don't want to do that.'

'Yes, I do. I'd love to.' She tilted her face up as she spoke, aware of the contents of the note. 'This Jack Fenner, he's a bit of an operator, isn't he?'

'Oh, absolutely. I've heard he does nothing for nothing.'

'What did he get out of it?'

'Evie said his usual double fee: information and lifelong gratitude . . .'

The night's flurry of snow had laid down three of the promised eight inches on the drive John had cleared the day before. Snow covered the landscape behind the yard, but Alex could hear the sound of the river a hundred yards away. The sun was a soft pallor in the sky, but the day was as fresh as if someone had cleaned it, removing all dirt. Alex breathed in; the air was charged with ozone and scented with pine resin, and it wasn't too cold to work. Slipping into her overalls and taking an old blanket from inside she slid underneath the motorhome and was soon tapping away.

Boots crunched their way over the powdered snow. The owner squatted down, dipping his head to look under, his face in silhouette.

'Haven't seen one of these in ages. Certainly not up here.' His dark, soft voice was tinged with amusement. 'Did you come in under cover of dark with your passport ready?'

163

'Yes. And my disguise.' Her voice was muffled and made even lower than usual by the strain of her awkward position. She glanced over to where her tools lay on a cloth out in the daylight. 'Hand me that wrench, would you?'

He pushed it under the chassis. The hand that delivered it was strong and masculine.

'I'm surprised Madame allowed it. She doesn't seem the type.'

'Really, why's that?'

'Everyone round here is so conscious of style. What's the problem?'

'Don't know. Plenty of teething problems on this thing.'

'Just bought it?'

'Just took delivery is more like it. I never had to do the driving before.' She banged away on a nut that wouldn't loosen.

'Where did you come from?'

'The coast. California.'

'Quite a journey. How did you find it on the hills? Cut out?'

'As a matter of fact, yes.' She banged her thumb and swore. 'God Almighty.' She shook away the pain, and peered up into the turgid black mess of oil and mud. She swept the flashlight round with despair. This thing was almost beyond her.

'Want a hand?'

'Don't need help, but thanks.'

Liam Gower looked at the small feet. The guy wasn't made of much, not someone he'd have associated with an attempted journey in this ancient wagon, but he'd obviously got spirit. He was not sure he would have tried it. It didn't look as if the wagon would stand the strain of five hundred miles, let alone three thousand.

'It takes a fair bit of strength to drive one of these things.'

'I managed.' Alex banged vigorously on the nut and at last it began to loosen. She worked it round. The thing had never been undone; now at least she could get at the carburettor housing.

'You know where I can find Alex?'

'Yes, as a matter of fact.'

'Fabrice wants him in to lunch.'

She smiled, realising the meaning; the engine could wait.

She slid out, and stood up. The black hair was untidily dragged back and her body was indeterminate in the clothes she wore, but undoubtedly slim. She had a blob of oil on her cheek, and her eyes were screwed up into the sun but her face was a perfect oval and her bones held the hallmark of beauty.

'*I'm* Alex.' She rubbed the heels of her hands on her overalls.

'I thought you were a guy.' He laughed and stuck out a hand. 'Liam Gower.'

'The Young Doctor,' she countered, smiling. He was tall, standing against the light.

'Your aunt didn't clue me in as to your sex.'

'Your second assumption.'

He listened to the soft sexy huskiness of her voice, intrigued, realising in part how he'd made his mistake. 'The first being . . .?'

'That a woman couldn't handle one of these.' She wiped her hands on a rag. 'You think women can't do these things?'

He looked her over. 'I thought so till today.'

'How very enlightened of you.'

'I'm always ready to have an open mind.'

'Move with the times, Young Doctor.'

'I try.' He grinned.

She shielded her eyes with her hand and looked him over. Eyes narrowed against the light, he was dark with a clever look about him, and he seemed to be very contained. He was big and husky in a worn plaid shirt and a sheepskin-lined parka. Goddamnit, he even wore a cowboy hat with snowflakes settling exquisitely on the brim.

'Where did you get that?' she said, suddenly amused.

'This?' He doffed the hat, revealing a sweep of black hair. 'Fabrice gave it to me.'

She laughed. 'It used to belong to her husband.'

165

But he did not see the joke, just the challenging humour in her eyes. Light accentuated the aristocratic planes of his face and the long deep scar on his cheek. Prompted by habit, she looked deeper and found that beneath the veneer there was something else; he was rough, a coldness there, a step you could not take beyond the smile. The eyes were grey and clear and of a steady, burning intelligence. Shadows at the corners of his lips showed a mouth that would smile easily. There was a lot to him, and that made her curious. He turned a moment towards the house and then back, reminding her.

'Are the others here?'

'Apparently they cancelled at the last minute.' Hillaire had advised against it once he knew Fabrice's plans. Their apologetic excuses had sounded genuine enough to her. 'Fabrice says she's going to try and rope in the next-door neighbours. She doesn't want to waste good food.'

His voice was measured, slow and warm. He'd put insinuation into a weather report. She laughed to herself, glad she was a girl with a broken heart and therefore not looking for adventure. Now she saw the smile. He was too sure of himself, and he seemed to be laughing at her. His eyes played tricks in the light, and she couldn't gauge their expression. Suddenly uncomfortable, she wanted to get away from their scrutiny.

'I'll just clean up.'

She turned away but he made no move to leave. He could see the shape of her, the sultry lips in profile, their dusky rose colour free of make-up, the strands of long gleaming black hair escaping the woollen hat. Her skin was very smooth. He parked himself on a post and folded his arms. He looked like a rancher in his faded jeans and time-worn cowboy boots.

'Tell me,' he said nonchalantly, as she put her foot on the first step of the motorhome. 'Why would such a feminine girl act such a tough role?'

Sparks flew from her eyes as she turned to face him. 'If you mean the motorhome, it's a preference for camping out rather than living in luxury.' She wasn't quite sure why she was so keen on making this point. 'Besides, it's mine.' He nodded quietly. 'I'm not here just to kill time.' There was clear insinuation in her voice but he did not react.

'I can see that. It must take a deal of spunk to drive that thing. It'd be hard work on these hills. Did you have problems with the changing altitude running the generator?'

She looked for the sarcasm, wasn't sure whether he was making fun of her, or going with it. She decided to believe in him.

'How did you know about that?'

'You have to change the mixture. Adjust it, it's probably set for the coast. It's a fuel/air mix. When the air thins out, the fuel runs too rich.'

'Well the generator certainly doesn't like being at 8,000 feet, I know that.' She looked him over. The cool grey eyes under their straight black brows were quizzical; a dash of black hair cast a shadow. Montana would have died for this one. 'The idle wouldn't hold on the last stretch. It would fire, but it was the devil to catch.'

'I could do it if you want.'

'That's OK, now I know.'

He shrugged, nonplussed. 'I gather you slept in it night before last.'

'That's right.' She put her hands on her hips.

'Must have been cold.' His smile caught at her; she felt its combustion. Powerful stuff. Pity she hadn't had that to fire her reluctant generator. Amused, the light touched at her eyes.

'I turned on the gas stove till I'd got a fug up, and then I slept in my long johns.'

He laughed, looking at her. 'Enterprising.'

She shrugged. 'Necessary.'

He drew in a breath, looked around at the yard, back at her. The early snow haze was lifting, and patches of brilliant blue showed in the sky. The late morning sun lay shafts of light upon the snow. 'So you didn't come to see your aunt.'

'No. I came because I promised myself once I would.' Suddenly curiosity gnawed at her. 'You seem to know cars.'

'I used to race a bit in my youth.'

'Is that how you got the scar? Souvenir of a plane crash in the Himalayas?'

'Nothing so romantic. I fell out of a tree when I was eight.' The smile came again. His steady eyes still seemed to hold her, which she found disconcerting. 'Racing was my form of relaxation. I had an old Sunbeam. My dad let me have it, as long as I learned how to fix it.'

'And all the other kids had BMWs, right?'

'Right.' He laughed a little, easing up.

'What did you do when you weren't racing?'

'Took medicine. I was at Oxford.'

'And now?'

'I'm a rookie surgeon, in New York.'

'That how you know this Bowman character?'

'More or less.' He parried her question. She saw pure steel. 'You?'

'I'm Fabrice's nephew. You know that.'

She smiled, her eyes slightly taunting, and moved away. Her looks were remarkably fluid, and she moved with athletic grace. Dark with a lovely smile, he wanted to see her without the severity of the hair pulled back from her face. There was something beyond, and it was the something that pulled him in. Her voice called out to him as she shrugged out of the overalls. 'Completely independent, you see,' she said. 'All mod cons.'

Tidying herself for lunch, she brushed out her hair, put on a touch of lipstick, a quick dash of Chanel and took the shine off her work-warmed skin with a dusting of translucent powder. Her eyes, with her arched black brows shaded by the fall of hair, gazed lustrously back at her, hinting at challenge in their depths.

Stepping out into the day, she almost wished she hadn't: he smiled in quite a different way as she came down the steps in jeans and soft chamois shirt, her hair loose around her shoulders, and his expression irked her; it was as if he had found her truth, that she was more feminine than she let on – as if he recognised her. Montana's words danced in her

168

head; this time she would be herself. *This time?* She collected herself fast as he stood back to escort her in to lunch. What on earth made her think that? This one was not her type at all; far too self-assured. She deliberately cooled her voice.

'Have you been here before?'

His expression didn't change. 'Only in the summer. I came for polocross. I know someone with a ranch up in Maroon Bells. He runs a team.'

'You've never skiied here?'

'No. It's not my kind of place.'

She let that one go. 'But you can ski.'

'Average.' He looked very physical. She sensed it was not the whole truth, and wondered at it. 'Where do you come from?'

'Upstate New York. Originally Toronto. I studied in New York, and took a house out of town. I don't care for cities.'

She walked beside him in the sun. 'You two work together? You and the Professor?'

He shook his head. 'Different fields. You?'

'I'm in between jobs.'

The conversation had died and neither was giving. They'd reached the front door.

'You think it's going to be good skiing today?'

'I'm no expert,' she said, evading the truth and wondering why. 'Just a punter.'

169

TWELVE

'. . . a lot was expected of you, Fabrice. You were the Queen of Aspen.'

'Too much. And enough of the past tense.'

'You threw it away, living alone after Boris.'

'Only in your opinion. I've lost nothing, Hillaire.'

'I never said you had. Beauty such as yours is never lost,' he intoned in his deep baritone as he helped her pass the plates. 'At eighty you will still have grace, hauteur, that still lovely smile; a knowledge of what beauty brings. Unfortunately, not all are so lucky. It's a way of holding oneself that the plain never know, as the rich do. Knowledge is like breeding, you can never acquire it except by rightful possession. What makes a teacher better than the rest? Children sense it. It's an inner calm. We sense each other's abilities just like animals do. In the world of genetic recreation, we can never be God entirely because conscience cannot be reproduced by science.'

The woman who sat at the head of the table put back her head and laughed. The soft lamps caught her and age did not dim her smile, nor her radiance at a compliment.

'Fabrice has always been a beauty,' he said to Liam, smiling. 'The sort that make ex-public-school boys with a penchant for Matron go weak at the knees. Or working-class boys like me with a sneaking longing for authority or a sweet for being good. We're the sort of men you can manipulate. The crackle of starch and a large bosom. Ah, there's something to be said for it!'

They all laughed, and Fabrice joined in merrily. She loved trivial talk in company, especially centred on her.

'Well the large bosom is part of the past, darling. That's memory lane, you naughty boy. I'm thin as a stick now . . .'

'Nonsense.'

170

'I owe it all to a good diet, exercise and fabulous friends,' she smiled as the steaming dish of vegetables did the rounds, 'not to mention a rejuvenation and counselling programme by a local herbalist we're all mad about. None of you young things need it of course, though the counsellor is dynamite – we all swear by her. Detoxification is the name of the game; she teaches rediscovery of the inner child that is in us all, building self-worth and healing of memories. Then when all that is taken care of we move on to self-care. Leaves you free to enjoy life, as I do.'

'Not to mention being born beautiful and with a perfect bone structure.'

'Hillaire, darling, you simply must come more often!' The bracelets jangled and her skin glowed with health. Fabrice was a handsome woman, and Alex marvelled at the effort that her aunt constantly made in the course of self-projection. She had never bothered, realising it was an art that took practice, and time. And a certain attitude to life.

'. . . but you should have seen Alex's mother,' Fabrice was saying as she tuned back in. 'Your mother was not only beautiful, dear, she had presence. What we used to call "it". When she walked in a room, everyone turned, men and women, and she charmed them all. I remember when we went through all the usual emotional traumas. She sailed through them, unheeded, making every event a situation that just made her even more interesting and attractive – whilst I had all the angst, and tripped over each and every one and turned it into a hurdle. People said, "Well, she would." It was said affectionately, of course, her life was always coloured by drama, she was never ordinary or dull; never boring – unless you can call constant drama boring,' she went on. 'But equally if she had had traumas, they would have said, "Well, she would, wouldn't she!" Everything she did became a conversation point. She was *always* dramatic. She flew her own plane at fifty for the first time.'

'I knew your mother, you know,' Hillaire said suddenly, and Alex found his eyes on her. He had a heavy, craggy face, black hair greying at the temples and a strong chin with intelligent probing dark eyes.

171

'Did you? What, here?'

'Well she used to visit Aspen when we were all young. She was colourful, as Fabrice says.' He cut his food. 'Used to think I was very staid.'

'You always were, Hillaire,' Fabrice broke in. 'Very driven.'

Given the lead, Alex opened her mouth to question, but Liam, his eyes on her, broke in.

'I'm sorry, you must miss her. She sounds wonderful.'

'Oh, she's not dead.'

'But you made it sound . . .'

'Just that she might as well be,' said Fabrice. 'Have another lobster tart, Alex, you've got nothing on your plate.' The manservant, John, was behind her. He poured wine into her glass; ice cold. It misted with condensation. As he moved away, Alex touched the surface, seeing the print of her finger remain. She felt Liam's eyes on her from across the table.

'Whatever happened to her?' Hillaire forked up his food. 'I never hear.'

Alex looked at him levelly. 'She joined a Buddhist retreat in the Himalayas.'

Fabrice laughed, sparkling in the shadows, reiterating her point.

'See – she would, wouldn't she!' She leaned forward into the light. 'We never hear from her, she was always entirely selfish and self-motivated.' She eyed her niece like an inquisitive bird. 'You're not a bit like her.'

'I'm not sure how to take that.' Alex bit into a piece of crisp unbuttered toast.

'You have something of her looks, but she'd never have done what you have done. Much too rough. And she always wore make-up . . .' She stopped, remembering their pact not to discuss Alex's life.

'Do you ever hear from her, Alex?'

'Rarely. Silence seems to be a part of her live now. Though I quite expect her to reappear here one day and just immediately involve herself in the social life and never mention Buddhism.'

'Except as a conversation point.'

Her mother had always been superficial. Perhaps that accounted for Alex's need to take life a bit more seriously.

'This family! So many skeletons in the cupboard you can't shut the door,' laughed Fabrice. 'Hillaire, have some more wine . . .'

Alex forked up her rice. 'Hillaire, what's your background?'

'Yeoman farmers, but my father broke away and became a minister.'

'No, I meant medically.'

'Ah,' he brushed it away. 'You don't want to hear about that. I just need to put my feet up, and tend to the internal Hillaire for a while.' He smiled at his hostess. 'And never better than when Benny is cooking, Fabrice. She was a terrific find.'

'I'd be devastated if I lost her. Luckily, I found John first, and he's such an old Aspenite he'll never leave. A little persuasion, a nice flat for them both and I think I've got them for life.'

'You're definitely a fixer, Fabrice.'

'They're too old to have children now . . .'

She watched the man as he ate with pleasure. She felt his flattery of her aunt was a way of deflecting the conversation from himself.

'Well of course that holds no guarantees any more, does it, Professor Bowman?'

He looked up at her, chewing thoughtfully to cover his reaction. His blithe manner and veiled eyes did not conceal his over-casual tone. 'In what way is that, Alex?'

'Well, isn't it true they can now even implant a womb into a man?'

'But who'd be the first to try it!?' His manner was purposefully jovial. A ripple of laughter followed.

'I gather two scientists at Jones University have managed to clone a perfect twin,' she pressed. 'Do you think this will become widespread, a gateway to the future?'

'Oh absolutely not,' he smiled, leaning back. 'There'd be an outcry.'

'But it's possible.'

He turned the smile to a chuckle. 'Not everything that's possible is probable, though.' He bent to his food, forking in a mouthful. 'Mmm, delicious. So, what do you do, Alex?'

He'd swung the conversation and she felt it. 'Nothing at present,' she said, determined not to answer. He was as adept at fielding close questions as Liam. 'Trekking, challenges. You name it. Whatever pays the rent.' Her voice was light and she did not look at her aunt. Out of the corner of her eye she saw Fabrice intent on her food. Whatever else, Fabrice was loyal, and family came first. She'd tell it as Alex wanted it.

He forked up another healthy mouthful. 'And they've been what?'

'An assortment of jobs.'

'Keep yourself busy.'

'Well, the English are notoriously underpaid.' She smiled. 'Try living in a cold flat in London. Only two years ago I had a shower installed. Before that I used a jug and bowl by candlelight.'

Hillaire laughed richly and then looked astounded. 'But surely they have electricity in England!?'

'You know they do,' she laughed. 'That part was choice. I thought if I was going to play the part it might as well be total.'

'How romantic.'

'People used to say "But who's there?" And I used to say, "Me, I like to do it, for myself." I like to be romantic. My house is full of candles.'

'Love it, and I thought I knew people. And you looked such a practical girl.' Now his eyes were distinctly amused. He'd caught her like a butterfly on a pin. She wriggled under his dark gaze until he switched to Fabrice. Pushing her, he'd led her to say something trivial that made her feel foolish. She felt the heat under her skin and he affected not to notice. 'Madness runs in families, doesn't it, Fabrice?'

But she waved his words away. 'You Americans are too used to mod cons. Our family is eccentric. For instance, I never pick flowers. I remember Boris cutting a vine once at the wrong time of the year and I told him to stop. I could hear screaming in my head. I felt the echo for days. More wine, anyone?'

'You're mad too, Fabrice.'

'Undoubtedly. But does that make you sane, darling? Have another piece of pie. Benny's cooking is so delicious, and she'd be offended if the plate wasn't clean as a whistle when we give it back . . .'

He lifted his hands as if to stop a train. 'I've had plenty. Delicious, as always. Just what the doctor ordered. And all here to enjoy – good food, lovely company and Christmas. Time to unwind.' He leaned back, hands to his girth; an ordinary man satiated by the ease of life. Alex lifted her glass of wine to her lips.

'Do you ski, Professor Bowman?'

'Wouldn't know a black run if I saw one, young lady. I'm no sportsman. I am here for the social life and to get away from reality.'

'Can you ever get away from the sort of work you're doing? Forgive me, but don't you look around you and see what is happening throughout the world? Excess babies there, none here. A tipping of the balance. If you can create sex, won't everyone want a boy? In many countries that's all that's important, surely.'

'It's an interesting point. Actually when we took a rough guide, 70 per cent wanted girls.'

'Really . . .'

'I'd like to go off on my own,' Liam intervened. 'Ski the back country. The mountain's at its best in early light, but by the time the lift lines open at nine, they are busy so quickly.'

'At this particular time of year it is busy, but forget the back country,' Fabrice said, grateful for the change of subject. 'It's so cold and unawoken back there. Timeless.' She shuddered. 'Not for me. I find it kind of spooky. It's so goddamn quiet, everything frozen. Boris and I went over the back of Buttermilk in a balloon. Actually, you could see it from the car park up at the top. They set us down up there. I

175

didn't last a minute.' She shivered. 'It wasn't the deadly cold. It was the sense of the mountain. Overwhelming power.' She looked at Hillaire. 'I'm surprised you never tried, Hillaire.'

'Jumping into ravines isn't my style, Fabrice. I like home comforts and I was never very adventurous. I leave that to the young.'

'But back in the fifties. You were young then.'

'I was never sporting in that way,' he said to her. 'I preferred to hunt, that's why I mostly came here in the summer. Track and discover, stealth not speed. It's far more interesting, to my mind. I tend to come here in the hunting season. This Christmas was a one-off.'

'So why did you choose it?' Alex ignored her aunt's raised eyebrow.

'To see my old friends.'

'But not to ski at all? It seems so alien. Aspen *is* ski.'

'My dear young thing, forgive me if I say you are just a little narrow-minded. Do we all have to ski? Can we not just say this place is heaven on earth, let's be there. Aspen is beautiful, a paradise. In the spring, in summer. Festivals, concerts, all year round. Has your aunt not enlightened you? Our old friends, the Paepckes, have ensured that we are never left unattended at any time. It is a centre of the arts. That's why I come, and for the peace and the lovely air. No, it is not all snow. That is only a part. As is everything. One has to look at the whole.'

'But –'

'Enough now.' Fabrice's raised eyebrow became almost vertical. 'Alex, help me clear, would you, dear?'

In the kitchen, she turned to her. 'What's up?'

'Nothing. Just curious.'

'Well, you're much too earnest. Go out and have fun, or have you forgotten that word, Alex? You missing the job, or something, darling? Get up the mountain, it's a beautiful day and you're young and without a care.' She became more serious. 'There's time for all this curiosity later. Find a lover; it's a perfect cure-all. I had a wonderful life with Boris. Loving the right man can be marvellous.'

'I'm sorry,' Alex said. 'You're right.' She gave Fabrice a big smile and a hug. 'He just seems so unreal, somehow. There's something . . .' she tailed off. 'Are you interested in Hillaire?'

'Hillaire? God no. The man's ten years my junior. At my age I'm free to be admired without the commitment. One never grows old, Alex; not in the mind, only in the body. Hillaire's right; good bones last for ever. Besides, I'll never marry again. Boris was hell sometimes, but it was often wonderful and never dull. I was always consumed with operatic jealousy when he was out of my sight. He was a true artist. Like all true artists, he knew he was the best, but with an ego so fragile a word could crush it, and a constant need for adulation. He wasn't perfect, and I was his strength but there'll never be another for me.' She set a bone china milk jug and sugar bowl on the tray. 'After him, all other men were insipid.'

Alex recalled her first sight of Liam, the dusting of snow lying artistically along the brim of his cowboy hat.

'That was a cheap trick with the hat.'

'But he's so dishy.' Alex did not miss the glint in her eye. 'Sort of reminds me of a young Boris,' she said, averting her eyes as she lifted down cups and saucers from the glass-fronted cupboards. 'Help me with these, would you, dear?'

She did, smiling wryly. The man, despite his broad shoulders and creased matinée brow, moved no mountains for her. The last thing she wanted was involvement, but Fabrice's obvious matchmaking amused her.

'I've planned for us all to go skiing after coffee,' she said, lifting the tray. 'You, me, and . . . um, Liam . . .' The blue eyes twinkled despite her attempt to keep a straight face.

Alex decided to take her at face value. 'Is he any good?'

'I don't know, dear. Not as good as you I don't suppose, but I don't imagine you'd know to let him win, would you,' she taunted, her words conjuring instant visions of Montana's admonishments. 'Now,' she said, placing both hands on Alex's arms, 'if you don't want people to know, you're not going the right way about it. You sound like you're holding an interview. Did your absent mother not teach you the art of conversation?' She wagged a finger, releasing her, and handed her the coffee pot. 'The poor man's just here to relax, so let him do that.'

And with that she swept ahead into the corridor to the dining room and Alex followed, the jug of coffee in her hand. It seemed fair enough: Aspen's exclusivity, riches and fairyland prettiness was far removed from reality right now, but still her journalistic senses prickled and when she returned to the dining room Liam's smile did nothing to alleviate it. She felt leaden beside her flighty, elegant aunt. But she still had her tongue.

'Isn't it a bit of a millstone?'

'What, dear?' Fabrice said as she pushed open the door with her foot, the set smile on her face as the room came into view and the devastatingly handsome man sitting beside her empty place.

'The boat race, aunt,' said Alex quietly using cockney rhyming slang. 'Good thing he's not a gynaecologist . . .' she went on, just loud enough for her to hear. It gave her some satisfaction to hear the coffee cups rattle precariously on the tray as the gentlemanly Hillaire stood to take it from a clearly discombobulated Aunt Fabrice. Alex sat down with satisfaction, even returning Liam's lopsided smile. Oh, that quizzical eyebrow; God save us. She decided right there and then to thrash him on the mountain run.

'Now, right after coffee we are going to get some air and we'll leave pudding while we work up an appetite,' announced her aunt, recovering her composure as she set small cut-glass decanters of whisky and liqueurs on the table. 'I suggest a dash of these for combustion. It's cold today. Benny has the car outside. We'll take the Silver Queen Gondola to the top of the mountain, and ski the Face of Bell for a start.' Her eyes flashed at her niece. 'Hillaire will meet the three of us at Bonnie's for apple strudel . . .'

'What happened to your other guests, by the way?' Alex recalled, as she passed the coffee round to Hillaire.

'Oh, they cancelled. Cream, Liam?' Fabrice poured carefully, swirling in a dash of cream. 'He brought the message round last night, didn't you, dear . . .'

Alex glanced at Liam, but his expression was nonchalant. Fabrice looked at him enquiringly, as she passed the cup. Alex caught a whiff of expensive aftershave when he took it from her.

'. . . after we went to bed, wasn't it? Were the lights still on?'

'Some of them, certainly.' He set the cup down, his voice honey smooth.

'Pity, you missed out on a nightcap,' she said, pouring her own, 'and an interesting discourse on Aspen. Didn't he, Alex . . .'

'I didn't want to disturb you,' he said. 'It all looked so . . . private.'

He gave a soft laugh that no one could interpret but her. Remembering her abandoned pleasure, the lusty singing and champagne and nakedness, her eyes were riveted to her plate. Clasping the stem of her glass for comfort, she looked up and met his gaze.

And knew now the cause of his amusement.

THIRTEEN

The mountain air was pristine. Her senses were catapulted into exhilaration that bordered on ecstasy as she jumped out into space and raced down the mountain. Her skis flew over the snow bearing her with effortless grace.

'Give me Rossignol or give me Head!' she shouted in an Aspen war cry, as she flew past a careful trio of snow bunnies in tight bright spandex ski suits. The spray was like steam as she jumped the blocks, the sunlight cutting through it. The snow spun out like icing sugar, a dancing wall of silver as she hurtled down the mountain. There was no sign of the others but for the moment she was only aware of the fabulous back-drop and the shimmering powder as she sliced through, carving a trail at speed, feeling joy and concentration and the pleasure of the adrenalin tug of danger, then braking gently as she saw the restaurant and skiing in amongst the crowds and spraying to an emphatic stop with a pleasurable sound of flurrying hard-packed snow.

Liam had watched her as she cut expertly through the crowds on the slope, saw the curve of her body. No doubt about the figure; supple and in perfect proportion, excellent qualities for an ace skier. He had known she was just as able as himself. He had sensed her resistance to him, the edge, and that had awakened his interest. He had also sensed her determination to win and as she had cut down the mountain on the quicker route of Pussyfoot and Pump House Hill, carving right down the centre, he had veered off to the left to challenge the more adventurous course, arriving just ahead of her.

For a moment he glimpsed a different Alex. Her skin was glowing when she came in, and she pulled off her goggles with a flair that emphasised the way she felt. Her ski suit was powdered with snow and she was free and breezy as the day itself, her cheeks brushed with colour and eyes bright. A smile of challenges overcome lit her face, giving her a touch of real beauty. Her nose was pink and snowflakes stood on her lashes.

He had been waiting for her, and he took her side as they moved through to a waiting table.

'You wouldn't need Fabrice's self-help here,' she said. 'What a place to start; you couldn't fail to succeed.' He could see her surprise at finding him there. 'Where did you go?'

'Summit.'

His eyes held hers. It was a known black run. He saw the flicker of acknowledgement with some satisfaction.

The crowd jostled, and they were quickly swallowed up in the fashion mayhem of the slopes: a blonde in a white fur headband and teak ski suit, edged in sable, a tight butt, a swinging wall of lush hair as she took off her goggles and laid hungry eyes on Liam. The people were shining, glossy ... and *rich* – in the way they held themselves: fur and neon, bright hot pink on not so perfect bums; pretty girls with loud drawls and dumb conversation; skinny matrons incarcerated in tight young suits and heavy make-up; three thickset guys from Hollywood in butch gear with mean hard faces talking overloud and attended by a bored guide; married couples bitching, whiny spoilt kids in outrageously lurid and expensive clothes; mums in turquoise and aubergine, lean ski instructors in tomato red.

They found the table and sat. Fabrice joined them a moment later. Alex smiled across at her.

'Did you manage to avoid the moguls?'

Fabrice, hosting the party, was still an excellent skier herself. She looked radiant at the centre of it all.

'Only Hillaire. And I've always found him difficult.'

'I meant the ones at the gate.'

The heavyweight trio stood there, Hollywood disdain stamped all over them. One started picking his nose. Fabrice turned away with disgust.

'Jesus, someone find me Telluride on the map.'

Liam looked over at Alex as she sat and pulled off her hat.

Her hair tumbled free around her shoulders. 'What was it you shouted on the mountain?' he asked, his eyes dancing.

She laughed, couldn't tell if he had heard or was curious; she didn't know him yet. *Yet*, implying *more*. 'Can't remember,' she said, the new thought not yet entering her conscious. 'I felt so good it could have been anything.'

She leaned back and felt the winter sun. She closed her eyes and did not see him studying her.

The woman who had just arrived, did. Ruth Lindstrom had taken the early afternoon to ski alone. As Alex swung her hair back to loosen it, her sense of luxury at the exercise and the ambience was uncontrived and unashamedly sensual. Ruth's sharp glance had immediately taken in Liam, the young man she had met earlier with Hillaire, and then she had seen the girl beside him, the one she'd met in the hotel. She'd sensed something about her, something she liked – and she seemed familiar, somehow. As Ruth stuck her skis in the snow and came in, pulling off her gloves, Liam saw her immediately and stood up.

'Ruth.'

Ruth smiled and came close. There was real warmth in her face. Alex sat up, her interest aroused by the new arrival. She had seen her earlier at the top of the mountain, alerted by the standard of her skiing, and had not realised she was the same doctor who had attended Darren in the hotel. Now she smiled, as did Ruth. Almost at the same time, Hillaire reappeared with a mug of hot chocolate topped with a spiral of cream. He stopped briefly, a warning glance in his eyes as Liam turned to take him in.

'Hillaire,' he said, in tune with the rules, 'you remember Dr Lindstrom.'

'Ah yes, how are you.' And he came forward, his hand outstretched.

'Do you know Fabrice?'

It was too late now. She palmed her gloves, inclining her head to the elegant woman.

'May I?'

'Of course, my dear.'

She sat, catching Alex's eye. Her face was now silhouetted against the snow. Liam turned to Ruth.

'And where is your husband, Wilhelm?'

'Shopping, sleeping. I'm not sure.'

'He doesn't ski.'

'Wilhelm's passions have always been reduced to a jam jar.'

He laughed, and so did the girl opposite her, her feelings burning in her face: curiosity, guardedness, *warmth*. A drift of long black hair was pushed back by one gloved hand and the memory jolted Ruth like an electric prod.

Ruth had been trying to place her since they had met. Seeing her again she had known she looked familiar, but where the dickens had she seen her before? And then as Alex brushed back the wisps of dark hair, the memory dropped into place. Television. News. Yes, that was it. And where . . .

Ruth stared. Their last stay in Munich. A slice of news from a British television station. In her mind's eye she recalled the words – *some scenes are too distressing to watch*. Alex, leading them around a veritable furnace in the snow, bodies lying everywhere, a mountaintop in some far-flung region; that same look of concentration on her face, that same deep passion . . .

Then why was she being so cagey? It obviously meant a lot to her. It could mean something to them too: danger to Hillaire's ideals. If the world's press got hold of what they were doing . . .

The crowds milled round, eagerly finding barely known acquaintances and calling them bosom pals. Fabrice didn't stay long. Social snob she was, but she hated superficiality. With a brief wave, she headed out across the deck. Alex's exuberant mood had passed in the silence that had fallen between her and Ruth; aware of their earlier warmth she felt sudden tension and she followed, snapping herself into her skis. With grace they both disappeared.

Ruth was still uncertain of Liam; he was too assertively handsome for early confidences, and she did not know what he was made of. She wanted to warn him, certainly, but was also unsure how much he knew. She had not yet had a chance to ask Hillaire, so she waited as the two men had a quick discussion. Liam, finishing his drink, stood up.

'I'm off too.'

Left alone, she paused a moment before zippering her suit. She wore a white polo under a black Head suit, and it flattered her. She pulled the green and gold woollen cap from her pocket and put on her gloves.

'Interesting,' she said.

'What's that?' Hillaire finished his apple strudel and pushed the plate away.

'That girl. Alex.'

'Fabrice's niece,' he stated. 'We just had lunch there.'

'You didn't recognise her?'

'Should I have?' Now the eyes, quietened for a moment, were alert. For a moment she wondered about voicing her feelings. 'Where are you going?'

'We shouldn't be seen together,' she said instead. 'It might become a talking point!' She made to get up. 'Besides, your rule . . .'

'You could always visit me at my house.' The dark eyes claimed her. His words stopped her and she laughed, but his eyes were too intense and she continued the move.

He stayed her with his hand. 'What about the girl?'

She held his look for just a moment. 'She's a reporter. More than that, she's the anchorman's feed-out on the BBC news. She reports from war zones, anywhere there's trouble. She's fearless.'

'She didn't seem fearless.'

'She didn't seem to want us to know either.'

He screwed up his eyes, assimilating the information. He was recalling the questions at lunch, placing the girl and her behaviour with the new information. Ruth watched his mind work and wanted to leave. This was the hard Hillaire, the bargaining one, the one who seduced with enticements. The Hillaire who always got what he wanted. She felt a shiver run through her. She saw the glitter in his black eyes as he returned his look to her.

'Maybe she's here for a Christmas break.'

'Like us,' she said with irony. She pulled on the hat and their eyes caught and went deeper.

'What about Liam? He seems to like her.' She watched the interest jump in his eyes. 'Shouldn't you warn him?' His answer would be her own. 'If a story like this got into the papers . . .'

'Don't worry,' he said, and his steady black stare spelled nothing she could read. 'I'll take care of it.'

Back in the house, Alex, now more than curious, picked up a phone and dialled a couple of numbers. The phone rang and rang in the London office; old friends in the trade were always very informative. She'd soon learn what she wanted to know.

'News desk . . .'

'Bill?'

'Alex! Where are you?'

'Skiing. Look, not much time to talk. Bill, you know of a guy called Kowolski in genetics?'

'Kowolski. Not *David* Kowolski?'

'Yes, that's the one.'

'Sure. I'm surprised you don't. He's been in the news.'

She felt her heart pump. 'I haven't been reading the papers lately. Give.'

'He's that test tube professor from UCLA. Causing all kinds of ructions. Some pretty incredible experiments have been taking place in his lab apparently, but it's all hush-hush. He did that thing on cloning, you remember. News, then no news. Someone shut it up . . .'

'I *remember* . . .' It was coming back, slowly.

'Remember those four guys, the scientists that got killed in Switzerland recently? Car went over a cliff. Word was out he had a lucky break. He was meant to be there. Got flu or something.'

'*Real* lucky,' she breathed.

'Yeah, well it all went quiet after that. When the journalists went round, they found the back door closed tight. All passed off as science fiction. He hasn't published a paper or anything, but I think some of the big boys sat on him . . .'

'That's right,' she said, her voice slowing with the memory of news cuttings from six months back. 'One other, as well . . . Ruth Lindstrom?'

'Yes, well she's another one. She's a microbiologist with an excellent knowledge of genetics. She's done a lot of close study work on a disease that is passed down the male line, Layton's Syndrome. Like Huntington's. Her hard work paid off, she's found a cure. They can check the DNA strand, find the culprit and switch him out of the circuit. Hey presto, a baby with no genetic imprint of the disease. Quite a clever lady; and just for extras, she's an Olympic standard skier *and* an ethicist. Did her training in the immune deficiency system. They think she's the one to watch for a cure to AIDS . . .'

'Whew . . . Hillaire Bowman?'

He laughed. 'Where *are* you? He's *highly* controversial. Thinks he's God. He's already aroused worldwide reaction with his views. Married briefly but divorced soon after, devoted to his work. He's considered by some to be the finest brain around in this day and age. Einstein of the nineties, a fascinating man, but too progressive for many as well. A bit of blue touchpaper, a dangerous guy. What is this?'

'I'm beginning to wonder.'

'Yeah. What's the scoop, Alex? If they're all meeting up, it must be big. Some people think that accident was no accident, if you get my drift, but there's no proof. If it was planned, it was clever; and if they're meeting and keeping it hush-hush, that makes me think it was true, or – they're running scared, 'cos they got something. They wouldn't take the risk otherwise; it'd be far too interesting to us greedy media and far too dangerous . . .' He listened to her silence. 'You sitting on this story, Alex, or you gonna give it to me? You being no longer on the beat and all that . . .'

That brought the truth home all too sharply. She straightened up.

'Later. If there is anything I'll be in touch. Thanks, Bill.'

She put down the phone, more than intrigued, knowing this could not be coincidence. Sinking back into the chair she let out a sigh of amazement. That dark-haired woman bending in the lobby to Darren's ankle, the clear intelligence and compassion in the brown eyes: a big picture emerged, as Alex remembered old newspaper broadcasts. Hillaire Bowman's relaxed and confident attitude, that of a very successful and powerful man. Kowolski, a boffin professor with his microscope practically attached to his character. And all here. She tapped the desk thoughtfully.

Of course. David Kowolski had been very much in the news, and quite recently, and if she had not been so involved in her own life she would have recognised him immediately. She remembered Hillaire's cagey and casual answers to her questions: these were the best in the field of genetics and she knew of at least three of them in one spot. She was intrigued as the picture cleared in her head, lining them all up before her. Her instincts had surely been right; now *why* were they here, and all acting so cool with each other? Was something going on? Hillaire had brushed away her questions far too glibly at lunch – *possible, not probable* – now it seemed the opposite.

Kowolski was *really* famous. If Ruth Lindstrom had genuinely not known him at all, her reaction that day in the hotel tending to Darren would have been quite different. Unless she was a real iceberg she would have been thrilled to meet him, and shown it. As with those of like mind, Alex had sensed heat and depth in the other woman; a passionate need of life. An iceberg she was not: Alex had seen her interest and compassion in her dealings with Darren himself and his parents. She'd seen her instant warmth on renewing what was clearly a brief acquaintance with Liam. So, she knew Kowolski. Yet she had all but ignored him in the hotel, pretended she did not.

Hillaire, so casual; Liam, so austere; Ruth – with that warning look in her eye.

Why?

She had found out no more about Liam Gower, the one

187

who interested her the most. However, she smiled as she realised she was one up on him. She knew about his friends and could bet they were up to something. Alone in the house, she wondered what, and, always an initiator, knew she would try to find out more.

She stepped outside on to the dark wood terrace. The day was brisk and cold. What were they up to? She leaned her hands on the terrace rail and looked out over the snow. Afternoon sun blazed from a brilliant blue sky and the craggy sea of peaks were capped with snow, the Rockies raw and primitive, beyond taming. As she planned a route to the truth, the young surgeon strayed into her mind.

FOURTEEN

'. . . two out of three people die because of their genetic inheritance. The day is right here when these people are going to be told of what and when they're likely to die. Now *that's* a pretty intimidating prospect.'

David Kowolski paused and reconsidered.

'Well, maybe yes, and maybe no . . . it's not as obvious an answer as it seems, but it's certainly interesting and clearly does a lot to concentrate the mind . . .' He pointed at them all. 'If you were able to give somebody a drug and say to him, "Look, at present the way you're going you won't have a one in ten chance of surviving lung cancer or cardiac arrest, you'll have a 90 per cent chance of premature death but if you take this drug you'll live not only a full lifespan, but even longer," my guess is, firstly that's going to do a lot to set you thinking, and, secondly, the person who patents such a drug is going to become a billionaire.'

The words spun in Wilhelm Lindstrom's head as he took the jeep and spun it down the short hill towards the black gates. They opened automatically and he swept through. A mile down the road he stopped beside the frozen river, in a small layby, and took out his cellular phone and the rest of the scene played over as he checked the number he was about to call.

'. . . if you're going to be in the position of a life-giver, dictating people's individual fates, then, whatever the ethics of it, you're going to get very rich . . .'

'. . . but equally, if you knew there was such a drug, the possibility that you might be destined for a genetically or environmentally premature death, would you be brave enough to take it? Do we want to live for ever, outlasting our kith and kin . . . isn't there actually some point where man has just seen enough?'

'. . . that is *my* point . . . *how much do we want to know . . .*'

Tension filled his face, and as he opened the window to take in the air of the cottonwood trees that bordered the river creaked beneath their sails of snow. He punched in the number.

'Wainwright . . .'

'Lindstrom. I'm in the car.'

'Did you get the tape?'

Sandford Wainwright swirled his heavy chair round. His sprawling multi-level ranch was set in an exclusive piece of realty spread across the mountains just south of Maroon Bells: a contemporary structure of wood and stone and soaring glass strewn with sun decks, terraces and balconies. He sat in a dazzling cathedral-ceilinged room, the sun pouring in over rich brown oak flooring and tinting the leaves of the forest high ficus trees. It was bold, sleek and contemporary; epithets that might have been applied to the man himself.

Wilhelm caught sight of his own pale blue eyes in the driving mirror as he checked the empty road behind him.

'No,' he said. He anticipated the exasperation.

'Why the fuck not?'

Dressed in his customary black polo and slacks, Sandford flipped his ponytail once with his hand, knocking the black leather string that held his glasses. He had been studying the paper. Now he let it fall to his desk, his eyes on the view outside, as Wilhelm's apologetic voice went on:

'You'll have to go with what I tell you. First, that guy's got the place so swept out it would have been impossible; second, you'd never have understood the lingo, very technical. Even hard for me. I got the gist of it though . . .' He paused a moment, remembering, and felt its import. Sandford Wainwright must have heard it too because his voice barked back down the phone.

'So, what is it?'

'First off, Kowolski's patenting that new drug.'

Sandford felt his interest stir. 'So I was right?'

'Well, yes you were; the rumour's true. Kowolski's research is pretty damn interesting.' Medical science was about

190

to make a breakthrough. He gave him the good news first: 'The drug can enhance life well past that as we know it, but it would be a life entirely dependent on drugs . . .'

Sandford Wainwright felt the initial glow of discovery. He'd been there when they'd persuaded the scientist in Basle to talk before they blew off his head. He'd been all too happy to inform on the genius who was due to arrive from California, but who by a stroke of luck had missed the conference due to a flu virus. Still, Sandford was now well aware of Kowolski's potential in the world of genetic discovery; word had had it that he had stumbled on something so stupendous it would change history. He lay back in his chair feeling the sun on him. He rubbed his fingers across his mouth and thought about what Wilhelm had just told him.

Longevity; a drug that prolonged life. It wasn't exactly earth-shattering but useful enough as a sideline. No, there was more; now he was sure of it. He felt the hairs on his arms tingle.

He was the head of a major subsidiary of the pharmaceutical giant, Wainwright-Feber; his offshoot was called WainCo. On his board, he had obtained the services of some very highly placed men in the medical profession, most recently Wilhelm Lindstrom. It had not been long before both men had discovered each other's real proclivities: symbiotic greed. Wilhelm had soon been elevated to the vice-presidency and all that it entailed.

Sandford also headed up many other companies, one of which was a large insurance company. He was very interested in modern genetic science, holding the reins of which would give him immense power. It was already suspected that genetic fingerprinting could enable insurance companies to create an uninsurable underclass, as well as huge premiums. Doctors on his board made him look good and legit; they also kept him in touch with what was happening to the medical world and averted the public eye from the truth. Drugs made a killing for him (a thought to amuse), so the last thing he wanted was a cure for any of the major diseases. He made an absolute fortune out of painkillers, lab equipment and incubating equipment for hospitals – but this, this was different.

Such a drug would be useful, but ... he shook his head. No, this was just the taster. Now he knew there was more to come and he felt the glow of real discovery.

'How's he done it?' he asked, ever curious, as his mind ran on.

'He's isolated a gene within the cell structure that slows the ageing process. This man is way ahead of his time. Basically, it keeps the skin youthful and reverses signs of age.' Taking animals with a degree of age and through genetic infusion, Kowolski had halted the process of growing old. He had found what caused terminal illness and within the chromosomes' genetic structure he could explore it, pin down the defective linking gene, isolate it from the main structure and synthetically reproduce it, infusing it with a counter-structure into the weak link of the gene. 'My question has always been: if it were possible to reverse the process of an illness, why not the process of ageing itself ...' Wilhelm's clipped voice had an excited edge.

Sandford nodded thoughtfully. 'This knowledge would be useful. Can you get a look at his notes, photocopy them?'

'Impossible. He keeps them close to his chest. I'm not even sure if I could interpret them. Probably need him himself.'

'Any skeletons in the closet?'

'Clean as a whistle. Loving family man, no crooked past.'

'It would be worth having though in today's market.' Sandford's voice slowed. 'The fountain of youth is the ultimate desire.'

'Nowhere more so than in Aspen.' Wilhelm's voice still held the note of excitement. 'With this knowledge you could name your price ...'

So true.

'You could rule the world, Sandford.'

Not true.

Sandford realised the potential of a drug that could prolong life. It was only a part of it. Kowolski might be a moral ethicist, and would only use it for a worthy cause, but Sandford imagined what it could mean to him: a generation could be born that would need to spend millions on maintaining their life structure. The drug company would be well endowed if he could patent it and of course money was always a hot commodity – as was perfection, which fell short without the final clue to the body's longevity. So this was all very interesting as a sideline. Ownership of this drug would be a nice little money-earner in the pharmaceutical industry – but it was not exactly what he had in mind.

Lengthening a lifespan could make a fortune for him in drugs, but Sanford was of another mind entirely; the megolomaniac in him did not just desire anything as brutal as amassing millions. No, he wanted purity.

The purity of creation.

That was his goal. He embraced it fully, feeling his heart swell with pride. That would enable him to have the power he craved. His smile was beatific as he gazed out across the room. Somehow he knew Kowolski, a man like that, held the key. Time would tell, and it was so close – and with Wilhelm sitting pretty, ready to steal, they were in clover. He inhaled the scent of near discovery as if it were a fine wine. Still, no harm in tagging on the other end as well:

'What's his price for selling the drug to Wainco, d'you reckon?'

'You're out of luck. That's the bad news. This is a man who cannot be bought . . . or bribed.'

'There's got to be something.' A weak link somewhere; there always was. He thought for a moment. 'That's all of it, nothing else?'

Wilhelm gave a short laugh. He watched the car that was coming up the road behind him, his blue eyes trained on the mirror. It drove past and he continued to watch its progress.

'Not for this morning. He only started out at midday. He's due to talk again after lunch.'

'Where do they think you are right now?'

'In town, getting something I need.'

'Well get back there. I don't want you missing anything . . .

and Wilhelm, try to enliven the proceedings, huh? Provoke him to talk. I want to hear it all when you call me back tonight...'

The sun began to peel back the film of soft grey cloud from the landscape, revealing a scene of dazzling white behind the barn and pole corral. In the fields beyond, the horses' breath clouded the air as the farmhand tossed bales of hay into their midst, and then broke and scattered them amongst the team.

Sandford saw none of this. He knew Kowolski would never start out the conference with his big guns; scientists they might be, but they were certainly not without their egos. He would save the best till last. That was what Sandford wanted to hear.

'Get a tape. I want it on record whatever it is – they won't sweep the room twice, I guarantee ... what are you due to talk about this afternoon?'

'Cloning to start out ... and then he's promised us something really special.'

The lone voice penetrated the room.

'Is this any better morally than Hitler's Arian race – ?'

Against the raised excited voices of the others who were all for progress, Ruth had half risen from the chair, her hand lifted to stop them, her voice striking clear through those of the men.

'I agree ...'

Wilhelm had been looking for that voice, and he played her along, knowing his wife. He wanted her to be controversial for a very good reason; it would draw Kowolski. He seemed to share her views as he backed her up, tempting the man out.

' ... it's hard to believe, David. We have all looked hard into this subject. But to create life from scratch. No, this is impossible ...'

'For God's sake,' she went on, warming to her feelings, 'we could reconstruct the genetic code of Hitler *himself*. It's not impossible if a frozen tissue sample were found ...'

Ruth had settled back in her chair again, but still her voice had touched them all, made a point. The Polish scientist seemed almost pleased by the controversial reaction.

'Precisely,' he said quietly. 'And we have just that . . .'

Even Wilhelm was surprised. 'Hitler?'

'No . . .' Kowolski drew breath in a room filled with silence as he crossed it, his shoes squeaking softly. 'But here is a point worth making . . .' He moved to the large blackboard and turned to face them. 'Why have dictators conceived large numbers of children? Cloning is appealing, irresistibly tempting to someone obsessed with a sense of his own self, and a child worthy of his destiny. What a fascinating adventure to watch himself grow up again forty years younger. But where do we step across the borderline of ethics? Because that is what this is all about, ladies and gentlemen,' his voice continued. 'Would we be advertising for sale to the richest, most dictatorial amongst us? Would that be the supperrace we would breed? Well, the whole thing is a minefield,' he said, his voice softening, 'today, this talk is between us, and us alone . . .'

He came forward to stand between them and the board behind him.

'There are no technical difficulties, my friends. The future is here . . . it is no more difficult to clone a human than it is any other mammal – ' His eyes held them as the light danced on the bottle lens of his spectacles – '*And we have done it.*'

Ruth looked to Hillaire, saw his silence. But it was the Italian, Mario Bene, who spoke first; excitement clear in his voice.

'The child lived?'

Kowolski nodded, smiling.

'What have you done with it?'

'Well,' he said gently. 'Now that's the point. You would like it to live, perhaps?'

'Surely you haven't . . .'

The doctor lifted his shoulders.

'*Why* . . .?' The outcry was collective, and he smiled at the shock on their faces.

'Ah, you see,' he lilted, his voice holding the familiar softness as the murmur died. 'You would draw the line at abortion,' he smiled gently and his voice held regret, 'because the world is not ready. We have succeeded, but we must now be seen to fail. It is not our ability, but the ethical difficulties that are so vast . . .'

He took a long moment before tapping the board, where his spidery writing mapped the surface. Sunlight streamed in and fell at his feet. Now he had them on the edge of their seats, and his voice grew brisker.

'First, we will talk about multiple fertilisation; time-warp twins, or triplets. You find no problem with this, I am sure. We already store fertilised human eggs quite routinely in liquid nitrogen at −196C. By implanting such eggs eighteen months apart, twins have been born with different ages. Not identical of course, because they developed from two different eggs fertilised at the same moment − simply an insurance against death. A survival kit. Call it what you will. A child that dies unexpectedly, leaving tragedy and heartbreak in its wake, can be recreated after the main body of grief has passed and the new baby reinstated in its place.'

'Like getting a new puppy to replace the old,' Ruth interjected. 'It's horrific.'

'But the same set of emotions,' he came back eagerly, his voice urgent, 'and look how easily the child is placated, and how quickly they adapt to and love the new animal. Their happiness is restored, the grief assuaged. Is there so very much wrong with that? And, of course, it would be very carefully monitored.'

'And you think it would stay that way?' She leaned back, fingers on the edge of the long table.

Kowolski shrugged. 'But, why not?' he provoked. 'Natural clones already exist in virtually every family tree.'

'It's *unnatural*, David.'

Kowolski shrugged again, his voice matter of fact. 'There's nothing unnatural about twins.' He took a beat, letting that ride, as his eyes swept the faces. 'We could not guarantee facial similarity, but with the cosmetic industry as it is, the child could be recreated to look exactly like the original.'

He took in the others, noted their attention.

'This is where environment would play a part. The clones would be alike. Maybe not identical, but like twins. And what is so bad about that? No one would detect the "clone" as being anything other than a sibling, or a twin, if close in age. We already collect aborted foetuses in our operating theatres, a very controversial move – and surgically remove various organs and tissues for transplanting. It is commonplace, and increasingly so, but we don't advertise it. Why not? Because the public can accept the latter but not the former.' His voice fell slightly, and his eyes drew them all to him. 'New parts for old bodies is a standard practice. Humans looking to buy spares. Spare part surgery is in huge demand. But it only works if spares are available.' He looked at Freddie and Valery Kalinin, the dour Russian: the spare parts team. 'So what do we see here?'

Freddie Renby-Tennant leaned back in his chair, hands thrust in his pockets. 'A new breed of human, genetically reproduced in the lab.'

'Exactly.' Kowolski used a piece of white chalk to thrust home his point. 'Imagine a scenario where a president is shot in the head. We are able to bring back brilliance from the dead. With tissue from an aborted human foetus the transplants have worked to cure brain damage. Foetal brain or spinal cord transplants in humans have overcome damage in human brains. All we need are surrogate mothers . . .'

The implication was enormous.

'A baby bank!?' Ruth's horrified voice held sheer disbelief.

The scientist shrugged again. 'What else have we all been doing, my dear Ruth, for years? It's just one stage further.'

'Yes, but at what stage do we stop?'

'Ah . . .' He held up a hand again. 'This is the point.' He nodded, and turned, walking again. He loved his stories; as did his students, always. Losing the technical, he painted pictures with his musical voice and they saw so much more clearly. 'Let's then take the simple yet standard case of a rich man who knows he is dying. He needs a kidney and none is available. He gives a blood sample and is told to come back

197

in about eight to ten months time for a transplant. He pays a very large sum for the privilege. The transplant is entirely successful, the only complication is that it takes quite a while to get going fully.' He took a beat. 'Could you agree with this?'

'Well, yes . . .'

He waved a hand in the air.

'Well, without realising it, he has just paid a private clinic for a cloned kidney. A nucleus was taken from a white blood cell in the sample he gave, and inserted into a human egg, which in turn was implanted into a surrogate mother's womb. The mother was hired for a small fee from the streets of a developing country. After nine months a cloned baby was removed by Caesarian section. Shortly after birth one kidney was removed and inserted into our wealthy friend. Twenty-four hours later the baby is adopted by doting parents in another country, who are told that the child has been born with a defective kidney that has now been removed.' He paused, letting it sink in. 'Fact or fiction? Well, it's fact. The cloning technology is all here. The demand is certainly here. Why not move on from spare part surgery into the whole kit and caboodle? Why stop at organs, why not recreate a living body of our own flesh and blood?'

Ruth exploded again. 'A subculture, a farm. That's what you're suggesting, David.'

'Blood samples could be taken from anybody?' put in Wilhelm, 'or from those who are in need and wish to pay huge sums?'

'. . . from those who are needed.'

There was total silence, then the mutterings began as the scientist's voice rang out.

'But,' he said, continuing. 'For the present there are two blocks. The first is obtaining a surrogate mother. That's not so hard to find in at least two-thirds of our world. A mother could be offered the equivalent of ten years' wages by an agent, or she could simply be used without her knowledge.'

There was a chorus of voices.

'That would be illegal . . . Regulations say . . .'

'When have you known scientists to be bound by laws and regulations. Our very nature is to explore –'

'But not like this . . . this is suggesting a trade . . . a . . . a . . . trade in human bodies!'

'And who are you speaking for, may I ask, huh!? How would you feel if your precious child was in a burns unit,' he said suddenly. His finger stabbed at Ruth, and then them all. Now his voice grew stronger and more demanding: 'Hideously disfigured, and needing skin grafts desperately?' He looked at Freddie, who nodded, brow wrinkled – it was a case he had come across many times: the weeping mother, the stalwart father. 'How far would you go to recreate its beauty so that for life people would not look on it and shudder? Would you worry about the donor, where the skin came from? And on a more sombre note, we all know of the mother who needed a bone marrow donor for her teenage leukaemia victim. When none was found *she* decided to have another baby to use it as a bone marrow donor. If it was a girl chances were the transplant would be 99 per cent in favour of being successful. She knew that though the operation would cause the new baby some pain, it would not affect its future health or well-being. The mother *herself* created her baby bank . . .'

Hillaire spoke out for the first time. 'I remember. The case caused great unease. What if cancer centres joined with fertility clinics to mass-produce embryos for tissue-matching purposes? What if babies conceived in this way and operated on were then regarded as surplus and offered for adoption?' He spoke with a slow authority to which they all listened, their expressions intent. 'Surrogate babies – or *designer* surrogate babies?'

Ruth threw him a curious look; it was the first time he had challenged David and his remark was intentionally provocative.

'Indeed.' David nodded his head fervently. 'The second, larger block is that a newborn baby kidney of course is much too small and immature to help a full grown adult much, isn't that right, Freddie?'

Freddie joined in, in his languid voice, his long legs stretching out before him, as he folded his arms. 'Quite right. Other tissues might do much better . . .'

'In particular bone marrow,' interjected the Russian, suddenly enthusiastic, to David's bobbing head.

'. . . and other rapidly dividing organs such as skin to cover grossly disfiguring burns,' finished Freddie.

His team now fully with him, David went into the penultimate stretch.

'So, having formed a complete baby kidney in the uterus, in the future we will be able to accelerate its growth in the laboratory using new growth hormones while connecting it to an artificial blood supply. Skin cloning is especially interesting because we can clone directly from cells without having to create a whole new human being.'

'*Cultivated babies*,' he said; 'babies for spare parts.' He held up a hand to stem the flow. He wanted his own words to shock them without interruption. 'We used to be shocked at stories of trekkers in deep jungle regions coming upon primitive tribes who cannibalised their own . . . Now *we* can plan spare parts for a human before it has even been born: a *cannibalised baby twin* . . . yes, *yes*. This is what we have to have. Is it not, Mario?'

The Italian's arms were thrust on the table before him. Now he steepled his fingers and looked down at their apex.

'What you say is very true.' He took a deeper breath. 'The ultimate step along this path, of course, would be reached when a newly fertilised egg was divided into two cells. One would be grown to the appropriate stage and then implanted into a woman, thus becoming in time the definitive human being; the other would be kept in a state of suspended animation in the frozen state.' Ruth dropped her head, but said nothing as he went on. 'If the adult human being at some period during his life was in need of an organ transplant, the frozen embryo could be implanted into a mother's uterus and, after birth, it could be allowed to grow until its organs were in a suitable state to be cannibalised for the sake of its more fortunate brother. We could do this . . . yes . . .'

His trailing voice left them in no doubt as to the business taking place in his research centre in Milan. Kowolski's soft voice came back in, Ruth no longer objecting. She had already sensed which way he was leading them – by making them all speak out, they had made his point for him.

'Yes, my friends, that day is here. That is why our meeting had to be kept so quiet. We can do it all, we have done it. We did in fact grow that first baby ... for a good few months.' The room hushed. 'We *had* to abort it,' he said in response to the questions in their faces. 'There was nothing wrong with it, except the *ethics*. Ah, you see, so where do we draw the line? Who is to say, but us? Is a vegetarian someone who eats only greens, or a little bit of fish? Or does he sometimes eat chicken so as not to offend his host? What is morality really? Isn't it simply the conception of each one of us? Who is to say that this is not a perfectly good and realistic future for us all? Was it wrong to deprive this perfectly healthy child of life once it had been created? It was just that *we* did the creating. *That's* the point. We thought it was wrong, but others will not. At what point do we let the baby go to term? Some day very soon. Human farming is just around the corner. All it needs is the triad: the unscrupulous, a great deal of money –' he listed them on his fingers ' – and a surrogate mother. We all know that each of these is all very much around; it is the chain that binds such a trio that is hopefully not. When this is created, we have mayhem. Giving birth has always been a way of recreating ourselves, but imagine – not only recreating yourself in your own image, but in your *exact* image ... think about it ... it's the ultimate ego trip. That is what we are here, in essence ... to *prevent* ...'

The faces watching, he slipped his papers into his briefcase and closed it with a soft click, obscuring the click of the tape recorder hidden in Wilhelm's jacket pocket.

Sandford listened to the tape, and as the voice finished and there was silence he reached forward and pressed the button. The hiss was silenced.

Quiet fell in the sunlit room. At the glass window, Wilhelm stood and looked out on the day.

'Choose sex, create sex,' he said dreamily into the silence. 'These men are able to build what they wish if they wish. They represent the prominent minds in future genetics and body manufacture. Modern Frankensteins with questionable morals. Their knowledge of each person's genetic thumbprint gives them the ability to play God . . .'

He turned away from the sunlight to take in Sandford's expression. The man seemed transfixed, as well he might be.

'. . . they're capable of anything,' he went on. 'But it's their "characters" you're dealing with, their ethical viewpoint. Some for, some against, some conditional, but all with expertise. It's why they were chosen.'

'And you?' He'd been wrong; Sandford was not in a trance, more, just riveted intensely in his thoughts.

'Pathology is an integral part of the operation. Besides, I'm a businessman far more than they are, they haf only dreams,' he said scathingly. 'They are scientists; money only means more research for them.'

'And for you it means power.'

He fell silent. Wilhelm's ego was at its best when such truths were out in the open. Where success had eluded him to date, scouring his heart and his wallet, Sandford promised him all his dreams at once.

'Yes,' he said quietly. 'There have been pockets of research worldwide, but it was Hillaire's insight that was the valuable link. He knew if he brought them all together they would fire off each other. It was a brilliant idea.' He paused. 'And it only works as long as it is kept quiet . . .'

Sandford shifted the little tag on his desk that he had had made. PROFIT OVER PRINCIPLE.

'They know they are able to talk and share because it is all being conducted in secrecy.'

Sandford laughed. 'Well, it has to be. There would be placards decrying it, anti-abortionists, gay factions, the lot, if the press got a hold of it. In Aspen these people are very strict. Don't I know it! I have had a home here for five years.' He tapped the desk and swung in his chair, ruminating over the contents of the tape. 'We can always use that as our weapon

if we don't get our way, but that is unlikely. I think we will.'
There was a very conservative feeling in Aspen: gays not allowed to take jobs, constant lobbying for its squeaky clean right-wing image, when underneath, like most pockets of paradise worldwide, it was anything but, inviting the worst of humankind along with the best.

'A baby completely free of disease, Sandford, its sex chosen, of perfect health. Genetically inherited disabilities prior to birth eradicated, a frozen spare parts factory on the side, a traffic in humanity.'

'So why has it failed before?'

'Because they were using animals as surrogates and the surrogates were rejecting human embryos.'

'So they need a human bank.'

'And from there . . .'

'From there . . . we will be capable of creation.'

His voice was hardly audible. He watched Carla, his stable girl, stride across the snow to the barn and pole corral. She wore a windbreaker and a cotton-knit polo shirt and jodhpurs.

He had the bank. His mind caressed the image of his chicken farm in Wyoming, but the grossly distorted bodies of his maternal production line upset him. A line of beautiful host mothers replaced it in his imagination: he wanted a queen for his gift to the world. The next question was a while coming.

'Can you do it?'

'Given the lab conditions and his research team, yes. I'd like to have a look at those notes though, give anything for that . . .'

'I thought cloning was outlawed.'

'Maybe. Regulations are one thing, persuading every scientist to abide by them is another.'

Sandford looked for the way in. 'You wife has found a cure for the Lengs,' he said.

'And no more than that. Forget Ruth. She's more of an ethicist than he is.'

Sandford pursed his lips thoughtfully. His talk seemed

idle, but it was anything but; his mind was working furiously beneath his benign exterior.

'Have you seen the wife, Mochi? She's quite something,' Wilhelm was saying. 'She was standing at the window when we arrived, like Lady Macbeth. He keeps her out of sight.'

'She's in New York today,' Sandford mused, eyes on the scene outside seeing nothing. Mochi was exquisitely lovely, it was true – serene and beautiful, she would make a perfect mother. He had already realised that.

'So I gather.'

'What's the word on their relationship?' he said casually, distracted by thoughts of her.

'You rarely see them together. But I chatted to Fenner last night. He said they lead separate lives pretty much. When they are together they're apparently quite formal with each other.'

'Really.' They way people conducted their private lives was often very useful, and of course this stage of his plan, unknown to Wilhelm, had already begun. Aware of the tenor of the conference beforehand, though not its content, he had been able to take out a little insurance. But her friendship with the barman was news, and interesting. 'She's talked to Jack Fenner?'

'They're old friends. She's worried, she's much younger. She's looking to her future, I guess.'

'Good, good . . .'

'They're not close.' Lindstrom warmed, passing the buck in envy. 'Many rich are like that. Money seems to make them false. Sex is the poor man's amusement.' He laughed, but it was not reciprocated.

The other man's dark voice held coldness.

'His disease has made him impotent. Might have something to do with it.'

'Yes.' Wilhelm's held apology. 'Of course.'

'This could be it for them. Make or break. And they're not telling each other the truth of their feelings, their real needs,' he murmured, half to himself, as if he forgot the other man. A highly unscrupulous man he had already found limitations on his own life. He needed money; he was beholden to shareholders and directors on his board. He was on a salary and it felt like a leash. He needed a route to freedom and the doctors were pawns in his game; he needed money such as Miki's – massive wealth, and the doctors' expertise. He planned to play on them all. Perhaps there *was* a route. He felt the pieces fall together as if in a psychic jigsaw: the man, the doctors, his money . . . his *wife*.

A weak link. One always had to look for the weak link. Where was it in this case? Perhaps he had found it. The germ grew in his mind, and as he turned he was anxious to be free of Wilhelm. Instinct told him there was more.

Wilhelm saw the look on his face. He had been waiting for it knowing it would come at the conclusion of their talk, and then . . .

He came over and leaned his hands on the polished desk. His pale and angular face was fever bright, and his pale eyes glowed almost dark with his final piece of knowledge. He smiled slowly.

'They're going to vote against all of it, Sandford.'

'Let them . . .'

'For of course, you were right. He did leave the best till last . . .'

Wilhelm recalled the scene for him. Watching their faces, Kowolski had slipped the folder back into his briefcase and closed it with a soft click, and he had spoken so quietly as he did so, his voice so full of the news he was about to impart, his *pièce de résistance*, that Wilhelm had been forced to switch off the recorder's telltale hiss.

As the scientist's words had flowed across the room, his gaze had wandered across Wilhelm's face and forward to that of Hillaire, then to Ruth. His expression said he would not use it, and no one would persuade him. He only wanted the information to be shared and for progress to be made, not damage caused.

But Sandford would use it.

Now as Wilhelm spoke those selfsame words he felt the pleasure that Kowolski must surely have felt as he shared his revelations, as Wilhelm did now.

When he revealed the extent to which Kowolski's lab had really gone with their DNA experiments – experiments which would never gain public knowledge or sympathy as far as the ethical doctor was concerned – he saw Sandford realise he had truly underestimated what was possible. What he was now hearing would change the world.

Science fiction. Life progressed beyond wildest imaginations. Man had stepped on the moon; now the miracle of life was no longer a religious concept, a creation of evolution and God. It was to be the work of man, and Sandford was to be that man.

The information he was hearing made the hairs stand on Sandford's neck. Information that promised riches and power beyond anyone's imagination.

When Wilhelm stopped speaking he could not move, as if to do so would shatter the fragile glass of the spell the man's words had cast upon him.

Sandford sat for a full five minutes after he had gone without moving, then he stood and walked across the polished sunlit boards, his head buzzing.

Like Miki Leng now, he wanted their research and their combined minds to go as far as they could, but for very different reasons.

He wanted to own the result.

His mind drifting to the oriental gentleman whom he knew well by sight and by repute, and whose needs he knew so very *very* well, he began to put a new and even more diabolical plan into action.

Miki was thinking about his own needs too as he sat alone in his library. He had been solely responsible for this gathering because it was his friend, Hillaire Bowman, who had introduced him to Ruth Lindstrom's work in the New York Brahms clinic, and had arranged Mochi's operation.

Now his wife was in New York and the team were here. He rubbed his hands gently feeling no pain, no pressure. He was able to think clearly. He had no idea what was going on daily downstairs, nor did he want to know. This was up to them all, and he needed no progress report, only an end result. It was all he had ever wanted.

To save his life, and protect his heir.

He took a glass of mineral water from the side table and sipped once, then again. He felt lonely. He had wanted them to isolate the gene that controlled his illness. Now he knew they could; but could they do it in time? He had wanted more, and understanding what was possible he had asked Hillaire to ensure that the child was a boy. There too, he had had his wish.

In return, and realising what part he could play in the future of research, he had set up this committee to see how far they could go. The two men had made a deal in a hot downtown coffee shop in New York, a month ago. Miki had provided all the funding in his gratitude, for Mochi and for the child who would perpetuate his line.

He knew that if they asked, he would give them more.
Much more.

He checked his watch. It would be time now, but Miki was philosophical and he never chased fate, just set it in motion and waited to see the result. Fate was in motion in New York and Mochi would call him, when she was ready.

FIFTEEN

In the comfortable main bar of Chasers, Montana chatted to the guests. Propped at the bar, she had a new job of sorts. She was supposed to take care of them – which she kind of did, kind of didn't.

Jack Fenner watched with amusement. It was exactly what he had anticipated and he knew what she was made of and liked it. The girl was ballsy and didn't give a toss about any of them. It had worked for him for years but he was no fool: he knew how much she needed this job as well and admired her for her nerve. For less, he could throw her out, but of course he wouldn't. She was making her niche in just one day, and they were two of a kind. She was not about to be seen as yet another leggy skivvy. She pretended to work as if it were her choice, something the guests were allowed to do, but the staff – never. A female clone: she would operate just like him and take the pressure off too. More time up the mountain for Jack, but curiously he was spending more time in the club. He loved to watch her, and she knew it.

She bent over the bar in her buttermilk shorts and he could see the cheeks of her very fine butt. His temperature rose. Only a matter of time before she found a man to take care of her and that man would be in his pocket, another coup for him. Just his style; he liked a hook on everybody. Only trouble was, tonight that man turned out to be Rowan Bader and he was not sure he liked that at all. He didn't mind the guys, he just liked to choose who; old buddies like Rowan were way too close. He frowned and his thoughts drifted as he watched her place her butt down square on the bar stool, waving hello to a newcomer. He screwed round in his seat to see who it was, too late. He was enveloped in a warm wrapped up hug that blinded his eyes. She reeked of her familiar scent.

'Hey, Jack . . .'

'Hey, Chiffon . . .'

'Ah . . .' she cried playfully, 'you guessed!'

The resident team mate had a new guy in tow.

'He calls himself Boxer,' she said. 'And don't ask why, but he packs a punch all right!' Perhaps his talents were hidden. She grinned and winked. Talent must be short on the ground, because this guy was not her normal type. He shook hands, feeling calluses – yep, had to be hidden talents.

Realising this was the place for gossip, Sandford's man, Boxer, had joined forces with a surefire certainty. He spotted Montana at the bar, the one he really wanted; this lean tigress was fantasy time for him. He had used Chiffon, having judged the girl's needs and her closeness to Fenner. It had been no problem to win her over; she was cheap and easy – a little flattery, a little come-on, and here he was. He guided a willing Chiffon to the bar.

Sandwiched between the girls, Montana's long long thighs spread wide on her bar stool, Boxer somehow managed to keep his mind on higher things as he motivated them charmingly to talk and that was where Alex found her friend an hour or so later, just past midday. By this time she was alone, Chiffon having shepherded her new lover away to her house for a heavy session. Montana was at the bar and talking to one of the waiters. His eyes were on her, and a piece of candy revolved around his mouth like a camel chewing. Montana slid off the bar stool as she arrived, making a meal of it. The man's eyes widened, as did his mouth, the revolutions slowing in awe.

'You still got your candy,' she said, her voice as provocative as if she was asking him to make love to her.

'Yeah.'

'I chewed mine.'

'You would.' His grin was gormless.

Her eyes smiled at him. 'You only say that because whatever I do is right. If I'd said I sucked it, you'd have said the same.'

Alex watched the pantomime with macabre interest. This

209

was Montana in her role-playing mode. The waiter squirmed and polished a glass, picking up the rhythm where the candy sucking had left off.

'Yeah, you would,' she said, picking up her coat from the opposite stool. 'Just like those general zodiac signs in the paper. You read one, you read them all. Every one is right. You take what you want to and apply it to yourself.'

'No, I don't.'

'Yes, you do. Shall I prove it?'

He swallowed. 'I guess you're right.' His eyes took in Alex, but Montana was like a heat-seeking missile.

'Sure I'm right. I can't do no wrong in your eyes. You're a man in love. Chew it, suck it, swallow it whole.' She watched his eyes grow round. 'Ain't I right?'

'Ain't it the truth.'

She left him then, laughing with her gap-toothed grin. Walking up to Alex she slipped her arm through hers as if the exchange had not taken place and they had never been parted. They walked out of the club. Montana was wearing a silk shirt with jeans, lizard-skin boots and the Coat. Morning had brought a powder blue sky and painted the trees with silver dust. Everything glittered. 'You're looking good,' she said, kissing her.

'You too. Is he in love with you?'

'Who?'

'The waiter back there.'

She looked back, as if she had just heard of him.

'Hell, I don't know, I was just being provocative.'

Alex snorted a laugh. 'Well, if he wasn't, he is now.'

Montana looked up and down the street as if his un-doubted puppy love was a hazard of life. 'Blondes have more fun,' she said, peeled a sweet and popped it into her mouth, tonguing it to the other side. 'Actually, I'm a sucker,' she said, her arm still threaded through Alex's, 'I just didn't want him to know that. Where's the car?'

'This way. But why did you want a car? This is walk town.'

'You'll see . . .'

They started to walk.

'That poor man's half dead already. What have you been doing to him?'

'Showing him I could wear his boots any day I wanted. Besides, it's a good education for Jack. We girls really are the stronger sex, you know.' Her eyes ran up and down. 'You could be just the same. If you wanted, that is?'

An unwelcome fast frame of Liam entered her head and she fast-forwarded it to a distant realm just as quickly.

'Not like you,' she said. 'You're a magnet.'

'Only because I send out signals.' She led her down Cooper Avenue Mall. 'That's all it is. You don't.' She paused. 'Why not?' The big black eyes absorbed her and the clothes shops around with equal voracity. Alex had forgotten the strength of Montana's colouring and vitality.

'I don't want men nosing round me. I'm sorry,' she said. 'That sounded rude.'

'No, it didn't. But why not? Just because you been hurt, or something?'

'Or something.' She found the fire red pickup and climbed in.

'Haven't you heard of traffic violations!' Montana jumped in the other side. 'You can't park just anywhere in this town. Get out of here quick.' Alex pulled it out into the road. Montana pushed in a track. 'Hotel California's' middle eight filled the compartment. 'Listen to that guitar riff. Man, I always wanted to play like that.'

'You're a child of the sixties.'

'Seventies.' She pointed ahead as they turned into the corner.

'Whoa, stop here . . . I have to get some of these.'

She hurtled her into Freudian Slip, buying Hot Chiles in hot colours and solids; then into Fast Eddie's for a cowboy hat. The Coat certainly impressed the salesgirls; they queued to serve her.

'Johnnie's wife must be feeling the cold,' said Alex in her slipstream.

'Johnnie's wife lives in the desert.'

She picked her way through a string of leather bands being held up by a hopeful salesgirl.

'What if they plan on Aspen for Christmas? It's not un-known.'

'They always go home to Florida for Christmas to see her aged mother. That's how Johnnie and I first got together. Bands are important,' she said. 'How about this one.' She held it up and fitted the black stetson to her head. It looked stunning over the fall of white blonde hair. 'Leather and con-cho hearts, my favourite . . .'

'I know, my aunt has one . . .'

'Stunning, aren't they?'

'Sure, but –'

'Yes, I'll take it.'

'Montana, how long's all this going to take . . .'

'Don't drag me away from a clothes shop, darling. That's tantamount to putting yourself up for adoption.' She fiddled deep into her bag. 'Now, I just have to hit PTs for some sexy undies. Rowan's invited me to dinner, and he expects dess-ert.'

'You going to give it to him? I thought it was Jack you were after . . .'

'No, of course not. But I'll strip off for a dip in the hot tub, let him see what he's missing. Word'll soon get around.'

'I would think it already has. I went up to Starwood this morning to see a friend I've met there, and she told me everyone was talking about this six-foot blonde in a bunny suit who's now ensconced as queen of the night at Chasers.'

'Didn't I tell you . . . what an image! Oh give me one of those as well,' she said, pointing across the rows of bands. 'Might as well ring the changes.'

'You need all this stuff?'

'Of course.' Montana laughed gaily as she gathered her shopping and pushed open the door. They went out into the snow light of the Aspen day. 'I have to look rich.' She grinned lasciviously. 'Goes with the coat . . . you know,' she said, and in one of her remarkable changes of direction sud-denly appeared to remember their trip. 'Hey, we never let off those fireworks.'

'With you around we didn't need to. Why do you want to

be rich? It'll just mean you can torture men on a grander scale.'

Montana chuckled.

'It's my contingency plan, I always have one. Now come along,' she grabbed her arm. 'I've got something to show that'll *really* make you laugh, and I'm late. This is where we need the car, so move it . . .'

'OK, class, now paint me a square orange. That's right. And try to make it look like an orange. Think of things that remind you and apply them to a different shape. Yes, *you got it . . .*!'

She pulled her in excitedly. The house was on the edge of town. Montana had climbed back into what she called her free-thinking gear, and now she wore a cowboy shirt cut off at the shoulders, glitter across the pockets and a pair of butter yellow chamois shorts – 'Got to dress for the part!' she'd whispered – she'd knotted her hair like it was summer in California and the silver blonde knot sat untidily on top of her head and fell in a pale waterfall around her face. She was barefoot; if anything the long brown legs looked even better here than they did in the desert.

'Montana. I need to talk to you for a minute.'

'What is it?'

'What are you *doing?*'

'Taking a class.'

The bunch of men and women were riveted; of various ages and credos they were ready to pray or hum – whatever she asked. They just needed a guru, and they hung on her every word. On their canvases square oranges sprung up enthusiastically all over the room.

'On *what?*'

'Self-help. What does it look like? It's all the thing here.'

'Yes, but why you? How did you get in? Whose house is this?'

'Oh, one of Jack's.' She waved a hand airily, used to gifts.

'He gave it to you!?'

'Lent it. Gave me the client list . . .' She smiled broadly. 'I told him I used to be in therapy.'

213

'But as a patient.'

'I didn't put it quite that way. But I know what it's about, don't I? Who better qualified?' Alex looked at her, recalling her talk in the desert evening. She had been very astute, clearing the last of the debris from Alex's mind.

'What are they doing now, then?'

'This is called replacement observation.'

'You're kidding.'

Montana pulled her in close and into a corner, hand on her sleeve, her breath in Alex's ear. 'Yes, I am, but don't tell the world. They wanted volunteers to take a class. To move things around. I'm their replacement observation in this case. Just a showgirl being an artist. Good, huh?'

'Montana, I have to talk to you, seriously. There's something going on here I have to share . . .'

'Can it wait? My class needs me. Come on, it's fun.' She clapped her hands. 'Now, let's try reincarnation,' she called out. 'What do you want to be in your next life? Write it down. Tells us how you *feel* about life. Yes, let it flow. Alex, do you want to join in?' she said, smiling her friend into the class. 'What would you like to be?'

'A copper beech.'

'They all turned and stared. Alex sighed.

'I'll catch you later . . .'

Miki walked on slippered feet across the black marble hall into the white drawing room. The telephone was ringing, and Lee was already bringing it to him. He bowed as Miki spoke into the receiver.

'Miki. It's all right.'

'Mochi, did all go well?'

'That's what I mean. The egg has been removed, we just have to wait now. There is no problem. The doctors told me that.'

He felt the joy, and then fear. 'Are you sure?'

'Everything is fine . . .'

He felt the bubble fill his heart. His chest swelled with it as he drew in a breath of pure pride, and relief. 'When are you coming home?'

'In two days, if all is well then they re-implant. The doctor said I should sleep tonight. I will be in the apartment, if you want me.' Her voice sounded young as a child.

'Good. Good . . .' He nodded, and again.

'Miki . . .' she hesitated, 'are *you* all right?'

But this was the part he did not want. Fully recovered, his memory was now only one of shame, not of his wife's care. His paternally proud chest deflated.

'You don't need to worry,' he said dismissively. 'Tell me when you are coming back, Mochi, that's all. I want to be there to meet you.'

'I will . . . Thank you, Miki. We're going to have our very own baby.' Another hesitation and she was gone. Her words rang in his ears as he replaced the receiver. He looked out on the view. It should have been glorious; this was the day he had waited for, the day to take in everything about his life as he looked out on the view that soothed and pleased him: his tranquillity.

Today, he didn't see it. He only felt his heart burst with pride and gratitude. For once, his cool approach to life had deserted him. He felt reborn.

He picked up the phone again. He would up the stakes for genetic research with a phone call to the leader of the committee: Hillaire Bowman. It was the very least he could do.

215

SIXTEEN

'Spare part surgery, a traffic in human trade. Well of course, Hillaire, none of this is new. If a living cell is needed, unscrupulous people are always ready to steal. I believe the going rate for a kidney is around £3,000, is it not?'

'£1,000 in a developing country such as India. But what about taking it a stage further? Who is to stop us taking that living cell from *healthy* patients . . .'

Hillaire eased himself down into the chair on his porch and put his feet up on the rail. Beside him, Liam sipped at his coffee, his hands around the mug. Steam rose from its surface. The day itself had not risen much above freezing and both men were well wrapped up against the cold. A Thermos of coffee stood on the table between them, and a bottle of whisky. Now, at his words, the younger man looked over at him, his expression intensifying.

'Yes, I can see you have guessed it.' Hillaire paused, letting it sink in. 'In third world countries it's a symbiotic, though ghastly, trade.' He recrossed his feet. 'Almost impossible to stop where there is need and little birth control and a shortage of money. But why just stop at kidneys? We already take the aborted foetuses from their mothers – laws do not prevent people from doing what they want.'

'But no one would sanction it publicly.'

'They wouldn't?' Hillaire shifted his weight, picking up a pipe and knocking it against the wall to disperse the ashes. 'Where wealthy clients can pay?' Trading in human organs may be illegal but to those living in squalor it is a chance for some of their family to get out. If you are Bangladeshi and can sell your kidney and thereby secure the survival of your sixteen children, why not.

Liam fell silent as Hillaire tamped his pipe down with new tobacco, and clamped it between his teeth. 'Cloning is the future, Liam.'

216

Liam looked him over. 'So why has it failed before?'

'Because animals have been implanted with human embryos and it has been unsuccessful. They needed human host figures.'

'And David has managed this?'

'So it would seem. The sky's the limit with this achievement, you see. Finding matches between organ donors and people needing them is extremely complicated and time-consuming; often we do not have time. Commercial pressures have resulted in this "trade" and payment to donors. I agree it does seem rather barbaric, but where there's need there will always be providers. With identical twins, by definition every organ is a perfect match. So it would be with clones.'

'Grow your own organ replacement,' Liam said drily.

Hillaire nodded, concentration etching the craggy features of his face. 'Absolutely. By taking a cell and cloning it we can put ourselves in a time warp. We can feed off our clones. Not only can our children be perfect, but we can extend our own pattern of life, if we so wish.'

Liam still held his mug between his hands, his strong face thoughtful. 'You open the door to the worst in human frailties, in mankind, with this, Hillaire.'

'Yes.' There was nothing else to say. 'But there is another side to human cloning,' he said. 'Just as you might have one old and beloved car, when it starts to go wrong or gets involved in an accident, as it inevitably does, what do you do? Buy a new one? Possibly. But do you sell the old one? Not necessarily. We humans become attached to all sorts of sentimentalities. We could advertise for a car of the same type. We buy it, we use the new car for which we have no sentimental attachment to feed the old car which has now become part of the family. Thus, our old faithful is restored and lovingly put back on the road. Even with sufficient organs available there can be an incompatibility between donor and recipient. With identical clones there would be no such problem.'

Liam's forehead creased as Hillaire spoke, his eyes intent on him, showing his seriousness. 'But wouldn't they have to be fully grown?'

'That's possible. Clones could be taken and grown within a sub-community. A spare parts factory of people. They would have to have a good quality of life, but they would be farmed. In exchange their sexual lives would be monitored but their lifestyle would be good, and children, otherwise afflicted, would be offered a chance to live. Parents will do anything for their children.'

'But only children from a privileged background would qualify. What about the ethical side of all this? You can't farm children just because they're of Third World origin!'

'Ah, yes, well that's what we've been discussing, of course.'

He drew on the flame, enjoying the more than casual discourse with his young friend. He admired and respected Liam. His field was surgery, his prowess legendary though he was still young. A brilliant academic record made for a bright future, and fiery idealism belonged to the young. Liam was a good sounding-board.

'It's rather too futuristic for me, Hillaire. I see medicine as a cure rather than a creation.' His voice held a trace of sarcasm.

'Well, it's not all Frankenstein.' He pulled on his pipe. 'There are some very good things to come out of such research. For example, we can now produce an exact photofit of a wanted criminal from a tissue sample found at the scene of the crime.'

'Genetic fingerprinting. Yes,' Liam agreed, 'now I agree that is useful. How exactly does it work?'

'Basically the genetic code is a text just as you might program on a word processor. You can alter the text in various ways: delete and retype the bits you want to change. Or wipe it out and start again from scratch. You can also borrow sections of text from elsewhere: text from a previously published piece can be lifted out and inserted into the new document. Designing genes is exactly like this. And it is far easier to copy all the genetic code of a cell than it is to rewrite it. At least you know the code works and what it will do. But you see we come back to the same thing – even easier than copying is to get the body to do the copying for you. We have the

218

power to create carbon copies of ourselves. Detection is almost impossible too. There's no way of tracing a clone from a perfectly normal baby.' The phone rang at that moment. 'Excuse me.' He went inside.

Liam sat, deep in thought as he listened to the murmur from within. Hillaire made the call brief, then rested the phone on its cradle and went back out through the storm door to where Liam sat, with his cup of coffee laced with whisky. He knew he had shattered him.

Hillaire eased himself back into his chair and pulled on his pipe again. A bird sang from somewhere high up in a tree.

'So what do you feel is the purpose of this cloning, Hillaire?'

'Well, in general it's an insurance for the future. Babies in deep freeze; if anything should happen to the one living, it could be replaced.'

'But what would that do to the one that existed? It makes every child expendable, so what happens to mortality if they are replaceable in every way?'

'Sadness if your child dies, but he's not lost. Some character maybe, some conscience, because this is individual, but with the same environment and upbringing the child will look and act more or less in the same way as his previous cloned host figure.'

'It has horrifying implications.'

'But quite safe in David's hands.' Hillaire allowed himself a small smile, recalling the heated exchange of the conference. It was all turning out as he had expected; as he had hoped.

'What about the whole nature versus nurture debate? Where does it end?'

Hillaire's smile was replaced by a dark look. 'Can't tell you too much, I'm afraid, but of course we acknowledge the part that nurture might play.' He put his own mug back on the wide balcony rail.

'Who's going to stop doctors?'

'True. The essence of their life is research. Exactly why I put this lot together.'

219

'And ego had nothing to do with it?'

'Some,' he admitted laughing. 'But I am assured of one thing: David's brilliance as well as his morality. Nothing comes close to him; I expect him to win a Nobel Prize any day. His research is extraordinary. And it would have dire consequences were it to fall into the wrong hands.'

Liam listened.

'Never mind David. What about the others? They may have a different view of the future.' He had integrity; a contained element as if he would hold the truth inside himself. It was why Hillaire liked his company, why he had invited him amongst all others to be his guest for the winter season.

He looked over at him. 'Well the question is, is there a market for human clones? Laying aside any ethical considerations for the moment, of course there is. It is an important question at this and in every other level of genetic engineering. If there is a market then they are likely to be made somewhere. Even without a commercial market they may still be created, just probably on a more experimental scale.'

Liam stood up and crossed to the rail, looking out. His voice ran deep.

'And limited only by the conscience of the experimenter.'

'Exactly.'

'Vast cultural and individual differences exist around the world, Hillaire. Personal ethics differ drastically between individuals and nations. Somewhere at some time, scientists will pursue what is physically possible – however undesirable.'

'And for its own sake,' Hillaire enjoined. 'Simply because such things are a challenge and intellectually fascinating. Or, they may be driven by personal, philosophical, religious, moral or political persuasions. Whatever the motive, the potential market for human clones is huge. Especially if they can be frozen – and they can – and only produced some years after the death of the donor . . .'

'A child with built-in guarantees.' Liam turned to him, apparently interested despite his misgivings. 'If couples could opt for donation of perfect characteristics to the host mother, why not cut out the uncertainties and plump for a complete set of guarantees? Intelligence, freedom from genetic disease, guaranteed abilities in other areas...'

'You could even have a series of photographs showing what the child would look like aged one day, two years, six years, twelve years. And as an adult,' Hillaire puffed on his dying pipe. 'Twin studies tell us a great deal about this area: twins separated at birth grow up with the same choices inherent and very similar characteristics. Genes pass by instinct, as seen in animals. These are not learned from observation; these are genetic characteristics. Humans are more greatly influenced by instinct than we care to think, with our scientific brains.' Liam watched as the flame was sucked in a long tongue into the bowl of the pipe, as Hillaire relit it. 'The only thing that we have not guaranteed so far in a cloned embryo for sale is the right environment for the child so that his or her guaranteed genetic potential could flourish at its best.' He watched the man's face carefully. 'Think about it. The perfect environment for the perfect child.' The sweet smell of Dutch tobacco drifted across.

'You could run an advertising campaign to all potential customers – describe the environment which usually produces excellent results with this particular set of genes, give a six year guarantee with the package,' Liam said with irony, and now he laughed outright. 'Come on, Hillaire. You surely can't support this as a plausible theory. But of course it won't happen, you would never sanction it. I know you better than that ... don't I?'

Hillaire's dark look eclipsed him. He would love to have included Liam within the group but he could not. Liam's intensity showed: the natural eagerness of youth, but something more. Hillaire felt it, and knowing his own dangerous side suspected it in someone else; Liam's idealism could be damaging if he knew about the rest of it. They had to keep it quiet: information so explosive it could rock the world. He did not dare to trust him fully.

'Liam, old chap. You are a remarkable young man by any account. But apart from the fact that it's almost impossible for any one person to understand what is right or wrong within this spectrum, I cannot share my views with you because they are not for general knowledge. We are still at the embryonic stage of our discussions. I will say one thing though. Whatever we might feel as a group is one thing, but what about an outside influence, some body of unscrupulous mien? Should we not share this knowledge so that we can construct a barrier against such a happening.'

'You mean, somebody already does know?'

'I think so. I strongly suspect somebody is already at work to make it a reality.'

Liam looked shattered.

'Now, I understand. This whole set-up is in the form of protection.' His face had paled. 'You're going as far as you can go in order to close it out.'

'Something of that sort. What we uncover will go no further than Miki Leng's conference room.'

'And what have you uncovered, Hillaire?'

Hillaire watched Liam's face as he sought to dull his interest. No good his becoming too curious: he was young enough to be too much the idealist. Ruth was of the same vein, but age had given her wisdom not offered to the young. Both of them good people, one just further along the road and able to understand the compromises that took the place of idealism as the years laid down their message. He fed him a last morsel to assuage him. 'I can tell you this, however. Miki Leng has offered us more funding. It's incredible how far he is prepared to let us go.'

'And will you accept?'

'That's what it's all about.' He fell into silence. Liam felt the brush-off.

'And what's Doctor Lindstrom all about?'

'Wilhelm?' Hillaire looked up.

'Don't act coy, Hillaire. You know I mean Ruth. I felt the flame. That's why I left the mountain. Did you two have something in the past?'

Hillaire looked down and away.

'We were at med school together, that's all. And we met

222

up here in Aspen when we were young. It's a great place for romance.'

'Bullshit. How did you lose her?'

How perceptive, thought Hillaire. Though somehow he had lost her, he had never been quite sure how. His feelings were still clear, especially now. Liam had sensed the love beyond the loyalty.

'I married someone else,' he said. And divorced within five years.

'You never thought of children of your own?'

'Never any time for a family.'

'There's always time for everything.' Liam turned and stretched, parking himself on the rail and eyeing his mentor. 'You only have to want.'

'Well, probably. She was wrapped up in her job, and I in mine. I don't think children came into it.'

'Would it have with Ruth?' he said, pointedly.

He thought of it. *Of course, yes.* 'Yes.'

'That's where love begins.'

'A brilliant thought.' Hillaire sat back comfortably, and smiled. 'It's what we've been discussing all morning. The need for children. Should that need be interfered with, how far should we go to create perfection.'

'It depends on one's concept of perfection. Human faults are what makes us lovable. Human truths.' Liam's eyes were shadowed by the light and Hillaire could not see his expression.

'Would you want a child with a defect to be born as such?' he said suddenly.

Liam swung a foot gently. 'Ask me that at the time. It's a difficult one. I'm not sure I'd want it planned in advance, though if it was on its way and it had a problem which could be cured in the womb, then of course.'

'It's an individual decision, isn't it?'

'Always has been.'

Hillaire smiled, trying to catch him. 'Always should be?'

Liam laughed, leaning back in his chair. '*Touché.* That's your department, Professor. And here comes your friend, if I'm not mistaken.'

The car had stopped in the shadowed spill of a glade of trees a small distance from the gate. They watched her look up at them, her face a pale moon surmounted by the crest of dark hair. She was dressed in a black jogging suit with a hood, and snow boots. Her body was lean. Hillaire's voice was suddenly quiet.

'Talking of friends,' he said. 'That girl, Alex?'

He saw the interest in Liam's face at once, though there was no overt reaction. 'Yes?'

'You know who she is, do you?'

The younger man kept his expression cool. He made a throwaway gesture with his hand, returning it to rest easily on his thigh. He looked over towards Ruth, and back. 'No idea, beyond that which she told us. An adventurer of some sort. Perhaps a spy for the Foreign Office?'

'No, but close.' Ruth had arrived at the garden gate and was smiling at them both. She opened it, and Hillaire watched her figure as she latched it carefully behind her. 'She's an investigative field journalist for the BBC.'

'No kidding.' Now he was alert, and amused.

'Apparently there was some ruckus with another reporter, a chap called Hart Bennett. They were fairly notorious, I gather,' he said, standing up to greet his guest. 'Turned up in every danger spot in the world. Obviously having an affair.'

'Danger spots?' he repeated.

'Every point of the compass. She even went on an Antarctic expedition, in order to get the news first as they arrived at the Pole. Amazing,' he laughed at the picture. 'Strong as an ox, quite clearly. Doesn't look the type, does she? Certainly she had me fooled with all that romantic candlelight business.' He breathed deep and recovered his primary line of thought. 'She's covered every war, so far. She gets right in there in her flak jacket with the bombs bursting and the terrorists fighting over the bodies. Puts herself in the front line. A girl who does that is no mouse.'

'I never thought she was . . .'

'No, but what do you think she's doing here?'

'Having a holiday?'

'Think again.'

'What makes you think we'd interest her.'

'The fact that she hasn't told us.'

'She may simply want a rest from the obvious questions, the blood lust.'

Now he turned prior to greeting Ruth.

'Liam, it's not that I don't trust you, but if the press found out about what we are doing, they'd be camping on our doorstep.It's essential there's no buzz. If you intend to see this girl, you have to deflate her. And remember, when you do, she's very very bright. You do it wrong, and all her senses will light up like that Christmas tree over there. Ah. Ruth . . .'

If she was surprised to find Liam there she said nothing of it, but allowed a small peck on the cheek from both men and settled down in the swing chair. Liam poured her a coffee from the jug. She looked up at him and smiled, then threw back her hair and enjoyed the view.

'It's so nice to relax.'

But it was clear that it was anything but. Liam knew she was burning to discuss things with Hillaire: her bright eyes said so, lit flames burning in their brown depths. He put the coffee back on the tray and stretched.

'Well,' he said. 'Think I'll go for a walk. Leave you two eggheads together.'

'Not on my account, surely.'

'No, stay.' This from Hillaire.

'We have nothing to hide.' She grinned. 'More's the pity.' She looked warmly at Hillaire. 'I just dropped in on the off-chance for a chat. We go back a long way. He always understood me so well.' She swung her dark hair, reminiscent of Alex. 'You know what they say. There's no such thing as one hundred per cent in a partner. At the most it's eighty, the missing twenty you have to find elsewhere . . .'

'And which am I?' Hillaire asked in his gruff voice, smiling like a boy. 'Eighty or twenty?'

She was in a frivolous mood. Or perhaps it was just for Liam.

'Whichever suits you the best,' she laughed. 'I thought you might like a drive into town, Hillaire. I rented a car for the week; my little bit of independence. I'm tired of sitting in that limousine day after day being swanned to and fro like a princess.' She stretched her long legs. 'Thought I'd pop out and take you up on your offer. Want to see the sights with an old friend?'

Liam saw the glances between them. He stood up. 'I'm going to head on into town.'

This time they didn't beg him to stay. But suddenly her eyes were on him as he set foot on the step. Feeling the kinship between the two of them made her realise the trust that Hillaire put in him; now she felt silly at her own worries.

'Did Hillaire tell you about Alex?'

'Just now.'

She looked at Hillaire.

'I don't think it's anything to worry about.'

They both looked at him together, and laughed. 'Good God, what is this!'

'Just keep any information to yourself.'

'I've none too share.'

She eyed Hillaire. 'Well,' she said carefully, and all their combined knowledge was in her dark eyes. She sipped at her coffee, her eyes watching over the rim. 'It's his baby.'

'I rather enjoyed the revelation, actually.'

'She's got more going for her than I thought, eh?'

'No. I did wonder, though. She had quite a bit of bite, didn't she Hillaire?'

'She certainly did.' He laughed, more relaxed with the lady scientist than Liam had ever seen him, and switched subjects. 'Ruth, Miki Leng has come up with more money. The baby's doing OK. I've been in touch with the clinic. His gratitude is showing; he's doubled the research money.'

The pleasure filled her face. 'Wonderful news. And manna from heaven to our research team. We have a long way to go yet. I just wish I could have helped him to live instead of just his child. It's dreadful to die on the outside with the brain still registering every humiliation.'

She showed her feelings easily. Liam could imagine her voice at the conference. He would like to have sounded her out in the same sort of conversation he had just had with Hillaire, but he owed it to Hillaire to be discreet, and equally, this was clearly not the time. He took his hat from the peg by the door, and his parka.

'Well, you two, I'm off. Can I trust you alone together?'

'Implicitly.' She laughed.

He strolled away, standing back at the gate to lift a hand in salutation, but he fell quickly into deep reflection as he headed down the street, walking with athletic grace down its centre, seeming oblivious to the rules of the road.

'Why, Ruth?'

'I wanted to drive round, see the area. Thought you might like to come too.'

'No, why didn't you wait for me?' His voice was dark with gravity. Liam had taken him too painfully back to a loss in the past for which he had never grieved properly, because he did not know its truth. He could see she was shocked by his direct approach, but he had to know. She recovered her composure and he saw her own hurt reflected in her eyes, and felt a quick sense of shame.

'Hillaire.' She turned in her seat. 'It was you who wouldn't wait. The world was out there. I didn't think you even saw me, and we always rowed.'

'I saw it as healthy discussions,' he remonstrated. 'I fancied myself in love with you.'

'Then you should have shown it,' she said, her eyes darkening.

'You only fight with those you love.'

She looked at him, a world in her eyes. Then she turned away and as she did she dropped her face so that her hair swung forward. It had been ever thus, and he felt the ache. An old man now, but emotions stayed the same. Bodies aged, but minds were sixteen. Medical science aside, he was an ordinary man.

'You were always so goddamn ambitious. You haven't changed either.'

'Would you want me to?'

She did not answer him and a silence fell between them.

'You should have told me,' she said at last.

'I thought I did,' he said. 'Some people talk. I've always found it hard to speak the words, except from a textbook.' He tried for a smile, and her eyes responded with quiet warmth.

'I always wondered what had happened to you,' she admitted.

'I never had to wonder. I always asked.' He kept his eyes on her. 'The medical world is very informative, especially of a brilliant star.'

'Didn't your mother teach you to look for the brightest star and then make a wish . . .!?' she countered, smiling, and in her smile was so much. A lifetime lost. The road was empty, the snow glinted, the imperious mountains touched on a Hockney blue sky: around them was that other worldly silence that beguiled the senses.

'I'll get a fresh pot of coffee.'

With the change of atmosphere they had found a change of subject. It was easier to discuss something with which they were both at least familiar.

'Animals don't interact like humans,' she said, sipping the hot drink. 'How do you know there won't be a hiccup?'

'It's a progression, Ruth. That's what we do.'

'Identical twins. One man-made? It's too dangerous.'

'David's way ahead of the field, Ruth.' He spoke steadily. 'If handled carefully, and for the right reasons, I believe in it. It's the way of the future.'

'Science fiction, Hillaire. Frankenstein. Your whole existence, not just physical, but emotions, your moral conscience, dictated by a scientist in a lab? It's unthinkable.'

'It's happening, Ruth.'

'I always knew there was something different about you,' she said in the face of his seemingly impenetrable belief. But he could not gauge her emotions clearly.

'Such as?'

'You're God, or think you are.'

'And Wilhelm?'

'He wants any money going spare for his own pet research subjects.'

'And for a clinic that begins with the letters of his own name.'

'Is that fair?' She tilted her head. 'Perhaps a charity.'

'Be serious. He's ambitious, and it's obvious. More than ambitious, Ruth. I sense hostility, ruthlessness.'

'Perhaps he's looking to protect me. And you're the fine one to be discussion ambition as a vice.'

He let it go. Ambition had always been his *bête noire*; it had divided them once.

'And what about your work?' she asked.

The conference had been convened to discuss genetics, but despite the clinic which he ran personally in New York, his particular curiosities lay elsewhere: the freezing techniques of cryology would possibly come into the picture somewhere when dealing with the frozen cells from which they would extract the drugs to be injected later into the human DNA, a secret only he was party to – for now. The laboratory which he and a group of doctors financed outside New York was coming up with some pretty incredible results; they were working closely with Kowolski on the other side of the country. He wondered if David ever really planned to disclose the whole unpalatable truth. He was not sure at this stage that he could confide wholly in Ruth, despite his regard for her. He had more in-depth knowledge of David's research than any of them could begin to imagine.

'The lab have been investigating patterns in brain tissue that's been preserved by freezing. They seem to be getting some pretty interesting results.'

Ruth looked amazed. 'You mean you'd been able to extract information from dead brains. Why, that's incredible. Does it follow a pattern, make any sense at all?'

'Oh, absolutely.'

'Good God . . .'

'There's definitely some sort of responsive impulses, we

229

just haven't worked out what they are, but we're getting close to decoding them. Just need that break-through.'

'They could just be random though.'

'No, none of us think so. But we've discovered a drug, Ruth. It triggers off buried memories much as neuro-surgeons have been doing for years, by accident, in the process of an operation. We think we have it.' He paused for a moment. 'Wainco have been developing a whole new generation of memory boosting drugs. The brain tends only to put into long term storage what it considers to be exciting or relevant. I've been working with chemicals to create better neural paths to those memories.'

'On real brains?'

'Yes.'

'Not on human guinea pigs.' She knew of the invasive techniques some scientists used on defenceless mental patients.

'No,' he smiled. 'On rats.'

She returned the smile. 'Who'd be a rat . . .' She pushed her hands into her fleece-lined jacket for warmth and let out the deep breath she had been holding during his revelations. 'Why bring us all together? You not worried about stealing?'

'I don't believe in secrets in science. Knowledge should be shared. We all have to work together.'

She smiled. 'Not a lot of people would agree with you on that.'

'Fortunately the guy who's paying for our trip, does.'

'You were never bound by rules, were you, Hillaire?'

'Too many scientists are in little boxes, Ruth.' He looked at her. 'You can't see out of a box.'

She had come up with something smarter than they had. He had most of his fertile ideas in his mid-twenties, and Ruth had retained that youthfulness. Most scientists lost it in the welter of information and academia. Youth had energy, partly because it hadn't learned all the rules. Ruth's built-in naivete had retained that, making her unusual, probably unique.

Too many scientists were stuck in a rut and he realized he

was falling into the same trap. He was growing stale with years of treading the same wellworn path and getting nowhere. He was disillusioned. He'd hoped for more progress, and this conference had brought it. Now he knew he had not wasted years of life going down that blind alley.

'We have that chemical,' he said. 'David has created it. Now we just have to patent it, fund it, and a whole new dimension begins. We know the future. Are you brave enough to have a genetic breakdown readout? Say, statistically you were to die at seventy. Are you prepared to accept that?'

'Statistically,' she repeated. 'And that's where your thinking goes wrong. You're not allowing for future advances in medicine.'

'You're right, of course. And with the manufacture of life-enhancing drugs I could live on; perhaps for ever. Doesn't the idea appeal to you? A rich man could finance its beginning, a foundation named after him. The most important breakthrough in science; longevity. We all want it. Religion is just a talisman to ward off fear. Right now it's survival of the fittest. We could change all that. You, and I, and the other members of the conference.'

'But you won't.'

'An unscrupulous man would.'

'Then you answer my question,' she challenged.

'It isn't over yet. I rest my case until it is.' He leaned forward, lifting a finger. 'Ruth, I deal daily in the genetic programming of offspring. I see family after family longing for a cure; rich or poor, to them their children or their old folks are everything. Tell me,' he said suddenly, 'why did you and Wilhelm never have children?'

She looked rather embarrassed, for the first time. She thought of Wilhelm's infertility. Despite his wishes, she had gone ahead and had herself checked out. Wilhelm had wanted to blame her and she had let him. She had been brought up to let a man be master, but her career had turned their marriage upside down. Never would she have wished for interference, even at the worst moments of sorrow. 'Wilhelm would not submit to testing.'

'Amazing. And you went with that?'

'He's my husband, Hillaire.'

'But you're at the centre of all possibilities.'

'And a moralist. Some things are better left alone. You equate science with no morality.'

'Oh, come now.'

'I equate it with God. Yes, it's possible. Man can walk on the moon and come back and embrace religion. It's science that opens our eyes to the miracle.'

'Only machines are immortal.'

'And God,' she said, looking pointedly at him. 'Only he can save himself.'

'Yes,' he said. 'That's what I believe in too.'

SEVENTEEN

As his butler announced his guest, Sandford Wainwright took three calls in his library. One was from New York, one from the other side of Aspen town and the other from Wyoming. All three made him smile. He left the library and went into his study ready to greet his guest.

In his suite high up in the house the doors whispered and no footfall could be heard. Everything was quiet. The girl's hips swayed down the hall under the tight material as she led Miki Leng to the study. She was blonde, with her hair caught back, and her legs were perfect. Her face bore just the right amount of discreet make-up and just the right expression. Miki wondered fleetingly what she was like when she was not pretending.

Her smile led him in. The man himself sat centre stage and he was writing. Miki was pleased; for the moment he would rather not speak as he took in the surroundings. Sandford Wainwright seemed set in space against the spectacular backdrop of the mountains. Reflected blue white light flooded into the room from where they reared up like great predators against the black night sky. The town sprawled below, studded with light through a floor-to-ceiling window, the reflection perfectly reproduced in the black desk that at first seemed the only object in the shadowed room, a spill of light upon the surface. Yet as his eyes adjusted there was beauty. A soft light on a painting, a dark gold vase of flowers.

Sandford was pleased at his interest. Turning, Miki found himself the object of his host's observation.

'You see, Mr Leng. I like beauty as you do.'

His eyes had lifted: bright cobalt blue against the sandy, sun-bleached skin. His face was square and flat, his hair appearing marine short, but in fact it was scraped close to his head and into a ponytail. It was not grey, but of indeterminate colour. He looked fit, lean and hard, despite his short stature. His age would not have mattered but he was around fifty.

'I watched a programme the other night,' he began as he stepped around the desk to shake hands, '... about a Japanese fellow much like yourself. Since he was a child he had wanted the brain of Einstein, a life's ambition. He was obsessed. I understand obsession, Mr Leng. I have felt that way, not about Einstein in particular, but about having something of value.' Their hands met; releasing his own, Sandford showed the way to a door beside an outside staircase. 'Would you care for tea?'

Miki bowed his acceptance.

Sandford smiled, pleased to be in the company of one such as himself. It was a novelty, and he meant to enjoy it.

'I have something to show you I think you might enjoy.'

Miki was led in gently, sensing the other man's respect. He was no fool; this was certainly no social call, but Miki was an old hand at dealing with those who wanted investment. It would not seem that this man needed that at all: his ranch equalled the Red House in almost every way, as far as realty was concerned. Of course, the contents of Miki's own house represented a fortune with which nobody could compete. He knew that for a fact: he had had them assessed to his satisfaction. Miki liked to be the best. But curious now, he was willing to be courted as a means to an end and he had infinite patience; sooner or later they would get to the point. Sandford offered to show him his string of horses, and outside in the heated two million dollar barn, he waited patiently, enjoying the spectacle. Seated high above the arena he watched Sandford's string of horses go through their paces. Tea came and went in the care of a silent, subservient maid.

The same girl who had shown him in was schooling one of the horses in the indoor ring. He admired the dark gold of her hair, the line of her muscled legs as she led the horse through its paces. She wore a cream silk shirt with narrow lapels and jodhpurs and as she leaned forward he could see the curve of her small breasts. She caught him looking and smiled.

So did Sandford.

'Drive and force get you what you want, Mr Leng. You only have to want it.'

'I understand this perfectly.'

'No, not enough.' The man's words surprised him, but he did not show it. 'Your band of doctors and their work have had spectacular results.' This elicited no reaction, but Sandford did not care, there was plenty of time yet. 'Genetic testing has been done before,' he went on, 'but never successfully. Now I know why.' He no longer bothered to beat about the bush. At a signal, the girl took the horse smoothly from the ring and they were left in silence. From his pocket, Sandford took the small black tape recorder. He tapped it. 'Whatever this doctor has, I want it.' He smiled carefully. 'I always win, Mr Leng. Always.'

Miki looked at the tape. Only now did he show a reaction.

'Where did you get this?'

Sandford's smile was hard. 'We'll talk about that later.'

And then he switched it on.

Sandford watched him carefully as the tape ended. Miki's expression had remained impassive throughout, but he had the trump card. He led into the possibilities slowly, widening Miki's mind and his horizons as he did so, playing on the rich man's only remaining vanity – immortality and world acclaim. Prestige; he knew all about that.

He let his words sink in as he thrust a little deeper.

'With the manufacture of life-enhancing drugs we can all extend our lives, and our health; the two are synonymous. Doesn't the idea appeal to you? A rich man such as yourself could . . .'

Miki ignored him for the moment, his mind on the tape.

'At some point in the future doctors will be able to reconstruct our entire bodies from the DNA coding in just one intact cell. This is something I know,' he said.

'That's what they've told us,' Sandford said, measuring his words, trying to contain his growing excitement. 'How would you feel if that was *now*?'

A moment passed. 'How do you mean?'

'With the help of DNA, Mr Leng, one of your doctors has even been able to take clothing and to cull cells from the cloth. *He has created a drug that can recreate from the dead . . .*'

'You are talking of freezing, or cryonic suspension. Of course, I know about this.'

'No,' said Sandford softly. 'I am *not*. I am talking about a drug that can literally bring anyone back to life – *without* freezing, that is the point. Anyone who has been a long time dead, Mr Leng. *Can you imagine what this means?*'

Miki stopped in his tracks. 'Yes. I can.'

Sandford was pleased at his knowledge, enjoying the man's company. Eagerly, he led him into the last part of the conference, the part omitted from the tape, the part that Lindstrom had whispered so salaciously across his desk.

'Well, cloning is not what interests me, Mr Leng. Nor does cryology, or a drug that produces an enviable lifespan.' He swept them aside like crumbs from a table. 'No, these are merely sidelines – useful, maybe – to the main issue. For me, and I would imagine for you, Kowolski has gone much further.' He paused a moment. 'He has discovered the use of organs of Arctic seals. These seals manage to live in sub-zero temperatures, freezing conditions, because they have adapted. Ecology has taught them how. The drug that he has extracted is the one that can literally recreate life from the grave. Not extend life, *create* life. Till now only God could do that. *We can ape that ability with Kowolski's drug . . .*'

Kowolski's research was extraordinary. DNA had progressed in his lab beyond the imagination: '. . . they have made it possible to take cells from a dead person and use them to create a living image or at least a very close likeness of that person. Now, if we were able to activate that with the famous of the highest possible order, what do we have?' He stood up, walked to the rail and looked down on the empty ring below. Turning, his eyes shone with a new fanatical light. 'DNA can be culled – *farmed* – from the cloth of the great and the dead and used to reproduce likenesses in future babies ... we have at our fingertips a *baby bank*: genius, creativity, beauty, brains, charisma – take your pick. Marilyn Monroe, John Kennedy, Albert Einstein – who do you want? It is the ultimate designer child,' he whispered hoarsely, his voice cracking with all the verve of a megalomaniac orator.

'And anybody who deals with taking living tissue from a person could be bribed to collect...' intoned Miki Leng, seeing it all.

'Indeed!' The pleasure belled in his voice. 'Well, what do you think?'

But Miki had changed tack; Sandford did not know his quarry as well as he thought. The small oriental man sat proudly in his chair. Now he had the information, the coal black eyes fixed on him with annoyance.

'Now tell me how you gained control of this information. Those doctors have my trust.'

Sandford felt a first pinprick of alarm, but nevertheless opened his hands wide, entirely unashamed. He would turn him around. 'Well, Mr Leng, I think you yourself expected this. You had the place swept after all, didn't you? However, once too few.'

'I see.' He seemed to accept that as a *fait accompli*, and moved on. 'And so what do you plan to do with this, and where do I come in?'

Sandford smiled. As if he hadn't guessed, but truly he hadn't – not as yet, and he felt a touch of amusement inside him as he played it out, waiting for the oriental composure to crack.

'I know where to get hold of these particular cells. But it will take huge money.'

'Who has them? Some obscure Brazilian laboratory? That is a bit hackneyed, Mr Wainwright.'

He did not flinch at his scepticism. 'Something similar. China.'

'China!?'

'Politically the two major powers are now China and the USA. China has some very immoral views towards ecology which we do not share here. Cloning would be very simply for them.'

'It is most strange that I have not heard of all this. Professor Bowman is my guest, his team financed by me. Why would they create anything behind my back?'

'Oh, I don't think they intend to. But it can be done.'

'Yet you had a spy in the camp, so to speak.'

'Though you are financing the team, Mr Leng,' he said patiently, 'they are doctors and are not going to tell you everything. Despite the fact that their progress or otherwise will be due to you, and you alone . . .' His voice was insinuating and silky; unsettling. '. . . with the help of DNA. Mr Leng, let me enlighten you. These doctors are thirsting for the future. Some little scrap of law is not going to stop them. What do you think they are doing with your money, just talking about your problem? No, of course not, they are taking a broader view, and one which would interest you greatly, I believe?' He walked as he spoke, easily embroidering with his hands a grander picture.

'For one thing, I know that in a lab in California the scientists have culled the cells of a man who might truly interest you: a very famous man long dead, and his cell structure is up for sale. They took a part of his brain when he was shot in a Kenyan hunting expedition, didn't even need to freeze it. It was splattered all over his safari suit. His wife gave it to the maid to be burned, and –' He palmed his hands wide – 'The maid has named her price.' He smiled. 'It's expensive, as you can imagine. With real money it can be bought – and brought to life . . .'

'Who is this man?' Miki said quietly.

'Who would you like him to be?' Sandford teased gently.

But Miki did not answer. 'How do you know all this?' he said.

'Through your doctors . . .'

'Through the Professor?' Miki played for time as his mind did juggling tricks. 'That would be hard to believe. He is a most moral man. I know this.'

'Moral or no,' Sandford shrugged, 'all doctors like to experiment and this one . . . just happened to go astray. I know where it is.' He felt Miki's eyes on him. 'But that is not of importance; what is, are the ramifications. With real money, it can be bought. Kowolski's lab know just how to do this. With anyone . . .' He looked at him. 'You realise what this means.'

'It means that no one is safe.'

'Precisely,' said Sandford with some pleasure. 'But for you it has special significance. Mochi is in New York. Right now, potentially your child could be anyone you want him to be.'

Now Miki looked at him, and his emotion showed for the first time. 'You know about that?'

Sandford shrugged. It was a private matter, but spies were legion when you were a rich man. Disgruntled employees, the sight of endless money making them at first almost ominously loyal, but daily subjection bringing envy, then disloyalty; then dismissal and almost simultaneously secrets were sold. He carried on:

'Of course, but you should be glad I know because I can help you – it means, my dear Mr Leng, that this need not be your last chance at a child. It means that despite a creeping illness, all crises can be cured. I'm surprised they have not told you, nor put you out of your misery. It is no longer a crisis point if you do not wish it to be. You can clone your child, you can create your child. Your child can be a development of yourself and your lovely wife – or it can be –' he spread his hands – 'a little bit helped along. A nip and a tuck, it's all the rage, why not start young? Why not make this child everything a child could be . . . it's still not too late . . .'

He saw that he had the man. He was standing like a deer in a forest that has smelled a foe, but he had no fear, he could see that, just a primeval interest in man's desire to re-create. Sandford fed the words in with care, pressing the buttons he had already seen light up under his scrutiny. His voice was pure silk and fed in at a low insidious pitch, but he need not have worried; Miki's mind was no longer on the present, but on the future.

'Any person in possession of an article belonging to a great person might be in possession of untold wealth. The implications are endless. Hospitals are always in need of benefactors.' He knew just which way to lead him. With his money, Sandford would become a beneficiary of Kowolski's hospital, and bribe a spy in the camp to give in to him. Miki knew this ploy only too well: with his assistance, his friend, Hillaire Bowman, had been able to enlist the help of a reluctant conspirator in Ruth Lindstrom, thus feeding Sandford into the system via her own husband. It was a perfectly woven, round plot, and he was ensnared by it.

'Your wish then, Mr Wainwright, is to control such an idea. Am I right?'

'Exactly right. I plan to patent the concept, injecting the genetic structure of anyone I choose.' He knew Kowolski would never do it, he was far too ethical. Sandford despised ethics: they were for the weak willed. He would set up Wilhelm, whose need for a place in medical history was powerful, with his own laboratory.

It was sinister; Miki understood that. He looked ahead, seeing the idea and its place in the environment. Like the old grave robbers, a thriving business could begin. Anybody in the medical profession could rake in a fortune during ordinary practice, if they were unscrupulous enough. Even those just in daily contact with the public – hairdressers, beauticians. Just a scale of skin, just a hair follicle, just a cell. That's all it would take. It opened up terrible possibilities.

'And to what purpose would I use this?'

'Your child could be anyone you want him to be . . .' He pressed the idea home. 'Given the right environment and a great deal of money, and that is precisely the point, the child would flourish. You have both, and that's all it takes.' He paused. 'I have . . . the bank . . .' Miki looked very directly at him.

'You have host mothers for this purpose already?'

Sandford's manner was that of a proud father. 'I have, but what I want more than anything is a mother of exquisite beauty to bear the fruits of what can be created – the world's first perfect designer child. Made to order.'

'Why don't you impregnate a young lady yourself? There would be plenty who are willing, surely?'

'Sadly I thought about this too late. Unlike me, you made provision. You have chances left, as long as your genes remain frozen in a cabinet in New York. But of course that too could change.'

Miki felt his blood freeze, and his expression changed.

'What are you saying?'

Sandford watched his quarry carefully. 'Nothing . . . specific. Just that I hold the key.'

'How did you discover all this information?'

'One of your doctors has been in my pocket for years. I understand need, obsession. I know how to milk it. He alerted me to you.'

'But the conference was my idea.'

'That's what you thought. A word here, a word there . . .' He examined his cuffs. 'I know it all, you see. Isn't it true that the woman, Ruth Lindstrom, was instrumental in curing your particular disease?'

'Yes.'

'There you are then. An easy route in.'

'Professor Ruth *Lindstrom*?'

'No,' he said with a smile. 'Not your Professor Lindstrom. And no guesses, please. I have some loyalty.' He smiled. 'I don't mean to alarm you at all. I just want to show you your vulnerability. I want to show you as well how to make yourself – and your family – secure for ever.'

'But then you also know my wife is already hopefully carrying our child . . .'

'Hope. Yes, I see, that is the right word . . .'

His implication was clear: if something should happen to this child – and it was by no means anything like clear of its obstacles yet – it might be genetically deformed, it might not even take. His sperm might never fertilise another, and then what?

Miki thought long and hard. His plans for bringing the doctors to Aspen had been twofold. One for his own power in being able to buy brains and their willingness to submit to

241

his money. And two, to see what could be done for him and Mochi. He knew the richest of doctors always needed funding for their research projects: they cost millions. Their egos were always vulnerable too. Any discovery had the stamp of their name on it, and discovery took huge funding. Money had corrupted him. He hadn't the moral or spiritual strength to overcome temptation of this calibre.

Sandford, motivated by greed and a rich man himself though not nearly as rich as Miki, had discovered Miki's great need. For Miki, the other interested party, it was the power of medical science, of discovery attributed to him, made possible by his money. It was the ultimate power trip for a man who had everything, and there was something for him in it too – if successful, Mochi might benefit, by being the mother of the world's first perfect child.

Sandford prompted gently: 'You *could* have whatever you wanted . . .'

Miki was torn: it was a morally ambiguous idea but the oriental mind was tempted; to date, he had everything but total acceptance, and this man had touched his nerves – he wanted political power. Imagine another woman bearing his child, brought on with his seed. Would Mochi mind so much if he did this? A child of his might not be acceptable, but a child who, for instance, resembled the Americans' adored public hero, John Kennedy, would have every chance; a child of his loins, genetically correct, matched with that of another to manufacture a replica of a great world figure. He smiled; he was not without his own self-deprecating humour.

'An oriental American president, however, is unlikely.'

Sandford did not smile, though privately he was amused at Miki's vanity.

'You're right, of course. Pearl Harbor's still too close for most to go for that . . . but he wouldn't be oriental,' he said ungracefully, 'that is just the point. He would be say John Kennedy.' He played perceptively on the man's weaknesses. 'Don't forget either that genetically *you* are at fault. Mochi would have no trouble with an alien sperm.'

Miki blanched. '*Mochi . . .!?*' He shook his head fervently. 'Oh no. She would never agree.'

Sandford's voice was silk. 'Forgive me, but I was under the impression she did as she was told.'

Miki held his look hard, waiting for him to continue, his expression giving nothing away.

Sandford forged on.

'What would be wrong with this idea? The child would have every advantage. It would be yours in every way.' He shrugged his shoulders, and his voice was coolly casual. 'And of course, it would be *perfect*.'

The words strung out into the silence between them. Miki's male pride and his need for the huge power that money and influence brought, conflicted. Whereas Sandford was corrupted by dreams of power beyond anyone's imagining, he watched Miki's mental wrangle and did not help him one iota. If he had judged him correctly, and he was sure he had, Miki was someone who saw everything through. Knowledge he loved; collecting the finest; to be the best – to have the best. To have the perfect child would be the best.

He did not answer directly, but when it came it was almost a question in the form of an answer.

'Mochi's a woman, and wants her own child, not something manufactured from a strand of DNA in a laboratory.'

'But forgive me,' Sandford laughed. 'Isn't that what is already happening? You were quite prepared to go to any lengths to perfect that baby for the two of you. It's all been pretty mechanical so far, hasn't it?'

Miki drew in a breath. 'No' was a word that had been coursing through him, though an inner devil persuaded him to think at least for fairness along other lines. But Sandford had misjudged him; he was not easily swayed at all. Especially where Mochi was concerned.

'I do not feel she would allow this.'

The insurmountable problem seemed to be Mochi. Sandford's look was intense. '*Would she have to know?*'

He was met by an inscrutable stare. Sandford found he simply did not know what the oriental mind was thinking.

He wondered if he had misjudged this man, and retreated as much as he was able whilst summoning up his next angle. But he was sure of one thing: he had read the flicker in the man's implacable eyes – Mochi – was the weak link. And Miki's reluctance had sealed her fate. Now he would go ahead anyway; he would have her.

Besides, he already had her. He was a businessman. He never made a move without a contingency plan. He would not place himself on safari without a gun.

It was time to quit – for now.

Reverting to charm, he eased the subject back on to the everyday, and after some small pleasantries he stood, ending the meeting. Time was of the essence; well, he would have to bend time. He avoided the pressure he longed for as they parted, knowing he definitely had the Japanese man's interest.

And that, he meant to play on.

'Mortality, Mr Leng. Think about it,' he said, knowing which button to push longest. It was all he thought about. 'It's no longer a word we need use . . .'

'Is that a Norma Kamali? It's fabulous.'

Alex and Darren followed Fanny into Tatou's after a morning's ski on Buttermilk. Fanny had whirled her along; hot chocolate and a croissant now essential. Conscious of social pecking order, Rowan, Evie and Jack were melting into the woodwork in a corner. Fanny had cruised in, ignoring all protocol, given Rowan the familiar rabbit punch and plonked herself down, squeezing Jack around the table. 'The house is magic, Evie,' she said. 'Thanks a bunch.'

As Evie and Jack had managed to fleece them, Evie was smiling. She'd checked Fanny for shopping labels as she sat down.

'A copy, I'd expect,' the northern girl said, giggling, her sense of fun infectious, as without trying she was accepted. 'Let's see the menu, then.'

'No menu. You have to be cool enough not to look at prices. Just order up and get the shock later.'

'In that case, petal, I'll have some of yours. You never heard we northerners are no fools.'

'You certainly paid enough for Evie's house!'

Lots of laughter, which Fanny ignored by joining in herself.

'Come in, Alex,' she invited in her usual 'introduce everyone' way. 'Waitress, could we squeeze two more chairs together. That's it,' she said, pulling it over herself. 'I used to do this job, you know. They can't pull any of that snobbish stuff on me. That's it, Alex love, settle yourself down. Darren pet, what'll you have . . .' It was her absolute gift to be totally oblivious of effect, so her *joie de vivre* worked every time: the self-conscious trio accepted her like an old pal. 'You'd never need a major-domo with me around. Oh, my aching butt, how many times do you have to fall to call yourself a skier – ?'

'Ask Rowan, he still can't stand up straight.'

'That's because I've been in your joint the night before, Jack.'

'Yeah, all night. You get on that gondola drunk at noon.'

'And don't I feel it. But it sure feels good, rocks me like a baby in a cradle . . .'

'How's Montana coming along?'

'Oh, Montana's coming along just dandy.'

'She around?'

'Took off early. Probably going up the mountain to come back down as a beaver . . .'

Hoots of laughter.

'Doesn't need to dress for that. You score last night, Rowan?'

He threw him a look. 'Whatever do you mean? Chrissake, Jack, keep your voice down.'

'Just wondering.'

'No. I think the lady's saving herself for another day.'

Jack's quiet went unnoticed as Fanny's sudden laughter lit up the room. Alex downed her hot chocolate; heavy socialising wasn't really her scene. Despite Fanny, everyone was too aware of position. She wanted out.

As she walked out of the restaurant alone she felt freer, and the smile spread over her face; it was all so clichéd. She remembered her aunt's words about the gossiping crowds; what she needed was two hours on the mountain. She looked up at its fresh-faced peaks with eagerness, the laughter and pleasure still in her eyes as she bumped straight into Liam.

'Hey.' His grey eyes glinted a message. 'I saw you coming . . .' He felt the jolt of electricity for the first time at the softness in her face.

'So you ran right into me?'

'You were so deep in thought, you didn't hear me shout.'

His eyes took her in. She wore a blue shot silk jacket, the collar turned up to frame her natural good looks, and her hair was loose, floating around her face. Her legs were superb in black leggings.

'Haven't you heard about the three-foot rule,' she said. 'Anything else is my territory.'

'Where you headed?'

'Ajax.'

He stepped back, amused. He knew her secret now, but it was not relevant. 'Want a rematch?'

She kept on walking. 'Can I stop you? Mountains belong to everyone.'

He fell in by her side.

'Don't you want to find out just how good I am?' The man was so provocative. 'Whether I can actually ski, or whether I simply flew down. You going to stick close and nose out the truth?'

He hadn't realised as he said it that it was deliberately challenging, but she must have thought her secret was safe, because her reciprocating expression didn't change.

She laughed, easing the tension.

'OK,' she said. 'Today, something difficult.'

He'd given her an opening to confide in him, but as he looked into her eyes they gave nothing away. Whatever need it was that kept her secrets too, she wasn't sharing.

'I thought you'd never ask.'

246

They were close enough to touch as they climbed into the gondola and she could not move away without looking stupid. But she was conscious that it burned her. She looked at the strong hand dashed with dark hair that now moved away of its own accord to rest on its owner's lap. Alex stared away then as his eyes checked her profile.

'Gentleman's Ridge,' she pronounced, 'and then the Jackpot.'

'If you insist.'

They headed up slowly. The long swatches of snow gleamed icy silver as if spread with a palette knife, huge and smooth, broken by the lines of skis and the flurry of their wake. The sunlight sparkled through on gentler, refreshing light spray whirling up around the downhill skiers.

'Tell me,' he said, 'does the guard ever come down?'

She gave him a good look over; her eyes shone.

'You have to earn it. . .'

It was pure grandeur. Blue shades of snow; majestic, frightening power. It needed deep heavy Wagner to go with it. They climbed higher and higher to where the air was thin. The snow was pristine pure, cakes and slices, ledges and valleys, ridges that bent soft and sheer: unbroken, but touched with black to remind you of the danger of the rocks beneath.

It was a different world within the clouds: the ridge was like walking a white rainbow high above the lilacs and blues. She headed down and jumped off the ridge into the canyon. The red of the skis flashed against the black and the white and the blue for a moment of primary beauty before she hit the powder with a gentle rush, and flew down ahead of him.

He lost her on the slopes but found her halfway down at the crossway of the Grand Junction, waiting for him. She seemed easy, freed by the exercise and the warmth. He'd seen many classically beautiful girls but her body was long and wonderful, and her soft laugh drew him in as he skied to a stop. He had known how her laugh would sound, he knew how her hair would spread on the pillow. She was a girl who made him remember his senses. He had begun to look for her cool and careless grace.

'So,' she said, the twinkle still in her eyes. 'What are they all up to?' Her eyes held laughter. She planted her poles in the snow, and pushed up her goggles. 'You can tell me, I'm a doctor!'

He smiled, but he had to deflect her.

'I don't know what you mean.'

'Oh come!' Her manner stayed light. 'Ruth knows you, and this fellow Kowolski and your mate, Hillaire. All in one place, it's too strange, and all pretending it's coincidence. Are you in on it?'

He took a breath. 'There's nothing to be in on.' And now he looked at her, keeping his eyes square on hers. 'Believe me, doctors need a rest too. You should know, being one yourself . . .'

He'd tried to bring the mood back and failed. He saw her close against him. She knew there was something and he wished he could have told her the truth. But the truth belonged to the old man.

For a moment she almost looked sad. Then the goggles went back, and she poled herself to the edge of the slope.

'I'll catch you later.'

And then she took off, making it clear she wished to ski alone. Liam headed down more slowly. When he reached the bottom of the mountain he half hoped to find her waiting, but her slim blue-clad figure was nowhere to be seen. It was three-thirty. The lift lines were closing and the late sun was softening contours. In the pub at the bottom of Little Nell he had a hot buttered rum while the sun went over the mountain. Then he joined the crowds that dispersed and headed back home.

Miki hit Chasers that night. There was so much on his mind and the house was empty. Calling the chauffeur, he headed downtown. It was always easy to sit with Jack. Jack had very few men friends, but Miki was one of them.

The first thing he saw as he came to the bottom of the

stairs was the girl sitting in his usual spot. And Jack had let her, knowing he was on his way. This had to be one very special lady.

Her legs went on for ever. Lounging in a big chair, holding court just like his friend, Montana's appeal was immediate. Her blonde hair glowed gold in the lamplight, her smile said that only the best would have her. And Miki had always been the best.

Jack and another guy were talking in relaxed fashion at the bar and the owner waved his arm and pointed at Montana, including her in the gesture. Their eyes met. On the floor Fanny was dancing hip-hop with a bunch of kids. She was laughing loudly and her dress, a red woollen mini studded with pearls and diamanté, glittered in the lights.

Miki needed to have her, to prove he still could. The feeling came over him with immediate and shocking intensity. There had been so much tension lately and Mochi was unearthly cool; this one was anything but. He needed a spectacular body to turn him on, a tigress in the flesh; a stranger with no emotional attachment.

'Hey, Miki.' The hand on his back was warm, the glass in his hand Miki's usual drink. 'Come along and meet Montana. She's my new girl.'

He smiled and bowed and she met his smile in a totally non-subservient way. She held out her hand as if she owned the joint.

'Do sit with me, Miki.'

He settled himself between them, the thought burning in his mind. He had to test it on somebody.

'Jack, let me ask you something. If you had a chance to father a child . . .'

'Now hold on . . .'

'No, this is entirely hypothetical.'

'As if – knowing you – you always have an angle. He always has an angle.' Montana smiled indulgently, but he had her interest at least.

'If you had a chance to father any child you wish, a child that would definitely make its mark on history, would you do so?'

Jack seemed a surprising choice for his confidence, but perhaps not so. As much as he was the 'keeper of secrets' he was also a moralist of sorts. Miki knew the man was a hedonist, but on 'human' subjects he seemed to be quite wise. And of course, he knew women.

'I wouldn't do it, not in any way at all.' He leaned back, cradling his drink. Around them the room buzzed with the tactile evening crowd.

'Why?'

'Because it would be unfair on the child. He would not be himself, not an original.'

This gave a new view of Jack. He was always painted in a careless vein, but it was self-created to hide the deeper man. Underneath, such a thing as morality was important to him. 'Morality, Miki,' he said, speaking his thoughts. 'You always have to remember that.'

'But if it was in a controlled experiment . . .'

'Miki, my old chum. The interesting thing about this is that though I cannot defend it, it is wrong. Forget it, old son. Have another drink and relax with the lovely Montana.'

Miki was not sure, but he was swayed by Jack. He saw what was there beneath the surface, and for that he trusted him. His inner knowledge that Mochi would not go for it was reaffirmed. And there was the rub. He knew suddenly then that if he was tugged in that direction he would deceive Mochi. Ultimately he was a coldly ambitious man. He would have his way once decided on; weighing everything in the balance first he would then act as he saw fit. Jack climbed to his feet to greet a new arrival, his rugged creased figure hugged by all and sundry. His laugh travelled across them and seemed to unite them as he walked away within a crowd. Montana caught Miki's eye and smiled.

Their expression held him; liquid black, and that pale sheet of hair. Tonight she wore a black dress that shivered like a snakeskin as she moved. It showed her bare shoulders and the long, sun-bronzed legs. She stood to get a fresh drink and towered over him. She was like a goddess, and her walk shifted the dress over her hips like nothing he had ever seen.

She knew who Miki was, though. A billionaire; shit.

Miki had always needed sex. It had been his release. Nothing could have been crueller than impotence for him. The doctors had said it was not impossible for him to regain his ability to make love, but it needed the emotional drive as well. A spark like a spark-plug. He was alone, tense and needing company; Montana was his ideal medicine. When she returned she sat a few feet away, giving him the space to join her or move. He liked her style. She wanted him to come to her. He stood up and walked across.

'May I join you?'

'Of course.' She grinned, showing a display of pearly teeth. 'Whatever the master says.'

'I don't believe that for a moment.'

He sat down, an old world elegance about him that she both admired and found enervating. She was giving off signals a mile a minute, and Miki's testosterone level was hotting up. He felt better than he had in months, and flexing his fingers found them fluid as before.

Soon they were involved in conversation, both fascinated by what they saw in the other.

'How did you get out here?'

'In a motorhome. We landed at Buttermilk.'

'A motorhome? Really.'

She had made a joke out of it, and it worked.

'With a girlfriend.'

'Ah. And you are now staying with Jack?'

'Temporarily.' She shifted her legs, and he heard the silky slide of stocking. 'Until I decide what to do.' She moved again. 'Would you like a drink? I'm going to get a refill.'

'Just coffee.'

She returned moments later, bearing a small tray. He admired the white gold shimmer of her hair, the line of her calves through the fine mesh of her stockings. As she leaned forward he could see the fullness of her breasts. She caught him looking and smiled.

'One lump, or two?'

He never took sugar. He held her eyes. 'Two, please.'

251

He still held her look as the crowd changed rhythm. Chiffon got up on stage to cheers of delight, and headed straight into a jam session. A long slow number that started with solo and no back-up, an earthy trembling cry of emotion. What an aphrodisiac. And such a little guy, so cute. She wanted to eat him up. Billions. She felt her skin tingle, and licked her lips with pleasure, her sultry eyes shining in the dark.

Miki could hear the sensuous purr and it turned him on like nothing on earth. Everyone was doing the 'does she, doesn't she' routine as Chiffon's manufactured body writhed around the mike. Miki's flatteringly intense look remained on Montana. There was something about oriental eyes, she decided; and the man was like a snake, his attention riveting, his quiet sure voice a magnet.

The number finished and Chiffon came off stage and into the arms of Freddie: the man who believed that everyone with money should have a fair crack of the whip in cosmetic surgery. They were old friends, though in fact their relationship was more bionic than social.

On the dance floor, they danced close. Freddie pinched her bum.

'I know where that bit went.'

She laughed, pouting her lips. Their secrets belonged to them. Her infectious laugh drifted over towards the bar where Jack Fenner was sitting. He was not speculating about her figure, he knew: she'd had everything done.

Another night at Chasers. They were much the same. In the end everyone reached the bar and told him their story; he was wondering whether it was not becoming a bit old hat. He was conscious of the two in the corner, whose eyes had not left each other.

But now Miki was standing, and he was giving directions.

Shit, he was asking Montana for a date, and the silly bitch was smiling, shaking her hair and nodding her head. As he left she looked up and smiled. Miki wanted to get to know her more, much more, but Jack, his friend and her protector, was on his way over fast. He eyes lowered as Jack made his way through the crowds, and she scribbled on a napkin and pressed the folded note into his hand. Her mouth said *call me*. Miki felt that he had made all the overtures; the sense of the chase was wearing. He was only to find out later that the plan had never been his.

In a lab in California, the glass at the long windows was broken carefully. A gloved hand reached in and pulled the catch open. Two shadowy figures snapped the security wires and climbed in. They knew just what they were doing.

Methodically, they began to wreck the place.

EIGHTEEN

In Chasers, Montana slid up behind Jack, who was sitting alone at the bar wearing a cowboy hat pushed on the back of his head. He had a worn chambray work shirt, sun-faded jeans and boots complete with spurs, though their jingle had never been heard beyond the streets of an Aspen mall.

'What are you reading?'

'Another pamphlet. Politically active meddling locals. Ban fur coats. Vote to wear or not to wear. Big deal. Who cares?'

'Clearly they do.'

'No, they don't, Montana. They're do-gooders. Pro-gay, pro-AIDS. They don't really care what it is, nor if it works. They're bored, that's all. This place is really about Lear jets and live lobster in January. Anything to be different. God forbid we're part of a crowd.'

'It's how you've made your money,' she said with wisdom. 'I shouldn't knock it, if I were you.'

'To be gay is not a sin, it's an option.'

'Here, it's a sin, not an option.'

He turned to her, and his eyes told her what she needed to know: she looked stunning.

'What have you done?'

'You like it, though.' She wore her hair in a quiff, like a teddy boy in negative. Very short, it emphasised her long neck and lovely face, and the body beneath it. Dark skin and white leather, black leggings and bright socks, and a black shirt with a motif. A canvas sports bag was slung over her shoulder, and the sable was dumped across the adjoining chair. It was never going back to its owner now.

'Miki Leng?' He knew Miki's taste, and tactics.

She fingered a bracelet.

'I've always like things small and Japanese. You know that.'

'Just take care.'

In the warning she heard a note; it was more than just words. Her answer was breezy. 'Relax, Jack. You've got to remember in life that everything reduces to grey. Just look at your washing filter.' She checked herself in the mirror over the bar. 'Christ, there's more tension in here than a psychiatric ward . . .'

He smiled.

'. . . you're normally the coolest dude in town. What gives?'

He circled his hands around his drink. 'I know the guy.'

'Yeah, well I'm planning on that as well.'

He tried to relax. It was her life. 'How are the lessons going?' he said, referring to her classes.

'Two kids have joined. The mother's a middle-class washout. Diamonds and minks make her salivate. She doesn't understand them at all, never will. She wants to invade them.'

'You do?'

'I do. I understand kids real well. I never grew up, you see.'

She grinned the infectious grin, and picked up the pamphlet he'd been studying.

'AIDS is a leveller,' he said, looking at it too. 'The famous die. The famous are as real as us.'

She looked at him closely, placing it back down.

'You *are* famous.'

He fingered the pages. 'Fame is a relative issue. You only assume I am because you're not. If you were, I'd seem ordinary.'

'You're mentally corrosive, Jack. You burn my batteries.' She slid off the bar stool. 'I'd call you infamous.'

He sat without moving, still hunched over his drink, his eyebrow raised. 'We're two of a kind.'

'We're survivors, Jack.'

He looked at them in the mirror together, at the arched eyebrow that was trademark Jack. 'The eyebrow's famous anyway.'

Beside him, she grinned. 'Like my teeth.'

'Like your ass.'

She howled and smacked his butt as she pranced out. In the bar, he watched her go. Rowan greeted her at the door, heading in with a hot collection of socialites just arrived. He jollied Jack along with a fun new story, his conquest of a girl they both thought unobtainable, and a hit off his joint – smoking was frowned on, but drugs were OK in Chasers – but for once, Jack seemed distracted; he had expected her to climb right into his bed.

Freddie was tucked in a corner now, talking to Fanny Mason, while Studley chatted to the ever-vibrant Chiffon. Freddie'd got bad news from the City; it was worse than ever. The last pay-up was going to clean him out, even his fee for the conference.

'I invested and I was badly hit.'

'Poor love.'

'This is the last holiday and I'm not going to tell her. I daren't. I was a Lloyd's name, Fanny. Now I'm being bounced out of every club in London.'

'Better change to Coutts, love. They don't bounce anyone.'

The blizzard spun around the car. And any speculation Montana might have been making about Jack was forgotten as she arrived at Miki's house in the car that had been sent to collect her. He had not come himself. She was aware of the slight, but not fazed by it; she had faith in herself. It was a revelation as they headed up the drive to see how the truly rich lived. She had had no idea and it took her breath away. As she stepped out of the car her eyes took it all in, her lips parted wide, and she looked at last to the chauffeur as if to include him.

The man, Juan, was completely expressionless, even as she smiled at him, as she hefted her bag on to her shoulder. He merely pointed up the steps and got back in the car. Montana, her boot on the first shallow step that the committee had used daily, stepped up to quite a different sort of meeting. The front door, eight feet high and a solid piece of oak, swung open slowly as she approached. There was no one to be seen.

Slowly, Montana went in.

The house was aubergine and black on entry; a palace of glass and rustic beams, arched ceilings and sprinkled lighting. A deep rose red carpet lay over the black marble floor. In the distance she could see reflections that danced on the surface of a pool set amongst a jungle of foliage. There was a wall of glass and a spectacular view. Underwater lighting threw translucent patterns on the walls. A telescope stood on the balcony. Soft music played throughout the house as she was taken into a drawing room by a manservant. There she waited.

The room was white, crystal white, dominated by a huge window: snow and mountains seemed to pull her into them and enter the womb of the house itself. She stepped down, fascinated. Against a purpled orange lush sky, tactile blue-white mountains dominated the view, with the deep bowl of the valley of Aspen and the soft golden star-like lights of town glowing beneath. There were no lights in the room itself, but two huge candles burned in the shadowed corners in black iron cathedral stands. The ice-cold mountain and the warm and comfortable room: it was eerie.

Miki joined her, silently crossing the room and taking her coat to slip it from her shoulders. The manservant appeared from nowhere and from a small ebony table began to serve them: caviare that was all about sensation, exploding tiny filaments on the tongue; Miki signalled her to drink an unfamiliar warm liquor; oysters sliding down her throat; slivers of avocado, and tiny morsels of *coquilles St Jacques*.

'You had no trouble getting here.'

'None at all.' She was driven, Chrissake.

Politeness because of the servant, Lee, made the food more poignant, their looks hotter, more intense.

'. . . have more of this one . . . where do you come from . . .'

Montana lost her cheekiness, overcome. The manservant was dressed in black and walked on quiet feet, and never said a word, seeming to know what his master required. Miki watched her reaction.

'He has no tongue.'

'But he has ears,' she said.

'And eyes . . .'

The word lingered with his look. He came to stand beside her, firelight and candles glinting on their lips and eyes that spoke it all. He led her to the door and slid it wide, stepping outside with her. Below a river burbled over warmed rocks; at the edge of the terrace a single Christmas flower bloomed in the snow.

He bent his hand into the snow, snapping the precious flower between his fingers. He held it to her.

'But there was only one.'

'Another will bloom.'

'My grandfather said never wait for bus or woman. Another along in a minute.'

'That's more Americana than Confucius, I'd say.'

'Perhaps.'

Humour filled the moment; always a prelude to sex. Both knew where they were headed and it made it far more erotic, an elixir more potent than anything she had known to date.

'Do you like beautiful things, Montana?'

'Yes.'

'Come along.'

Miki wasted little time. He was elemental in his approach, and it included a tour of the house. He wanted her to be completely spellbound, and then he would be master. Miki was an expert; it was a tactile seduction of the mind and taste. His silence was an aphrodisiac, the sumptuous house both temple and altar prepared for an offering of herself.

As they arrived at the exotic setting of the black marble hot tub lushly surrounded by its rich green jungle, he dimmed a switch and tiny stars studded the black walls all around. He looked up and gave a gentle clap, and very slowly the huge roof began to slide back. Montana gasped as the snow fell in an opaque sheet around them, tiny crystalline flakes settling on their shoulders. On her lashes and her tongue as she poked it out to taste the melting crystals.

'Would you like to try it?' he said, pointing at the tub.

Montana held his look and slowly stripped, discarding her clothes with no haste, but without the bump and grind of which she was quite capable. This was a graceful undressing, as if she prepared for him. Quite naked, she let him see her for a full moment before she stepped down into the exquisite warmth of the tub, slowly letting its blackness eat up her long golden body.

Now the snow fell soft and steady, a diaphanous white curtain with no wind to stir it. The visible swell of her breasts met his eyes above the waterline. The water's heat and the contrasting sensation of the icy snow sent a *frisson* along her skin that left her gasping with pleasure. His eyes darkened as he saw, drinking her in. Water jets began to throb against her, touching her just where she was most vulnerable. Montana could hardly breathe as his eyes trained on her, watching. He waited until the air was charged with her need.

'Come along, now, they are ready for you.'

She did not ask who; nor did he touch her as he handed her a soft robe and she followed him, entering a room of semi-darkness and feeling mildly surprised to be met by a smiling, also silent girl, and led gently forward to a table.

Miki was quite ruthless. It had led him to the top, and then some. He had decisions to make and sex had always cleared his head. He had made the first of them when he had seen her in the club, and had known what sort of girl she was exactly. He had to fire both her pleasure and his before he entered her. This ritual was his prelude.

A man joined the girl, and invited Montana to lie down. They stroked her with oil, gently whispering over her pliant skin at first and then approaching in swirls and finally touching the points so aroused by her sensations. The woman was dressed as a geisha, the man in an oriental black robe; both had impersonal expressions, but both of them had hands that knew everything about her body. Miki had stood in the shadows of the room and listened to her growing sighs, then moans of pleasure. Montana had responded far more to the woman's touch, though they were equal in their exploration.

A soft movement and they were gone.

'Now I know you,' he said at her side. He wore a black and silver kimono and it suited him. 'Bend over the bed, Montana.'

He stood behind her, and she saw his robe slip to the floor.

'Spread your legs. Do as I tell you, don't look, don't touch.'

She laid herself over and spread her legs, waiting for him. He entered from behind and she got an immense and pleasurable shock. She had no idea it would be like this. A mirror would have told her the truth. She was so stoned, and crying out so hard with her delight that she never heard the buzz.

Just as well: a second-hand dildo with a sucking action simply wasn't her style. The little guy couldn't get it up, as she was to tell her close friend, Jack, much much later, when she found it abandoned in the bathroom afterwards.

But it was a helluva way to get round two out of an old bloke.

As she found out, sore but happy, returning to the Hotel Leonore two hours later, with $5,000 plumping up her handbag.

NINETEEN

David Kowolski received the phone call in his hotel suite. He put down the receiver, and went straight to the window as if he had hoped to see Jackie and the kids up on the slopes waiting for his signal.

There was nothing of course but rooftops, snow and the ever-present mountain, dotted with tiny figures. His family was somewhere out there up on the slopes, and he could not let them know about the emergency.

His team had tracked him down; they knew he'd respond. He was of serious mien, a professor of deeds as well as morals. From a Polish ghetto he'd had to use his ability to get to the top, but he had not forgotten his poor beginnings – he dealt with real people, he knew street life. He was an eminent specialist in his field, and an expert in medical ethics. What Aspen represented was anathema to him. He was all for life in its purest form. He was going but he was worried about the moral issue in his absence. There was one person who immediately sprang to mind.

'Can I come in?'

Ruth had opened the door to the Lindstroms' suite; her calm face changed when she saw his worry. The door opened wide.

'Of course . . . whatever's wrong . . . ?'

He stepped in, explaining. 'Ruth, I've got a real problem back at my lab –' Behind he saw Wilhelm turn at the window. 'Hello, Wilhelm.'

'Hello, David. What's up?' He came casually across.

'Oh, trouble, trouble. Terrible trouble.' He threw his hands in the air. 'Someone broke in and smashed up my laboratory, ruined everything . . .'

'Oh no!'

Ruth took his hands in hers.

'Equipment, experiments, everything. It's all ruined.'

'David, I am sorry.' Wilhelm stood above him as he sank to the sofa, shaking his head in distress. 'Is there anything we can do?'

'Nothing.' He addressed them both, but his attention kept returning to her. 'Look, Ruth. I have to go back. My team need me,' he explained gently. 'I was never able to delegate too well, now I'm the only one who can put it all back together . . .'

And with one of my students watching how you do it, thought Wilhelm. *Perfect . . .*

'I've heard your arguments,' he went on, their hands still linked, now in urgency from him. 'Despite your natural interest, my dear, you're for the moral voice . . .'

'Absolutely David. I'm for genetic repair, not creation.'

'I'm asking you to hold for the moral voice in my absence.' David's eyes took in Wilhelm quickly, and danced back. 'Both of you. Unfortunately Jackie's halfway up a mountain with the kids, and I'm not sure which one. I've left a note for her, but would you explain?'

'Of course.'

'I'll straighten out things as best I can.' He shook his head again.

'How long will you be gone?' Ruth's voice was worried.

'Ah, well that depends . . . I won't know until I assess the damage. Apparently it's pretty bad. Maybe they did not know what they were looking for exactly, if anything. It seems to be just vindictive, pure vandalism.'

'Someone who'd heard about the experiments,' Ruth ventured gently. She turned her worried face to her husband, and he returned her look with one of suitable concern.

David made a face. 'Possibly. It was why we toned it down in the press.' His sad eyes took her in.

'I'm so sorry,' she said again, and held his hands tight.

'Yes, well.' The briskness was back. He patted her hands and stood. 'Now, there is just one more problem. My notes . . .'

Wilhelm felt himself step forward mentally.

'Yes?'

'I only plan to be gone a day or so, but,' he shook his head, 'the conference has to continue. There are not many days left to cover all the subjects. I really should leave my notes for Hillaire's talk-through tomorrow . . .'

'You could leave them with us.' Wilhelm cleared his throat. 'They'll be safe enough.' He gave a half-smile at Ruth, who smiled back.

'Absolutely, David, we could keep them for you . . .'

'Oh, no, no . . .!' He shook his head again. 'You are too kind, but it's not necessary. Really no problem. No,' he stood up. 'I shall leave the notes with my good friend, Hillaire.' He spoke with sarcastic humour; their views were not necessarily known to coincide. The thought amused him. 'With instructions to select and deliver just as I would myself.'

'Well, if you wish, but . . .' Wilhelm held his smile.

David closed it out with a wave of his hand. 'I know you are concerned about safety, and quite rightly. Better in the hotel safe, but what about our work? This is so important.' His voice grew more serious. 'My notes are very relevant to the conference and today holds another big debate. I cannot leave the meeting high and dry. No, I've decided to entrust them to Hillaire until my return in the next day or so. He'll know what to do.'

He smiled, and thrust out his hand.

'Well, I must be going.'

'I'll go with you.' Ruth turned to Wilhelm, who stepped forward as well.

'I'll come.'

Ruth turned to him, as she took her coat from the chair. 'I thought you had an appointment,' she said, her forehead creased with confusion. 'Didn't you say?'

'Oh yes.'

'So, I won't be long.' Her hand was comfortably on David's back as they went out together. 'I would like to go along for the ride with you, talk things over,' she was saying as her husband watched impotently from behind her. 'We haven't had a chance . . .'

Alex had left their house until last. Fabrice had made Christmas puddings for all her friends and asked her to deliver them. Looking at her list, as if she needed to, she was in a dual state of mind. Too often, Liam popped into her consciousness; Hillaire's address had burned a hole in the paper.

Driving down the winding streets, looking for the signposts, she felt her heart hammer as she saw Riverside Street. She had been sorry after she'd left the mountain so fast hurt by his lack of confidence in her, but had checked herself often later in the following hours – after all, he had showed loyalty: that at least. She'd transmuted it into humour; her journalistic skills were piqued, and what else – that was the sobering thought. She had chosen this moment to confide the truth about her past. She knew how much she was looking forward to his company.

As she drove up, another car was standing at the kerb. Long, sleek and black, she did not recognise it, but the men were familiar and it was too late to turn back. David Kowolski was talking on the porch as she arrived and she could not leave. They had seen her, but she felt awkward because it was clear from their glances that she had arrived at a bad time. No chance to talk to Liam here. Damn. Why hadn't she come here first? He might just have been alone.

She stepped out, seeing their eyes all stray to her. Instantly she was conscious of tension as she proceeded with the informal visit, opening and shutting the gate and walking up the path to where they stood collectively silent as if awaiting something.

It was Liam who moved first, though not hastily. He ambled down the steps and walked to her, hands deep in the pockets of his parka.

'Are we little Red Riding Hood today?'

She looked at the basket over her arm. 'Oh, that.' She laughed, lifting the red chequered cloth. 'Fabrice's idea of occasion. She's made Christmas puddings for all of you,' she said lamely, feeling like the gatecrasher at a party. His eyes were shadowed and she could not read them, but the tilted smile was there.

'I'd invite you in, but we're kind of busy . . .'

'Oh, of course.' She looked past him to the scientist. He was dressed for travel, a briefcase in his hand, with his initials stamped in the corner. As he turned in whispering conversation with Hillaire, the gold print caught the sun and gleamed.

'Shall I take it?' he was asking, amused by her instant curiosity.

She brought her attention back. He seemed to stand on guard, but in the most casual and friendly way, and though she could not take offence it was nonetheless quite clear he was barring the way to further pleasantries, yet not without regret.

She kept her voice cool. 'I wanted to talk to you.'

'What about?'

She had his interest. She could feel it, as surely as she could feel the tension on the porch, a discussion that had moments of raised voices. 'About something important to me,' she said.

She looked into his eyes, and saw – something. Only for a moment, and it was gone.

'Of course,' he said quietly. 'How about later? Over a cup of hot chocolate. Sorry it can't be now, I've got to hold the fort whilst Hillaire and David go to the airport.' She saw Hillaire look her way; though distant, she could feel the dark enquiry in his eyes. Her curiosity would have to take a back seat. He wanted Liam to get rid of her. But his unhurried protégé was keeping her. 'Shall we say four, outside the Wheelers Opera House? There's a café near there. It's quiet.'

A man ran past, an oddball in tights, jogging bare to the waist, his gear in two large bum bags; he wore a brightly coloured bandana, neon glasses and headphones and gave an air of being totally in a world of his own. Brightly coloured plumes flared from his waist as he loped on by.

'God,' she said.

'Yep, they're all here.'

And they both laughed, watching him go. As their look

came back the warmth stayed. It was a moment neither wanted to break. 'Well,' she said at last. 'I've got to go.' She turned away.

'Alex?'

'Yes?'

'The cake.'

'Oh!' She laughed, and lifted it out. 'It weighs a ton. But I guess it's good. Benny cooked it. It's a pudding.'

'Right.' He took it. 'If it's anything like the other day . . .'

'. . . it's bound to be good.'

'And full of calories. Fabrice likes people to *eat*.'

'Yes. Well, see you later.' Pleasantries; she found herself wanting anything but. The tension was as alive between them as between the men on the porch, but so different. The moments spoke volumes. She saw the line of his lips and how they sat; she'd got to know that little quirk far too quickly and watched his lip lift now in a half-smile, the level raking eyes looking deep into her. She wanted them to see her, what she was; to see what he would think when he heard her story.

Beyond him, she saw the Polish doctor hand his briefcase to Hillaire, not letting go as he gave a final admonishment. The initials DK winked in the sunshine, and the moment seemed to click in frames as if she was in a film, or a time warp. Words drifted out over the still air, accompanied by a chuckle and a handshake.

'I was always a fan of Roosevelt . . .'

'. . . ah, there you have the edge! I was too young, an embryonic refugee . . . I only knew that American ice-cream was the best thing in the world . . .'

More laughter.

Liam had not left the path and was watching her go intently, and as she tried to read the message in his eyes she briefly wished she had taken more trouble with her appearance, but the other more arrogant side of her said no: this time she wanted to be appreciated for herself. Unsure, she had been burned once already, she was too shy to hold on to his look. Breaking it, she raised her hand to him and headed for her car, warmed with an inner glow as if she'd had a swig

266

of brandy. On the porch, the two men separated and started to walk down towards the waiting car.

Backing up, her inner smile evaporated as looking into her driving mirror she saw into the shadows of the limousine. There in the back, quietly reading, sat Ruth. She had not announced herself, and now her eyes were on Alex, watching. It said she was not a part of this.

'I've left my notes because you're going to need them, Hillaire, but I challenge you to respect the moral voice . . .'

'. . . I called the members of the conference specifically with adverse viewpoints in mind, David,' he reminded him. 'Medicine versus ethics versus morality versus discovery and science. It's all part and parcel . . .'

The car had drawn into the kerb at the airport and the two of them were in heated exchange. As yet David had made no move to leave, but his hand lay on the door handle. The chauffeur stood impassively outside, waiting for a signal.

'I wonder. You're a devious bastard,' David said. 'Try to remember that as Miki Leng brandishes seductive promises in your face. You've always been so goddamn ambitious. It isn't everything, Hillaire.' Accusing him in this way he was quite unafraid to stand up to the autocratic chairman. 'You're too easy to seduce, to my mind. And far too good at seducing. Are you coming with me?'

Hillaire paused. 'You go on ahead. I'll follow.'

David smiled to Ruth. 'I'll be in touch.'

Now he left, and Hillaire looked to Ruth, his departing words floating on the air between them. She was saying nothing, nor did she have to. To him, she was as seductive as anything Aspen had to offer, and it was his own infamously ambitious personality that had caused him to lose her so many years ago; now he knew. He felt her thoughts.

As David walked away from the car she turned her face to him, shadowed within the elegant car. The soft smell of leather mingled with her perfume. With sudden clarity, he saw her again at the conference, unafraid to voice her feelings, her body half rising in her seat in protest against the unfairness of life.

'You're sentimental, Ruth,' he said suddenly.

'And that's a vice?'

'No,' he said softly. 'Quite the opposite.'

She studied him.

'Did you ask me to join your team on my merit alone, Hillaire?'

He felt her gentleness. Alone in the car together a very provocative atmosphere had built up. A long moment passed. This time he was determined to kill it, not only because of her words. She had to know her priority in his mind. The rest: well . . . she was married, after all. He had to remember that.

'I told you before, you're the best in your field.' He put his hand on the latch. 'You have to believe that, Ruth, or you're no good to us, or yourself.' The day rushed in. Outside he bent his head down. 'I have business overnight in New York. Take the car back, I'll see you first thing in the morning.'

She watched him walk off, the wind blowing the tails of his coat. He pulled it tight over his backside in an old and suddenly painfully familiar gesture. He was a young man again, and she was watching him leave.

He did not look back. She signalled the driver and they left.

Wilhelm was where she had left him, in their hotel suite. A tray of coffee and biscuits stood untouched on the table. As she came in, bringing a small dash of cold air with her, he rose to his feet.

'How did it go?'

'Oh,' she smiled, drawing off her gloves. 'Fine.'

'The case?'

'What?'

'The briefcase. Did he give Hillaire the notes?'

'Yes.' She ran her fingers through her hair, and sloughed off her jacket, throwing it over a chair. 'He did.'

Wilhelm could hardly stand her lack of urgency.

'Well, and what did he do with it?'

She shrugged. 'He kept it, of course.'

'With no security?' His voice held incredulity.

'Why not?' Now she was looking at him properly, sensing his concern, a crease on her own previously untroubled brow.

He pushed his hands into his pockets, lifted his shoulders. 'Seems a bit risky.'

She smiled, understanding. 'Oh, Wilhelm. It's no problem. The briefcase has a combination lock.'

'Someone could –'

She came across and placed her hands on his arms.

'David has a sense of humour, Wilhelm. Not only the lock, but inside a laptop computer with a secret access code. A secret to die for . . . nothing could be safer.' She was smiling as he looked down into her face and the room seemed to still for him as he asked her the question:

'Did he tell it to you?'

'No, Wilhelm.' She looked him in the eye. 'Only to Hillaire . . .'

TWENTY

'Hillaire . . .?'

'David. How's it going? Are you on your way back?'

'A terrible mess here, Hillaire. Somebody certainly knew how to hurt us. All our lab equipment is destroyed, thousands of dollars' worth. We've got insurance but it's going to take time to set up the experiments again. Besides, my research team need me here; they're a sensitive bunch, falling apart right now.'

'I understand completely.' He checked his disappointment. 'What have the police said?'

'Oh, usual stuff, taking notes and such, trying to find the perpetrator. They think we're all mad, and when we try to explain what's missing we have to spell it all out. It's taking hours, and they're not too interested. It's Christmas, lots of break-ins and robberies, what are we to them?'

'They don't realise the importance, of course.'

'No. But listen to the worst, Hillaire. They knew what they were looking for. They took the culture . . .'

'My God . . .'

'Yes.'

'What stage was it at?'

'The most vulnerable, I'm afraid. In the wrong hands, it simply won't make it. It's all we can hope for.' He sighed, his voice sounding flat, while Hillaire's worked furiously overtime.

'David . . . if they knew what they were looking for, surely –'

'Yes, you don't need to spell it out. Somewhere right now, they'll have to implant or lose it. Look,' he said, as if hurried and unwilling to talk further, 'I don't know how my lot got hold of me. I did a disappearing act for the sake of the press *et al*. But I'm staying, I'm needed here. Only I can get it all moving again. The conference will have to go on without me. Maybe, God willing, I can clear this whole mess up . . .'

'What about your notes? Can I carry on for you?'

He paused and thought it through. 'They're not for general viewing, Hillaire.'

'No, of course.'

'Despite what I said yesterday, I trust you. Especially now, you can't let me down. Think carefully, Hillaire. Everything I said yesterday was true. We are responsible for the new world. Us alone. Screw this up and we create a master race out of control, with all the wrong people in command. You know what I'm talking about. Put that feverish excitement about progress out of your head and remember progress is for the positive, and must be handled with expert care.'

'I'll go carefully. Can you get back in a couple of days?'

'I'll try. Perhaps within the week would be more realistic. I'm leaving Jackie and the kids to enjoy themselves.'

'Fair enough. I'll look in on them. Any advice on the notes?'

'Pick only the most salient points, and do not elaborate on my research.'

'Right. I have to go back into surgery. Miki Leng's wife . . .'

'Ah, yes.'

'I'll ring you later, before I go back down. I'm flying down first thing in the morning . . .'

Hillaire strode back down the corridor towards the operating room, then slowed as if in thought, his fingers pulling at his chin with worry. There was a phone box right beside him. He fiddled for change, dialled the number of the Jerome in Aspen. He was put through to their hotel suite. It picked up on the third ring.

'*Ruth . . .?*'

'Hillaire.' Wilhelm's voice was cool and guarded. 'Where are you?'

'Oh, hello, Wilhelm. In New York.' His emotions cooled off a little at the sound of his voice, her husband. 'Look, David's lab's taken a helluva hit. They've stolen the culture . . .'

'Oh, Jesus, Hillaire.' He could hear the man's worry in his voice and realised the success of their mission. His hard eyes held a pale glow. 'How's the lab itself?'

'Totalled.'

'Shit. Where do we go from here?'

'Alone.'

'Without the rest of his information?'

'I have it.' His eyes on the theatre, he saw the concerned face of the nurse look out, see him, and signal him to come. 'We'll progress without him.' The eyes that met hers were dark and intense; he raised a hand to say he'd be there. 'I have to play both sides from now on, Wilhelm, the moralist and the progressive. What do you think of that?'

'You'll manage.' He wiped his mouth with the flat of his hand.

'I wonder how his lab found him?' mused Hillaire. 'He left no address.'

'Beats me.'

'Well, excuse me, they're calling me for theatre. I have to go.'

'Hillaire —'

'But there was an answering buzz only, the man had gone. Wilhelm called Sandford directly.

'I just heard from Hillaire. I gather it went off all right . . .'

The flat vowels monotoned down the line. 'They stole a couple of things, made it look like a random burglary, but the important stuff was all plugged into the power supply. The idiots destroyed what was left, which is a pity because we could have done with it — still it can all be done again.' The well-buried pure scientist in Wilhelm turned over in his stomach. 'Bowman's up in New York, is he?' Sandford chuckled. 'Soon be in hand then. My boys searched for notes, but there were none. Kowolski's assistants either take them home, or he's got them on him.'

'He hasn't got them on him.'

There was a new note in the voice. 'Where are they?'

'In his briefcase.'

'And where's that?'

'He left it behind. With Hillaire.'

'Can you get it?'

'I'm going to guess not. Hillaire's not going to let it out of his sight, he's probably taken it with him to New York, and even if not, as for breaking and entering, I'm not your man. Besides, he's got a young fellow staying in his house who does *not* have a routine life. He's in and out like a yo-yo.'

The voice ran cold, telling of a man not to be trifled with. 'We have to have those notes, Wilhelm. It's not enough to just get the culture. With Kowolski now out of the way, our oriental friend is next. And Miki's financing is the next important thing. But we want to know how to do the experiments now we've destroyed Kowolski's lab.'

Wilhelm paused. 'Did you find the eggs?'

'Yes.'

There was a satisfaction there, and Wilhelm's heart stopped.

'They're being well looked after . . .'

The lab's rookie male nurse heard it first.

Sunlight was blocked by a reedy paper-thin light that fed down between the buildings. The high window was dusty and closed and showed the bricks of another building two feet away. Mochi was wheeled into the next-door room and he caught a glance of her as the bed smoothed by with the squeak of rubber wheels. He looked at her, her pale face turned to his. She smiled and was gone.

In this tiny anteroom, a row of green surgical gowns and overshoes hung on pegs above a wooden bench. Through the next door which had a round protective glass window like a porthole, the room was lined with large freezers, oxygen monitors, a water purifier, and a battery of hi-tech machinery. Thick pipes ran across the ceiling to a duct in the wall.

In the lab there were freezers and the low hum of motors. The door had a heavy rubber seal around it. As he opened it, there was a strong current of cool air: the purifier made a barrier for germs. It cooled the sweat in the fine down of his upper lip.

In the next room, lit by a single low-wattage red bulb, it was very hot and there was a sour reek of chemicals. Microscopes were ranged on the surfaces. The high steel cabinets and hi-tech machinery there cost thousands of dollars.

It was towards one of these machines that he was now moving, bent on a course of action that would change the life of many, many people. Now it had to be stolen. Now. It was the opportune moment: the incubator had done its work. They had seen the first cleavage and the egg was healthy. Embryo transfer would take place within the hour. It had been fertilised, and it was clear. He had taken care of the senior nurse whose job it was to man this precious division; a strong laxative mixed with her food had kept her home with the runs on this very important day for his own special project.

In this corner lay the extra incumbent, brought in with great care under the cover of dark and with the help of his own pass-key. The two doctors who had entered with their cabinet on wheels were unknown to him, and remained so.

He'd been promised ten thousand. It would pay off the loft conversion and he would marry Elaine, but he had a conscience. He knew from the records how much the oriental girl needed this. He'd been told. Rich women had it all, he'd told himself that. But Mochi's smile had jabbed at him: a look of such pleasure and need it had unsettled him. He thought of Elaine and his future too. The pictures shifted in his mind – did he want it built on this? But *ten thousand*.

Now, now was the time to switch the dishes.

In the next room was the great man himself: Professor Hillaire Bowman. He was no fool, and renowned for the tremendous care with which he handled his patients. He would oversee the operation: any moment he would be wondering why there was a delay . . .

Ten thousand.

He saw them walking up the aisle; he saw Elaine's proud smile; but as she lifted her veil and turned to look at him he saw the pale and peaceful face of the oriental girl smile trustingly in her place.

Thing was, he knew the inside story on both women in here today for embryo transfer; knew both were healthy, knew about the third dish as well, knew what it contained. His heart fluttered;plans had changed. He was no longer to swap hers into the black lady but to implant the contents of the third dish into the oriental. He did not know why; he had not asked. The oriental girl's egg would be taken back to some place in Wyoming and implanted there. It was diabolical, but . . .

Ten thousand. So easy. No one would ever know it was him.

He opened the door of the incubator.

In Wyoming, at the converted chicken farm, Mrs Carinic was rushed into surgery.

Her baby was due.

Outside, a very special cargo was arriving, and in her bedroom, the healthiest of the old ladies was being given the de-luxe treatment as she was being pre-opped.

'You're a very special lady,' said the nurse, as she pushed the syringe into the woman's well-fleshed arm.

They rang the owner of the clinic right away once it was all over. It had gone smoothly, so far.

He'd want to know; he'd said so.

He wanted the baby to grow despite the switch. It would ensure their silence and their infinite cooperation should anything happen meanwhile.

TWENTY-ONE

Sandford received Juan Fernandez in his study. A little cash and he had hit paydirt. He knew the ranch was impressive and would intimidate and influence the Mexican chauffeur.

'Juan Fernandez.' He looked nervous.

'You are Mr Leng's chauffeur.'

'Thas right.'

'And he trusts you completely?'

'He tell me to always say nothing. So I say nothing. I pick up, I drop. I open doors, I drive. I watch, I listen, but I say nothing.'

'But you see a lot and hear a lot, eh Fernandez?'

'That's right too, *señor*.' He looked around at the closed door behind him. He went no further.

Sandford sighed and reached into his drawer. It was always the same; how did these people learn so fast? Leaning over his desk on his elbows he counted out $1,000, starting at one and folding them down slowly. He saw the greed leap into the man's eyes.

'This is an instalment. You will work for me further. Tell me what you know. I need a hook on this man, Fernandez. You understand.'

'Sure. My wife and I, Maria, we work for the master two years. No pay rise. But is good job.' He was clearly nervous of being found out, and did not want to lose it. That was good. It was a cushy job with the Lengs. But so much money was too provocative in a place like Aspen.

Sandford smiled at him as if he liked him, but in fact he despised him. 'Go on . . .'

'Last night I pick up a girl for Mr Leng. Mrs Leng is out of town.'

'Go on.'

'She is from Jack Fenner's bar, Chasers. She work there.'

This was interesting. Sandford leaned forward. 'Not the tall blonde one?'

'Yes, her. She stay quite a while. She spend time in hot tub, and then have massage. She like the girl quite a lot. Mr Leng take her into bedroom after. He use machines on her, I know about this because my wife tell me when she clean up.'

'Machines.'

He swallowed. 'Mr Leng is impotent. He and his wife no longer make love. He cannot. But he have this machine.' He described a penile attachment of a good nine inches. 'It is tube, with small motor, for men of his problem. It suck up the penis inside and he can make love.'

'But not with his wife?' Sandford was tempted to laugh. This was too much.

'No, she would be shock. He treat her like delicate, like flower. He call her Orchid. No, he keep this for moment such as this girl from the club, Montana Marr.'

'What d'you suppose she thought of that?'

'She think it great. He go on for hour, never go down. She cry with pleasure. He tell her not to look. She think he great stud.'

'How do you know this?'

'All rooms have intercom. We use it in kitchen, because we are bored, *señor*.'

Sandford roared with laughter. A plastic dildo with a battery pack; what a way to get an erection! He almost felt like ringing him and asking for the manufacturer! Well, I never. What a hoot. He simply could not imagine the superior elegant little oriental getting to grips with this. But what a handle on the man. He would never want this to get out.

He reached into his desk, and yanked out another bundle.

'Here.' He slapped it across the desk watching the man's face split into a smile. 'You've earned it. This is the most fun I've had in years.'

'And the tape, sir.' He fished in his pocket as he replaced the space with the money. 'I think you like this too.'

He had been right. Hillaire, Ruth and David: he had their conversation taped. And then the two alone: Hillaire and

Ruth. He listened to the mellow note in their voices and did not have to put too much together. He had Wilhelm too, now. He smiled broadly and leaned back in his chair, his square dark face florid with humor. Little Fernandez had done well; what a lesson in management. The black eyes under their deep hoods snapped with dark laughter.

All interesting stuff. He had wound his net in and caught all but the slipperiest big fish. He needed something on Kowolski but the man was gone, and his lab was clean. He needed some serious bait to catch a fish like Miki, and he thought he had it.

'How do you think he feels about his wife?'

'He scared of his wife. Scare to lose her. She a very beautiful lady, very calm, very ... cool. They very distant with each other, but I think he love her very much. Just never show it. He expect everyone to be reserve, even her ...'

So he had been right: Mochi was the weak link. He felt the thrill of discovery and leaned back, his eyes on the nervous Hispanic.

From his eyes, he could tell there was more.

'Yes?' he said, prompting. 'There is something else.'

Fernandez twisted his hands together.

'Señor ... I have to collect Mrs Leng today. While her husband is out of town. He fly to coast for business, just a few hours.'

Sandford sat back wondering for a moment.

'No, Juan. I have a better plan. You bring Mrs Leng to me ...'

Now he had them both in his pocket. With his hold over Mochi, he had Miki too. Whichever way he looked, he had a winner; it was too amusing.

This time he had really tricked them both. A cloned egg, a culled egg for his Messiah.

He got back on the phone.

The storm that had affected the rest of New York did not affect Mochi. Stepping out into a swirl of snow and ice, she felt sunshine in her heart. She was delighted for the moment

278

with a secret that was hers alone, though the doctor had told her this could be her only chance. Of course, there could be other chances, but who knew – each one was so precious, and this egg was healthy. Miki's terminal illness also made them short of time. She was so sure everything was all right. She telephoned the pilot *en route* to the airport, and told him to get ready. She was going home. Conscious of the doctor's pleasure for her, his instructions to take care of herself, and the fact that Miki had already been informed, she headed home to Aspen. He would be longing to see her, and she had never felt so proud, and good. She would arrive early and surprise him.

She stepped off the plane in Aspen, happy. A spring in her step, she headed for the taxi rank, lost in her own world. She had caught an earlier plane in order to surprise Miki, and intent on her homecoming was hurrying to find a taxi as the midnight blue Range Rover drove up in front of her.

The passenger door opened and the ponytailed man spoke to her from the shadows.

'Climb in, Mrs Leng. We have something to discuss. No, don't look around, it concerns your husband, and your visit to . . . the *clinic* . . .'

Despite the tension he could see around her eyes and in her manner as she looked around before climbing in, Sandford looked at her admiringly, up close realising his obsession at last. He was immediately jealous of Miki. He would love to have possessed her, obedient and perfect, bearing a perfect baby, unblemished, hand-picked – *chosen*. The petite Japanese girl had caught him because of her beauty; her face was pale, but perhaps it was simply her delicate colouring. Hit her early was his ploy. Now he had her in his car and before he was out of the airport he was already halfway through the story:

'. . . I have been very fair, in fact, Mrs Leng – may I call you Mochi? – I know this is a tense time for you. I have not told you before partly because I do not want to endanger your child . . .'

How he had manipulated her life, a puppet on his strings

as she entrusted her precious cargo to the staff of a New York clinic, how her body had been used and invaded as he wished. Now her pleasure had slipped away to a dark place never to return; he had swapped the egg with that of an unknown woman – kept it – replaced it – what? Russian roulette, and he wasn't telling . . .

'. . . this is just to let you know you're mine.'

'Blackmail.' She drew her coat closer. Inside its winter warmth she shivered uncontrollably. But he was not abducting her, he was threatening her as they drove into town along familiar streets and it was far more frightening. 'How do I know you are telling the truth?'

'I don't play games, or take chances. Ask tomorrow after the young lab assistant who was there. This is a family concern, Mrs Leng, but if you want proof of my intentions, do this.'

She stared ahead through the window, not wanting to look at him, at his heavy flat face and thick black brows and staring eyes, and his soft ominous voice which sounded like Darth Vader, as if he spoke behind a mask. He terrified her, the reverberating sound of his voice especially.

'Why would you want my husband to help you? WainCo is enormous; it's part of Wainwright-Feber.' She knew of the pharmaceutical giant. God help her, they were the drugs that Miki took; she had seen the name on the packages. 'You must have the money you wish.' She tried for sanity.

'Not enough. WainCo is owned by a conglomerate of which I am merely the chairman. There are cousins, executors. I won't bore you with the details; enough to say it is a family concern too. My father started it, distributed it around the family so that none of us could take control. I *want* control.' His hands on the driving wheel slid, and clamped themselves tighter as if he would drive home the point. 'Money will give me that: my own company, a hospital where I can recruit the finest minds for laboratory research. Research that will finally hamper the drug industry in general, except me. I will be sitting pretty with the knowledge. I will patent it, and I will be in control.'

'Have you not got a family of your own?' she tried.

'I am not inclined towards marriage. It's an irony that your husband should be financing this venture here in Aspen, as right-wing and reactionary as they come. If they knew. It's amusing to me that not only do they not suspect, but I shall steal the one thing they want right here in their midst.' He looked at her, feeding her gloves despairingly through her tiny hands. She was exquisite, despite her nerves. So beautiful; he did not want to frighten her, so he kept the threatening tenor of his voice from her. Only the words were terrifying.

'Why do you tell me all this?' she said, and now her jewel black eyes swung towards him in the porcelain doll face.

'Because I want a great deal of help from you.'

'How?'

'Basically to persuade your husband to part with his money, and –'

'And what?'

'In time I'll tell you,' he said, smiling. 'When the babe's a bit stronger.' The smile was more sinister than the words.

'Why should I not tell everybody, Miki especially? As you say, he is powerful. He would hate you for what you are doing to me, to us. And what if I don't believe you . . .'

Sandford laughed softly as the car entered Main Street and the town which was her home and yet so far from her right now.

'Ah, the answer is very simple. Why don't you ring the clinic in New York now? There's the phone.' He pointed at the car phone wedged like a red hornet in the blackness between them. 'The baby is my insurance that you will do what I want. Or are you afraid to discover I am telling the truth? A truth that will honour you to keep silent.'

'I don't know the number.'

'I do.' And he gave it to her. 'Sorry, you'll have to do it, I hate to take my eyes off the road.'

Mochi wanted to know. Reaching down, hands shaking, she lifted the receiver and dialled the lab. She needed both hands to hold the mobile. All too soon she heard the receptionist's familiar voice. Hesitating, she announced herself, and heard the kindness and the offer of assistance. She started on a story, any story. Just to know the truth, and yet the last truth she wanted.

'. . . and that young man,' she was saying, surprised her voice was not quivering as she was inside, '. . . he was very kind. I wanted to send gifts to you all. Could you give me his name?'

Respect and embarrassment coloured the voice. 'Oh, I am sorry, Mrs Leng. I'd rather you had not known. He committed suicide. He was found in his room just hours ago with an overdose of drugs. There was a note. His girlfriend said he had some serious problem on his mind.'

She had to ask. 'What did he take?'

The receptionist mentioned the brand name. 'Paracetamol content. I'm afraid many people don't realise just how dangerous they are.'

'Thank you.'

She looked up. She saw the glint in the corner of his eye where the light caught it, a half-smile on his wide mouth. He held a bottle aloft. Her eyes blurring as she rattled the receiver back into its cradle, she could hardly see the label, but he told her anyway.

'Made by WainCo Drugs.'

A family concern, he had called it. It really had become that now. Made more poignant because of her recent happiness, Mochi shed bitter tears.

Miki, only recently home himself, was amazed to see her alight from the cab and was already hurrying down the steps to greet her, with Lee moving away to pay off the driver. His face was warm with smiles and his arms around her felt good, yet she felt like a traitor to her own body and him. Thrilled with her news he did not quiz her too closely about her method of transport, but greeted her with a real love he had not shown before.

Mochi, lost in her own misery, missed the depth of these feelings, allowing herself to be led up the steps to the house, with Miki believing that her fragile state was due to her condition. He had never had a child before, nor knew what to expect.

282

In the hallway of their house, he lifted her coat gently from her shoulders.

'Mochi.'

She turned to him, her pain standing hard in her heart. She was completely to blame.

'You have done this for us. I am honoured and proud, but more than that . . . Mochi, perhaps I have not told you often enough how I feel for you. You are the most important thing in my life.' He hesitated but now, listening, watching his face, she saw it. The cloud moved away, and there was pure joy in his eyes as his hand travelled gently over her stomach. 'I love you . . . and our baby . . .'

Weeping, she let him hold her in his arms. Now she could never tell him. Love had moved in and she could not disgrace them, could not take away that look in his eyes. Whatever the man wanted, she would do. Mochi would face her dilemma alone and it tortured her.

For Miki his night with Montana was sexual only. He was able to divorce it from the overflowing joy he now felt for his wife. That he was considering any form of deception was between him and his conscience which he often dictated, by moving fate into his own hands. If he did it, he would justify it as being right for them both. In fact, were Miki to go ahead with the cloning, she would not even need him to penetrate her, so there could be many chances; but she did not know that.

All she knew as she lay there within the circle of his arms was that she was pregnant and it could be her only chance with her husband. Miki represented everything to her in lifestyle, tradition and love. She hated herself for it, tearing herself apart with her mixed feelings of guilt, but it was what she had come to know; she needed wealth and position, it was an essential part of her. Abortion would take away everything. Miki's child would be 'perfect' – and Japanese – if she helped the man. She let Miki lead her upstairs to her bedroom with strict instruction to his staff to bring her anything she wanted, and to her, an order to lie down and rest and he would return to her shortly.

In her bedroom, with Miki downstairs ordering her yet another expensive gift, she thought about love and laid it against the hospital visits and the mechanics of her love life with Miki. Touching one of the many furs in her wardrobe and feeling its silky seductive texture, she gazed out on the snowy panorama. Mochi wondered about her future, and what decision she would make. Her mind raced on: with Miki's faulty gene eradicated the child was on its way, potentially perfect. But was it someone else's; that of an unknown woman? She stared out of the window as twilight kissed the slopes. She couldn't lose Miki. She wanted to run tests, but it would be too obvious. And who would she trust? and where would she do it? Miki would find out; she would lose everything. She had to know. She needed a doctor, but which one? Her mind whirling, she heard Miki returning, and turned from the window, a carefully practised smile on her face.

'We are invited to the Rushmores tonight, but I will cancel.'

'No. You see I remembered.' She was already dressed. Mochi kept a very strict diary and was conscious of protocol. Wearing black and a string of pearls, her hair coiled silkily on her head, her look was simple and devastating.

'As long as you feel up to it.'

'I do. I feel fine, truly, Miki.' She went to him and took his arm. Better this than staying at home and driving herself mad. At least with people her crazed mind would have a chance to slow and she could talk inanities for a few hours, before they came back to the quiet and her fears. Every moment the baby grew inside her, and every moment it might or might not be hers. It was like a living death. The emotions tore her apart.

At the party Miki was solicitous and every inch the proud father; he never left her side. His hand at the small of her back he guided her to groups of friends, sharing the good news. One group stood by the door, and in its shadow a man entered, freezing the polite smile from her face.

And Miki was guiding her forward.

'Sandford,' he was saying, and his voice seemed to hold a certain significance. 'I want you to hear the good news. All has gone well. Mochi is with child.'

Sandford smiled and bowed, taking her cold hand in his.

'Well . . .' he spaced it. 'Congratulations.'

Mochi looked up into his face slowly, her face paler than the pearls around her throat and he smiled, the smile broadening as he looked from one to the other. He never attended functions; hated 'do's' but he knew which parties to attend. This one, to remind them both of his presence; to see them both together and to know he had them in the palm of his hand.

Sandford looked at the beautiful Mochi, knowing why she did not share her husband's extreme joy. It was not the time for discussion, but his mind was working overtime. He frowned: he was far more interested in how Mochi was holding up. Her nervousness told him that so far she had not confided, and coupled with Miki's announcement he was sure of it – but there was something else, something less certain he could not decipher. Having put the gears in motion he wanted to drive it forward, but another group pulled them into its periphery, and Miki's slim hand was pressing his wife beside him to greet more guests.

She'd managed to slip away; but he watched her carefully, with only half an ear to the group around him, yattering uselessly about nothing, which for once made it easy to see what she was up to, and how she was reacting. As she turned in profile he saw her eyes on someone at the other side of the room, and followed her gaze with interest.

Mochi recognised Liam at once. He was too handsome to forget; besides, he had been up at the house. He was a doctor, she knew that much, but not one of the doctors in what she thought of as 'the group'. He had not been involved in their conferences. She knew not to talk to them by instruction from her husband. But this one – she watched him laugh, and noted his strength. Instinctively, she liked and trusted what she saw. Feeling Miki's interest stray slightly, she looked around for the ponytailed man and saw no sign of him. This might be her only chance and she had to trust to her own instincts, instincts that to date had never let her down.

She'd seen Liam only that once at the house. She'd heard about him, knew he was talented, and probably had contacts. He was young too, like her; perhaps he would understand.

Sandford watched her thread her way through the crowd, saw Liam's face turn and look down at her, watched her mouth move in rapid conversation and the young man smile, and respond. She had a sublime beauty, and the young man looked shrewd and sincere, but as she talked to him it seemed more than that. Suddenly they both laughed, after which she seemed to relax and started to talk. The young man lowered his head and listened. Sandford edged his way slowly through the crowd, pretending to join in conversation but reading the body language. It was getting serious; he didn't want the bitch happy, he wanted her on tenterhooks.

'. . . oh, Mr Wainwright, can I interest you in a raffle ticket? A very worthy cause. You get a run named after you for ever $30,000 contribution . . .'

'What . . .?'

He turned to the woman, gilded in diamonds and wearing a dress that had clearly cost thousands and had to be from Valentino's fall collection.

'I just *know* we can count on *you!*' The voice was kittenish, ridiculous. His quarry was slipping away.

'. . . *can we talk, somewhere private . . .*'

In the midst of a story of little consequence, her sudden words were a whisper he hardly heard. Liam turned his face to look down on her. She repeated herself.

'Can I talk to you?'

'Of course.'

'I need your help.'

He inclined his head to listen. 'I can't imagine I could help, but I'll try.'

'We need to talk elsewhere. Can you meet me in my car, it's the dark blue Cherokee outside. I don't want my husband to see.' She was beautiful, loaded with diamonds. In stunning black, and a figure to match he wondered anew about her. She looked at the raised eyebrow, the tilted mouth. 'No,' she said, with the smallest tone of regret, 'it's nothing like that.'

Now he could see the worry in her face, and his own expression mirrored hers. 'Two minutes? Right outside?'

'Across the street. Follow me out. I'll flash the lights when I see you.'

Ponytail had rid himself of the woman with a pledge. Now his face behind his glass was cold as he watched the charade. First her, leaving by one door; then, coolly but unmistakably following by one opposite, him. Liam even brushed by him as he left with a curt 'excuse me'. A man with a mission.

It was impossible to follow them, but his senses were alert. He would find out who the young man was and why Mochi Leng had an interest in him. Why him?

Liam had listened carefully to the torrent of words. The car heater ran with a sound of rushing air; she had it unbearably hot. He didn't want to tell her and stop her talking. He leaned over and turned it down a notch, but she hardly seemed to notice.

'And what stage are you at now?'

'A few days only. How do I know if it's mine?' she wailed.

He looked at her, deep with concern. 'You don't. You can't even know that the egg will develop. And I'm not sure we can check the blood group this early. It's not straightforward, but there may be a way. Do you know your blood group, and Miki's?'

'Yes. I'm A. I think Miki is the same.'

'That's a plus. It's unusual. The "O" positive is the most normal. With any luck we can strike home here. Apart from that, it'd have to be DNA testing, and that's time consuming. Let's take it stage by stage. I know someone in Denver. I'll book it for you, but don't hold out hope, Mochi. It's early days. In a few weeks, maybe ...'

'I can't wait that long. I'll kill myself.'

He laid a hand briefly over hers. 'I'll see what I can do.'

'Thank you.' He stepped out of the car and came round to her side. He placed a hand on the window.

'Don't worry. It's probably fine.'

His smile was reassuring, and he was handsome. Fleetingly, she thought of Miki and compared them. His body would be hard and he would dominate her with those killer eyes. But she had chosen, long ago. And a young man such as this one would never have given all those things which nowadays she could not do without. Impulsively, knowing her lot, she kissed him, settling for the germ of friendship that had already begun to grow.

'Thank you, Liam . . .'

Sandford moved closer to the window of the house, his finger to his lips as he watched the two talk close in the street outside. Would she take the chance to abort the foetus? He knew human nature and he doubted it. So what was she up to? He tapped his finger gently against his lips and thought it through, letting his mind reel in the past scenarios.

The young doctor and her earnest face filled his mind for the second time that day. Not a pick-up, she was too uptight: *she had been asking for help*.

Even if she planned to terminate the child, which he doubted, he could prevent her doing so. Boxer and the chauffeur, Fernandez, would report on every one of her movements. A few checks, and he would soon discover what she was up to. He knew he would get Miki's cooperation, and this was just one more grip on Mochi's neck. Just as long as she did not find a way of determining the true genetic blood group of the baby. He wondered; was that what she was up to . . .? If she did, he lost everything.

He needed to twist Miki's arm, needed him to put his money, his weight – and his wife – behind the project to make it work for him. He was going to use Mochi to persuade her husband to do the deal with him. He had sussed out Miki well. And he had learned one very important lesson: the spies were right. Neither of them was telling the truth. She did not want Miki to know what she was doing; clearly she felt guilty. *Perfect*. The only stumbling block to Miki's going along with his plans was whether or not Mochi would play ball. And he had to play them both so carefully. Maybe he had just had to frighten her a little more; she had more gumption than he'd imagined.

Sandford crossed the street from the party and watched as she ran quickly back into the house and the young man headed off down the sidewalk.

He already knew who *he* was. And at a signal Boxer detached himself from the shadows and began to follow the man.

Back in the party throng, Miki searched the jam-packed crowd for his wife. He had seen how unsettled she was, and now he knew what he would do. He had no option; it was odd that he ever thought he had. He loved Mochi. Winning was no longer important; coming first? He already was: he was going to be a father.

TWENTY-TWO

The room was filling up with people when they walked in. Heat, and laughter, and the clatter of china. Liam pulled out a chair, ordering for them both as he did so. Alex did not argue; it was what she wanted anyway.

Small talk. He stirred his cappuccino, and she watched the froth till he laid down his spoon and looked up quizzically at her. 'So – what's up?'

His eyes were shadowed, but their cool grey interest was not hidden from her. She was conscious of all the planes of his face. Casting her fears aside, she went for it.

'I had something to tell you.'

'Fire away.' He didn't move.

She squeezed her lips together and took a breath.

'I'm not exactly who you think I am.'

'Really?' He felt an immediate tension and then an eclipsing rush of warmth towards her, knowing she was going to confide, absorbing all that that meant, and badly wanting to hear it from her own lips. For a moment, his emotions quite overcame him. Her mouth caught the sheen of sun from the window, and he could hardly tear his eyes away from the soft texture of her lips.

'I was working as an investigative journalist, Liam, till I came here.' She licked her lips and he felt the warmth steal into him. 'I covered Bosnia, the Sudan, Rwanda.' She looked down, and he felt the scenes, imagining them as she described them. As she talked, he interpreted her confidence correctly, and as she looked up his eyes told her what she wanted to know. That he trusted her, that he had known already and was simply waiting for her to tell it like it was.

She saw it in their depths like an understatement of his feelings, and felt a flood of gratitude that he had not pressed her for this information. Respect; it was what she looked for. What she had not found to date.

Her reasons for leaving the Beeb were skipped over, but he read between the lines: she did not want to talk about the other man; not here. Not now.

He seemed an irrelevance, she thought, yet at the time he had been so all-consuming. How life changed in a few short months! Ugly feet; she laughed and it added to the intimacy of her voice.

He took her hand briefly, and she felt its warmth.

'Alex . . .'

'You knew, didn't you?' His hand lit all her nerves with the *frisson* of their skin touching. It seemed to glide around hers, fingers finding hers in a sexual litmus paper that had her reacting so quickly that it reached into the pulses and nerve endings of her skin. Her face seemed to soften.

'Hey, Alex . . .'

The young boy slid in beside her. 'How you doing?'

'Hi, Darren.' She ruffled his hair as he sat beside her, looking up and smiling. 'Where's your mum?'

'Shoppin'.'

They both laughed at the rueful expression on his face; laughed together, as one. Eyes lifting to Liam's, the warmth stayed. She saw discovery, *recognition*. Her breath caught, but her words sounded sane enough. 'And she sent you off, right?'

'No, I got bored. When me mum goes shopping, I hate it. Dad said I could go walkabout, and I saw you come in here.'

'I'm glad you did. Darren, this is Liam.'

'Hello, sir.'

'Good manners. The English school, right? I remember that.'

Alex's eyes queried. He went to school in England? She wanted to *know*. But the boy was talking.

'No Mum. She says it's important in this day and age to remember our good manners when the world is progressing so fast.'

'You'll have to meet Fanny,' Alex laughed.

'I look forward to it.'

'Well come on then,' said Darren, standing up. 'She said to get back to the bar by twelve and find her there.'

'You planning on skiing?'

'Not today. Weather's not good enough. Mum's taking me to a movie later. Want to come over?'

'Sure.'

She saw Liam's equal interest in the child as he paid and left, walking down the street with him. Suddenly they were both aware of each other with the chaperon of Darren volubly talking between them and marching them down to the Jerome; they exchanged smiles in his wake.

She was moved to see how naturally good Liam was with the boy when most men might have wanted her exclusive attention. Ruse or not, she dismissed the cynic in her, finding it drew her closer to him. She felt only good.

Fanny was at the bar, ordering, fed up with waiting. She never stood on ceremony. There were two men standing there, and they paid her little attention. One was drinking fast, as if about to leave once he'd quenched his thirst. She'd seen both before; not together, but around. One had a pony-tail. Suddenly Fanny remembered: climbing into the blacked-out Aspen chic Range Rover. Rhino bars, she thought, laughing to herself. She felt as if she knew him, as if he might share the joke. Of course he wouldn't, she was far too friendly with strangers. She shut her lip and instead smiled at the waiter.

As the drinks came, she fished for money and slid her hands around them, laughing inwardly as she heard the exchange: 'Everyone's corruptible, you just have to find their price level, Boxer . . .'

What a goof; as if that were true. He meant nothing to her, just another cynic in town. Fanny rejoined her table, flashing the photos she'd pulled from her wallet. The new group gathered round; there was always a group with Fanny.

'Here look, this is me and Stud on the day of his operation.'

'Looks like a wedding photo.'

'It is! Poor man thought they were going to shrivel. Drop off one by one when he got caught in matrimony!' Squeals of laughter. 'Just a joke, he couldn't wait, *really*!'

Skis stacked in the hall, hot cider in the silver tureen in the lobby, the soft chatter of the elite; light laughter as Alex and Liam entered and Fanny's raucous chuckle could be heard.

'That's me Mum,' said Darren.

'Oh, I see.'

'*You will!*' It felt refreshing to Alex as she sought Fanny out and a reunion with the family; delivering a rosy-cheeked Darren back to his mother, she introduced Liam.

'Fanny, this is –'

'Alex, darling. Guess what –' Fanny's delighted face was wreathed in smiles. 'Jack Fenner's announced his theme for this year's party. Everyone's to come as their private fantasy. Isn't it *great . . .?*' she said, strangling the word.

'. . . Liam.'

'Hello, pet.'

Alex sat down. 'What are you going as?'

'Well, I'm going with two hunky ski instructors in thongs and nothing else. Me own private Chippendales.' She eyed Liam playfully. 'Want to audition!?' He smiled, raising her blood pressure. 'Wow, all yours, Alex love, too hot for me!' Fanny didn't wait for the answer; punctuation and pauses were not for her. Now a valued member of the 'in crowd', she rattled on, confiding loudly. 'Rowan's going with three of his wife's best girlfriends. That's his fantasy!'

'And Jack?'

'Jack's not telling.'

It was fun, and typically Jack. Fancy dress exposed people; they showed up in their *alter ego* – which was sometimes surprising: quiet girls lit out in jungle dress, outrageous flirts in men's suits. But fantasies, what a winner. Fired by the idea of freedom in a closed setting, the exclusive guests would not see his tactics. They were all getting ready to party, unwittingly revealing themselves and their sexual fantasies to Jack Fenner, amateur psychiatrist and exponent of people's needs.

Fanny's group did not notice the two men watching them from the bar. Sandford's eyes travelled over them, taking in Liam and, at his side, the interesting-looking brunette. For a moment his gaze became hard. It was as well no one noticed: it was too revealing.

293

He left to the signal from the door. His car waited outside and he had an appointment.

Once again, Wilhelm had put down the phone as Ruth entered the room upstairs.

'David's not coming back. All his stuff's been wrecked.'

'Yes, I know.'

'How?' She closed the door behind her, and he noticed how good she looked. Trim, and with a lift to her head that was always there these days. 'I only just left off talking with Hillaire in New York; he didn't mention telling you.'

'You're so thick with that guy.'

Her eyes widened. 'Who *told* you?'

'What is this, Ruth, an inquisition? We're all part of the same team.' He picked up his gloves and headed for the door. 'Hillaire himself did; does that surprise you? He was probably looking for you. Sounded disappointed to get me. Ruth, don't be so territorial – just because you discover a cure for a minor disease does not gif you the right to question me.' He palmed the gloves into one hand. 'The important thing is that we haf to go on without him.'

The accent again. Only when he was under strain. Ruth felt it for just a moment, and then the despair that was increasingly there these days when she confronted her husband on any issue. He saw every question as an attack, never a query. She took a deep breath, feeling the divide between them.

'It'll be difficult without Hillaire.'

'He took David's case, of course.'

'No.' She sounded surprised, and then levelled her voice, as if challenging him with something she did know. There was a sense of defeat too; why did it always have to be a battle? 'It's at his house, I told you.'

'Still!?'

'Of course.'

'And I suppose you know when he is coming back too.'

'Yes, as a matter of fact. Tomorrow morning.'

Out in the corridor, Wilhelm waited for the lift and felt

irritation burn inside him. He was uneasy. He banked on the fact that he controlled his wife; had thought to get her to get a sight of the notes via Hillaire and earn a few points, but she was fighting back. Maybe there were more obstacles than he realised. The lift doors opened and he walked in, pressing the button with more firmness than it needed. At least now he knew where the case was, and they would find the access code. He would call Sandford from the lobby.

Obstacles were removable. He wanted his clinic. He saw his name set into a brass plate on a walled pillar, then a long tree-lined drive. It would be elegant, unassuming. It would be talked about the world over.

Now was the time to steal the briefcase while Hillaire was still out of town. He had already had the call from downstairs from Sandford, who was leaving for a few hours but would be back in the early evening. He was to go then under cover of dark with Boxer.

He would be back in control.

In town, Mochi was unable to face going home just yet. She found a small bar where she was not known and sought solace in a drink, for once not thinking of her child. She had gone in to make a telephone call, to avoid using the phone at home. She knew how lines were monitored by Miki's staff.

Denver had drawn a blank. The doctor had told her on the telephone that as she was under such close supervision from her doctor in New York, there was no way he could interfere. Ethically, she would have to return to the clinic where she was being treated for any treatment connected with her baby. Anything else was impossible.

Distraught, Mochi was lost in her sorrow as Sandford, working on the division factor, put the second part of his scheme into action. As she sat there, a man she had seen somewhere before slid into place beside her. Boxer talked, and Mochi listened.

She left with him a moment later.

The small Lear jet took less than forty minutes to reach the Wyoming smallholding. Sandford strode in ahead of her, leaving Mochi to follow in his wake. She pulled her fur coat around her, horrified by what she saw in the passageways of the house: slatternly women of ancient years with bulging pregnant stomachs, weeping and moaning and pulling into the walls as they passed. Nurses led them away, gently protesting, into side rooms.

'Can't have them getting upset,' said Sandford as he turned his proud face towards her. 'No good for the babies at all. They have to go to term, or at least pretty close. Come along.'

A monster amongst monstrosities. Mochi, feeling sick to her stomach, did not argue, could not say a word, but her face must have shown her feelings and for once Sandford lost his supercilious look as he led her into a room.

'I'd rather the cloned babies were born to beautiful surrogate mothers,' he said, closing the door. The bosomy matron smiled and whispered away. 'Come,' he said, propelling a shocked Mochi by the arm. 'Can't have you fainting on me.' He led her to a chair, and took one opposite, his eyes on her. But he could not wait to talk, despite her appearance.

'Yes, I understand your feelings, my dear Mochi. Turning out these creations from these wizened old mothers seems obscene. Even I have limits.'

'Elderly mothers with implanted eggs? It's disgusting. What about their relatives?'

He laughed, pleased she was showing interest.

'Oh, no relatives. They've been offloaded.' She turned her face away. 'This is not exactly an asylum, you understand. More a place for unwanted geriatrics.'

He watched her face. 'Even worse,' she said, horrified.

'Not really. Even more reason for you to help.'

'Me?'

He walked in a semicircle. 'With you, if you feel so bad about it, old ladies will not be necessary. The nurses will be pleased to let them go. They wet the bed, cause a nuisance. The old dears are a bit ga-ga and so no one really takes much notice of what they say, but in fact the babies are being incubated in them, brought to term and then removed by

Caesarian section, and sold.' He could not help but brag. 'As they are drugged and since old ladies appear to have quite rotund stomachs anyway, they don't give cause for alarm to their relations. And many do not get visitors. These are women who are truly left alone in the world and so are very vulnerable. We feed them very well, give them lots of attention, more than they would get at home.' He closed the door. 'It's really not so bad.'

'They *live* through this?' she asked, her voice a shocked whisper.

'Most of them.' He parked himself on the edge of a bed. 'Now . . . Mochi . . . let's not talk about them, let's talk about why we're really here . . .' His eyes were deadly black, looking deep into her, and Mochi felt her will being sucked away. 'Do you have any idea what is going on in the ground floor of your house?'

'Some, I –'

'No, you don't, so I shall inform you.' He sat by the window, with the sun slanting across his face. He folded his arms and legs astride, he stared up at her. 'Your husband has a tiger by the tail, Mochi. His money has set up these doctors to discuss a progression of genetics such as you and I know it. But, they have gone much further than that.' He smiled. 'So far,' he breathed, a glitter entering his eyes. 'They have discovered something I have wanted for a long time. In easy laymen's language, these doctors not only have the ability to cure, and extend life beyond the grave; there too they have found out how to create it . . .'

'In . . .'

'Yes.' His whisper was a smile. 'From the cells of the dead they know how to literally make a new human being. Thence to the lab, and to the baby farm. Out there –'

'*No!*'

'Oh, yes. But even more fascinating is this they can create from the dead! The cells of dead people, frozen in a time warp. Can you imagine what this means? We can literally make what we want.'

'You're *mad*.'

297

He gave a small irritated shrug and stood up.

'Enlightened. And you should be honoured.'

'Me?' She touched her chest lightly. 'Why me? I have nothing to do with it.'

'Yes you do, Mochi. You are not carrying the baby you think.'

'What are you talking about?' She lifted a face that was moon-white, her eyes two horrified shadows as she took in what he was saying.

'I have taken it from you. I told you ... but ... I lied a little ...' He smiled. 'My young friend – erstwhile friend, in New York ...'

She stared at him. '*What have you done with it!?*'

He smiled to think it was just in the next room. 'Oh, I *have* it. As insurance ... elsewhere.'

'So what am I carrying!?'

He shrugged airily 'Another one. One far better.'

Tears welled.

'I shall get rid of it.'

'No.'

'How do you know I have not aborted it already,' she said, bravely.

'You haven't.'

She kept her chin up, her black eyes smarting.

'I *know* where you've been you see, what you've done. Ah yes, Denver, wasn't it? Mochi, you have to realise that because of my connections in the drug industry I can buy the right people. I have spies everywhere.' He smiled. 'The doctor in Denver is now planning his own winter fortnight in Aspen. So, do we have a deal. Will you help me?'

'No,' she said, obstinately, her mind racing.

'Now look,' he said patiently. 'Stop thinking ahead of me, I've already been there. You can't win, and – you have too much to lose. I have all Miki's frozen seed, besides. I own your future: they're mine for as long as you cooperate, and don't tell him. I shall tell him at the right moment. He's impotent; this is his last chance. *And* yours.'

'But I thought you said I was no longer carrying our child.'

'You're not.' He opened his hands wide. 'I'll explain. I have implanted a cloned egg already, a *culled* egg. Such a vessel for my first Messiah. Mochi, you are beautiful. Are you not proud? What riches! I feel as if I am the father myself. I am fit, and not bad looking I'm told, but unfortunately infertile. This is my way of giving birth, birth to an idea, a *creation* wrought by my hand and my invention. And with Miki's money.'

'He will *never* help you.' Her head reeling, her words were futile.

'No?' He got up. 'Well, we'll see. You are going to persuade him that this is what you want and that he will want it too.' She was terrified of Miki's finding out. He would hate her. She would lose everything. What was growing inside her? Nothing? Was he fooling her? Her own child? An abomination? She laid a hand on her stomach as if to know. She felt as if it was a parasite; what was to stop her aborting, believing this man? But she wouldn't do that. She couldn't take the chance he was lying. She had to do what he said. 'I already found about the doctor, Mochi, so no tricks. You have *no* secrets any more.' He laughed, and spoke as she pressed her hands to her ears, blood rushing, but still she heard him: 'I even control your body, and as long as I do, you will be a good girl . . .'

Slowly, she nodded.

'Good,' he said, watching her. 'Now, first: Professor Bowman has a briefcase hidden in his house. I know you are friends with the young doctor who lives with him,' he said, watching her face tighten and her eyes widen, wondering if she had misplaced her trust; the more unsettled she was the better. 'I want you to get it for me –'

'I *couldn't*! What, walk in there, and – no, I couldn't . . .'

'No,' he said slowly, thinking, 'I don't suppose you could. You wouldn't know how to steal, would you . . .' Forcing her against her nature might be counterproductive; a little knowledge and all that just might make her bold enough to talk to her husband. 'In that case I'll find something else for you to do. I want you to seduce him . . . now, you know how to do that, surely . . .'

TWENTY-THREE

Sandford crossed the hall, a big strong man in black Armani, his grey ponytail flipping over his collar. His feet were bare, since his house used tons of fuel per month to fight sub-zero temperatures.

Miki was going to turn him down, he knew that. He felt it in his bones, but he would never let them know. He could tell right away by the tone of his voice; a company man, he had learned to read his cue on the telephone as much as by handwriting. The face-to-face interview was often contrived but the other two were fallible if you listened well.

'Mr Wainwright . . .'

Sandford's smile pulled across his face, and the heavy eyes flickered over his surroundings and back. He let him go first.

'Mr Wainwright, I have been thinking, and this is what I have been asking myself. There are no guarantees with your idea.'

'I have to disagree, I –'

'No, please let me finish. Delighted as I would be to have a child who could rise to the highest position in the land, even if you were to clone an exact copy of Abraham Lincoln's DNA structure you could not hope to reproduce the man.' He lifted his hand, thinking about Jack Fenner's simple words. 'The missing link is *conscience*. Charisma is given to many but there are no guarantees; academia perhaps, beauty even can be manufactured or encouraged. But my wife *is* beautiful, and all the money I have made is through my own ability. So you see, with my son now well and on his way we have no need of this – as long as, of course, he gets his inheritances the right way round!'

Sandford could hear the smile in Miki's voice at the mild joke, but his face was set as stern as stone. This was not a man who changed his mind, he had made it up after much deliberation. This then was his answer. Sandford decided to pour on the ice a little.

'Your . . . baby . . .'

'Yes. A son. We have given in that much to genetic engineering.'

'I have that baby, Mr Leng.'

Miki's pause was immensely pleasurable; Sandford leaned back in his chair, smiling.

'I'm sorry, I think I misheard. You said . . .'

'I have your baby. Impregnated by you.'

A long pause. 'What are you talking about?'

He told him; never mentioned Mochi, knew he didn't have to, knew she hadn't told Miki. That much he banked on. Good for him not getting close to his wife, it helped him immeasurably.

'I needed to know you would cooperate. A threat was clearly not enough with a man such as you.' He said it as a compliment. 'As you say, you have everything. No, the only way was to do as I have done and move on my own volition – before you answered me, as you have done. A little insurance.' His voice held pleasure. 'And it turns out that I was right in my judgement of you, Mr Leng . . .'

And of your wife.

'You have *stolen* my child?'

Not stolen; put it on ice. He chuckled; finalised the news with his *coup de grâce*.

'Possibly; the truth of that is my insurance . . . but not only that, Mr Leng, I have stolen your own future samples as well. There is nothing genetically frozen that is your stock in any sperm bank in New York any longer.'

The shock must have bowled him over and Sandford, leaning back and smiling, wished he could have seen his face. Give the man his due, he did not crack, but his voice was so cold a whisper could have shattered it.

'How do I know this is true?'

'Can you take the risk?' He listened carefully to the silence and thought of mentioning the 'machine' to show just how much he knew, but decided against this little intimacy; better

301

to hold a few cards back. Opening up all his senses to read the man's voice, he went for the *pièce de la résistance*: 'And you cannot tell your wife. Think what it would do – what she might do once she knew. You have to support my actions now, just in case ... and silently.'

This time he was prepared to say nothing. He knew the inner man would be wrestling with this. He understood need, ah yes, and obsession; and Miki Leng was obsessed right now with reproduction because his biological clock was running out – just like a woman! Or as women used to be. He allowed himself a small inner smile. He was counting on his knowledge of their relationship: a couple not close enough to discuss this in honesty. Marriage was indeed a trap he was glad he had avoided; bound together by everything but what really mattered. But he couldn't wait.

'Do I have your answer?'

Another gap in time, and then:

'What is you want me to do?'

Music, sweet music. His unfocused gaze embraced the dreams dancing before him in the air.

'I want *you* ... to finance a clinic. To put all your money, your billions shall we say, into it. I shall run it. It will be the pioneering clinic for genetic engineering: few will know what it really contains until I am ready to make our happy announcements to the world.' He smiled paternally. 'The deal is to be finalised within the next six months. All in place before you have a chance to change your mind.' *His* own private joke – that in a Wyoming smallholding an oriental baby would be about to be born; one he would keep his eye on. 'Oh, and the last thing – the greatest honour. I want you to do some persuading ... but not just yet.' He paused for a moment, amused by how he held them so separately in his hands. The truth was it was already in progress but he wanted Miki to sanction it first. From there they would both learn to live with it, given time. '*Mochi will have the honour of being first in line . . .*'

'Where are you going?'

Alex stood at the foot of the stairs, and looked up. Fabrice appeared out of the shadows of the landing. A row of matched hide luggage stood in the hall.

'Wanderlust, darling. You know how that is. I never stay here too long.'

Alex looked at the half-dozen assorted valises.

'Where are you going? And for *how long*?'

'California, my angel. Just for a few days.' Laughing, she touched Alex's face gently with her leather glove as she reached the foot of the stairs. 'And the house is *all yours*. Use the pickup if you want. It'll suit you,' she grinned naughtily. 'Go and buy a couple of things on my account too. Dress up.' She touched her shoulders. 'You are a beautiful girl, you need to show it off.'

'Anyone who's interested can already see it.'

'Anyone I know?'

Alex pulled out of her embrace. 'I wasn't being specific.' She sat on the edge of the hall settle. 'Why the sudden departure?'

'I never stay long. Itchy feet. And I miss the sun. This place is full of deadbeats at this time of year,' she said breezily. 'I'll be back in for the fun crowd. You've got it for a few days at least. Now, be a dear and drive me to the airport.'

Alex stopped off for a drink after the commercial jet had taken off. A girl sat in the bar; a girl she'd seen before in town. She remembered her for her fragile beauty. Alex smiled at her, but she hardly responded. In fact, she looked quite ill, and as Alex sipped her drink she watched her more closely. She seemed distracted and confused, and as she reached for her own drink, she knocked it clumsily with her hand.

Alex waited, and as the girl bent her head and wept she went over, spoke gently: 'Are you all right?'

'I . . . I . . .' She put a hand to her head. 'I just need to get home.'

Mochi had always been cosseted, and this last confrontation had left her unable to deal with anything at all, even driving herself back home. Alex sensed her confusion.

303

'You want a lift?'

'No, no I can manage.'

'I'm happy to drive you,' she offered. The girl turned her tragic tear-stained face up to hers. 'I've seen you before,' she said.

'It's a small place. Do you know Fabrice Strauss?'

She sniffed like a child. 'I think so. She lives in the West End, doesn't she?'

'That's right. She's my aunt,' Alex said as if to reassure her. 'So, I'm just leaving. I'll run you home if you wish.'

'Yes.' The smile suddenly appeared like sunshine, giving the pale face a transcendental beauty. Alex gazed at her. She found victims hard to deal with, especially when they were dressed in ranch mink right down to their boots and were clearly as privileged as this one was. She had seen real victims, but this girl seemed truly distraught, and she had a soft spot for those in difficulties.

'Where do you live?'

'Red Mountain.' And with that she leaned forward and sobbed, sniffing hard.

Alex put an arm around her, paying her bill. 'Come on.' She led her out to the pickup, and wondered if this girl had ever been in something so ordinary. But she climbed in, pulling the folds of the coat around her, but then suddenly turned in a panic as Alex put the car into gear.

'But I don't want to go there.'

'Where do you want to go?'

'Anywhere else.'

She seemed terrified. 'It's so big and empty and right now I just don't feel like being there. I cannot face my husband.'

'Tell you what,' said Alex. 'I'm going back to my aunt's house to make some cookies. Chocolate crunch, I've got an order in for a little boy homesick for his mother's cookies in England. Want to come and sit with me while I cook?'

She nodded, speechless, and Alex made her decision for her: she was going home with Alex.

As the girl drove her, Mochi felt at least the tip of her fear subside; for a while it had been impossible to deal with. Now the peak had gone, and she could see something of her feelings. She knew for a start that for once she did not want to be alone in that splendid isolation; she wanted to be somewhere safe and comfortable, just like her mother's house used to be with her family all packed into the one tiny room. She was terrified of Miki and her return to their house, her guilty conscience making her tearful and nervous. She had done nothing wrong, but she had this dreadful secret, for which she was sure she was to blame; now she just wanted someone to lead her by the hand and make it all right again, the way it was before. She didn't want to find briefcases, or deceive the nice young doctor, or her husband. She just wanted to be a baby. The tears threatened again, and her lip trembled.

Back at the house, Alex parked her in the breakfast bar with a hot drink while she pulled ingredients from the cupboards.

'So, you live in Red Mountain. What's your name?'

'Mochi Leng.' Alex nodded; the name meant nothing. She feathered flour, and as she rolled the dough and whisked eggs Mochi saw some sort of down to earth reality. After a few moments, she even slipped off her coat and felt a surge of interest grow. The disciplines, the lies, the poking and prodding in New York had been too much for her. The warmth and comfort of Fabrice's cosy breakfast nook, the normality, and the pretty girl so easy to talk to and so much her own age, broke down her defences. She sensed her compassion, and felt brave.

'So Mochi, what's the problem? Could I help?'

'Not really,' she said. 'I don't think anyone can.'

'They say it's quite good to try a stranger.' Alex beat the mixture in the bowl, wiped a stray mark of flour from her cheek with the back of her hand. 'I'm willing if you are.'

Mochi bit her lip and thought about it. A moment later the biscuits were in the oven, and Alex was tucked up in the bar beside her, her feet up on the cushions and a warm cup of tea between her hands. The delicious smell of baking filled the room, and it must have taken Mochi back to her childhood. She took a deep breath and relaxed, feeling safe.

'Who are you, Alex?'

'Just a girl like you.' She held her softly with her voice.

'If I tell you . . . it mustn't go any further. It is too – ' she drew breath – 'dangerous . . .' Alex nodded, drawn like a magnet. 'But I have to tell someone, so . . .'

She leaned a little forward.

'This man is blackmailing me,' she began. 'And I cannot tell my husband.'

'I think you should if you can,' Alex began carefully. 'That would defuse things, wouldn't it?'

'No, you don't understand.' Then she began, and as she talked and told the story, Alex's hair stood on end: the players were all the people she knew, coming together on stage as if she had seen the first act and now all the characters were revealed in their true guises in the second. She held her breath, hardly daring to stem the flow as the small tinkling voice told the tragic tale.

'. . . Miki would blame me, you see. So I went to a doctor here in town and asked him for help. He sent me to another doctor in Denver, but the man already knew I was coming there. This Sandford Wainwright had told him. I wanted to run tests on the blood group of the baby but he wouldn't do it. He said I had to go back to the clinic in New York, but they would tell Miki,' she said sadly. 'Alex, I don't know what to do.'

'And he says he has the egg you were carrying? That it was taken by this lab technician?'

'Yes. I rang the clinic on his car phone. They told me he was . . . dead . . .'

'He gave you the right number, I presume. I mean, it wasn't a put-up job?'

'No, no,' she said, sadly. 'I know the receptionist there. She is always kind, we have spoken before.'

'I see. And you think Wainwright murdered him.'

The eyes came up bright. 'I *know* he did. He made no hesitation about letting me know that. It was to scare me, to let me know how dangerous he can be. He wants me to have this other baby, to convince Miki that that is what I want.'

306

Alex thought furiously. 'And there is no way to find out the truth?'

'No, he seems to know every move I make. I don't know what I am carrying. He talked about the baby being . . . being somebody else's, then about being . . . a clone. I don't know. What should I believe?'

'What hold has he got over you?'

'Precisely this knowledge, and therefore a guarantee of my silence.'

'What does he want?'

'A briefcase. He talked about a briefcase.' She did not add how she was to get it. In any case, Alex had shown immediate interest. She sipped her hot drink, miserable, as Alex looked her over intently.

'*A briefcase!?*'

'Belonging to a doctor . . .'

'Not at Professor *Bowman's* house?'

She recalled the balcony scene, Liam's nearness. She pushed it away as Mochi's tear-stained face came up, alight.

'Yes, yes,' she said eagerly. 'That's the one. How do you know about it?'

'Well, let's just say that I keep my eyes and ears open, Mochi,' said Alex. 'But how does he think you're going to get hold of it? You can't just walk in there.'

Mochi shook her head, looking down at her hands curled around the mug. She did not say how.

'He thinks the briefcase will be a way of getting your husband to cooperate,' Alex guessed. 'Is that it?'

Mochi nodded.

'Did he say what's in it?'

'Obviously something very important.'

'Yes, important to him,' Alex mused softly. 'I wonder what . . .' She came back to her, looking for the clue. 'Who is your husband, Mochi? What does he do?'

And then she told her, and Alex understood. Money, billions of dollars; the doctors all in their house, Ruth finding the cure for his genetic defect, Kowolski offering more information than any of them had dreamed. The man was after

307

the money; the briefcase had to contain medical information of some sort that was so original that this pharmaceutical guy wanted it for himself. She longed to have a look at it so badly she would have gone over there and stolen it from under Liam's nose ... *Liam* – her heart closed. What did he have to do with this? Was he faithless, after all? She thought about him laughing in the sunshine as they walked with Darren, catching her eyes across the table. Mochi was talking:

'Miki is stalling on some deal with Sandford and this awful man wants my influence. It's something to do with the conference.'

'What's it about?'

'I don't know the full details. Miki and I do not discuss this sort of thing, he keeps business separate, though it is medical, I know that, and I feel to do with his illness. This man, Sandford, kept talking about his first Messiah, and my being the mother. I'm scared ...'

Her lip trembled and her head went down again.

'This Professor Kowolski, he has this new discovery, that is all. Frozen babies. Oh, it's terrible. And I may be carrying one ...'

And she burst into tears, her head on her arms.

Alex, with her first real pull on the story, again thought of Liam. Her head spinning with all this information, and her emotions unsteady she wondered if she'd done the right thing by talking to him. She had fondly thought of him as being on the periphery, as he had said; whatever they were involved in, he was clear. But *was* he? She remembered her glow of pleasure at being with him, then felt the brush of fear as she thought that information might have been all he wanted. And now she had to ask. Bringing her thoughts back under control, she looked at the weeping girl:

'Did you meet a doctor called Liam Gower?'

'Oh yes,' she said tremulously, 'he's the one who sent me to the doctor in Denver ...'

Back in the car and heading for his luxurious home in the hills, Sandford relaxed. He had wanted to own Miki; now, through Mochi and blackmail, he could. Mochi was terrified of Miki's discovery, he could see that. He had total power over her, had dominated her since childhood, and Sandford saw the humour in what had happened; he, Sandford, now had power over them both. Having got to know the man a little he was secretly laughing at the threat he had implanted in both their minds separately; he had got what he wanted by playing on their disparate weaknesses. It had worked perfectly. A little added piquancy to his plot. But, leaving humor behind, Sandford's mind was working overtime: how to keep the pot boiling until he had the contents of the briefcase and Wilhelm could see the notes and they could begin work on the first cultured baby. He could just send the heavies in, but that might go very wrong. Here in Aspen, Neighbourhood Watch was at its zenith.

Mochi had to do it. All he really needed now was to keep her terrified of Miki's discovery, have her deeper in his clutches through her subterfuge and gain Miki in his pocket through her persuasion. His evil mind turned it all over. One thing at a time. First, he had to draw Mochi in, and throw out all other influences. A thought crossed his mind regarding the man who had put her in touch with the doctor in Denver.

He could have laid a bet it was the handsome doctor she'd been so chatty with. He frowned, recalling him. Seeing him with the second girl in the laughing group in the lobby. The fellow seemed to get about a bit. He would put tabs on him.

He picked up his car phone and dialled.

309

TWENTY-FOUR

Alex made her way through the snowdrifts in the soft afternoon light, her head full of her discoveries. She needed a
little sanity, such as only Montana could provide. Montana,
despite her crazy ways, had a remarkably clear head when it
came to seeing straight through to a subject – if she could
just pin her down for five minutes. Alex meant to try out her
theories on her friend. Jack had said she had gone shopping.
She saw her way up ahead at the end of the street and her
heart lifted.

'Montana!'

But she was too far away, and Alex broke into a gentle run
a she saw her figure disappear inside a clothes shop.

As soon as she opened the glass door, felt the warmth and
the smell of clothes and saw the glitter, Montana was
hooked; she was never immune to the lure of Aspen, but
clothes shops had always done that to her since she was a
little girl, and she had this one incurable habit. She stared at
the bikinis on their racks: expensive, stashed amongst the ski
gear, they would be easy to slip under her coat. More and
more she wanted to acquire beautiful things, but Aspen was
so expensive. She looked at the price tags and her heartbeat
soared – it would be so easy. Glitter and delicate fur, not
ever meant for swimming, but so lovely to recline in one of
those long chairs beside the pool, a glass in her hand, eyes
admiring her. Miki's house, his lifestyle had destroyed her
resolve. Her hand reached out to touch. She had no need to
steal, but it gave her such a buzz . . .

Behind her, Alex entered the almost empty shop, passed
the bored salesgirls, and headed down to the back where she
could see Montana's blonde head. She'd creep up on her
and then jump, hear her scream the place down. It would be
a hoot. Montana's scream was ear-splitting at the best of
times. She knew it would make her laugh.

She saw her lift the bikini from its hanger and crept closer. And stopped. Christ, Montana was pushing it inside her jacket and she was looking furtive; another followed. Talk about standing out: she was dressed in bright turquoise with pink flashing and a pair of pink earmuffs for shoplifting.

'*Montana*,' she whispered.

She had no chance to say anything to stop her, without alerting someone. She watched helplessly as Montana headed round the other side and out of the shop with a smile and a quip for the girls as she hit the street. She forgot all else as her heart went out to her friend.

Montana put a little extra into her step, her pulse racing.

The first time had been years ago. The shop assistant had kept aside a dress for her; it was reduced. She was running out of money in those days but nobody knew. She was used to the good life. She'd tried on the dress; it needed a belt. The girl brought her one. She seemed so nice, then she told Montana she was going off duty. She'd never thought of it, but she loved the belt, and it was so expensive. She could put it aside for later, come back. But the price was so high, and she had it in her hands, round her waist, on the dress. It was black velvet, studded with pearls. It had no store check. The girl had gone to lunch. It fitted on the black woollen dress; it looked beautiful.

She'd looked up as she did this time: no cameras. Careful not to let them see her looking, so if she was caught she could plead innocence. As she looked deliberately casually, she'd realised what she was intending again. And it had grown. The richness of this place – she hadn't done this in years. What had Aspen done to her? She'd held the bikini against her face: it was perfect. She'd never bought something so expensive or so useless, but useless was almost the point. The thrill was the kick as much as anything; the thrill of those first few yards, of getting away with it.

Twenty-five yards and closing on the end of the street, her head felt as if it contained a swarm of hot bees.

Knowing what she was thinking, she had worn it, that dress; it had suited like her a dream, pearls and diamanté all over the bodice, a short short skirt.

It was heaven.

At the cash desk was a new girl. She'd been nice too. Montana had hardly been able to breathe. Still time to turn back, thought it was narrowing. She was wearing the belt then. Looked odd the longer she left it to take it off, to ask them to put it by. The girl was wrapping up the dress, putting the rejected stuff on hangers. Time to hand over the belt.

Two hundred and thirty nine dollars, please. *Shit.*

She'd handed over the money. For the dress.

Around the corner, and down into the mall, her step jaunty, almost a stride. Ahead was the hotel and Chasers, but her mind was on the past.

The queue in that dress shop had been building. Was there some secret alarm on the belt? Had they watched her through the air vents? Were they waiting to see her walk, then catch her?

She hadn't given it back. She'd gone down the stairs, her cheeks flushed. She'd even stopped a moment to admire a painting before heading for the door. Pushed; it said pull. It worked. She was out of the shop and remembering what a friend had once said, a friend who had shocked her: the first twenty yards of the street were the worst and the best. It was the ultimate high.

Like sex.

She'd walked across the promenade. Headed for the large store opposite, wanting to get lost. She hadn't rushed, she hadn't thought about it. Just felt purposeful. She could still be called forgetful. The belt was around her waist; she could feel it tight, like a pair of hands. She waited for the tap on her shoulder, on the small of her back. The skin froze there as she went on walking, walking, not noticing the crowds just walking, breath racing, skin tingling.

Through the glass door watching her reflection and that of the square behind her, on through another store, every man a challenge in her eyeline. Out the other side – could they even challenge her now? Up in the escalator to her car, she was walking fast. At her car. Perhaps they'd waited to catch her quietly. No one. She had a ticket. Justice. She deserved the belt, everything evened out. The store charged ridiculous prices. The salesgirl was so nice to her – would it come off her wages? Would she even suspect the young girl with the nice face and smart clothes? They'd laughed together. She'd even left her number, in case any more came in. It made her look less suspicious.

When she got home she'd call, say she'd made a mistake. She started the car and drove out. She knew that was not true. On the freeway she'd felt free. Had she felt exhilarated, euphoric? No. She'd felt a mix of free-flowing emotions, none outstanding. Surprise, perhaps.

Surprise now too as she hit the street and her room across it. The Hotel Lenore was Alpine quaint, wooden steps up off the street. She ran up them, pushed open the door that held her reflection, and headed straight up the stairs; she couldn't wait to get through that door and close it.

The past always came back. She'd done it and had not got caught, and once again felt surprise that it was so easy. She burst through her door and slammed it shut, leaning against its surface, her chest rising up and down with exertion, but the moment of real sensation had been in the first part of that street. Euphoria came with anticipation not with action. She crossed to the mirror and checked her eyes. They burned darkly in her face, her cheeks flushed, her wide lips open, and the tousled blonde hair with its pink quiff was stained with sweat. She looked glorious, just like she had had fabulous sex.

Would she do it again? Wasn't it a one-off? Aspen was too incestuous. No, given a set of circumstances anything was possible.

She ripped off the tag feverishly as if she were starved. The bikini was no longer stolen. It was hers. She stroked it, it looked beautiful. Meant for her. Was it a better prize because it was stolen? No, just different.

She stripped and put in on quickly. The fur and the glitter enhanced her skin. She turned this way and that.

She wouldn't tell.

Anyone.

Then came the buzz on the intercom.

'Montana, guest. You decent?'

Heart in the throat. 'Who?'

'Alex.'

'Sure.' Wide smile of relief. 'Tell her to come up.'

'Hey, sport.' Montana lolloped down the stairs to get her.

'Christ, what have you done to your hair?'

'Well, it's Christmas, isn't it.' She gave Alex a big hug. She wore a short leather skirt with a huge sweater.

'Been out shopping, Montana?'

'Gotta ring the changes, babe. Shit, have I something to tell you . . .' She practically propelled them up the stairs.

'I'd hoped you might.'

Montana looked puzzled as she pushed Alex into her room.

'You know about it?'

'Yep. I saw you.' She folded her arms, and pushed her tongue into her cheek.

Montana made a face. 'You saw me at Miki's?'

Alex found her voice. '*Miki's!?*'

'Where I went the other night?'

'You've lost me. Tell.'

'Red Mountain. What a spread. Guy's a fucking billionaire; little guy, a Chink. What a house, and what a lover. Man, he kept it up for an hour. I wasn't allowed to look. Weird, but wonderful.'

Alex's interest level was up.

'You were at Miki's house?'

'Oh, spoilsport. You did know.'

'I didn't know. I just know of him. What happened?'

Her interest was maintained as Montana went into full salacious detail.

'You saw the whole house?'

'It took almost as long as the sex. It's the biggest thing you've ever seen, and I do mean the place they live.'

Alex left her prime thought aside as the new information eclipsed it. 'You see the boardroom?'

314

'How d'you know about the boardroom?'

'Montana, this group of doctors I mentioned. They meet there.'

'Yeah, he said something about that. After we had sex he was up, fired, you know. Seemed like he's one of these guys who need the sexual edge to get them going on all manner of things. He started in about doctors and meetings and stuff. And his needs. Reckon I'll be going back.' She pulled the pocket of her bag wide. 'Check this out. Five thousand dollars.'

'Shit . . .'

'I think he had something on his mind and he was grateful to talk it over. He wanted to boast too, I knew that. So I brought him out. He let slip something strange. Apparently he's a bit of a sick guy, and he and his wife have got the group working for them to get a cure. He's got the chance of fixing everything for them, but he didn't say what. I think it's a bit suspect myself, way he suddenly clammed up like he'd said too much.' She grabbed a bottle of whisky by the neck and poured a couple of shots, handing one to Alex, who shook her head, her mind reeling.

'Have you met a guy called Sandford Wainwright?'

'Now that name rings a bell. He's something to do with the man we talked to at the bar. Remember?'

'*Yes.*'

'Jack looked real worried. I've never seen him that way.' Clearly she was worried too. Montana was suffering rejection – Miki had not been in touch. No man had ever dispensed with her without an immediate callback requiring more; everyone always wanted a replay of that wonderful body.

'So you didn't need the dress shop just now. Were you getting it for him?'

Montana went white and sat down hard. 'You were there?'

'Yes.'

'No one's immune to what money can buy, Alex, least of all me. And I don't have it.'

'Is it so important?'

She hung her head. 'Shit, Alex, it's part of the reason I left Vegas. I got caught.'

Alex consoled her. 'I'll put the stuff back for you.' She went over to the cabinet and picked up the whisky, refilling her glass. 'Here, drink this. I'll do it before anyone notices.' She sat beside Montana on the bed.

'You're mad, Montana. You don't need to do this. Jack would be devastated. You'd lose everything you hope to gain in this place, you'd lose face.'

'Oh, it's not that. It's a compulsion. It's like a drug. I need therapy myself. That's what I was doing.'

'Look, *I'll* take it back. I'm going back that way. Just don't do it again.'

'You are a real pal, Alex. I'll curb my drivings for you.'

Having sorted out Montana and not without some spine-tingling qualms herself, she was turning back to the exit of the shop when she saw something through the window that stopped her in her tracks.

Liam and Mochi, their eyes for no one but each other. Mochi's face turned up to his was all too familiar. They were deep in conversation, at the end of which Liam laid his hand gently on her shoulder. Alex stepped back. Mochi had held back at one point – was her real secret an unknown lover?

Not wanting to spy further, feeling their shared moment just too painful, she headed back home. It was silent and beautiful, a soft snow falling, and at every corner an old iron street lamp. There was little sign of modern life; old lace at the windows, and picket fences. Suddenly she realised that all those families must once have come here, to this very spot, and most likely built in the same area. Of course it made sense – in the old Victorian West End of Aspen, now the most expensive part, were the earliest of the smarter dwellings. It was natural they would all live close, before the roads were carved up the mountainside to build Starwood and the steel and glass edifices on Red Mountain. Earlier they had lived near the heart of the town where they could get their food on horseback and water from the Roaring Fork. She speculated on how it must all have been before Aspen became so greedy, as she wandered along. It would have been perfect then. In summer too, she could have walked across the river, jumping the boulders, heading through the trees across the grass now piled deep with snow-drifts.

She also realised something else almost as suddenly – just how close their house was to that of Hillaire and Liam. Driving, it was longer, because she had to negotiate lanes and crossroads, but in fact Fabrice's land almost backed on to that of Hillaire. If one cut out the road, a couple of hundred yards of grass and river made them almost next-door neighbours.

She went quickly inside, ran up the stairs to the attic and climbed out carefully on to the slippery roof. There was a small balcony, and out on the roof she could see Hillaire's front door.

It gave her the idea. Sliding back down the attic staircase, she almost broke her neck trying to make the telephone.

'Oh hi, Montana . . . yes . . . everything's OK.'

'Could you meet up for a drink?'

'Tonight?'

'Just feeling a bit blue.' Montana, hooked by rejection. 'Miki hasn't called.'

'I could have told you.' She leaned back against the wall. 'His wife is back, Montana.'

'How do you know.'

Alex blotted out the all to vivid picture. 'I just saw her in town.'

'Johnnie always called when Clarice was in town. He just sneaked out.'

'Miki is not Johnnie. You should forget this, it's not your style.'

'He's *sooo . . . rich.*'

'Montana, next time I'm just going to let you drop yourself in it.'

Montana laughed. 'You're making me feel better already. I'll go and annoy Jack instead. Meet me tomorrow?'

'Sure.'

Alex retired, the thoughts milling in her mind.

Wilhelm Lindstrom stood at the hotel window watching the darkness fall. The rosy hues of sunset gave way to an inky blackness streaked with vermilion, beneath which the snow-clad Ajax mountain was bathed in a soft eerie blue. He looked up into the sky, sensing the tight gathering of an impending snowstorm. He pulled on his gloves, and checked his watch. He had arranged to meet Boxer out on the street in exactly fifteen minutes. He took a deep breath, feeling the tension. This was not his sort of game, and he would be glad when it was over. The cosy hotel suite made him feel claustrophobic. With a sudden movement he strode across the room and went out, banging the door behind him. He would have a drink in the bar to steady his nerves.

The lift doors opened as he walked out into the lobby. Across the deck the hotel porter picked up the telephone.

'Hotel Jerome, how can I help you?'

Alex smiled into the receiver, masking her nerves.

'This is Dr Ruth Lindstrom. I wonder if you help me out with a small problem . . .'

'Certainly I will try, madam . . .'

'Would you please contact a Doctor Liam Gower for me. Here is his number.' She read the number over the phone. 'I have been trying to reach him at his home to ask him to meet me in the bar for a drink, and he is expecting my call. But I have to dash out now for a couple of minutes. Would you be so kind and try the number a couple of times for me . . .?'

She had delivered the same sort of message earlier to Ruth, who was sitting in a bar across town right now; it would ensure she didn't appear in the Jerome and spoil Alex's plans. All she needed was half an hour at the most.

'Of course.' She could almost hear the man bow. 'I will try straight away . . .'

TWENTY-FIVE

Alex put down the phone and went to the back door, opening it swiftly on to the night – all in one movement, no time for reflection. It was a clear, crisp evening. The snow from the branches tossed down on to her bare head as she pushed their leaves aside and walked through. The lights of the houses around were like soft candles burning in the darkness.

She walked through the trees at the back of the house, following her sense of direction. She was right: they opened out into Hillaire's yard and she almost walked straight into the long black limo that slid up in front of the house. Alex stood back quickly, pressing herself hard behind the spiny trunk of an ancient snowclad fir. Mochi climbed out and Liam ran down the steps and greeted her as if he had been waiting. Putting his arm around her he got back in the car with her. His comforting gesture seemed to be that of a lover.

Alex felt her eyes burn as she watched them set against the snow: their gentleness together, his faithfulness now a fact that caused a dry lump in her throat. The car pulled away from the kerb silently and glided down the street. He was bringing Mochi with him or else he had simply ignored her call from the hotel porter. Either way, it satisfied one of her wishes: he was gone – but what about the other one? Her breath pumped out against the cold air, and she was conscious of her red nose and cold feet. She had been almost stationary, transfixed by the sight. Now she was free to do one thing – lose her guilt for betraying Liam in any way. Not questioning why she should care, conflicting emotions tearing inside her, she knew one thing: she had time on her side.

Bracing herself, she pushed him out of her heart and, dashing across the road, slipped into their house, through the door and into the sitting room, looking around desperately, an intruder.

There was nothing but a friendly cat to greet her. She started to look, searching for the briefcase she remembered, the one with D.K. on the side. Opening doors, she found a scullery, a dining room; and up on the first floor, Hillaire's study.

Endless cupboards, and none too tidy. There were stacks of folders – any of them could contain the information. She leafed through them, bent down to check the back of the cupboards, closed the doors and looked across at the desk. Here she checked all the drawers and found the bottom two on the right-hand side to have a united false front. Naturally it was locked.

Another frustrating five minutes were spent looking for the key. She sat down at the swivel chair, exasperated, laid her hands on the green blotter, ran her fingers distractedly over its surface and knocked its leather edge. The glint of brass caught the soft light.

Alex flicked it out quickly. A tiny key, a desk key. Fitting it to the lock, she marvelled at the obvious place when she had been searching, losing valuable time. The drawer slid open. The briefcase lay alone in its depths, cradled by two files of paper.

She placed it on the table and tried the catches. Combination lock; a circular dial. She would never find out the numbers. She fiddled with a couple of combinations. Dates, it was always dates. But what dates would he choose? Now slow down. It had to be something Hillaire would remember, because she would take a bet he could not chance writing them down. She closed her eyes and imagined, trying to relax but aware that she was anything but. She thumped the table in frustration.

Birthday? Hell, she didn't know his birthday. What was he – mid-forties; that would mean born in '40, '41, and she'd never been into star signs even if that would give her a clue. Jesus, there was nothing to do but get out, take it, and try to sort it out later. Her hand was on the handle and she was standing, turning, as she remembered.

Like a flash of sunlight itself, the two men standing half

hidden by shadows, the briefcase turning in the light as they shook hands. The initials D.K. catching the sun, the heavy-set men chuckling in the snowy landscape in the porch. The handshake, the words:

'... I always was a fan of Roosevelt ...'

Her fingers touched the dial as if it would reveal its secret. Roosevelt. A birthday, a famous date – it had to be. He had revealed a clue at that time, she was sure of it. Neither of them would have chanced writing it down. With a sense of excitement she thought, and thought hard.

Roosevelt ... land reforms ... history lessons ... long-forgotten facts. She tried every alternative. Why, she had never been good at dates, had always had to stay in for extra prep learning the damn things. Now, what had she learned about Roosevelt?

She closed her eyes.

Pearl Harbor.

7 December 1941.

Nineteen forty-one! Yes, that had to be it. Kowolski's birthday, emigration to America, whatever. Something around that.

7.12.41. her fingers were trembling as she clicked through the numbers, held her breath, pushed the switch.

Nothing.

Oh shit, what could it be then? What else had he done? She looked around the room: history books, reference books. There were plenty of them, but time was definitely not on her side now. Her eyes scanned the room for a clue and fell upon the calendar. The month was stored first. Of *course*. The American way.

12.7.41.

The answering click was like heaven.

And now she was faced with the second obstacle: the lap-top. Switching on was easy enough, even the model – a Macintosh. She had one at home. She clicked in the familiar instructions, looking for the information she sought ...

ACCESS DENIED

Of course, a code. He would have one. Thinking along the

same lines, she clicked in 'Pearl Harbor' – nothing. Franklin D. Roosevelt – nothing. Japan – Second World War – Hiroshima – Variations on both.

ACCESS DENIED

She sat back, fingers on the keyboard, staring at the screen, willing it into life.

She was sure it had to be connected. It was the way the man thought. By all accounts a factual man, a scientist ... but one with extra depth and sensitivity. She remembered her history; a phrase that had stuck in her memory.

Day of Infamy.

Day of death, but also of birth, a new beginning, a freedom from tyranny ...

The letters clicked under her fingers.

The screen rattled into hieroglyphics right in front of her eyes. She scanned the information, trying to read. It was here. All of it. There was referred access to another file, and another. And at last, in layman's language, the truth ...

Clicked open, and laid out before her, the notes were stacked neatly one beneath the other. She ran through the file, feeling more hopeless than ever. The notes were indecipherable; even the headings were double Dutch. Long unintelligible sentences which she would never be able to interpret; mathematical formulae; diagrams. *Some of babies.* Heart pounding, she read through carefully and found a cross-reference.

Notes. Headings to refer to for the conference. Spelling it out, spelling it out for a collection of doctors not always entirely *au fait* with the intricacies of genetics. Notes just meant to inform – about the experiments, the discoveries, the current *achievements* of Kowolski's California laboratory.

Totally absorbed she found herself sinking into the chair and not noticing the time passing by. Could she believe what she was reading? Shadows seemed to gather and press around her as chilled, she read on.

A time bomb. She couldn't make head or tail of the contents of the files, but this one made some sort of horrible sense. Instinctively, even though it was still in doctors' jargon, she knew most of the truth: genetic designer babies grown in lab conditions. Twins for spare parts. Horrible. Flicking through the files once more she thought she understood the graphics now: this was the formula then, the lab reports; in a carefully listed set of research experiments was the formula for creating life. Miki's money, Mochi's body – the elements fired through her mind. The two were to be used for the purpose of unforgivable procreation, she was certain of it.

Sick to her stomach, and armed with the briefcase, Alex had just one thought: she had to get the information out of here. Not because of the doctors' involvement – she could deal with that and them later, but because Sandford Wainwright was on his way like a big black tidal wave about to engulf an island. Mochi might not have the guts to steal, but Alex did, and this was nothing like Montana's need: she had to save something here from being destroyed. She didn't understand, but knew it was terribly important to get the case to safety and ask questions later. She clicked out the program, switched off the machine and, throwing it back into the briefcase, fastened the catches.

She had to trust somebody. And Liam was the one she thought of. It hurt, but just because he'd got a thing with Mochi didn't mean he was untrustworthy. He was the one she needed; she knew he was her best bet. He was the obvious choice; he would interpret the information, suggest what to do with the case until Kowolski returned; a halfway house of truth.

She felt the dark then, gathering all around her. And froze, suddenly certain someone was in the house. Heart in mouth, she stood up, tripped over the edge of the rug, reached out for the lamp and felt it topple over as the hand covered hers like a trap.

'What the hell are you doing?'

Mochi reached the plane and found the steps down awaiting her. The pilot did not greet her, and that was strange. In the pale blue light she hurried across the wet tarmac to the Lear. She was grateful to the young man who had seen her to the airport; she had needed his comfort and a strong shoulder. He had arranged for her to see someone reliable in New York, a real friend this time. This time it would not go wrong. She put her foot on the first step, looking up into the open hatch for the pilot to welcome her.

'Mochi . . .'

She gasped, hand to her throat. 'Miki . . . what are you doing here?'

He looked at her, the question in his own eyes. 'What are *you*?'

'I just planned a trip to New York.'

'Without telling me. Mochi, what is going on?'

She had never gone into Aspen itself without an itinerary before. Now a trip to New York.

'Overnight? What am I supposed to think?'

'I . . . was coming to visit you . . .'

He came slowly down the steps. 'Why, when I would be on my way home anyway?'

'I . . .'

'Mochi, what is going on?'

Sandford had imbued in her husband just the right amount of concern; too much and he would be alert. When he confronted Mochi she was terrified. She tried to wriggle out of it.

'I'd planned another trip to the clinic, Miki.'

'But for what? There's a schedule set. You're not due back there for a week or so. Tell me what you are doing Mochi? How could you think I would not find out?'

'I'd only be gone for the afternoon, Miki. I often go into town for a few hours.'

'But I always know where you are. Do you think this is responsible – flying?'

'Oh come.' She tried to make a joke of it. 'There is no danger yet.'

'There's always danger if you're foolish, Mochi, and don't think things through.'

Of course he was right, but he was the one who had taught her she never had to think for herself. She knew all too well

324

that his staff were in his pay, and she could bet Lee, Maria and Juan were spying on her. She felt firmly in the grip of the ponytailed man. Now she was facing the biggest challenge of her life and trying to deal with it as best she could, and failing miserably. Mochi, feeling the pressure of it all, put her hands to her face and wept.

Miki took her home in silence. In the mirror, Juan Fernandez watched the two of them, taking notes for his new benefactor.

Miki probed his silent thoughts. Already, he was bound up in looking for a way out of his dilemma, and felt guilt towards Mochi for his subterfuge. It did not help that she was acting oddly, and his own anxiety made him angry. It came across as coldness.

Miki was certain she was hiding something: it took one deceiver to know another. There were no signs of running away or accusation, so she did not know about Montana. But she was very frightened; she was shaking in her corner of the car, pressed into the leather as if she wanted to disappear.

He longed to put his arm around her, but they had lived their lives too long in parallel. So he sat, unsure of what to do, and beside him she suffered. When she had gone to Liam's house she had thought of inveigling her way in, trying to seduce him and then running off with the briefcase. Her softness as she stood outside in the snow had been a prelude, easy with his handsome good looks gazing down on her. But she was just not made for that sort of thing; she wouldn't know how to start. She had never had to fight for anything or use any form of manipulation in her life. But she would have to, to survive.

As the limousine sped them home and her plans were ruined, she realised just how far Sandford would go to get his way.

'Hand me the briefcase, Alex.'
He held out his hand to her.
'No.'
She put it behind her, held it firm.

'No!?' He laughed coldly. 'When you're trespassing in someone's house?'

'I won't hand it over, Liam. Not until you listen.'

He folded his arms, but his manner was icy. The fallen lamp cast awkward shadows on his face.

'I'm listening.'

He was also barring her way. There was no way she could get past him, so he had to believe her. Her mouth had gone dry; it was too early in whatever they had between them for mere trust to survive this. The tension was palpable; it came from many different sources.

'Do you know what's in this case, Liam?'

'Not exactly. I do know it's private property.'

'And someone wants it badly enough to steal it. No,' she said, to the sarcastic expression in his eyes. 'Not me . . .'

She hesitated. Either she trusted him or she didn't. Instinctively she looked inside herself for the answer. Though the facts pointed to the opposite, she did trust him. She would.

And she began to tell him.

On the sidewalk outside the Hotel Jerome, Wilhelm flipped his coat tails around him as he slid into the back seat of the car. Boxer, at the wheel, eyed him once before the two pulled out into the light evening traffic.

Neither man had said a word.

TWENTY-SIX

'Just read it,' she begged, as she finished explaining. 'Read what I have read . . . see if you agree . . .'

He stepped forward, and eyeing her, sat down at the desk and turned the fallen lamp upright towards him. As he read, it was like an electric beam and almost immediately he felt the sense of discovery. He saw it reflected in her face, the excitement – and the fear. The message was clear.

'His lab was broken into, Alex,' he said softly.

'Now we know why.'

Here was the full formula, and it was far more advanced than he had imagined: the secret of the body's longevity, and even more, the explosive practice of retrieving bodies from the dead by injecting a drug. The process was fully described, but mostly indecipherable. *A drug.* He studied the hieroglyphics on the page, but they meant little to him. One thing he knew: Hillaire had certainly not told him everything. Liam's interest was intense, but his knowledge of such formulae limited.

'We need someone to interpret this for us. This in talk is gobbledegook.' Seeing his awed reaction, trust had returned to her. And to him. She came close, leaning over his shoulder.

'But who?'

'Ruth Lindstrom,' he said, looking intently at the screen.

She stepped back. 'You must be joking. She'd go bananas that we were looking at it. Besides, she probably already knows. This lot are ready to set the world on fire.'

She paused, aware of him.

'I don't think so. I've got a feeling that Kowolski is keeping this time bomb. He's the best in the business, and Hillaire has simply called him and them together to see what *could* be done, not what will be done. It's tremendously exciting.'

'Are you *crazy*?'

'This is a formula way ahead of its time, Alex,' he said, screwing around in his seat.

'No wonder this mad man wants it. He probably wants to create his own master race.'

'It's possible the notes relate to a revival of a practice long gone, but with the addition of a new discovery, DNA.'

'Bodies for sale ... farming from the dead ... *Resurrection* ... ?'

'Well we don't know for sure.'

'Oh yes we do. And only from a hand-picked litter.'

She was ready to run out with it, and him; had not known that the real dilemma would come now.

'Alex,' he said, stopping her in her tracks. 'I have to tell you why I'm really here. What the conference is all about, what this information could mean if it is what I think it is. Though I am not a part of it, Hillaire has confided in me. He always does. We're in different fields, but we get along real well. We use each other as a sort of sounding board, as it were ... for new ideas ...'

As he spoke he got up and stepped towards her, but Alex retreated, her tension heightening in a very different way. She could not stand this constant ping-ponging with her heart. Excited by the discovery, he did not notice until she exploded:

'You lied, Liam. You *knew* what they were up to.'

'Not exactly, but it's invaluable research, Alex. If only you could understand ...'

'No.' She put up her hands as if he was about to strike her.

But it was words only.

She was furious. First because he had not confided in her the nature of their business, which she saw as morally wrong; secondly there was her own growing alarm; and thirdly, all her senses told her there was something going on here, something she did not understand. But she knew she was not about to hand over such valuable information and have it get into the wrong hands. She was certain there was some sort of link between the body of doctors and Mochi's blackmail. It was the only bit she had held back; she was not yet ready to confide that in him, though from his affair with Mochi he probably knew.

'What is the difference between this and Hitler's idea of a perfect race that began on the makeshift and hideous operating tables of the war camps?' she asked angrily. 'Appalling deeds were done then in the name of *furthering* medicine.' Her outrage and anger were inflamed by her embryonic trust in this man and her feelings for him. 'It appears that history is about to rear its head in a similar way, and even if any prospective operations that come out of the conference are done under different conditions, the ethics are still questionable. The same as those being accused of war crimes; playing at God . . .'

'That's a very simplistic way of looking at it, Alex. So black and white. The grey areas in this are the ones to be looking at: how this research can be used for the good of mankind –'

'Spoken like a doctor, Liam. And you know where that will get you.'

'And how about you, Alex? Do your journalistic feelings have nothing to do with this? A good story – isn't that why you've been hounding the truth out of everybody, chasing up the doctors' angle to see what's going on? Now you've found out, what are you going to do with it – let it ride? Somehow, I don't think so. Not when I find you in here trying to take a sneak look at this briefcase . . .'

Their angry words tore at the air, then stilled, leaving behind them the stain of their distrust, and of their burgeoning feelings all hardened into one ball of hurt.

'The world *should* know: lives will be saved; morality will win when it comes to using it for the proper process. The world is not fuelled by opportunists, though they are there. In the right hands proper use will be made of this excellent information.' He was trying to argue the point with a surprisingly difficult Alex. 'Ruth and David are holding for the moral voice . . .'

'You're naive, Liam.'

Yet even as she spoke she admired him, understanding his character and her own. It would make her a better journalist if she ever got back to that in the future, might give her the 'soul' she needed, and she reflected that perhaps this was why it had not worked out for her and Hart. Alex was torn by her own feelings of being a journalist. And now he had pointed that out to her, none too kindly. The truth hit hard. She was trained to respond to the story – and what was she going to do with it? She hadn't thought. But this confrontation revitalised her; confrontation – and Liam. Quickly, she thought back again to her relationship with Hart. Did Liam want recognition the way Hart did ... didn't she want the story? Simmering down, she looked into the strong face before her, saw the integrity standing there in his eyes and the firm set of his lips. His flaming words were not those of a liar, a self-seeker. No, Liam was almost entirely altruistic: this was a man who was not self-congratulatory. She saw suddenly that, although he had a will of granite, he was a true doctor, pursuing the greater human good, not his own. And ironically it was she that had always chased a story.

'You're right,' she said slowly. 'Though this time I am not thinking as a journalist. The press can be very damaging.'

'No doubt about it,' he said, calming down. He sat on the back edge of the sofa. 'If the contents of this briefcase become open knowledge there could be huge dangers ahead.'

'You never know people, Liam.'

'You're right.' He pushed his hands into his pockets, his body relaxing. 'You have to go on instinct.'

'All right.' She took a breath, feeling the burning in her eyes diminish. 'I have to trust someone, and it might as well be you.'

'Thanks,' he said drily. But he made no move. It was she who clicked out the program, she who made the step forward to close down the laptop. Liam sat with his bottom still parked on the edge of the small two-seater sofa. She fastened the catches on the case as he watched her.

Aware of the bright light in his eye, and his hand as he put it out and took the briefcase, and the way he ran his fingers over its surface as if it were precious, a valuable cargo, her heart caught as she watched him. Whether it was the strength in his long brown hands, the determined profile or the cool grey eyes with their glinting depths – was it interest, challenge or winning? – she did not know if she trusted him completely. She swallowed, her feelings were so mixed. She hoped that she had not just handed over dynamite to the wrong party.

'I've arranged to meet Montana and I have to go.' She fastened her jacket. 'What are we going to do?'

'First we have to find out where we stand. We have people to protect here. They could be hurt badly if we get it wrong,' he said, looking up. 'Mochi, for one.'

'Right.' Her eyes caught his. 'What about Mochi?'

She met a stone wall. 'What about her?'

'She and her husband are involved here, aren't they?'

His voice was level. Mochi had trusted him with herself. This was not a point he cared to discuss. He saw the girl's eyes flare again, and felt his own response.

'She seems very much in awe of Miki,' Alex went on.

'She's been ruled by him, it's true, but she is intelligent,' he said carefully, protecting her confidence. 'Enough to think for herself, if necessary.'

'And most attractive.'

'That too.' Now he smiled.

'I saw you two together. You seemed . . . very close.'

'That is simply not your business.'

The reasons why she should even bring it up stood there between them. The fact that it mattered made him smile, slowly, and the smile met an answering flush in her face. But she didn't drop her eyes despite her infuriating reaction.

'Are you her lover?'

He came over, placing the briefcase down. His hand stayed hers on the zip of her jacket, and pushed it back down. He slid his arms into the warmth and pulled her close. He seemed to tower over her and she felt the strength and the passion in those eyes.

331

'Why would you want to know?'

He saw the answer in her face; she could not hide it.

'Alex . . .?'

She put up her hands to try and hold him away, but he was dominant enough to unnerve her. She did not want to break Mochi's confidence; it wasn't hers to share. She pulled herself free and walked away, putting the sofa between them, changing the subject, anything to still the trembling that had begun when he touched her. And now there was something else; reality. Like a cold chill she realised it. She swung around to look at the window, where the curtains stood open to the darkness. They had to get out. Standing there with the briefcase between them, any second someone might come in and catch them.

She did not want him to know how he affected her; did not feel ready for this. Her body betrayed her, she had felt pliant and willing, longing just to melt into him, and a liquid heat had poured through her as she imagined his kiss. Her eyes, despite herself, went straight to his lips as she turned, to his hands. She tried to gather her shaking thoughts. He was still standing where she had left him, that supercilious smile on his face.

'Let's get out of here. Discuss this some place else.'

She headed swiftly for the door, the briefcase in hand, and he came with her, heading out over the snow to the back of the house.

The car that swung up in front of the house stopped, cutting its engine as Liam held the last of the low pine branches back for Alex to make her way through. The branches closed behind them with a swing of white powder as the two men climbed out of the car and looked around.

The lights were out in her aunt's house. Alex drew the curtains and laid the briefcase on the table, smoothing away a small dusting of flour with her palm. Suddenly Mochi's face came back to her, and as quickly she brushed it away.

She switched on the lamp as he came into the room, very tall and seeming to fill the space. In the soft light his eyes seemed to find their way into her, watching her without any form of pretence.

As he sat at the table, he placed his hands in an apex from above which his eyes gathered her in.

Alex plugged in the kettle out of habit, pulling down cups as he watched her intently. She spoke as if to save herself, though from what she had not as yet put into words.

'This Sandford Wainwright wants that information, and somehow plans to use it, that's why I came to take it. Not because I'm a journalist.' They had not known who to trust, but they wanted to tell, to clear the slate with each other. She did not think why as she ran on: 'The briefcase anyway is dynamite. I want to take it with me. Get it out of this house, away from here. I think it should be delivered to Hillaire tonight. At least we know where he is. Or at least hidden until we can get the first flight out in the morning.'

Alex had always acted on instinct, it had made her what she was. But Liam did not share her fears; he'd been schooled in the lab.

'The briefcase is not ours to remove,' he said infuriatingly. 'Hillaire is responsible for it. Besides, he'll be back in the morning.'

'Not until lunchtime, and Hillaire does not know about Sandford,' she argued, 'nor his unethical plans – if he did, he would remove the briefcase immediately.' She was bound by her oath to Mochi and could not involve her, but it would be a good point: if Liam cared for her he would want her out of danger. He was being so obstinate and it was frustrating; she felt the net closing, danger nearby. She'd seen it coming often enough in her job to sense its approach. 'There is only one way, and that is for me to take it out of the house before Sandford gets wind of our involvement. Hillaire can decide what to do with it from the safety of New York. Sandford will use strong-arm tactics next and it'll be too late. I know what I'm talking about. He'll look for it here, Liam. He doesn't know I'm on the track, but I bet he knows about you. He seems to have spies everywhere. Let me hide it somewhere while we think what to do.'

'All right, on one condition. That I run it over to you later – I want just an hour or so to read, myself.'

'But you said yourself that the bulk of the material is double Dutch to you . . .'

'The major notes are not. Alex, just an hour. I can't let this pass me by. Understand?'

Whether she did or not, he had decided.

'All right.' But it was with reluctance. 'Meet me at the Motherlode in an hour, Liam, or I'll start to worry.' She pointed to the street. 'Put the briefcase in the wheelhouse compartment of my aunt's car. Go through the back door into the garage and no one will see. I'll take the pickup into town.' She rezipped her jacket, and the remembered warmth of his hands on her made her shake.

'I can't help feeling someone, somewhere, is orchestrating this more than we know and we're in the middle of a large plan that we don't fully understand,' she said, keeping her voice cool. She stepped away a pace, felt the loss and stopped. His voice came from behind her.

'It's quite possible, and Alex – I don't plan to simply put this in the wrong hands. I just want to read it through. Then talk it over with Ruth. Find out what the hell is going on.'

'She probably knows already.' Her voice was caustic.

'I think you're wrong. I reckon she'll be as surprised as we are.'

He stood up then and without averting his eyes came closer. She felt his breath on her cheek.

'Talk to Hillaire. He will convince you I am right,' she said. His hands touched her shoulders and spun her round. He took the cup from her hand and placed it, carefully, back on the counter.

She looked up at him.

'I think I should get out of here,' she said. But his voice was too soft, his nearness too inviting. She backed slightly and found herself imprisoned by the counter. Her small gasp of surprise brought him nearer, his arms slipping possessively around her, a darkness she understood in his eyes. His hips moved in against her, near enough for her to feel the

334

heat of him, the cloth that brushed her. The hand that cupped her chin was warm as he lifted her face to meet his. Her strong resolve had been weakened, and this time . . .

'In a moment.'

This time as his lips came down on hers she did not back away.

'*Señor* Wainwright. I have news.'

'Talk to me.'

'Mr and Mrs Leng are now home. They did not talk, all the way.'

'Good . . .'

'But before, she travel to the airport with a young man, after your phone call, she go to his house and pick him up.'

Sandford sat forward, the chair leather squeaking. He crouched over his desk like an animal, intent. 'Who?'

'I don't know his name, but I know where he live.'

'Well, what did he look like?'

'Tall, handsome, a white Americano. Very charming to her, and – '

'Goddamnit . . .'

Sandford thumped his desk. Though she had been diverted from her task, someone had helped her, so she had confided in the man. This could well thwart his plans. It didn't take him long to find out who.

'That's not good enough, you idiot! I'm not paying for half-assed information. Have you seen him before?'

'I was about to say.' The voice sighed with patience. 'I have seen him with Professor Bowman. I tink he live in the same house as the doctor, *señor*.'

The young doctor.

'That's better. That's what I want to know.' Sandford's evil mind swung around and lit on Liam.

It was time to take action. He pressed the buttons rapidly on his desk.

'Boxer . . . where are you . . . ?'

'We just left the house. No one there, no case. Looks like someone's been searching already. Couple of papers on the floor, footsteps outside in the snow. They led into the trees, but it's dark – we lost 'em.'

Sandford's hand fisted on the table.

'Both of you get over here right away. Come get me. No more soft touch. I want somebody dealt with – now.'

TWENTY-SEVEN

The kitchen lamp shone on the screen. Liam read avidly, deep into the subject. A knock at the back door made him jump.

He went over cautiously, opening the door a fraction.

'Ruth!'

She smiled warmly. 'Don't act so surprised. Didn't you call me to meet up?'

'No.' Puzzled, he looked back into the room, back at her, but didn't open the door wider. She looked pointedly at the handle, her own hands fisted deep into her pockets against the cold. She was still smiling, but some of the warmth had turned to query.

'I got a message from the hotel porter that he couldn't get hold of you. Something about a drink in the bar?' He looked blank, but she went on. 'I drove over to get you, found you gone and as I came around the corner,' she said, freeing one of her hands to point, 'I saw you and Alex come into the house.' She tucked the hand back in, and said to his silence: 'I could still do with a drink. Any chance I could come in?'

'Oh, yes . . . of course.' He stood back, then remembered as she came around the edge of the door: 'Ruth, in fact I wanted to call you but . . .'

He never finished. As Ruth stood there in the edge of the lamplight, her smile was dying fast.

'Ruth . . .' He went to close down the computer, but she had seen.

'Isn't that David's case . . .?' Open on the table beside him. 'Liam, what are you doing? Did Hillaire say you could do this?' She saw the gleam in his eye, the intense interest. 'What have you seen?'

She made to go over, but he barred her way.

'Do you know what's in these papers, Ruth?' he said, bypassing her question.

'Yes.'

She took him on now, straight up.

'Did Hillaire tell you why he wanted to set up this conference?'

'To get us all together. But Liam, look, it's in the interests of knowledge, not of use of that knowledge. David and I are the balance here . . . Hillaire chose us for that reason. You don't need to worry.'

Once again her eyes searched, tried to view the screen, as if by exposure the world would print off their message and run it free.

'Ruth,' he said, 'tell me what I think I already know . . .'

'What do you know?'

'Not as much as I'd like to,' he said, standing back. The top notes now read through, he had been trying to decipher the attendant research papers. Ruth could not help herself; the scientist in her stepped forward as if in a dream, reaching out for something that was the lodestar of discovery.

Fastening her glasses to her nose, she scanned David's screen. It was her subject and she was tempted. Not long enough for her to memorise all of it, but she read enough for her to confirm their feelings, gathering the whole truth to her.

'I knew it,' she said, straightening up. 'David has gone further than any of us knew. He cannot only recreate from frozen tissue, not only can he recreate from the long dead, but . . . *there is a child living* . . . *oh God,*' she whispered, 'he didn't tell us . . .'

'Do you think he meant to?'

'Probably couldn't trust himself, or us. Look what he has found: experiments on living flesh, taken from the dying . . . November, 1972 . . . host figure . . . *God,*' she said, her mind racing as she pressed the keyboard buttons feverishly to close down the message. 'No one must see this. If this got out, we would have horror on our hands. Grave robbers, pieces of long-dead dictators being sold on the open market. Even Hitler, if a small piece of his flesh could be found. So he *wasn't joking* . . .'

'The moral voice, Ruth?'

Her eyes met his, their excitement, but also their fear, catching. It was real. If it was true, the future was here in their hands. He was excited himself now, knowing he had been right about her, knowing she had interpreted his own feelings correctly. There had been far more than Hillaire had let either of them know. Had he planned for her to know, or was it just between him and David . . .

She seemed to read his thoughts.

'At least let me borrow it for the evening, it can't hurt anyone. David would have been planning to share it with me anyway, as I was at least part of the team.'

'Perhaps,' said Liam, but despite the challenge in her eyes, he did not hand it over. 'This thing's going to run away with itself. David knew it would, which is why he left it with Hillaire. He had a level head. He probably already knows.'

'*I* already know.'

'But not how to recreate all of this, Ruth,' he said, perceptively. 'It's all in *here*, isn't it? You've already heard but not seen,' he said accusingly, and she lowered her eyes fractionally. 'And only a part of it, not the whole. These introductory notes do not relate to the full extent of David's research –'

'Christ, Liam, you don't know how much this means to me,' she remonstrated, but Liam was steadfast.

'It has to remain fiction, Ruth. Now, let's go.' He took her arm and led her out, pulling the door to behind him. 'Alex was right. I think there is some dirty work afoot, and I'm going to hide this particular little piece of dynamite.'

'Alex?'

'Yes.' His eyes held hers. 'You said there was no need to worry, right . . .'

'But with *this*.'

'I wish you two would stop distrusting each other. You're both of one mind, if you'd only realise it.' He headed down the steps, guiding her reluctantly beside him. 'She's not going to read it, just stop worrying. She can't anyway, you know that.'

'Where are you going?' she said, her eyes on the case. She didn't want it out of her sight.

Laughing, he pushed her into her car. 'Get going. I don't plan to tell you.'

'Don't trust me, Liam?'

He leaned into her window. 'I don't trust myself either, Ruth. I'm going to put it somewhere where it's out of both our hands. Then ... I'm going to have a word with my old friend, and yours ...'

Wilhelm closed the door quietly as he came in, brushing the snow from his shoulders. Sandford had disbanded them in order to try and find out the truth. His troubled mien would have been obvious to all but his wife, who sat engrossed at her dressing table, poring over some paperwork.

'Christ, Ruth. I thought you said you'd be down in a couple of minutes. I've been sitting at the bar waiting.'

She hardly raised her head.

'Work isn't everything. Come along ...' She was so immersed in scribblings and notations she did not hear him. He leaned over and startled her. 'What *are* you so involved in?'

She jumped. 'Wilhelm?'

'Yes, *Wilhelm*.' He looked at the jottings on her paper. 'What *is* this?'

'I ... er ...'

'Come on, Ruth. I *am* your husband. *Tell* me ...'

'Wilhelm, you must promise to keep a secret.'

'Naturally.' He sat down beside her. The information was gathering doctors like trees in a brushfire. But he was her husband and why should she not tell him? But she would not tell him how she got it; that would infuriate Hillaire. She would have to say David had let it slip.

She shared it with him, words tumbling over themselves, and was gratified that her normally fractious husband did not criticise her once. Wilhelm listened with extreme interest, his heart pounding. Jesus, right here on his doorstep – she knew where it was. Gathering his words and manner carefully, he knew he would get the truth out of her. Then he must tell Sandford right away.

'Where did you get this information?' His voice was over-casual. 'I thought Hillaire had it under lock and key.' That was the question she had dreaded. His eyes now held both an accusation of conspiracy and desire.

'David told me.'

'Come on, Ruth, you can do better than that.' His eyes were ruthless with need that he knew he could not disguise, though he tried. He would simply have to bully her into submission; it had always worked better than persuasion. 'David wasn't about to share this with anyone. You'd have told me yesterday. Who found it for you?'

She swallowed hard.

'His houseguest, Liam Gower.' Wilhelm nodded, accepting this answer. 'No one else knows. He left the case there.'

'And Liam looked through it.'

'Er no, a friend of his.'

'Is it still there?'

'No, they've taken it.'

Wilhelm's senses jumped into alarm mode, but not for the reasons she thought. Anger brought him to his feet.

'What business did he have taking it!?'

'I think as Hillaire's friend, he felt – '

'They had no right.'

'No, listen, Wilhelm.' She rose to her feet and now she whispered the truth. 'There is far more in those notes than you and I suspect. And Liam and this girl believe there is some sort of conspiracy going on.'

'Conspiracy?' Guilt and fear pulsed through him; he saw the loss of his own future, and it fired him into anger. 'What *are* you talking about, Ruth? And you believed this, and let it happen? Hillaire will be most annoyed. We should tell him.' He banged his forefinger repeatedly against the palm of his other hand. 'We must get it back quickly now that Liam has spilled the beans to this girl; we are after all the experts on this subject the world over. Go and get it, Ruth. Bring it back and I will fly it up to Hillaire immediately.' He drilled his eyes into hers; it was a *fait accompli*. And he would take care of the case *en route*.

But Ruth's answer surprised him.

'No, Wilhelm. As a matter of fact I endorse their decision,' she said gravely. 'This is too incestuous, and it needs an impartial jury. Alex is going to take a flight out of town tomorrow, and she is right to return the briefcase.'

'To David?'

'To Hillaire – he's closer, and because she feels the contents are too volatile.' Wilhelm heard the warning note, and pressed a little further.

'Why should she worry? He'll be back soon.'

'Well, according to them, it's not that simple. As I said, they think there's something up. Alex is afraid of the notes getting into the wrong hands. I must say I misjudged her,' she said, getting up. 'I thought she was just another nosy journalist. I warned Liam off.'

'She's a *journalist*?'

'One of the best.'

Wilhelm was amazed. The information they were after was sitting somewhere in Aspen and they didn't even have it due to his stupid wife. And the bitch who had it was a fucking *journalist*...

'Well,' Ruth was saying as she took his arm, 'what about that dinner you promised me? I'm famished after all that excitement.' She walked him to the door. 'And afterwards we'll tell Hillaire. I've already put in a call to him. His housekeeper says he'll be home in an hour. He'll be quite happy, don't worry, darling; he trusts Liam implicitly. So do I...'

Wilhelm let himself be led down the hall, his anger a living thing contained within him as he tried to stop himself from grabbing her and throwing her against the wall in frustration. Then, she would never tell him. Deep inside her, Ruth was made of steel. He sensed that; it was only the periphery that he conquered so often. This time she would fight back. No, he knew of another way.

'He'll be back tomorrow,' she said. 'If I know him. We'll have it all sorted out by then.'

'Yes, we will...'

Downstairs, the bar was half empty. They settled into a corner. One drink, and he was begging off.

'Damn . . .'

'What is it?'

'I've just remembered some important notes I left up at the Red Mountain house. I want to go over them tonight. Look,' he said, wiping his lips with his napkin. He patted her hand: 'You finish your dinner and meet me in the lounge for a liqueur. Perhaps we'll go out for dessert, yes?'

'All right.' She frowned. 'Can't it wait till morning.'

'Ah well. You know how it is, Ruth. When you need to work . . .'

The blue eyes were cold. He patted her hand.

'. . . I'll be back soon.'

TWENTY-EIGHT

'Jack, can I borrow your car?'

'Sure, but . . .'

'Cool. Check you later.'

'Montana, wait . . .'

But the door had slammed, and the softly lit street was empty. She had gone.

Montana looked up the slope towards the massive house set on the lip of the mountain as she switched off the engine and the quiet motor died into silence. There were dim lights on in the upstairs room and in one downstairs; the conference room, she thought. It looked hostile but exciting, the grand setting seeming to spell a warning to keep out. She could not have driven in anyway, the gates were locked, but there was a pedestrian passway, built for the maids, she imagined. She knew there was a security beam there, because he had told her.

She bent low to avoid setting off the alarm, then walked up quietly in the darkness, her eyes on the house. No one came out to kill her: no mad guard dog or trained karate-chopping servant. Montana paused a moment, and tossed her keys gently in her hand, getting her bearings. Ah yes, over there.

Always straightforward in her actions, she'd decided to pay a visit to Miki. Unused to the oriental mind, she felt he was moving too slowly. She had an hour or more to kill before meeting Alex, and Jack, with his ear to the wall, had told her that Mochi had just headed out of town; he'd seen her on her way to the airport. She saw the long black limo in the drive but it did not bother her – presumably it had just returned from dropping Mochi off – and entered the house quietly through the lit door of the conference room, the route in from the hot tub that she remembered. She meant to creep up the back stairs and surprise him.

As she headed down the corridor, she heard the man's voice.

'*Shit*,' she said softly.

She'd have to pass the door, and she'd be seen. Think up some story. From what she knew this bunch were not part of the house in general. Walk past, head in the air as if she owned the place. Why, even if she bumped into Mrs Leng herself she'd say she was delivering flowers, or something.

She stepped forward, about to place her foot in the beam of light, but something – perhaps remembering the rat from the desert and Alex holding her back, or an inner gut re-action to the man's tone of voice – made her stop.

And she was glad she did. The conversation was not on the telephone as she had thought, but being held with a man so silent she had not realised he was literally on the other side of the door. She held her breath as he spoke. A shrewd operator herself, Montana was not thrown by the sinister voice, but listened in silence.

'. . . so he's got the case.'

'No, I don't think he has. The girl has. And she means to take it out of town in the next twenty-four hours.'

'What girl?'

'Alex is her name, I gather. She's a fucking journalist too.'

Montana froze, on full alert.

The man shifted from the door: she saw him clearly, and pushed back against the wall. She'd seen him before, in town. His name was Wilhelm.

'Well, get rid of her.'

'I plan to. Soon as I find her.'

'And if she hasn't got the case on her, find that too. Any way you can. This is your future too, Wilhelm. I'll put Boxer at the airport, just in case she slips out.'

Alex was in danger. The man moved across the room and his voice echoed. She pressed a little closer to the hinge of the door and peeped in. The second man had his back to her, but his voice was awfully familiar. And now she saw there was a third: she knew who he was immediately – the

guy she and Chiffon had chatted to so freely, more than
once, in the bar. Oh, Christ. Placing her hands each side of
the crack she watched them; there were long gaps between
their sentences as the main man clearly thought his way
through this, leading the triad; the room echoed so much
she could hear his shoes squeak. She tried not to let her
heavy breathing give her away.

'What about your wife?'

'Ruth?'

'You got two of them?'

'She won't be any trouble. She believes in me totally. I
put on a good act. She will get the papers off them. They
trust her.'

'But she doesn't trust you, right?'

She could hear him smile. Her heart beat fast.

'I can talk her into it.'

'Then do it. She's your wife, Wilhelm. She'll do as she's
told, or we'll deal with her as well. Got that?'

Silence fell beyond the door, and Montana closed her
eyes, willing her heart to slow. For a moment she glanced
towards the lit staircase that led up beside the door and then
down to where she had come in. So easy to get out of here
... but she had to hear it all.

'What will happen if this fails?'

Another silence, this one distinctly unpleasant. She interpreted fast: Montana had been in all sorts of trouble in her
life with Johnnie, and she'd got used to pregnant silences.
And then of course there'd been that time with the cops ...

'I will get hold of the papers, don't worry.' Because his
life depended on it.

She watched as the ponytailed man turned his face. She
knew him now, she'd seen him often and never liked him.
He'd always looked at her strangely.

'Now I have Mochi Leng in my hands, I plan to use her,'
Sandford concluded. The words were eerie. His speculation
over Liam now rested also on Alex. He saw them as a dual
threat. He remembered the girl with the strength in her
face. So she was a journalist. 'I wonder how much the girl
knows of the experiments.'

'In connection with Liam,' Wilhelm informed him, 'she is probably very well versed in the extent of what is possible, and more than probably now knows all about your blackmail of Mike's wife.' He felt no loyalty to the young friend of Hillaire's. Ruth thought of him too highly. He saw it all slipping away as he realised Liam's involvement with Mochi, and Alex, who had found all of this out.

'These two have got right in my way.' Sandford's voice held menace.

Wilhelm filled in with more information.

'She's the niece of Fabrice Strauss, Ruth recognised her.'

'Ah . . . yes. *I* know the one.' Sandford recalled the girl further, the shade of toughness in the feminine face. He knew he had someone in his way, someone who must be eradicated. The rest he could control. 'Boxer . . . do you know this Alex Dawnay?'

'Yes. She came into Chasers when I was there. She travelled in with Montana Farr, Fenner's friend. The one who hit on Miki.'

The circle connected, and Montana jumped out of her skin.

'You know where she lives?'

'I can find out in no time.'

'Get rid of her, but be smart about it. The doctor too. They're going to cause me no end of trouble. First, find out where the briefcase is. Wilhelm will help you. Check the airport for outgoing flights, then get on the phone and track them down. They shouldn't be hard to find. This town is not exactly New York. Someone'll tell you where they are.'

'Right.'

'An accident on the slopes would be perfect.' He sliced a finger across his throat in mime. 'Take them into the back country and drop them out of a chopper into a ravine. Anything; but Boxer . . .'

'Yes, sir.'

'Make sure they have skis with them when they fall – we want it to look authentic.'

Montana's shock was diverted as she heard a door open

upstairs, and Mochi's unmistakable voice which was tearful. Her eyes stared upwards as if at any moment Mochi would come downstairs. The door closed again, but the distant voices continued. Shit: Jack said she had gone out of town for the day. Mochi had told him that in case anyone had asked, knowing Miki frequented the bar. For some reason the trip had not happened.

Now all Montana could think about was getting out. Prising herself softly away from the wall, she paused for a second to see if she was safe, and grimaced at the silence that had fallen between the three men. Even more reason to get going: any moment they'd be out here. That thought motivated her more than anything, and glad of the thick carpet that ran down the centre of the boards, she headed for the door, turned the knob with the greatest care, and was out, pushing it closed oh so gently. Heading like a wraith down the drive, she stumbled once and then ran as fast as she could on the balls of her feet on the icy downward slope. Through the gate, only remembering the beam at the very last minute, she ducked as though she'd been shot then stumbled along the outside road in the dark, snowflakes whirling down into a silent world. Her footsteps would be visible – but who'd be looking?

Luckily her car was at the end of the road, the lock smothered in snow. She brushed it away and pushed in the key, letting herself into the warmth with a rush of sound. Just as well she had not wanted to alert Miki, and she couldn't have driven in through the gates with their alarm system. Clearly, Wilhelm had a key. To have slipped in the way she did had probably saved her skin.

She pushed the car out of the lay-by, and jumped it out into the road as her snowy boot slid on the pedal. Nerves; she had to calm down. Even running away from Johnnie wasn't as nerve-racking as this. As she drove away she had another thought; she faced her own dilemma, and she had the whole drive into town to think about it. Driving slower once she was away, she checked the mirror then her own feelings. It was going to destroy her ambitions when she told

Alex. She didn't know the full story nor to what extent Miki was involved, but one thing was clear to her: Miki would never forgive her, nor would the clannish Aspen elite if she somehow got this wrong. But there was no other route; she saw the end of all her dreams as she headed towards the meeting with her friend. She knew she had to tell Alex: not only was she in danger, but she'd been there for her when the chips were down – wasn't that what a friend was for? Montana deliberated on this all along the road into town, but knew there was no alternative. Alex had saved her ass. Now it was her turn.

'Shit,' she said. And hit the steering wheel with her fist. 'Shit, shit.' This was where she came in.

The gates swung open and shut just behind her as Wilhelm, Boxer and Sandford headed into town in Sandford's car. The man had insisted on meeting at the Red House: an unnerving request with the owners in residence. But he had said he had them in the bag – if they came downstairs, which they would not. It was part of his diabolical humour that he could come and go as he pleased . . .

Wilhelm chewed at the side of his thumb as they drove. There'd been total silence in the car as they drove away; Sandford's tension did not allow for small talk. Wilhelm had known he must tell Sandford right away, but his dilemma was that his own wife had encouraged the information to slip away from them. He was in awe of Sandford, and kept this to himself – after all, Ruth did not know of his double trade, so he had learned to tread a middle road. Wilhelm believed he was right too: there was a swing to the right these days, more than apparent here in Aspen, a backlash against postwar liberalism, and he and Sandford were simply part of this corrective process.

He had to tread carefully with Ruth, and show himself as sympathetic. The pharmaceutical tycoon would want the software for himself and there was no way he would give it to the world. It was worth a great deal to him to keep to himself and use at his own discretion. Wilhelm knew that he would have to run off a copy for himself as insurance. He did not trust the man at all, but he needed him.

Now they were all on the way to visit his wife. Wilhelm did not see himself in the role of thug, but his friends did. Worried, he sat in the back of the car, his silence attributable to fear.

The birds had flown. But Sandford had a plan.

'Ah, Ruth . . .'

He'd found her in the lobby and bent over to kiss her cheek; his was as cold as ice.

'Wilhelm, wherever did you get to?' She looked at his hands. 'And where are the papers you went for?'

He sat down opposite her, his hand sliding across her shoulder as he did so. He kept his eyes on her, and it wasn't hard. Her cheeks were a little pink from the fire and her eyes glowed. The dress she was wearing was simple and black with a rope of pearls, and her stockinged legs were elegant in simple courts.

'You look wonderful, Ruth.'

She smiled. 'That doesn't answer my question.'

'I turned back halfway. I thought – why work tonight . . .'

'Well that sounds like a great idea. But you took ages.' She put down the book she was reading.

'I sat and thought about what you were saying for a moment. Realised how I've been neglecting you lately.'

She laid a hand on his. 'Wilhelm, how sweet of you, but we've both been busy, haven't we?' she offered. But she appreciated it, he could see that.

Wilhelm dreamed of riches; it helped with his subterfuge and his conscience as he sweet-talked her, and he still loved her too. She was attractive, willing and very smart. And normally cooperative. In many ways, this was a means to an end, not something he felt too bad about doing. For them both he would gain riches such as she had never dreamed of; certainly *her* work would never provide it. She worked for the clinic and took a wage. It was a small way of thinking. His way was big.

350

He took her hand between his.

'Ruth ... this couple, Liam and Alex ...'

She looked at him quizzically.

'Do you know where they are?'

She shook her head. 'No idea, why?'

He gave a short laugh. 'Because of the briefcase.'

'Well no, I don't know.' His urgency was making her uncomfortable. The softness had gone from his eyes – if it had ever been there – and he seemed nervous. It had an effect on her.

'So how would we get the case back to Hillaire?'

'Well, we wouldn't,' she said, explaining gently. 'She's taking it to David.'

'Can we trust them with this?'

'Absolutely.' A sickeningly trusting smile lit her face. 'I spoke to Hillaire while you were gone ...' Wilhelm could have kicked himself for forgetting that small point; he should have taken her somewhere, anywhere, where Hillaire could not have spoken to her, endorsing her decision: '... he told me I had done the right thing, that Liam could be trusted implicitly. He was very worried about the idea of someone trying to steal the notes, but not altogether surprised. After all, there was that break-in at the lab. He put two and two together. Wilhelm ... what is the matter?'

He had paled, and his hands had tightened into fists that he now balled against his face.

'Somehow you have to take them into your confidence, and somehow get hold of the papers, or at least find out if we could have photocopies before the notes are taken away ...'

'Why?'

'Because I want to know! I'm a scientist – like you. I'm interested, goddamnit ...'

But Wilhelm was too eager; he had overplayed his hand. For some reason she could not name, Ruth felt uneasy.

She withdrew her hand a little. 'Why, Wilhelm?'

'For us, Ruth,' he said, with an almost desperate sadness.

She took a long pause. 'I told you, I haven't a clue.'

Alex was toying with her drink as Montana arrived at the Motherlode bar. Her knowledge was an irony which amused her, but she'd always been a fatalist too. She'd been on her way to screw the guy, and she'd got screwed herself. Still, at least Alex would be safe, though she'd never ever thought of herself as altruistic before – it had always been a one-way stretch for Montana.

Alex turned her head as Montana came close. She stood up, the tension breaking into something of a smile. Montana pushed her back down into her seat and clambered on to the chair beside her, pressing close.

'Sit down, Jesus, have I got something to tell you! I just went up to the – Red House, you know . . .'

'To see Miki?'

'Yes, and – '

'But Mochi's in town, isn't she?'

'Yes,' she said, stopping in her tracks. 'How did you know? I thought Jack, the fount of all knowledge, was infallible.'

'Well, I knew because . . . look, Montana, you know, you were right – there is definitely something going on here. Liam and I dug out a real scheme. You won't believe this. I have to head out of town right after he gets here, but – '

'No no, listen. *You* don't understand, Alex. You're in – '

'Oh, here he is . . .'

Liam came in, eyes searching, and found her right away. The heat in his eyes mirrored her own, and the quick nod told her he had done as she asked. She felt a flood of gratitude, and for the moment there was nothing else in the room but him. Montana looked into her face and saw like a revelation the warmth and the real beauty that is rare touch her. Staring, she turned quickly to look at its cause. He was coming over, walking with an athletic grace, ruffling his dark hair free of its damp pelt of snow.

Shit, *handsome* . . .

'Jesus, what a gorgeous guy.'

'I knew you'd like him, but hands off. He's mine . . .'

Alex smiled brightly. Montana realised her friend's feelings very quickly as their eyes met. And he was there.

'Got rid of it?'

'Yep.' He lounged at the bar, and his eyes took in Montana, who posed automatically under the scrutiny. 'In the place you suggested . . . Hi . . .'

Alex introduced them, the smile still hovering. A new gentleness was in her face and the hair was down, Montana observed wryly. Two in one spot, just as well.

'Liam, huh. Listen, you guys, and listen hard –'

'Oh, Liam, thank goodness I caught you up. Thank you for lending me your scarf . . .'

'Ruth, hi.'

He stood to offer his seat.

'Oh no, it's OK. I'm not staying.' She glanced at Montana, then at Alex, and she was distinctly nervous. Montana's face was brittle with distrust, her eyes like those of a cat about to pounce when the mouse made its first run for it.

Ruth felt disappointment, and the hostility. She'd known where he'd be, because of course he'd told her. This was a brand new avenue for her, and one she had never travelled before, for Ruth believed implicitly in loyalty. Confiding in her husband had always come naturally. Ruth was ruled by him; despite her professional ability, she had an emotional Cinderella complex, a need to be loved, so she always capitulated to him. And he had always played on this. Going against him, getting the confidence of Liam and Alex, went against the grain.

Alex turned to her friend, once Liam and Ruth fell into idle conversation.

'Isn't he something! What was it you were going to tell me, Montana?'

Montana downed her drink, and touched Alex's hand. 'Meet me round the back in two minutes . . .'

'Why, what . . .?'

'Just do it, OK. There's a tow-away zone round the back. Meet me there. It's important . . . bye!' she said, lifting a hand. She stood up, eyes level with Liam, and hers were cold. These two were in league, and Alex was in danger.

She believed Ruth was as operational as her husband and, keeping her secret to herself, she left. 'Nice meeting you. Gotta run . . .'

Five minutes later, Alex was there. Breathlessly, Montana let her have the whole story, ending with the bit about Mochi, and the disposal of the baby. Alex was horrified.

'Now I know how Sandford means to make his plans work. Wilhelm knows we have the briefcase,' said Alex. Then her blood ran cold. 'How on earth did he find out?'

Montana answered for her. 'Liam told Ruth.' She stared into her face. 'Liam was the doctor Mochi saw, Alex.'

'No, he just steered her in the right direction.'

'The right direction? Straight into her husband's arms, with nothing done?'

'But that wasn't his fault.'

'Wasn't it?'

'He was as upset as I was. Why, I even accused . . .'

And then she remembered: that look in his eye, the way he wouldn't answer. The way he'd kissed her, and she'd fallen for it.

Alex felt a chill – neither of them had confided this in her. She should not have trusted Liam after all. Why had she? Her instincts had told her she could. She was torn by wanting to believe him, to trust him, yet why had he not told her about his involvement with Mochi? Had it been Liam who had leaked the report to Sandford?

Alex was on her own as she struggled, wanting to believe in him, with Montana's eyes on hers looking disbelieving.

'But then it was also Liam who sent Mochi out of town,' she tried. 'To another doctor in New York.'

'No,' came the answer. 'You told me yourself – Mochi is up at the house with her husband.'

Of course. 'Who the hell can we trust, Montana?'

Montana pulled a slim black cellphone out of her pocket. 'Jack.'

'Jack!? The reprobate Jack? Are we speaking the same language?'

'He's got more class than you think. He gave me this in case of emergencies. Thought I'd get myself in a few.'

'He gave you a present, and you think you can trust him? Christ, Montana . . .'

'Well this sure as hell is an emergency. You got any better ideas?'

Alex shook her head, consumed by thought. 'Just don't tell him *everything*,' she muttered, half heard by Montana who was already speaking.

'I thought not . . . Jack?'

She related the bare outline of the story at speed. Jack took it in fast. His answer was immediate.

' . . . the one I'd put my money on is Fanny Mason. You want me to ring her?'

'Good plan. Would you? We'll be right over there. Just got to head back to Alex's house for the –' Alex shook her head briefly – '. . . for some clothes.'

She got off the phone. Alex nodded. 'We'll tell Fanny. He's right. But I don't trust anyone else, OK?'

Montana waggled her head. 'OK, OK. Back to your place.'

They started to walk to the car. Alex grabbed Montana, stopping her mid-stride.

'Oh, what about Liam . . . he's waiting for me.'

Montana grabbed her arm and broke into a fast walk.

'Fuck Liam. Man that looks like that deserves to sit on a cold stool and wait. If he's genuine it'll turn out right. If not . . .' She chivvied her along. 'Come on . . .'

The house had been broken into. Papers were scattered over the floor and it was clear that someone had been searching, because nothing of value had been taken. Heart in her mouth, Alex went to the car and found the briefcase. She was grateful, because of the way she felt about Liam.

'The case is here, Montana. Where I asked him to leave it.'

But Montana was far more cynical.

'Double bluff. He wants you in his pocket. Liam has reported to the Lindstroms, and this is the evidence of it. He's probably on his way back for the briefcase, hoping to pull you into his plot with him. Grab it, pack a couple of things, and let's get out of here. He'll be on his way fast once they realise you're not coming back to the bar ...'

They threw the room into some sort of order. Then, armed with the briefcase, got in the car and headed up to Fanny's.

TWENTY-NINE

In the car with Montana at the wheel, Alex was silent. A blizzard threatened to sweep them away, but Montana handled the icy roads and Jack's big old four-wheeler as if she was born to it. Alex was glad she did not have to drive. This encompassed every anti-humanitarian thing she had ever striven against. Hart had broken her trust, and now Liam, a man she hardly knew, was asking her to trust his word and she couldn't. Every instinct told her she could, but Montana's words had blown all that away. She had to believe that right now she was doing the right thing.

As Montana drove her further and further away from the chance of trust – and maybe more – between her and Liam she felt her heart break. He'd have left the bar by now. He knew she was not coming back, that she did not trust him. And why should she? Except for the way she felt inside. Alex stretched out her legs and sighed, eliciting a sideways glance and a pat on the leg from Montana.

What was the difference between human experiments then and what they planned to do now? She felt it was morally wrong to play with life and death, but as a journalist she knew it was not her decision to make; it was the world's right to decide, not hers. It was a story, and Liam was a doctor. They both knew what discovery could mean for medical science. That was the road he had chosen, then. The only part she found hard to take was the way he had used her. The kiss still lingered on her lips; it had glittered under her skin, and the light had not diminished at all. She only wished it had, but it had reached her heart and shone there like a beacon.

Montana had blown it too. She had been about to capitalise at last on her assets, assets that had a limited timespan. In ten years she would not have the beauty she had now. And now she was 'in' with the in crowd, the very centre, the nucleus, accepted as one of them. She'd come from a small Midwest town, her cheap background something she had also tried to hide as she recreated herself as the showgirl, Montana Farr. Now she'd told all – she'd lose financially, gain morally. It was her test.

Laughing to herself, she remembered all the homespun philosophies she'd fed Alex out there in the desert. But Alex was a pal, and a friend was a friend.

The gates swung open slowly as she headed up into Starwood and Fanny's house: Jack had given her directions. The house lights were on and the door was opening. She didn't want to stay and socialise; she'd done her bit and knew where she was going.

'You'll be fine now,' she said, as Fanny appeared in the doorway and ran across to the car.

'Hey, you two . . . come on in . . .'

'I'll check you later,' she whispered. 'I'm going home,' she said, not thinking how she'd phrased it. She put the car into gear. 'If you want me, ring Jack. That's where I'll be.'

'Oh, petal. Am I glad to see you. Come in, come in . . . tell me everything . . .'

Safe for the moment, Alex followed her, briefcase in hand, into the house, and settling down by the fire with the two of them, drink in hand and a dish of corn chips and guacamole in front of her, told her the story to date. They sat, faces etched with concern, holding hands, Stud occasionally stoking up the fire without interrupting then sitting back on his knees to listen. He shook his head, and his eyes caught those of his wife at times. Alex, lancing her worries, envied them their love. As her voice trailed to a close, Fanny leaned over and touched her.

'At least none of them know where you are, pet. And for my money, I'd go with the bloke. Seemed a nice guy to me. And ever so good looking. I wouldn't mind.' She grinned as Stud left the room.

'You're trying to make me feel better.'

'Kind of, but I mean it too.'

'Thanks, Fanny.' But the slight nagging doubt in her mind about Liam's authenticity remained. She knew she was falling in love; Fanny had seen it too, and it hurt. 'It's clear that Ruth and Wilhelm are hand in glove with Sandford; he's the blackmailer, and she at least is a good friend of Liam. The way things have turned out, it's hard not to believe it.'

'But he left the case, didn't he?'

'Montana said that was just a ruse of some sort. He'd clearly arranged to meet Ruth in the bar.'

Fanny stepped into the future. 'What's your plan then, Alex, love?'

'I'm dangerous to the guy, Fanny. The sooner I get out of town the better. He has the hook on Miki now, the lean he needs on a powerful guy. He's not about to let it go.'

She nodded, kneeling down by the fire to poke at the embers.

'Being a journalist, you'd be dangerous to him, wouldn't you?'

'How did you know I'm a journalist?'

'Oh, me and Stud remembered you some time after from the nine o'clock news.'

'You never said.'

'Nor did you. We didn't think it worth bringing up.'

Alex took her in, the lovely warm face, and smiled.

'You're so wonderful, Fanny.'

'So are you, love. I'd hate to see you hurt, in anything. So tell us what we can do, and we'll do it.'

She looked out of the window. 'Well, now I'll have to go by car. But the blizzard is too bad to let us get down the hill tonight. It'll blow out by morning, and I'll leave first thing.'

'Alone.'

'Yes.'

'As you wish, pet. Though my money's on the good-looking fella. Doesn't look the type to give up easy, not once he wants something, that is ... Look, you're OK for the moment, I just have to have a word with Studley about something.'

'Sure.'

Fanny left her alone for the moment, curled up by the fire. She envied their closeness: no move was made without the other. Tucked in by the fire, Alex watched the storm outside the window, and was glad she had the papers and intended to leave for New York in the morning, alone.

She was now very alert to Sandford. With her knowledge, the sooner she got out of town the better. He had what he needed on Miki, a powerful and immensely rich man. He'd looked for the weak link and now he'd found it. Alex, as an investigative journalist, was dangerous. Once the briefcase was safely returned to its owner, she would be no less dangerous; with nothing to lose, she might go to the press. Sandford didn't know how strongly she felt about Mochi; he'd judge everything by his standards and would see a need to dispose of her. She knew that, and watching the night through the window, wondered how close he was to her. He would know she could not leave until the storm had passed, probably at dawn when the world so often went quiet. Thank goodness no one but Montana knew where she was. She would spend the night with Fanny, whom she'd trust with her life. Come to that, she might have to. She shivered and drew closer to the flames.

Montana pushed open the door of Chasers and ran down the stairs. She felt like a little security right now, after blowing her own luck, and did not question why she believed Jack was the guy she needed to give her that feeling.

She saw his back hunched over the bar and her heart lifted. She got ready with a flippant remark, but it died on her lips as he looked into his face. Worry stood in his eyes, and relief filled them as he saw her again, the smile spreading slowly and staying.

Montana waited a moment, eyes on him, then slowly pulled a roach from her pocket. She climbed on to the bar stool and straddled it as if she were an old cowboy.

'Hey, Jack . . .'

'Montana.' His eyes were all hers. 'How the fuck's my car?'

But for the moment she was still cooking over the situation in her mind. She knew now she need not have worried about ditching her chances: she and Jack were cut from the same cloth, and being here felt just right. Home. She laughed deep inside herself. Men were sometimes hardest to handle at the last moment, like a tricky steer. Rope 'em in, then give 'em a stroke and they'd kick you.

'Am I glad to discover how good it is to see you, Jack. Sitting at the bar in your usual spot.' Her voice was light, her eyes narrowing as she lit the joint in a masculine manner.

'Losers and winners are often thrown together by developments, Montana. Have a drink?'

'Don't feel like it right now,' she said, smiling. 'Just wanna smoke some.'

He didn't ask any more; knew she wouldn't tell. Just: 'Alex OK?'

'Sure. She's heading out of town.'

Jack nodded. It was just the two of them right now, and he was glad to have her back. Gauging her mood, he cupped her cheek in his hand. He knew the girl well, knew the front was exactly that. It meant she cared when she was acting tough.

'Cheer, up Montana. You're my best girl and I rely on you, honey. Go get into your "fantasy" outfit, while I get into mine.'

She was not in the mood for a party, but it was all a part of her.

'Sure.'

She kissed him on top of his forehead. 'Thanks a million, old chum. I knew you'd work it out right.'

She slid off the stool, seeming tired, and headed out to her room. Jack watched her go, and his face held a softness that had never been there before. He caught it in the mirror and laughed.

'Well, I never . . . old Jack . . .'

The misrepresented Ruth trekked back through the streets. Liam had waited in the bar for a mere five minutes for Alex to return and Ruth had seen his worry. She had not asked

361

about the whereabouts of the case or mentioned Wilhelm. They had talked about the contents, but not at length. Both seemed to have a bit on their minds; she didn't know how to start either, racked as she was by worry.

Crossing the road she saw the car head by. She recognised Sandford right away, but not the two heavyweights sitting in the back; henchmen was written all across their foreheads. She felt nervous, and drew her coat closer as she hurried down the sidewalk. He was a man she had never liked.

Back at the hotel, as she closed on the front door, she was certain she recognised the car again. This time it was empty.

The lift doors opened and she hurried out, making for the room. Fiddling with her key in the lock, she let herself in fast as if to put something between her and them.

'Wilhelm are you here? Oh!'

She saw the broad shoulders and the ponytail at once. He was in the centre of the room looking out across the street. At her voice, the three men turned to look at her all at once.

Instinctively she turned back towards the door, but Sandford glanced across, and the second man was between her and the door in a second. He stood behind her. Wilhelm sat on the sofa, and his thin pale face was the colour of the walls; he looked like he belonged in a morgue.

Sandford looked her up and down. He was smoking a small cheroot.

'Where is Alex?'

'Alex?'

'Yes, *Alex*.'

'I don't know.' Her eyes looked wildly from one to the other and rested on her husband. 'Wilhelm, what is going on?'

But he looked away.

Sandford stepped forward, his black eyes burning in his head under their heavy lids. His square face was dark as thunder.

'Where are the papers?'

'How the hell should I know?' She moved out of his space towards a table, placing her hands on its familiar top. Her flowers, her books. 'Look, what is this?'

As she stalled, she saw three things. The henchman's fractional movement, Sandford's mild rebuke to him, and her husband's fear. It was enough for her. Some fighting spirit she did not know she possessed built up in her. Her hands left the table top, and she felt anger jet into her eyes.

'What have you been saying, Wilhelm?'

Sandford answered for him, stubbing out his cheroot in a small ashtray and practically grinding it into the glass. 'He told us everything, Ruth. He always has. I know exactly what's in those papers, but we need you to obtain them physically. Your husband did ask you to get them, didn't he?'

Ruth held back a gasp. Wilhelm was the saboteur?

'And I refused.'

'Well now I'm asking.'

She lifted her chin. 'And I refuse with even more certainty.'

She felt the tension. To hell with them. 'If they are that important to you, God help anyone who helps you get them. Now I understand what David meant, and I'm damn glad for one that I voiced my fear of men like you.'

Wilhelm had deceived her, she could see that, and his deception fired her more than anything. For a moment she knew that she had them. Her outburst had stunned them, where he must have led them to believe she would capitulate.

Sandford went to the door, but his eyes were on her husband.

'You get her to deal with us, OK, Wilhelm. I want cooperation. You know what I mean, and how it stands if I don't get what I want.'

The door shut softly behind them.

'Wilhelm, how *could you*?'

'For us. You can't imagine, Ruth, what this would mean to us. It's not what you think.' Fear made him eager to change tack.

'Isn't that what the traitor always says?'

'Ruth – money beyond your wildest dreams, money to build a hospital, to have any sort of research you want. Our name on the gate, our clinic. Fame worldwide.'

'For what? For selling chunks of human bodies, flesh for sale! Are you sick, Wilhelm? I am a doctor, even if you are not any more. I believe in helping the sick, the poor and the needy. Just like David. His brilliance meant he stumbled on something he simply wanted to share in essence with us, so that we could prevent it happening. To band together. Don't you see, that's what Hillaire wanted too? That was what it was all about!'

'I see progress too, Ruth.'

'And riches, and your name in lights. And with a toad like that one who has just left,' she said, brandishing a hand at the door. 'How long before he kicks you out, Wilhelm, and takes it all for himself? All the glory. Do you think he's going to share with you once he has it all? Are you stupid?'

He rose to his feet suddenly, at breaking point: the goal for which he had sold his soul was suddenly disappearing.

'You're jealous, Ruth. You always have been. I'm the one with the flair. With the genius. You married me because I am a star, and you're nothing but a plodding fool who stumbled over something in your research and tagged your name to it. Probably one of your students even found it.'

'Wilhelm, get out –'

'Yes, I'm getting. But I will not share it with you, Ruth, not now. I'm going to do what he wants, and keep it all for myself.'

'Do that, Wilhelm. Just go.'

The door slammed and she was alone. She trembled with the fight; she had fought for all she was worth on this subject. Left alone, she saw the danger Alex was in. She found Fabrice's number in the book. The telephone rang and rang and no one answered. She grabbed her coat and ran out of the door.

THIRTY

The torchlight parade made its serpentine way down the mountain, and the small mining town was alive with activity. Golden party lights had sprung up everywhere, bathing with colour the snow and the faces of the strollers who roamed the streets. Amongst the party-goers out for Aspen's winter carnival, Liam had been searching for Alex for over half an hour. The night was full of people. It was the night of Jack Fenner's party. Threading his way through the revelry, he could not find her. His concern grew.

He headed past the bouncers in Chasers, pushing the men aside. Montana was at the bar with Jack. Montana was dressed as a man in pinstripes, and Jack as one of his nubile in-house maidens in high-cut shorts and pinny. The rest was bacchanalia, amongst which they seemed to be a happy duo. The woman he had seen on the slopes with Alex came up to him. She wore a full-length mink and a matching fur turban, with a sparkling diamond pin at the throat of her black face-framing polo. Her face was all invitation; it said she had not forgotten. It only reminded him of Alex, of when he had first become aware of her freshness and her real beauty. He pushed past her to the man at the bar.

'Montana. Where's Alex?'

She eyed him. 'How should I know?'

'Because you asked her to meet you. And now she's disappeared.'

She wasn't inclined to be rude to such a dish even if she did distrust him. After all, life was life, and she was still living it. And she could have been wrong.

'I'm not her keeper, Liam, now am I . . .'

She angled herself against Jack, who stood quietly smoking and taking it all in, but now her eyes gathered a hard light as she saw the woman appear behind him.

'You two always seem to appear together. *Strangely* enough.'

'Do you know where she is, Montana? She's in danger.' Ruth, dressed in her black tracksuit, looked pale and strained.

'You're telling me . . . !?'

Montana laughed. There was definite hostility between the two women, but Ruth had found her strength of character, and ignoring Montana, she turned in quick conversation with Liam, letting him gather quite a bit more of the picture.

'She was reluctant to confide in you, Liam, but I know why now. I'm not surprised. She must wonder who to trust. But I'm telling you, she *is* in trouble, and if you care about her you'd better track her down. I think Montana knows exactly where she is too, and I think I know the key to her sudden disappearance.'

Montana angled herself again, taking Jack's cigarette and smoking it herself. 'Something I said?'

'I suggest that Alex cares very much for you,' said Ruth, ignoring her but speaking to Liam for them all to hear. With a woman's instinct she suddenly turned and said, 'Jack, where is she . . .'

He got Ruth to drop him off at home, and went in to use the telephone, almost tripping over the startled cat. As he dialled he looked around him at the chaos. Someone had come calling.

'Liam . . . that you?'

'She with you, Fanny?'

A pause.

'Look –' she sounded as if she had put her hand around the receiver – 'You've taken it upon yourself to call, chuck, and God help you if I'm wrong, but I reckon it means you're upfront. Alex is here with me and I reckon she just might need you right now.'

He held the receiver close. 'Where are you?'

'Up in Starwood.' She gave him the address. 'Tread carefully when you come up here. She's all of a dither.' She did not give away anything of their own discussions, but as she spoke she confirmed her distrust of Ruth. 'Don't talk to anyone, especially that Lindstrom couple, Ruth and Wilhelm. Not a word, mind.'

'I won't. I'm not in league with them, Fanny, and I can't imagine Ruth would be involved. What's she told you?'

'Little, except this Sandford is a megalomaniac who will stop at nothing. He knows that Alex is capable of ruining everything. Now don't ask me how, 'cos I don't know the story. She's just resting, poor love, but I know enough. Get up here and help her, she needs a friend.'

He knew what she meant. He knew too from Mochi that by telling Miki, or persuading Mochi to come clean, he could screw it all up for Sandford. Sandford clearly wanted to get to Miki before Mochi managed to get a blood test on the baby and find a truth that would defuse his plan one way or another. If she found out that she was carrying Miki's baby for certain, Sandford could no longer threaten her. He wondered what the truth was and whether it was all bluff; but the man was clever, it was impossible to know – at this stage anyway.

'I reckon anyone who got in his way would be in extreme danger,' Fanny was saying. 'I've seen the man, heard him talk. He's amoral . . .' She was a basic girl from a tough background and she knew his sort.

'I'll be there soon as I can.'

Alex filled his mind so much that he was in the garage before he remembered that Hillaire had taken his car to the airport.

'Damn . . .'

He looked around, as if hoping for salvation, but there was nothing but the creaking of trees, the soft drifting sheets of snow and silence and the blue shadows of night. He ran across the streets through the woods where the tracks of cross-country skiers sliced between the trees; treading deep in drifts he headed for Alex's house. He knew of one car that would be available, and he knew where the absent owner stashed the key.

Fanny was already waiting on the porch as he drove up in the pickup, her curvy figure backlit by the warmth of the house. Ignoring the snow she ran out in her baby pink tracksuit. She was shouting as she came, snow petals falling on her blonde hair, and screwing up her face against the wetness.

'She's gone, Liam love!'

He was climbing down into the snow, his boots treading heavily.

'Gone!?'

'Yes. A few minutes ago – you must have passed her on the road.' She pointed back the way he'd come. 'She took a cab, I couldn't stop her. Suddenly got the wind up and she said she had to go tonight. I think she felt she wasn't safe.'

Realising the seriousness of the situation, he longed to be there beside her. Fanny's next words filled him with dread.

'I think she was heading back to the house.'

'I wish I'd had more faith in her instincts.' He climbed back in. 'I'm very worried about Alex being back there. I've got to get going.'

'I'll hold the fort, lovey.'

He remembered the devastation back at Hillaire's house – the upturned chairs and emptied drawers, the cupboard doors swinging open. She did not yet know just how brutal these men might be, or how determined. It confirmed for him once and for all the truth of his feelings.

'Where's your husband?' he asked.

'He's up the hill visiting, why?'

'Get him to come home, OK? Will you do that? And lock the door.'

As she nodded he was already backing the pickup to the edge of the drive. He raced down the hill and along the road back into the West End of town.

As Fanny came off the phone to Studley she heard the noise outside. She replaced the receiver slowly, listening. The sound of voices, voices that she did not recognise, and the gate intercom had not gone. They must know the number: friends of Evie's.

368

Fanny went to the french windows and peered out. She ducked and screamed as the fist came flying and smashed the glass. A gloved hand reached through for the clasp and undid it before she had time to leave the room. The man in his balaclava and jogging suit was at her side as she reached the door. Another followed.

'Where is she?'

'Who?'

'Don't play dumb, sister. You know who.'

'I've no idea what you're talking about,' she said, shaking herself free. 'Now if you're friends of Evie's I don't think the joke is very funny and my husband will certainly not think it amusing.'

The man stood still, and his voice grew cold.

'Your husband isn't here, or he'd be in here now, with you. Has he taken her somewhere?'

Her eyes grew round, praying for time; for Studley to return and throw them out. Then she looked at the size of them and prayed he wouldn't.

'You clearly don't know about the alarm system, do you, smartarse? The minute you broke in here, you set it off. Half the cops in Pitkin County are probably climbing up that road right now. If I were you I'd get out while you can.'

She showed her mettle, smart enough to try and divert them and keeping quiet about the truth. She'd almost got away with it, saw the man hesitate and look to his mate and then to the window, expecting flashing blue lights.

'Mum . . .?' Darren appeared in the doorway, rubbing his eyes.

'Oh, pet . . .' She ran to him, putting her hands on his pyjamaed shoulders to shoo him back upstairs, but his next words froze her to the spot.

'Did Alex stay, Mum? Is she taking me skiing in the morning?'

Half asleep, he suddenly noticed the men. And they saw him. Coming back from the door almost in one stride the first man took him by the shoulder.

'Ow, that hurts!'

'Get your hands off him!' Fanny screamed.

'Where is she?'

Darren was lifted from the ground by his ear. 'Ow ... don't! *Mum . . . !*'

'She's in town!' she shouted. 'She's in *town!*' Fanny had her point of vulnerability, and it was her child. When he was threatened, she had no option; she gave in.

Darren was dropped to the floor, clutching his reddened ear and sobbing. She was down on the ground beside him in a flash.

'You bastards,' she said, cuddling him.

'Where in town?'

She held Darren tight, her heart torn, but there really only was one choice. She gave her at least an extra five minutes with a lie, and prayed it was enough.

'The doctor's house.'

The hunt was on.

Snow flurried in the headlight beams. A curve and an icy patch and he was ploughing through drifts and sending a spray of blinding snow over the windshield. Liam gunned the car, but the back wheels spun uselessly, slanted into the open night air. Liam stepped out; the pickup was deep in the ditch.

Sound was magnified by the surrounding silence and the hush of softly falling snow. It was below freezing but it felt all right; it was a dry cold rather than damp and he was wearing a heavy sheepskin-lined parka. He jammed on a ski cap, pulled up the hood of his sweatshirt, and as a couple of cars passed him started to run.

He was glad he did; the snow softened his steps. At Hillaire's they were already searching. He sheltered under the protection of a tree and watched for half a second, saw the lights spring on upstairs. The snow was deepening rapidly and drifts were starting to build. There was little time. Soon they would be on the scent. Retracing his steps slightly, he headed in a diagonal across the lawn, falling deep into the drifts. No time to go by the road where they might catch him

370

up, so he pushed through the tough snow-laden branches of the firs that smacked back into his eyes, leaving the stain of pine resin on his face and hands. Crossing the frozen river he climbed the opposite bank.

Huge snowflakes melted down his face. A good eight inches and it was coming down hard. Outside the house he saw the motorhome: its door stood slightly open and there was a light on inside. He'd taken the pickup, and now this was her only option – *their* only option. Stumbling through a drift four feet deep, he found it empty, but there was no time to run into the house and get her.

'Alex!' he shouted against the dark. 'Alex!'

He wiped the snow off the windshield, blinded as the downy drifting flakes melted into his eyes.

On the porch, Alex stamped the snow off her boots, listening to the bark of coyotes. The chimneys tainted the night air with the smell of wood smoke and lights glowed a warm welcome from the windows of the old house. It should have been a night to tuck in and watch the world lighten in another splendid dawn, but she had work to do; her backpack over her shoulder, she heard the voice calling from the other side of the house, and her face turned swiftly.

The door opened wide with a splintering tumble of ice and Liam was in, kicking the snow from his boots and jumping into the driver's seat. He found the ignition and twisted the key with such urgency it bruised his finger. Flooring the gas pedal he choked the engine so that it coughed and died then, as he swore at it, lumbered into reluctant response. The sound would bring her out, if nothing else; he didn't want her arguing with him in the house while the heavies had their chance to drive the all too short distance round the corner and find them like sitting ducks.

Snow was still falling heavily, and a wind was getting up. It was very early morning now, soft blue-yellow lightening the dark just before dawn. The snow whirled around him as the motorhome fired and rumbled into life and oily exhaust fumes blasted out the back. The lights were on in the motorhome, its thundering engine filled the quiet moments before

371

Alex came running out. She stopped immediately she saw him, but he leaped out and took the bag, hurrying her, and with the grasp of his arm, the swift kiss he gave her and the mix of vulnerability and tension in his face, she knew it was all right. As urgently as Liam she climbed into the passenger seat, and they reversed out of the drive.

A snowplough motored along slowly, its warning beacons flashing blue light. They damn nearly hit it, as with his face pressed close to the misted screen, windscreen wipers battling with the cloud of snow, and rubbing a circle of vision in the condensation within, Liam threw the old machine out on to the road, shoved it into gear, then blasted forward, an endless flurry of snowflakes hurtling out of the darkness at them.

Once out on the road, he held her hand, and checked the mirror behind him for any stray cars. There were no words for the moment. Like his mentor, with Liam actions spoke loudest.

None too soon; as the old motorhome trundled out of town, a sleek black car swung and slid on to the main street of Aspen and drove out as fast as it was able in the same direction as them. It was followed by a small grey Toyota, skis strapped to the roof.

Ruth put her foot down on the pedal and followed at a half-block's distance. She was dressed for the cold, her equipment stashed in the back, ready for anything. She had been waiting since midnight for any sort of movement, and thanked God for the rental car she had taken out in order – she had to face this fact – to be free to see Hillaire. Conscious it was she who had alerted her husband and therefore Sandford to Alex's discovery, Ruth wanted to help redress the balance. She'd overheard from Wilhelm's phone call moments earlier that they were going to follow them and deal with them on the lonely mountain road that led out of Aspen; the couple were headed out in the motorhome. At much the same time she heard the weather forecast and knew they'd never make it: the report was for heavy snow and the lanes leading to Aspen would be snowbound – Alex and Liam would be caught with ease.

Ruth was an Olympic skier and she knew the mountains; had skiied them often as a young woman. She knew the back passes, and had once skied the back of the mountain when competing in the Powder Eight. No one was better than her. She could lead them out.

With Wilhelm gone Ruth had wasted no time. She had slipped out of the hotel room, hurried to her car ready to go and here she was, following them down the road out of town and heading for Buttermilk.

Alex and Liam were now fully aware of what they were up against as they headed out of town in the snowstorm. As he took a left and headed up the hill alongside Buttermilk, Alex knew they would be easily caught on the road down the mountain, and knew too that this was the team she should always have been a part of. There was only one way.

She knew about the back country beyond the mountain. Liam did too; he drove to a vantage point as high up the mountain as he was able and then, cutting the engine, he took her swiftly into his arms and kissed her. There was only time for a lingering moment, a look that sealed whatever it was ahead that they shared. Even in the midst of it cars stole up the mountain road, throwing long spears of yellow light on the mountain snow.

The snow was deepening rapidly and more drifts were starting to build as the wind churned down the slope; the blizzard had cut visibility to a few yards, but in some ways that was on their side.

They fastened on their ski boots, and pulled their jackets down tight over their gloves, their hats down to their brows and adjusted their goggles. If they were protected from the wind and blocked inside a wall of snow they had a fighting chance of surviving through the night. They had not played right into Sandford's hands as he had expected. The motorhome would have broken down on the hill, caught in the rapidly piling snow, but this way they might make it.

Alex had grabbed a second parka from the seat behind her for extra warmth. Pulling it on and searching for mittens she found the fetish in the pocket; visions of Montana's face in

373

the desert and her words of wisdom came back to her. She gave it a squeeze and a prayer. It had to help them now.

The precious computer software was inside her jacket as she came down on to the last step and Liam lifted her into his arms. His whispered words were brief, and caught at her, but there was no time to respond or even to feel them. They headed out as the first glimmer of dawn broke in the eastern sky.

Snow swirled among the trees, the wind wailed forlornly through the treetops and they were off. As they blundered through trees and snow, finding the way, they heard the first of the cries that followed them.

Now it was just them and the mountain.

Ruth parked her car right behind the two men as they climbed out and headed swiftly after their quarry: Sandford and Boxer – she was close enough to recognise them. Her last climb up the hill had been in darkness and she had prayed that the little car would make it. Her prayers had been answered – and she had not been seen. Slipping the skis on her feet, she braced herself and pushed off from another spot, one far more dangerous but quicker. Although she knew the back passes where they had practised it had never been in half-light nor conditions like these; the blizzard was no longer so thick but the light was deceptive. No one was better than her, and this she banked on as she swooped down the first stretch. She could lead Alex and Liam to safety if she could just get ahead. She knew of a way to cut them off: skiing almost blind, she followed her memory and her conscience.

The couple were in no doubt as to the outcome if they were caught, but they had discovered that together they were like two pieces of a jigsaw: both strong, both determined and athletic and both loyal. Side by side, swerving down the icy slopes, that loyalty showed for Liam as she spotted the distant black figure heading down towards them, skiing expertly. He recognised it as Ruth. Despite Alex's early misgivings, he'd trusted his friend, so as she pointed the way out for them to follow, they did so in a hair-raising chase, slicing through trees and off precipices, bright with dangerous ice in the early morning. Light was painting the air, the shadows giving way. Dull grey clouds hung like a pall over the mountains. There was a cold and bitter wind blowing off the peaks. The clouds lingered and then snowflakes began to fall lazily, adding a breath of whiteness to the air. Snow fell in light half-hearted swirls, and as the sky streaked with pink against the grey, the first thin rays of sun bounced off their polarised lenses as they dipped and flew over banks and into valleys of snow. Twisting and turning, they were ahead. The weather was improving, and with it their chances.

Down through the canyon the gunshots rang out. Immediately, they skied wide, separating slightly; and Ruth, acting as decoy, sliced off to one side. The two pursuing men took the easier run along with her, clearly mistaking her for Alex.

They all heard thunder at the same time. The avalanche caused by the gunfire cracked the mountain and slid. A tidal wave of smoking flying ice, thundering, rolling chunks of imploding snow, came down the cut like a raging white wall, fingers of snow scooping down the smooth terrain and flying up in a cloud on the slope below. As it smoked down the hillside all of their skills were utilised; far enough apart to feel separated, they jumped from one icy crag to another, plummeting down on to pillows of snow in a desperate and dangerous escape.

Sandford came after them, dancing his way down the mountain, flurrying the snow. A soft thud as he hit the snow behind them and he was closing very fast, a powerful skier and very determined.

Finally, a cliff of ice. They flew from the sky, straight down like plump birds, and hit the precipice below, with its trailing fingers over jagged black rocks. Liam jumped from the ledge to the crest beneath and fell, rolling over. Alex, holding her breath, jumped, behind him. A fan of white crested in their wake as they went over the edge. A metallic gleam as Ruth hurtled past in black and silver. The edge of the avalanche gathered up all in its path, hurling it in front of it like a giant ball down to the bottom of the ravine. Alex found herself tumbling into the mouth of an old mine, grabbed by Liam, as it thundered past. Sitting on their ledge, holding each other tight, they finally managed to recover their breath as they watched the almost slow-motion wall of white gather up the mountain vista in its frightening power. Together and silently they wondered about those who had flown by within it. As the last rumble died Liam turned and looked at the place where they had landed.

The entrance had been boarded up, but he pulled a couple of boards loose and they pushed their way in. He pulled out a flashlight and shone it.

'It's an old silver mine.'

'Ugh.'

'Not what I'd planned . . . but still.'

It was musty and cold, and smelled of dank earth and age. There was a distant drip of water way back in the darkness, and the torchlight shone on a limitless hole, bordered with more of the same rotten boards that faded into a darkness that was absolute; festooned with spiders' webs. Surprisingly it wasn't impossibly cold, though the rough walls glistened with damp where the flashlight danced around. Alex touched the timbers and found them crumbling under her fingers. She wiped the dirt off on her suit.

'Is it safe?'

'Safer than outside for now. I think we should wait a bit, don't you? Let them think we're buried under all that snow.'

'You did pretty well out there.'

He turned to her, undeniably handsome with the devil may care smile. 'Thank you. I tried.'

'You only pretended not to be as good as me, didn't you?'

He put his arms around her and kissed her gently, on her lips, on the tip of her nose. And again, eyes closed. 'So that you would see me again.'

'Never thought it would be like this.'

'No.'

'Serve you right,' she said as he drew her in closer. 'Get what you wish for.'

'Do I?'

Her arms were around him, the light kisses gathering momentum, as she murmured: 'Say it again . . .'

'What?'

'What you said up the mountain.'

He pulled back slightly. '"Jesus, the goddamn engine's stalled"?'

'No . . .' Her eyes held their heat. 'Right after that . . .'

'Oh. *That* . . .'

He stroked her face with the back of his hand, making her wait, filling up the moment with his eyes.

'I love you . . .'

And suddenly the amused light in his eye became something else as her upturned serious face moved him too deeply for restraint. His mouth came down on hers with a hunger that both of them had longed for. Humour, need, adrenalin and fear – the mixed emotions brought them together; henchmen and documents forgotten, driven by physical need, they forgot all else as with the first touch they found each other.

He opened the catch of her parka. Kissed her throat, building the tremulous heat inside her.

'It's freezing,' he whispered against her mouth, tasting her with his tongue. His fingers pushed in under her parka, touching her breasts and making her head swim.

'I can cope,' she sighed, and her knees bent as he bore her to the ground. 'I spent some time in an Antarctic field camp.'

'So I heard.'

'I always slept naked. You didn't freeze, not as long as you kept a hat on. You stay warmer that way . . .'

'I'm glad that you warned me.' He found the zip of her jacket beneath the parka. 'God, you're covered in these things . . .'

His smile warmed her. She unzipped the rest herself.

THIRTY-ONE

As they made their way down the mountain Alex's momentum swept her up to the crest of a gentle slope and she carved a stop at its edge to gaze out over the beauty of the valley below.

Sparkling now in the early sunshine, the virgin snow had laid a fresh smooth dusting of powder over the land, and at its centre far below a small lake shimmered.

Exhilarated from the run, she turned to Liam, who had swooshed to a stop beside her, her pleasure alight in her face. The snow had the glitter of diamonds, and the sparkling mountain wore a tiara; a low cloud that held the pink blush of sunrise. Together they drank in the vista, hushed by the awesome silence that surrounded them: two alone yet so together, perfectly at one in the midst of this magnificent landscape.

'This is how it should be.'

She felt for the fetish in her pocket and sent it a very private thank you as he leaned over and pulled her into his arms.

Later they reached the road and a fire red snowcat clearing a path against black spruces and blue sky with puffs of cloud.

'Wonder what happened to Ruth?'

The mountainside had been clear as they came out; morning sun bouncing off their polarised lenses, the snow blinding under the light of a clear blue sky.

'I imagine she made it. She's a dynamite skier.'

'And a good friend.' Alex pushed off towards the snowcat. 'You got the disk?'

She patted her zipped pocket. 'I got the disk.'

Breath steamed the morning light as they stepped up the slope to the road.

'Hey . . .!'

It was the best sight they saw as they hitched a lift to the airport and caught the first flight out.

Hillaire took the call in his office. The girl was immediately shown in. She was called Elaine. She told him what the man had done, what he had confessed to her before his death; told him the truth.

Ian, her fiancé, had never switched dishes. Morality had held out, and in her tear-stained eyes there was pride for his sacrifice. Sandford's Messiah was not and never had been a part of Mochi, but down in Wyoming on an insignificant chicken farm it was growing in the body of an aged woman who would bear it to term.

Hillaire made a quick phone call. Others were able to take care of this – the FBI, who had been notified at once. He knew a moment's uncertainty; the man called Boxer was still missing, his body unrecovered from the valley floor. That could mean that he had got away, managed to warn them. It was possible that even if the inmates of the atrocious 'hospital' had been taken away, they would never find out where that culled egg had ended up, or whether it would live to term. Hillaire pushed the disquiet from his mind; that particularly immorality would have to be dealt with later.

For now, he had his priorities. Ruth had been in the Aspen Valley hospital. She had been flown by chopper out of the mountain town, with a newly determined Hillaire beside her, and straight into the clinic in New York; one run by himself.

He went down the corridor to her door.

Intensive care. She was almost surrounded by tubes as he came in, the door closing softly. He went over to the bed, and took her hand gently. If Ruth pulled through, as they thought she would, Hillaire would not make a second mistake. He sat beside her bed and used the phone.

'Bowman. Call Mrs Leng, would you?' A moment passed in which he watched Ruth's face silently, then the gentle buzz.

'Mochi? Listen to me . . .' And then he told her. 'It's backed up by the tests I ran on you. The young fellow in the lab never switched dishes. Nor did Sandford do anything to you. You're safe, and Mochi – the baby's well.' Hillaire, in the best place to do so as Mochi's doctor, had run an easy test on her. The baby was Miki's – thanks to the young man and his conscience.

Hillaire stood back from the bed.

'Confide in your husband as soon as you are able,' he encouraged her. 'There is nothing more important than sharing. Given what has happened, Miki will understand.'

'I'll try. We will both have to change. But the news is wonderful. A way to start, more than you can imagine.'

'Well, my dear. The answer is up to you, but the threat is gone. In every way.'

He put down the phone. Sandford Wainwright had died on the mountain; Wilhelm was in custody. The medical group had been voluntarily 'disbanded' – the wives' pleasure increased at having their husbands suddenly out with them and the children on the slopes, enjoying the most exclusive ski resort in the world, their job done.

He smiled to himself and felt the pressure on his hand.

Ruth's eyes were open. 'Hillaire . . .'

He bent over her, covering her hands with both of his.

'This time I'm never going to leave you . . .'

The party was over. Montana climbed into the jeep beside Jack. She'd lost nothing. She was a natural in Aspen and Jack had admired her from the start. He turned the dial for the weather report.

'. . . and today, ten new inches on top of Ajax . . .'

He switched off. 'I'm going to get Rowan for that.'

'Excuse me . . . not *now* please . . .'

He took her in. She grinned lasciviously. She was still wearing the pinstriped suit, but it looked a bit the worse for wear; mid-morning the white shirt straining under its buttons as she leaned back, her arm around his shoulders, looked as if it was time to give up trying. There were sleepy dark shadows under her eyes in the hard daylight and she looked sexy as hell.

'Is it true about the weather report?'

'Care to find out? Back at my place.'

'Ah yes, and where is your place? I never did know.'

'On top of Ajax, of course.'

They laughed as the engine turned over.

'I'm right there with you sugar, you're speaking my language . . .'

She had always had a contingency plan.

On the California beach the couple strolled barefoot in the sand, and the Pacific waves rolled dramatically alongside. They headed back to a small beachhouse lent by a grateful David Kowolski.

Alex was sitting by the window on the long seat strewn with cushions as he came back from the phone. Her hair was loose around bare, sun-kissed shoulders, a glow of colour that had not been there before. Her dark eyes were soft and there was a gentle smile on her face.

'Who was it?'

He lifted a strand of dark hair gently from her shoulder and brushed it back, feeling the smoothness of her skin.

'My department . . . I've been offered a post with Médecins sans Frontières.'

'Are you going to take it?' She could not understand the glint in his eye. Perhaps she had misunderstood the depths of their feelings. She had wanted to ask for more from him. It was on the tip of her tongue, but now this job – taking him away.

'I'm asking you.'

'Is it what you want?'

'In one way. How did your day go?'

Alex had just come back from the news office in downtown LA. She'd been in touch with Bill and he'd called to let her know the latest.

'Oh, pretty good . . .'

'Well,' he prompted. 'Any news?' He took her hand, playing with her fingers. The *frisson* of his skin shimmered all the way through her.

'Actually,' she said, 'I've been offered a job too.'

'Really, where?'

'As Foreign Correspondent with a major English daily newspaper . . .'

She was surprised at his interest; she herself was feeling devastated at the thought of separation.

'Where?'

'In Africa,' she said.

'Same place as me, how strange . . .'

'You *knew*!'

His laugh provoked her, and she swung the pillow at him. He chuckled and sidestepped, grabbing her as she came after him, and throwing her back down, seducing her with long molten kisses.

'How did you swing that?' she asked in lazy pleasure.

His lips came down on hers, unable to leave her alone, as his arms pulled her in and they lay back on the sofa together. She felt the sun on her face, and the warmth of his arms as gently he undressed her, with a slow unbuttoning and a shirking off of soft cotton and restraint.

'No bulky snowsuits . . .' A whisper against her skin . . .

'No zips . . .' . . . that made her lift in pleasure.

This time it was skin to skin. The laughter soon stopped as passion took over.

'I told you,' he said, as his lips travelled down over her. 'I always get what I wish for . . .'